PETER ABRAHAMS

"There are basically only two kinds of crime stories: the ones where you know what's coming . . . and the ones where you don't, which applies to just about everything Peter Abrahams writes. . . . For all their originality, his suspenseful plots invariably turn on the complex interaction of good and evil in a self-aware modern society. . . . Abrahams writes . . . scenes that can curl your toes."

New York Times Book Review

DELUSION

"[A] taut new novel. . . . Abrahams constructs a powder keg of suspense, using vivid characterization and underwritten prose. He manages to imbue this page-turner with themes of racial and economic injustice while conjuring the ghost of Hamlet's father to hover in the wings. This is another stellar mystery from one of [the] best."

Boston Globe

"[A] contemporary master offers unique new twists on the classic whodunit. . . . The novel's power derives from delving deep into the characters' lives. . . . [Their] fates and the integrity of justice itself seem to swing in an unsteady balance, with Abrahams keeping the tension taut right through the end."

Washington

By Peter Abrahams

DELUSION
NERVE DAMAGE
END OF STORY
OBLIVION
THEIR WILDEST DREAMS
THE TUTOR
LAST OF THE DIXIE HEROES
CRYING WOLF
A PERFECT CRIME
THE FAN
LIGHTS OUT
REVOLUTION #9
PRESSURE DROP
HARD RAIN
RED MESSAGE
TONGUES OF FIRE
THE FURY OF RACHEL MONETTE

For Younger Readers

DOWN THE RABBIT HOLE
BEHIND THE CURTAIN
INTO THE DARK

Peter
ABRAHAMS

DELUSION

HARPER

An Imprint of HarperCollins*Publishers*

This book is a work of fiction. The characters, incidents, and dialogue are drawn from the author's imagination and are not to be construed as real. Any resemblance to actual events or persons, living or dead, is entirely coincidental.

HARPER

An Imprint of HarperCollins*Publishers*
10 East 53rd Street
New York, New York 10022–5299

Copyright © 2008 by Pas de Deux
ISBN 978-0-06-113800-3

First Harper paperback printing: April 2009
First William Morrow hardcover printing: April 2008

Printed in the United States of America

Visit Harper paperbacks on the World Wide Web at
www.harpercollins.com

10 9 8 7 6 5 4 3 2 1

To Laura Geringer

DELUSION

CHAPTER 1

The man they called Pirate heard a guard coming down the cell block. Pirate had excellent hearing. He could identify the guards just from the sound of their footsteps on the cement floor. This one—Hispanic, bushy salt-and-pepper mustache, dark depressions under his eyes—had a tread that was somehow muffled and heavy at the same time, and once in a while he dragged a heel in a way that made a little scuffing sound Pirate found pleasant.

Scuff, scuff, and then the footsteps stopped. "Hey," the guard said.

Pirate, lying on his bunk, facing the wall—a featureless wall, but he'd grown to like it—turned his head. The Hispanic guard with the mustache and tired eyes—Pirate no longer bothered to learn their names—stood outside the bars, keys in hand.

"Wakie wakie," the guard said.

Pirate hadn't been sleeping, but he didn't argue. He just lay there, head turned so he could see, body curled comfortably, one hand resting on his Bible. Pirate hardly even opened it anymore—the one section that interested him now pretty much committed to memory—but he liked the feel of it, especially that gold tassel for marking your place.

"Come on," the guard said. "Shake a leg."

Shake a leg? Pirate didn't understand. It wasn't chow time, and besides, weren't they in lockdown? Hadn't they

been in lockdown the past two or three days, for reasons
Pirate had forgotten, or never known? He didn't understand,
but didn't argue, instead getting off the bunk and moving
toward the bars. Keys jingled. The guard opened up, made
a little motion with his chin, a quick tilt. Pirate raised his
arms, spread his legs, got patted down. The guard grunted.
Pirate turned, lowered his pants, bent over. The guard
grunted again. Pirate straightened, zipped up. The guard
made another chin motion, this one sideways. Pirate stepped
outside.

They walked down the corridor, the guard on Pirate's
right. On the right was bad, his blind side, made him uncomfortable. But there was nothing he could do.

"You got a visitor," the guard said.

A visitor? Pirate hadn't had a visitor in a long time, years
and years. They went down the row of cells, Pirate's good
eye, his only eye, registering all the familiar faces, each one
more or less wrong in its own way; and around the corner,
more cells, four tiers, on and on. It reminded him, when he
thought of it at all, of an experiment he'd seen in a movie,
one with rats. The difference was he'd felt sorry for the rats.
Pirate didn't feel sorry for anyone in here, himself included.
That part—no longer feeling sorry for himself—was his
greatest accomplishment. He was at peace, in harmony with
passing time. That was the message of the gold tassel.

"Who?" he said.

"Who what?" said the guard.

"The visitor."

"Your lawyer, maybe?"

Pirate didn't have a lawyer. He'd had a lawyer long ago,
Mr. Rollins, but hadn't heard from him in years.

They came to a gate. Pirate's guard handed over a slip of
paper. Another guard opened the gate. They went down a
short walkway, through an unlocked door, into the visiting
room.

There were no other inmates in the visiting room. The
guard took a seat at the back, picked a newspaper off the

floor. On the far side of the glass, by one of the phones, sat a young woman Pirate had never seen. She smiled—smiled at him, Pirate. No doubt about it—besides, there was no one else around, no one she could have been smiling at. Except the guard, maybe; but the guard, opening his newspaper, wasn't paying any attention to the woman. A big photograph of a man with his arms raised in triumph was on the front page. Pirate didn't recognize him.

"Ten minutes," said the guard.

Pirate moved toward the glass wall, a thick, shatterproof glass wall with three steel chairs in front, bolted to the floor. He sat in the middle one, facing the young woman. Her skin transfixed him. No one inside—inmates or guards—had skin like this, smooth, glowing, so alive. And her eyes: the whites of them, so clear, like alabaster, a word he'd come across in his reading and now grasped.

She raised a hand, small and finely shaped, with polished nails and a gold wedding band. He followed its movements like a dog; as a boy, he'd had a very smart dog named Snappy, capable of following silent commands. Some time passed—his mind on Snappy—before he realized what she wanted him to do: pick up the phone.

He picked up the phone. She spoke into hers.

"Hello, Mr. DuPree."

His real name: When had he last heard it? "Hello," he said; and then, remembering his manners, added, "ma'am."

She smiled again, her teeth—more of that alabaster, like works of art, having nothing to do with biting, sparkling even through the dusty, smeary glass—distracted him, so he almost missed what came next. "Oh," she said, "just call me Susannah. Susannah Upton."

"Susannah Upton?"

She spelled both names for him. "I'm a lawyer."

"Yeah?" said Pirate. "Are you from Mr. Rollins?"

"Mr. Rollins?" she said.

"My lawyer," said Pirate. "At the trial."

Susannah Upton frowned. That meant one tiny furrow

appeared on her brow, somehow making her look even younger. "I believe . . ." she began, and opened a leather briefcase, taking a sheet of paper from a folder with Pirate's full name written in red on the front: Alvin Mack DuPree. ". . . yes," Susannah continued, "he passed away."

"Died?"

Susannah nodded. "Almost ten years ago now."

At that moment, Pirate felt a strange feeling that came from time to time, a squinting in the socket where his right eye had been; like he was trying to see better, get things in focus. "What of?" Pirate said.

"I'm sorry?"

"Mr. Rollins. What did he die of?"

"It doesn't say."

Pirate tried to picture Mr. Rollins, estimate his age back then. He'd had graying hair, but that didn't necessarily mean . . .

"But my visit has nothing to do with Mr. Rollins," Susannah went on. "Are you familiar with the Justice Project, Mr. DuPree?"

Although he couldn't form an image of Mr. Rollins's face, Pirate had a clear memory of Mr. Rollins's breath in the courtroom, boozy little rising clouds, almost visible. Was it the booze that killed him? Pirate was about to ask, when Susannah spoke.

"Mr. DuPree? The Justice Project?"

He shook his head, although he thought he remembered a band by that name. Pirate had played guitar at one time, traveled with a bar band that covered country hits, and once, at the Red Rooster, even backed up a singer who was going to be the next Delbert McClinton. The chords on "You Win Again" went E, B7, E, A.

"We're a nonprofit legal advocacy group," Susannah said, "dedicated to freeing the innocent."

"No innocents in here," Pirate said.

Susannah blinked. "But you, Mr. DuPree, you're in here."

"Yup."

Susannah gazed at him for a moment, then cradling the phone between her shoulder and chin, she leafed through the folder with his name on the cover; a thick folder.

"I don't have any money," Pirate said.

"Money?"

"For lawyers."

"No money needed," Susannah said. "We're funded by private donors. All expenses associated with your case will be taken care of."

"My case?"

"That's what brings me here," Susannah said. "There've been some exciting developments—all on account of Bernardine, which is the weird part."

"Bernardine?" Pirate knew no one of that name, never had.

"The hurricane, Mr. DuPree. In September."

"Oh, yeah," said Pirate, trying to recall the details. Bernardine had passed over the prison—a hundred miles inland, maybe more—at night; he hadn't heard a thing.

"You're aware of the extent of the damage?" Susannah said.

"Damage?"

"Down in Belle Ville. Half the town got flooded, including Lower Town and the whole business district."

"Yeah?" Pirate said. "Princess Street, too?"

"I think so," Susannah said. "Why do you ask?"

"I had a job on Princess Street once," said Pirate. Bouncer at the Pink Passion Club, a good job, possibly the best job he'd ever had, partly because of the tips the girls gave him, never less than twenty dollars, but more because of the good feeling he got protecting them. Pirate had been jacked in those days, ripped. He was still big, but the jacked, ripped part was gone.

"What kind of job?" Susannah said.

"Just a job."

Susannah nodded. "In answer to your question, Princess Street got flooded, too. Everything south of Marigot was under six feet of water for days and days, including the courthouse, police headquarters and the state offices. The cleanup's still going on, but FEMA found something—we're still not sure exactly when—that pertains to your case. And that's putting it mildly."

Pertains meant . . . ? Pirate had no clue. "Something from when I worked at the Pink Passion Club?" he said.

Susannah shook her head. "This goes back to the night of the murder."

"What murder?"

"The murder of Johnny Blanton," said Susannah. For a moment her voice faded, the connection going bad even though they were in touching distance. All calls were recorded; Pirate knew that, had temporarily forgotten. "Why you're here," Susannah added.

Pirate no longer denied he'd killed Johnny Blanton. Not that he confessed, or made any kind of admission; he just no longer denied it. What was the point? That way lay turmoil; he was at peace.

Susannah shuffled through her papers. "Do you remember why you didn't take the stand at your trial?"

Mr. Rollins's orders: something about how his criminal record—including a robbery where no one got hurt but resembled the Johnny Blanton case in other ways—made it a poor idea. Pirate shook his head. His memories from that period were blurry; long ago, and he'd been coming off two or three years of booze and drugs. The only really clear trial memory he had was the length of time the jury had been out—twenty-three minutes. "Just long enough to polish off the doughnuts," someone, maybe a reporter, had said as they'd led Pirate away.

"Tell me about your alibi," Susannah said.

Pirate didn't feel like doing that. "Why?"

"Since you didn't take the stand," Susannah said, "your alibi entered the record only in the state's direct examination of the detective—what was his name?"

"Couldn't tell you," Pirate said. He yawned; normally this was nap time.

"And evidently Mr. Rollins didn't see fit to cross," Susannah said, "meaning it was never presented in its best light."

"What wasn't?"

"Your alibi."

Why all this talk about his alibi? It was a piss-poor alibi; Pirate had known that from the start. "No one to back it up," he said. "No witnesses."

Susannah smiled again, a quick little smile. "Run through it for me anyway."

Pirate shrugged. He ran through it, his puny alibi, a night alone in his apartment, drinking, drugging, watching TV, passing out till the middle of the next day. When they'd asked him what he'd watched on TV, he hadn't remembered a single show. The man he'd been was puny, too. He was much better now.

"This was your apartment at 2145 Bigard Street? Number four A?"

Pirate nodded, although he'd forgotten the apartment number and the address, too; only a memory of the building itself remained, brick, with an odd yellow stain down the front.

"Approximately two blocks north of Nappy's Fine Liquors at the corner of Charles?" Susannah said.

Pirate nodded. He remembered Nappy's all right, with its tiny slit windows, like a fort.

"I've got something to show you," Susannah said. She reached into the folder, took out a blown-up photograph, held it to the glass.

Pirate gazed at the photograph, a close-up of a young man, midchest to the top of his head. The young man looked angry about something, his mouth open like he might have been shouting. In fact, he was a mean-looking son of a bitch, with hostile eyes and a snake tattoo wound around one of his huge biceps. Pirate had a tattoo just like that, now faded by the passage of so much . . .

And then it hit him, who this was. He glanced at—what was her name again?—Susannah; he glanced at her, saw how she was watching him, the way you watch someone unwrapping a present when you know what's inside, and then looked back at this picture of himself, his much-younger, two-eyed self. He gazed at that pale blue right eye—an angry eye, the pupil dilated as though he'd been on something, but there, intact, whole.

Pirate's eye, his only eye, shifted back to Susannah.

"Well," she said, "do you see?"

"See what?" Pirate said.

"What this means."

Pirate stared at the picture. He noticed that this younger self of his was holding up something, a card or . . . a driver's license. His driver's license: he could just make out the tiny picture of himself, a still-younger version, last year of high school.

"No," Pirate said. "I don't know what it means."

"Check the bottom right-hand corner."

Pirate checked the bottom right-hand corner. He saw one of those time codes, in computer-style lettering: *12:41 AM July 23*. And then the year, twenty years before. All these numbers swam around in his mind, then clicked together in a way that made his steady, plodding heartbeat speed up a little. He was looking at a photograph from the night of Johnny Blanton's murder. Pirate turned slowly to Susannah.

"It's a still taken from a security video camera over the front door at Nappy's Fine Liquors," she said. "The store was closed at that hour, of course, but you wanted in. You even showed proof of age."

"I . . . I don't remember."

"The way we figure it, you woke up in the night, perhaps not very sober, went out for more to drink, came back home, blacked out."

"I just don't . . ."

"That's the beauty part," Susannah said. "It doesn't matter whether you remember or not. According to the trial testimony, Johnny Blanton was murdered between twelve-thirty and twelve forty-five. It might even have happened at that exact same minute, twelve forty-one."

Pirate stared at her. He got that squinting feeling in his non-eye, stronger than ever before, strong enough to hurt. For a moment, he thought he was actually seeing out of it, out of an empty socket. The beautiful skin on her face dissolved and the bones underneath appeared, clear as day, very fine. Yes, he was seeing out of his former eye.

"As you may recall," Susannah said, "the murder took place at the Parish Street Pier on the Sunshine Road bayou, not far from Magnolia Glade. That's six point three miles from Nappy's—or rather, from where Nappy's used to be. I measured it myself, Mr. DuPree. Do you see what this means? No one can be in two places at the same time. You didn't do it, end of story."

Tell me something I don't know. Pirate kept that thought to himself.

"Time's up," said the guard.

CHAPTER 2

Light slanted down through the gently heaving water in sunny columns, one of which illuminated a little fish swimming near the base of the reef, purple and gold, like a jewel on the move. Nell breathed deeply through her snorkel, filling her lungs, and dove straight down with slow, powerful kicks, her upper body still. Near the bottom, she stopped kicking and glided the rest of the way, hovering over the fish. A fairy basslet, or possibly a beaugregory, but Nell had never seen either one with gold so bright, purple so intense. It looked up at her, tiny eyes—most colorless of all its parts—watching her, void of any expression she could define. The fish was hovering, too, its front fins vibrating at hummingbird-wing speed, filagreed fins so close to transparent they were almost invisible. And—this was amazing—the two front fins didn't match: one was purple, the other gold. Nell, transfixed, lost all track of time until she felt pressure starting to build in her chest. She checked the depth gauge on her wrist: fifty-five feet. Nell was a good breath holder. She turned back for a last look at this special fish, perhaps one of a kind. It was gone. She kicked her way back up.

Nell broke the surface, blew through her snorkel, sucked in the rich air. Bahamian air: it had its own smell, floral and salty, her favorite smell on earth, and this was her favorite place. She turned toward Little Parrot Cay, a coral islet about fifty yards away: from this angle, tropical paradise pared down to the simplest components—white sand beach, a few palm trees, thatched hut—all colors bright, as in a child's version. In fact, hadn't Norah, her daughter, now in college, once come home from school with just such a painting? Nell was trying to remember the details when something down below grabbed her leg.

She jerked away, a frightened cry rising up her snorkel, a cry she smothered when her husband burst up through the surface, a big smile on his face.

"Clay," she said, pushing her mouthpiece aside, "you scared me."

He put his arms around her, sang a few off-key notes she took to be the shark theme from *Jaws*.

"I mean it," she said.

Clay stopped singing. He glanced down. "Hey, what's that?"

"What's what?"

"On the bottom."

Nell dipped her face into the water, gazed down through her mask. She saw something black lying on the sand, something man-made, maybe a box. She turned to Clay. That big smile was back on his face. She noticed he'd had way too much sun; this was the ninth day of vacation, their longest in years, maybe ever.

"Too deep for me," he said.

Nell got the mouthpiece back between her teeth, dove down. Yes, a box, not big, not heavy. She carried it back to the surface.

"What's inside?" Clay said; still that big smile.

Nell raised the lid. Inside, wrapped in waterproof plastic, she found another box, this one blue, the word *Tiffany* on the top. She opened it, too.

"Oh, Clay."

"Happy anniversary," said Clay.

"But it's months away."

"I couldn't wait."

They bobbed up and down, the swell pushing them closer together. The sand beach on Little Parrot Cay pinkened under the late-afternoon sun. A flock of dark birds rose out of the palms, wheeled across the sky and headed north.

"I don't want to go back," Nell said.

"Maybe one day we won't," said Clay.

"When?" said Nell. "Be specific."

Clay laughed. "June," he said.

"June?"

"The thirty-third."

She laughed, too, pretended to throw a punch. He pretended to block it.

They ate dinner on the patio of the house on the back, rocky side of Little Parrot Cay—spiny lobster, speared by Nell, conch fritters, cooked by Clay, white wine. The lights of North Eleuthera shone in the east, a fuzzy glow like a distant galaxy. Clay's lobster fork clinked on the glass table. A shooting star went by—not an uncommon nighttime sight on Little Parrot Cay, but this one was very bright. Nell caught its reflected path in Clay's eyes.

"Life is good," he said.

Their bare feet touched under the table.

Little Parrot Cay belonged to Clay's friend—their friend—Duke Bastien. Nell and Clay spent one or two weekends a year on the Cay, free weekends, if Duke had had his way, but Clay insisted on paying. He'd researched Out-Island hotel prices, paid Duke the top rate. That was Clay, at least the professional side: by the book. In other parts of life he could be unpredictable—the shark episode, for example; and sometimes in bed.

Like tonight. They'd been married for almost eighteen years, so it wasn't surprising that he'd know her body. But to know things about it that she did not? After, lying in bed, the ocean breeze flowing through the wide-open sliders, Nell said, "How do you know?"

But he was asleep.

Nell slept, too. She'd had the best sleeps of her life on the Cay, untroubled visits to some deep, rejuvenating place. And she was on her way when Johnny appeared in her dreams, stepping out from behind a coral reef, but somehow dry. He wore pin-striped suit pants—Nell remembered that suit— was barefoot and naked above the waist. The red hole over his heart was tiny, almost invisible. So long since she'd seen him, in life or in dreams: she wanted to lick that tiny red hole, make it go away, but the scene changed.

Nell awoke at dawn. The breeze had died down, leaving the bedroom cool, almost cold, but she was hot, her face clammy, an actual sweat drop rolling into the hollow of her throat. She glanced at Clay. He lay on his side, his back to her, very still. Light, weak and milky, left most of the room in shadow, but it illuminated a vein in Clay's neck, throbbing slowly.

Nell rose, saw herself in a mirror: her eyes were dark and worried. She went into the kitchen, dug through her purse, found her cell phone. No missed calls, specifically none from a 615 area code. That calmed her for a moment or two. She imagined Norah fast asleep in her dorm room, safe and sound. Then she began to find bad interpretations for the absence of a call, turn all the nonevidence upside down. She checked the time: 6:35. Too early to place a call of her own, not without appearing to be checking up, and Norah didn't like that. Nell's index finger trembled on the buttons. She made herself put the phone away.

A bird chirped in the flamboyant tree that stood near the back door. Nell walked down the crushed-shell path to the beach side of the Cay. The sea lay flat and motionless as it often did at dawn, more like jelly than water. Nell slipped off her nightgown and dove in, half expecting viscous resistance, but there was none. She found a nice rhythm right away, body riding flat and high, hips controlling everything, forearms loose, stroke soft on entry, speeding up at the end, and most important, feeling the water, mantra of her college coach. Feeling the water came naturally to Nell, was the reason she'd been drawn to swimming in the first place; and no water felt like this. Nell swam around Little Parrot Cay.

By the time she climbed back onto the beach, a light chop had ruffled up, as though her own motion had got things going. The sun, two or three handbreadths above the horizon, was already warm. Nell walked to the dock at the south end of the beach, turned on the hose and held it over her head, streaming the salt away, feeling fresh as this perfect morning. The truth was that back in her racing days, despite her love of the water and how coachable all her coaches said she was, she'd never been quite fast enough—a winner of heats now and then, but never a champion. Johnny, on the other hand: she remembered how she actually rocked in the water when he flew by in the next lane. She took a deep breath. He'd rocked her in the water. Remnants of some kind of bad dream came to life in her brain. The worried feeling, washed away, began to return. She turned off the hose, and was walking back up the beach to get her nightgown when she heard a faint drone in the sky.

A plane appeared in the west; a seaplane, floats glowing in the sun. The wings tilted and the plane came down in a long, curving arc. Nell put on her nightgown. The plane skimmed onto the water with a splash and coasted up to the dock, pushing a silver wave. The lettering on the tail read: DK INDUSTRIES. Nell went out to the end of the dock. The pilot's door opened.

"Hi, darlin'," said Duke Bastien. He threw her a line. Nell caught the end, looped it around a cleat. "Sorry to bust in," he said.

"Duke," she said. "It's your place."

"Bad manners is bad manners," said Duke, stepping onto the dock. Duke was a big guy; it trembled under his weight. "Clay up?" he said.

"I think he's still sleeping."

"You had one of your swims?"

Nell nodded, at the same time hiking up the shoulder strap of her nightgown, the fabric not transparent but very light. Duke was looking at her face, not her body; he actually did have good manners.

"Are you two going fishing?" Nell said. Duke had a thirty-two-foot inboard with a tuna tower, tied up on the other side of the dock. "Clay didn't mention it."

"'Fraid not," said Duke. "Mind getting him for me?"

Nell walked up to the house. A warm breeze sprang up, blew some deep red blossoms out of the flamboyant tree and across her path. A phone rang as she went inside. Two cell phones lay on the kitchen counter, his and hers. It was Clay's. She answered.

"Hello, ma'am. Sergeant Bowman here. The chief handy?"

"One moment," Nell said.

She went into the bedroom. Clay opened his eyes. He saw her and smiled. She knew that under the covers he was hard, all set for her to climb back in. That would have been nice. Nell covered the mouthpiece. "Sergeant Bowman's on the phone. And Duke just flew in—he's down at the dock."

"Duke's here?"

Clay sat up. He was one of those dark-haired, olive-skinned men who looked ten years younger than they were. The only sign of aging she could see on his face was a slight vertical groove on his brow, between the eyes. It deepened as he took the phone.

"Hey, Wayne," he said. "What's up?"

Clay listened for a second or two. "What the hell are you—" Then he went quiet, listened some more.

"Norah?" said Nell, moving closer. "Is it something about Norah?"

Clay shook his head, waved her away. He got out of bed, started pulling on a pair of shorts with his free hand, his erection deflating fast. Then he hurried out of the room. Nell followed.

Clay sped up. He was a very fast walker when he wanted

to be. Running after him down the crushed-shell path, she could barely keep up. His shoulder muscles stood out like ropes, rising to the base of his neck. He was still talking on the phone. She heard him say, "Just sit tight." And: "I'm on my way."

"On your way where?" Nell called after him. "Is it Norah?"

He didn't seem to hear. Duke watched from the dock, arms folded across his chest.

Nell ran faster, caught up to Clay, touched his back. "What?" she said. "Tell me."

Clay stuffed the phone in his pocket, whirled around. "Nell," he said. "Go on up to the house."

"But—"

His voice rose. "Did you hear me?"

He'd never spoken to her like that, not in eighteen years. It stunned her. She stood on the path, frozen in place. Clay seemed frozen there, too, face flushed, mouth a little open. He started to say something, something quieter, but Duke, coming toward them, interrupted.

"Just give us a minute or two, darlin'," he said. "Everything's fine."

"Is Norah all right?"

Duke shot Clay a puzzled look. "Why wouldn't she be?"

Clay reached out, squeezed her hand. "I told you. It's got nothing to do with Norah."

"Is it a business thing?"

"Yeah," said Duke. "Kinda."

They looked down at her, two big men, somehow reassuring just from the amount of space they occupied. Duke was an important businessman and one of Clay's biggest supporters, went way back with him, but they weren't in business together; Clay was the chief of police, not in business at all. Nell went back to the house, wondering what sort of business it could be.

Her phone was ringing. She grabbed it: not Norah; a Belle Ville number, slightly familiar although she couldn't place it.

"Hello?"

"Nell? Lee Ann Bonner."

Lee Ann Bonner, a reporter at the *Belle Ville Guardian,* had a daughter Norah's age. They'd been sleepover friends in grade school, but Nell hadn't talked to Lee Ann in years. She stepped onto the front terrace. Clay and Duke were talking on the dock, their heads close together.

"Nell?"

"Yes?"

"I know this must be an . . . unsettling time," Lee Ann said, "but I wondered if you had any comment at all, any reaction I could quote."

"I don't understand," Nell said. "Reaction to what?"

Pause, a long one. A big fish jumped clear of the water, not far from the end of the dock, but neither man noticed. "You mean you haven't heard?" Lee Ann said. "Alvin DuPree—they're letting him go."

Nell lost her balance, caught hold of a patio chair. Alvin DuPree was serving a life sentence without parole. "Letting him go?"

Lee Ann started in on a complicated answer Nell had trouble processing, all about something called the Justice Project, Hurricane Bernardine, FEMA, video cameras. Only the last sentence stuck in her mind, stuck like a fact sharpened at one end.

"He didn't do it."

CHAPTER 3

The seaplane rose in a long semicircle. At first Little Parrot Cay was clear in Nell's window. Then it got mixed up with other cays in the chain, and soon they were all just specks, and finally gone.

Up in the cockpit, Clay and Duke sat side by side. The backs of their heads had a similar shape, Clay's perhaps a little finer in some way; although their faces were very different, from this angle they could have been brothers.

"What's the Justice Project?" Nell said.

Because of engine noise, or the fact that both men were wearing headsets, they didn't hear.

She spoke louder. "What's the Justice Project?"

Clay turned, raising one earphone. "You say something?"

Nell repeated it once more.

"Lawyers," Clay said. "Don't know much about them."

"But they're wrong," Nell said. "It's all a mistake."

Clay nodded. He had fine eyes, soft, gentle brown and normally very clear, but now they looked blurry, and no particular color at all.

"What kind of lawyers?" Nell said. "How did it happen?"

"That's what I'm going to find out," Clay said, lowering the earpiece back in place and turning away. The plane entered a cloud, first wispy, then thick. A dull grayness closed in, taking away all dimensions, driving her into herself.

* * *

"Did you get a good look at him?"

"I was right there." Which explained the blood on the front of her white T-shirt.

The detective—she didn't catch his name for the longest time—had a gentle manner and a soft voice. "Think you could identify the killer?"

How could she not? She'd been right there.

Back in Belle Ville, a squad car was waiting to take Clay to his office downtown. Duke drove Nell home. They— she, Clay and Norah, when school wasn't in session—lived in the Heights, nicest neighborhood in Belle Ville next to Magnolia Glade. The route led through Lower Town, where the cleanup still went on, trucks, graders, front-end loaders—some bearing the DK Industries logo—clustered here and there. The stink of mud, rot, decomposition, hung in the air. Duke slid the windows up. From the porch of a lopsided house, the flood line halfway up the front door, a man watched them go by, his eyes expressionless but his posture accusatory, as though she or Duke, or people who rode in cars like Duke's, were somehow to blame for all the destruction. She was seeing that posture more and more.

"How long will it take for things to be normal?" she said.

Duke frowned. "What things?"

She gestured out the window.

"Oh," he said, frown fading. "Sewer piping goes in next month. After that the sidewalks and then it should be pretty quick."

Nell hadn't been talking about sewers and sidewalks; she let it go. Duke dropped her off a few minutes later.

Nell loved her house: Mediterranean-style, not too big, at the end of a cul-de-sac called Sandhill Way. Her favorite features were the terrace in back—a loggia, according to the real-estate agent who'd sold them the place—overlooking state-protected woods, and of course the lap pool, a Christmas present from Clay years before. She went inside, stepped over piles of mail on the tile floor. The message light was blinking on the hall phone, the word *full* in the little window.

She entered the kitchen, noticed fruit flies hovering over a bowl of fruit on the kitchen table. It wasn't like her to go away without putting that bowl in the fridge. Maybe she had put it away, maybe someone—

"Norah?" she called. "Norah?"

The house was silent. Nell went to the table, saw the fruit was rotten. She was in the garage, dumping it into a trash barrel, when she heard the front doorbell. Nell walked back into the house, stepped over the mail, opened the door.

Lee Ann Bonner stood outside, although Nell didn't recognize her for a moment. She'd never seen her wearing glasses before, and these were of some new, distracting design. They made her eyes look more intelligent than humanly possible, as though her IQ were three or four hundred.

"Oh, good," Lee Ann said. "I was hoping you'd be back."

"How did you know I was gone?" Nell said. A question that came blurting out without any thought on her part, but a sharp one.

"Called One Marigot." One Marigot was the address of police headquarters, finally habitable again—the reason Clay and Nell had been able to get away. "The chief's whereabouts is posted on the daily sheet."

"Oh," said Nell; maybe not a sharp question after all.

"You're looking good," Lee Ann said.

"Thanks."

"I like your hair that way."

"I like yours, too."

Lee Ann patted her own hair; she had a spiky cut, pretty edgy for Belle Ville. "Still with the museum?"

Nell nodded; she was assistant curator at the Belle Ville

Museum of History and Art. "But we're closed until the insurance comes through."

"Any damage to the paintings and stuff?"

"No. We lost one of the pieces in the sculpture garden, that's all."

"Which one?"

"*Cloud Nine.*"

"*Cloud Nine?* With those arches?"

"Yes."

"That's my favorite."

"Mine, too."

Behind those strange glasses, Lee Ann's eyes narrowed. "Wasn't it made of metal?"

"Bronze."

"How does something like that get washed away?"

"It was stolen," Nell said. "In all the chaos."

"What's it worth?"

"We paid twenty thousand dollars, but his stuff has gone up."

"Christ," said Lee Ann. She took off her glasses, didn't seem quite so intimidating. "How's Norah?"

"Good."

"At Duke, right?"

"Vanderbilt."

"Always did have a head on her shoulders."

"And Layla?" Nell said.

"Partying her ass off at LSU. I only hear from her when she wants money."

Nell remembered then that Lee Ann had gotten divorced somewhere along the way. A bee came buzzing by. Lee Ann blinked.

"Speaking of the hurricane," she said, "I wondered whether you could help me out on a few things."

"Like what?"

"This business with Alvin DuPree."

"I told you on the phone, Lee Ann—I really don't know anything about it."

"But you must—" The bee, or another one, whizzed right between two of those spiky tufts on Lee Ann's head. "Ooo," she said, ducking away. "I hate bees—swell up like you wouldn't believe."

"We can't have that," Nell said, stepping aside.

Lee Ann laughed and went in.

They sat in the sunroom, looking out on the lap pool, and drank lemonade.

"This is nice," Lee Ann said. "Reminds me of the old days, when the girls were little. They were so different— Layla such a chatterbox, Norah so quiet. Remember?"

"Yes."

"She was a deep one, I could see it," Lee Ann said. "Bet she's at the top of her class."

"Not quite." In fact, Norah was on academic probation.

"Gets those smarts from you," Lee Ann said. "No disrespect to your husband, of course." Nell didn't correct her on any of that. Lee Ann reached into her bag, took out a spiral notebook. "I really think the story here, the crux of it, the human story, is your reaction," she said. "How would you describe it?"

"For the third time, Lee Ann. I don't understand what's going on."

"But the simple fact that he's being freed, that he didn't do it, must—".

"He did it." Nell's voice rose in anger, taking her by surprise.

Lee Ann nodded, wrote something in her notebook.

"You're writing that down?" Nell said.

"For accuracy," said Lee Ann.

"But I don't want you to."

"You don't want me to be accurate?"

Nell shook her head. "It's not that. But I can't be quoted in the paper. Is that what you're planning?"

Lee Ann smiled. "I am a reporter. And this is shaping up to be a big story."

"It is?"

"An innocent man in jail for twenty years and all of a sudden exculpatory evidence comes floating up out of One Marigot? Sounds like a big story to me."

"Exculpatory?" Nell stumbled a little over the word, a word she knew but had never spoken before. "That's impossible. I saw it with my own eyes."

Lee Ann's pen was moving, although her eyes, now behind those glasses again, were on Nell. "You're referring to the murder?"

"Yes. But I'm not going to talk about it. There's obviously some big mistake—and I'm sure my husband is straightening it out right now."

Lee Ann's pen stopped in midstroke. She closed the notebook, put it away. "Fair enough," she said. "But how about a little chat on background?"

Background? "Meaning?"

"Off the record. No quotes, no reactions, no story in the paper. Just so I can understand better."

"I don't know," Nell said. But what harm could there be? The story—her part, at least—must have been a matter of record.

"It would be a big help to me," Lee Ann said. "I was still in Atlanta back then." She raised her lemonade glass, took a sip. "Mmm," she said. Just a little thing, but the atmosphere in the room changed, became more social. "I've forgotten whether you're from here or not."

"From Dallas originally," Nell said. "But we moved here when I was six or seven. My dad took a job at Mercy."

"He's a doctor?"

"Was. They're retired now, living in Naples."

"Yeah? My dad's in Sarasota, with wife number four. She's five years older."

"That's not too bad."

"Than me," Lee Ann said.

Nell laughed, drank some of her lemonade.

"I take it," said Lee Ann, "that the victim—the original victim—was your boyfriend?"

Nell put down her glass. "Yes," she said, wondering what Lee Ann meant by *original victim*.

"John Blanton?"

"Everyone called him Johnny."

"Was he from Belle Ville?"

"New Orleans," Nell said. "We met at UNC. He was writing his Ph.D. thesis."

"Art history, like you?"

"Geology," Nell said. "And I actually didn't even complete my master's. We were spending that summer here, but I never went back."

"The summer of the murder?"

Nell nodded. One of the biggest regrets of her life, not going back, abandoning her studies, but she kept that to herself, always had; a minor matter, after all, compared with what happened to Johnny.

"Do you ever regret that?" Lee Ann said. "Not going back?"

"No," Nell said. It hit her for the first time—why now?— that going back to Chapel Hill, finishing the degree, was what Johnny would have wanted her to do.

"But you ended up with a good job anyway," Lee Ann said, as though she'd been following Nell's thoughts.

"I love the museum," Nell said.

"Best thing in the whole town, if you ask me," Lee Ann said.

"I wouldn't go that far."

"No? You like it here? Don't find B Ville a bit slow?"

"I like it. Especially the way it used to be."

"Before the murder?"

Nell paused. That wasn't what she'd meant, but it sidetracked her. "Before the hurricane," she said. "The goddamn hurricane."

"It wasn't just the hurricane that did us in."

"What do you mean?"

"Nîmes got hit just as hard and they had barely any flooding at all."

"But aren't they higher up?" A long-ago conversation with

Johnny, something about the geology of the region, stirred in her mind.

"Not much," Lee Ann said. "We'll have to wait for the report."

"Report?"

"From the Army Corps of Engineers—the levees, the Canal Street floodgates, what went wrong and why, et cetera, et cetera. And who knows how long that'll take?" A cell phone rang in Lee Ann's bag. She took it out, glanced at the number, frowned, put it back. "What can you tell me about the murder?"

"It was horrible."

"You were an eyewitness?"

"Yes."

"The only eyewitness?"

"That's right."

"Where did it happen?"

Nell took a deep breath. All at once she felt nervous, as though about to take a big test, or give a speech. At the same time, she found she wanted to talk about it, a desire she hadn't had in years, maybe not since the trial. "Just south of Magnolia Glade," she said. "We—Johnny and I—were living in my parents' guesthouse for the summer." One odd thing about that summer: hot, like all Gulf summers, but for some reason the humidity never came, making for soft, warm nights, one after another. "Johnny spent the days on his thesis—he'd reached the writing stage. I was teaching swimming at the Y camp. At night we went for long walks, sometimes all the way to the levee."

"Levee?"

"The old Sunshine Road levee. It all got changed after they built the canal." Their favorite spot in Belle Ville: from up on the levee, they'd had a clear view of the Gulf, with the lights of the shrimpers and the freighters moving slowly in the darkness.

Lee Ann's phone rang again. "Damn," she said, ignoring it. "Go on."

Suddenly Nell had a clear memory of the moon that night,

a full moon, very bright, and how Johnny had explained that the moon had probably once been part of the earth. What had he said? *It's like a little ghost brother stuck up there.* He'd had a head full of thoughts like that, rocked her with them once in a while, the way he'd rocked her in the pool the first time they'd met. Love at first sight, no doubt about it. Falling in love with Clay had been different, longer, slower, perhaps sweeter; and darker, of course. But Lee Ann didn't want to hear any of that.

"We were on our way back," Nell said. "Following the creek. Do you know the pier at the foot of Parish Street?"

"Gone now," said Lee Ann. "Bernardine."

Nell hadn't known that. "We were just passing the pier when—"

She paused. What was that? The front door?

"When what?" said Lee Ann.

At that moment, Clay walked in. He'd changed at the office, was wearing a dark suit—the one she'd got at the Brooks Brothers outlet—white shirt, blue tie. "Hi, baby," he said, and then noticed Lee Ann, in the corner on the wicker chair.

"You remember Lee Ann?" Nell said.

"Wouldn't take much of a memory," Clay said. "Lee Ann was in my office not two hours ago."

Nell turned to Lee Ann, a little confused. Lee Ann's face was expressionless, but she'd shifted her legs under the chair, as though about to rise.

"Where I told her," Clay went on, "I had no comment on the DuPree situation and that I didn't believe my wife would either. So I assume what we have here is a social call."

Lee Ann was on her feet. "This is a big story, Chief," she said. "There's no way to keep it under wraps."

"Keeping things under wraps has never been my style," Clay said, "as I think the *Guardian* knows."

"They've backed him in every election," Nell said, unnecessary since Lee Ann had to know that, but it popped out anyway.

"Then why this new approach?" Lee Ann said.

"It's not a new approach," Clay said. "We always make sure we've got the facts before going public."

"Is it a fact that the D.A.'s going to oppose the motion to cut Alvin DuPree loose?" Lee Ann said.

"You'll have to ask her."

"I plan to."

"That's your right," Clay said. "Even your duty. We won't keep you."

Lee Ann slung her bag over her shoulder, turned to Nell. "Good to see you," she said.

"I'll walk you to the door," said Nell.

A silent walk. When Nell returned, she found Clay in the kitchen, buttering a cracker, his hands not quite steady.

"Those are stale," Nell said.

Clay didn't seem to hear. The cracker split in half. He reached in the box for another one. "What did you tell her?" he said.

"Nothing," said Nell. "I've got nothing to tell. What's going on?"

Clay sat at the counter, rubbed his eyes. "I wish I knew." He kept rubbing them, much too hard.

"Don't," said Nell. "You'll hurt yourself." She went over to him, pulled his hands away. His eyes still had that blurry look, and now they were bloodshot, too. She kissed his forehead. At the same time, she caught a whiff of that downtown stink that Bernardine had left behind, most noticeable when the breeze blew from the west. Had she left the front door open? She went to check. It was closed.

CHAPTER 4

A little ghost brother, going round and round?" said Nellie.

"Yeah," said Johnny Blanton. He took her hand. They walked along the Sunshine Road towpath, the road on one side, the bayou on the other, moon overhead. A breeze drifted by, leaving the air the way it had been, soft and warm, so strangely unoppressive for July, and now smelling of flowers. "There must be some great paintings of the moon," Johnny said.

"*Starry Night*," said Nellie. But other than that she couldn't think of a single one.

"That's it?" Johnny said.

"Maybe painters didn't want to do landscapes at night," Nellie said.

"Because it's hard to see?"

"And colder."

"Hey!" said Johnny. "Now you're thinking like a scientist." He stopped, faced her. She saw the moon in his eyes, reflected twice. "On the other hand," he said, "it's night and I can see you fine." They kissed. "So that shoots your theory."

"Then let's go home," Nellie said. "And try getting practical."

"Like how?"

"Maybe you can come up with something."

They walked back in the moonlight, unhurried. Nellie's parents' guesthouse stood in the farthest corner of the property; they had privacy and all the time in the world. A quiet summer night: nothing to hear but their footsteps, their breathing and the water, making sucking sounds in the bayou.

"Tide's coming in," Johnny said.

"There are tides in the bayou?"

"Sure," said Johnny. "This one anyway. And it'll be a high one tonight."

"How come?"

Johnny pointed at the moon. "Full," he said. "Kind of poetic, if you think of it, the ghost brother still clinging on."

"Better explain the tides, Johnny."

Johnny explained the tides.

"Who figured all this out?" Nellie said.

"You mean what causes the tides, and the mathematical framework?" he said. "Newton."

"When was that?"

"Sixteen-ninety, give or take."

"Wow."

"Wow what?"

"Think of all that time before, when people had no idea," Nellie said.

"That's you."

"What do you mean?"

"That reaction, imagining a whole vanished world. Me, I'm in 1689, trying to find what comes next."

She mussed his hair. "My very own Sir Isaac."

"Not even close—there'll never be another Newton," Johnny said. They were arm in arm now, the Parish Street Pier a dark slanting oblong in the distance. "Fact is, I've been thinking about tides a lot lately."

"For your thesis?" Nellie said, trying to see some connection to geology.

"No," Johnny said. "But being down here got me interested."

"In what way?"

"Everyone knows how low the land is around here," Johnny said. "But there hasn't been much research on the topography of the sea bottom, especially as it relates to the shore contour. There are some obvious conclusions waiting out there, but no one seems in a hurry to—"

"Topography?" Nellie said. "What's that?"

"Land shape," said Johnny, "but I'm just interested in elevation differences on the sea bottom. Accurate data are a little hard to come by."

"But the charts must go way back."

He put his arm over her shoulder; she put hers behind his back; they fit together perfectly. Nellie loved the feel of his back, sinewy, the spine in a deep hollow between two long muscles, swimmer's muscles. "They do," he said as they came to the Parish Street Pier, a rickety old structure once used for launching little catfish boats, back when there'd been catfish in the bayou. "The problem is that the bottom changes over time—the whole earth's so dynamic, that's what keeps jumping out at—" He cut himself off. "Am I boring you?"

"Never," she said. "'The bottom changes over time' and therefore?"

He smiled, his teeth pure white in the moonlight. "And therefore—I've actually done some modeling on this—let's suppose you've got contours basically acting like a giant funnel, when along comes—"

A man stepped out from behind a support post on the pier. The movement startled Nellie. Johnny's hand tightened a little on her shoulder, strong and reassuring. The man came forward; a big, dark form.

"Evening," Johnny said.

The man took another step then paused. There was something wrong with his face, something horribly misshapen. He took another step, turning slightly into the moonlight, and Nellie saw she was wrong about his face. It wasn't misshapen, just covered by a bandanna pulled up to his eyes.

* * *

"Norah? Hi, it's Mom. Everything good? Give me a call. When you get a chance."

Clay came out of the bedroom. He'd changed out of his dark suit, wore shorts, flip-flops, a polo shirt. "Let's go for a walk," he said.

"A walk?" Nell said. They never went for walks; on the beach at Little Parrot Cay, maybe, but not at home.

"It's nice out," Clay said.

They went outside. It didn't seem that nice to Nell. A wind blew from the north, driving a line of clouds across the sky, and the temperature was falling. Clay took her hand as they walked around the circle at the end of the street and followed Sandhill Way's gentle downward slope. His hand was so much bigger than hers; she thought of her father walking her up to the diving board at the Y, long ago. The neighborhood was quiet, parents at work, kids at school; a dog barked in someone's backyard, and a gardener leaned on his rake, touching the buttons on a handheld device with a toothpick.

"Haven't got much to tell you yet," Clay said.

"But this tape," Nell said, "or picture, or whatever it is—it has to be a fake." A statement, but her voice rose a little at the end, on its own.

"Goes without saying. But how it happened, who made it—I'm not getting anywhere on that. All we know is some FEMA worker found the tape in a locked file cabinet that got sprung open, or that somebody sprung open, in a basement storage room at One Marigot. From there it gets to these justice people, by steps unknown."

Nell gave her head a little shake, as though that might unscramble things, restore order. "Anybody could have made the tape," she said. "Anybody with the right kind of know-how."

Clay glanced down at her, looked away. "It's not just the tape," he said.

"What do you mean?"

"There was a note along with it."

"What kind of note?"

They came to the cross street, Blue Heron Road, turned right. The mail truck appeared, the driver waving as she went by. "Purports to be from the guy who sent the tape, Napoleon Ferris, owner of the liquor store."

"What did it say?"

Clay took a deep breath, let it out slowly. When he spoke his voice was so low she could hardly make out the words. "Something to the effect of 'You've got the wrong guy.'"

Nell squeezed his hand. They passed the tennis club, all the courts deserted. A small lizard lay on the baseline on court one, flicking its tongue. "Does this man, Napoleon, does he have some grudge against . . ." She left the sentence unfinished, having no idea how a grudge might explain what was going on. Was this some kind of conspiracy? Her mind didn't work well in areas like that.

"Be nice to know what he was up to," Clay said. The wind rose. "First we have to find him."

A raindrop struck Nell's face. "I don't understand."

"Looks like he's a refugee." There were hundreds of Bernardine refugees, gone to Houston and Atlanta, and many of them hadn't returned. "No one's seen him since the hurricane and vandals tore his store apart."

"Are you looking for him?"

"Oh, yeah. There's no way they'll hold the hearing till we find him."

"Hearing?"

"On DuPree's status. Whether or not to free him."

"That won't happen, will it?"

"Freeing him?" Clay shook his head.

Rain started falling, light at first. The lizard had vanished. Nell and Clay headed for home. The rain fell harder. They sped up, and soon were running, no longer holding hands. They'd been surprised by sudden squalls and ended up running like this before, but all the other times had led to lots of laughter, and feeling younger than they were. Thunder boomed in the north, and the full torrent, icy cold, caught them just as they reached the driveway. They hurried to the side door, sheltered from the rain under the breezeway roof. Clay unlocked the door, turned to her, water streaming down his face.

"One other thing," he said. "That locker belonged to Bobby Rice."

"Bobby?" she said. Bobby Rice had been Clay's partner, back in his detective days, back when Johnny got murdered. "What does that mean?"

"Don't ask me," Clay said. "But the envelope the tape came in is postmarked a month before the trial." He went inside.

A month before the trial? Meaning it had sat, undisclosed, in Bobby Rice's file cabinet for twenty years? How was that possible? Or, if it was all a conspiracy, someone had made it look like the tape had been there all that time. These new facts, if they were facts, refused to line up in her mind, form a narrative. And there'd be no explanation from Bobby: he'd drowned in the flood, rescuing a baby from a rooftop in Lower Town, and lay in the Old Cemetery, integrated at last, not far from the town's Confederate heroes.

Nell stood in the breezeway, rain pouring down on both sides, splashing on the stone walkways. One of the first things she'd noticed about Clay, in those days after the murder when she began noticing things again, was how well he got along with Bobby. With Belle Ville's racial history the way it was, that nice, easy, respectful way they had with each other caught her attention. A full year had passed before she spent even a moment with Clay that didn't relate to the case, but what had come later, what they had now, had probably started then.

The detective introduced himself and his partner, but Nellie, sitting in the family room at her parents' house, didn't catch the names. She couldn't stop shaking and all the colors in the room were wrong, every tone darkened down.

"Ma'am?" said the detective, turning to Nellie's mother. "Maybe she'd like a cup of tea."

"Oh, yes," said Nellie's mom, and she hurried away.

"I want this animal caught," said Nellie's father, his voice much too loud, loud and ragged. "Caught and lethally injected."

In dinner-table conversations, he'd always been an opponent of capital punishment. Nellie started crying.

"Perhaps, sir," said the detective, "we could have just a few moments alone with your daughter."

"Get us out of here much quicker," said the partner.

"I'm her father. I'm also a physician. Can't you see she's in a state of—"

"It's all right, Dad." She pulled herself together, at least to the extent of stopping the tears.

Her father left the room, half closing the door. She could hear him pacing in the hall.

"Mind if we sit down?" the detective said. Nellie noticed his voice—maybe because of the contrast to the way her father had been talking—deep but gentle.

"Please," Nellie said.

The detective pulled up her father's brass-studded leather footstool; the partner sat on the couch beside her, leaving plenty of space. They didn't speak, just sat there, almost like churchgoers waiting for the service to begin.

"I was so slow," Nellie said.

"Not sure I'm following," said the detective.

"If I'd been quicker, maybe—" She began crying again.

"One thing you can't do right now," the detective said, "now or ever, is blame yourself for anything."

"You survived," said the partner. "Survive something like that, you're a hero, plain and simple."

"But you don't understand," Nellie said. "We're swimmers. We could have swum away. We could have swum all the way down the bayou."

"Swimmers?"

And she began telling them about the swimming, how

she'd been on the UNC team, how Johnny, as an undergraduate at Texas a few years before, had put up the third-fastest one hundred butterfly time in the nation, how they'd met in the pool. She went on and on, all this irrelevant stuff about Johnny and her, but suddenly there was nothing more important than getting it on the record. Nellie sat on the sofa in the old family room, blood on her T-shirt, and saw that everything about Johnny and her was made official. She almost included the fact that she was pregnant, but she and Johnny had decided to keep it just between themselves for a while; announcing it now, by herself, somehow felt like a betrayal.

"What is it you want?" Johnny said, backing away, left arm around Nellie, turning slightly to shield her.

Behind the bandanna, the man's lips moved. "Money," he said.

"All right," said Johnny. "You can have my money." With his free hand, he reached into his right front pocket, where he kept his billfold.

That left him with no free hands, and his chest exposed. The man stepped forward. Moonlight flashed on a long blade. Then came a horrible sound of steel on bone, in bone, through bone, and Johnny staggered.

Nellie caught him. The knife slid free of Johnny's body, still in the man's hand; Nellie heard a faint hiss of air leaking from Johnny's chest. *But no blood, thank God.* The man raised the knife. Nellie kicked out at him, an instinctive movement, but with all her strength. She hit him right on the knee. He grunted in pain. His leg buckled. He twisted around, and at that moment the bandanna slid partway down and she caught her glimpse of his face, at least the upper half: a white face, possibly round and fleshy, with pale blue eyes, almost colorless. Then headlights shone way down Sunshine Road, and the man raised the bandanna and ran, at first with a limp and then not, over to Parish Street and into the woods.

"Johnny?" He was still leaning against her, but now started slipping down her body. She lowered him onto the path. "Are you all right?" she said, kneeling beside him, cradling his head.

"I think so," he said. That was when the blood came.

CHAPTER 5

Pirate opened his Bible, read the following passage several times. His lips moved as he read and a whispery sound came from his mouth. He already knew these words by heart; this was more like harmonizing than reading.

> And the Lord turned the captivity of Job, when he prayed for his friends: also the Lord gave Job twice as much as he had before. Then came there unto him all his brethren, and all his sisters, and all they that had been of his acquaintance before, and did eat bread with him in his house: and they bemoaned him, and comforted him over all the evil that the Lord had brought upon him: every man also gave him a piece of money, and every one an earring of gold. So the Lord blessed the latter end of Job more than his beginning: for he had fourteen thousand sheep, and six thousand camels, and a thousand yoke of oxen, and a thousand she asses. He also had seven sons and three daughters.

Turned the captivity: Pirate had determined long ago that this was a way of saying God set Job free. He remembered a line from somewhere: *A test. This is only a test.* Was it from Job? He thought not, but couldn't be sure. Pirate hadn't been quite sure of things since that visit from the lawyer woman with the beautiful skin, her name now forgotten. If it hadn't been for her beautiful skin, Pirate might have decided that he'd imagined the whole meeting; but his imagination wasn't good enough to picture skin like that. Also, there were rumors in the prison, rumors about him. Fourteen thousand sheep, six thousand camels: he knew that was crazy. And the she asses, whatever those were, gave him bad thoughts.

He reread the entire Book of Job, fondling the gold tassel while he searched without success for: *A test. This is only a test.* That carried him all the way to exercise period.

Pirate had a tiny weapon he preferred to take with him to exercise period. It was probably too small—just a spear-point-tipped razor-blade fragment with a safe edge on one side for gripping, an edge he'd made from hardened chewing gum—for actual killing, useful only for cutting and slashing. Not that he'd ever cut and slashed with it: Pirate was at peace with the other inmates. But after what had happened to him at exercise period one day in his second year, he'd fallen into the habit of being prepared.

Pirate was concealing his weapon just as he heard the click that meant his door was about to slide open. A tiny weapon, wrapped in a tiny bit of cloth: Pirate raised his patch, folded up his eyelid—he still had an eyelid, the way whales still had bones for feet, a fact he'd read somewhere—and placed the weapon in his socket, where it fit, but barely, if he got the angle just so. Pirate folded his eyelid back down, lowered the patch, and went to exercise period.

Exercise period took place in a big, open-roofed cage with a dirt yard and a basketball hoop at one end. For some reason, Pirate arrived a minute or two early. There was only one other inmate on the yard, sitting slumped against the fence as though ill, and as Pirate went closer he saw that this lone inmate was Esteban Malvi. He and Esteban Malvi went way back. Pirate's heart started beating fast, despite how at peace he was with everything. His heart beat fast and he felt the tiny weapon in his eye.

* * *

Year two. In those days, the exercise yard was bigger and uncaged, on the other side of C-block, bounded by the walls themselves. C-block was the oldest part of the prison, and there were a few odd corners in the old yard, hard to see from the towers. Guards patrolled the yard, so those blind spots shouldn't have mattered, but they did on the morning that Esteban Malvi decided that Pirate—still called Al at the time—had disrespected him.

Pirate was a much bigger man than Esteban Malvi, and at that stage of his life still jacked and ripped besides. The catch was Malvi's position: his father headed a Central American drug gang, the Ocho Cincos or something like that, a gang unknown to Pirate until too late. They lured him into one of those blind spots in the yard with an offer of a cigarette. For a moment, everything looked friendly, Malvi sitting on a bench, eating yogurt with a plastic spoon, other inmates lounging around: one of those misleading first impressions. The other inmates turned out to be Ocho Cincos. The next minute Pirate lay helpless on the ground and Malvi was scooping out his right eye with the plastic spoon. Impossible to do that with a plastic spoon, of course. The eating part snapped off right away, but what remained had a sharp point, and Malvi finished the job with that. A minute later, Pirate was alone and the guards were on their way. No witnesses stepped forward, and Pirate, now more experienced, knew enough to keep his mouth shut.

And here, slumped against the fence in the new yard, was Esteban Malvi, all pale and clammy, looking ill, and for a moment or two they would be alone. Pirate went closer. Esteban recognized him, understood the situation instantly, tried to squirm away. But he was weak, and there was nowhere to go. Pirate crouched beside him. Esteban's eyes shifted here and there, maybe searching for help. But Pirate knew there would be no help. Everything was lined up right.

"What's the matter, Esteban?" he said. "Got AIDS?"

"A little bit," Esteban said.

Pirate put a hand on Esteban's shoulder. His hand looked huge and strong, Esteban's shoulder weak and pitiful. The tiny weapon in Pirate's eye itched to get out.

Esteban pushed against the fence, as though his body could flow through the holes. "What—what can I do for you?" he said. "Maybe make things easier?"

"Things couldn't be any easier," Pirate said. "I'm easy."

"Oh, right, I hear you're getting out. Be a shame to ruin that."

Pirate shrugged. "Do I care?" he said. A funny question: he didn't know the answer himself. He let go of Esteban, raised his eyepatch, folded back the eyelid, produced the weapon. Esteban's eyes got very big. They suddenly began exerting magnetic force, and the weapon was steel. What else could it do?

"Oh, God," said Esteban.

And at that moment, Pirate understood the story of Job, but completely, the last bit of meaning falling into rightful place: he knew what it felt like, not just to be Job, but to be God as well. Had he ever felt happier in his life? Pirate laughed out loud. For some reason that scared Esteban even more. Yellow liquid pooled in the dirt between his legs. Pirate wrapped the tiny weapon in its tiny scrap of cotton and put it back where it belonged. He rose.

"This is your lucky day, Esteban," he said.

Esteban gazed up at him.

"But don't push it too far—I'm not going to cure your AIDS."

Esteban's face turned unpleasant; he let his natural meanness get the best of him. "You nuts?" he said.

Pirate froze for a second. Then he bent over and patted Esteban's clammy head. After that, more to demonstrate God's unpredictability than anything else—how could you spend time with Job without learning of God's unpredictability?—Pirate thumbed up one of Esteban's eyelids, licked the tip of the index finger of his other hand, just to be sanitary, and stroked Esteban's eyeball, stroked it lightly, the way he'd stroke a kitten. Well, maybe a little harder than that. Then came some sort of cry on Esteban's part, not too loud. Pirate gave a brief explanation: "This is only a test." He walked away. Other inmates were arriving, plus a few guards. Pirate spoke to one of them.

"Esteban's AIDS is giving him a hard time today."

The guard glanced over at Esteban, slumped against the fence. "Christ," he said, and reached for his surgical gloves.

Pirate lay on his bunk, fingers on the gold tassel. Time passed. He was at peace. Footsteps sounded outside: light, with a slight offbeat rhythm—recognized by Pirate from his guitar-playing days—as though whoever was coming had a song on the brain. Pirate already knew: it was the CO with the modified dreds, a big man but soft on his feet.

"Pirate?" he said. "Visitor."

Pirate didn't feel like a visitor—he was having a nice quiet time—but he didn't argue. Keys jingled. He went through the steps: raised arms, spreading, dropped pants, bending. Then Pirate and the guard walked past all the caged rats.

"Lots of talk about you these days, Pirate," the guard said.

"Don't pay attention to gossip, myself," said Pirate.

They went into the visiting room. The woman with the glowing skin was waiting on the other side of the glass. Pirate sat in the middle chair, like last time, and picked up the phone.

The woman smiled. "Hello, Mr. DuPree," she said. "Holding up all right?"

Holding up all right? Pirate wasn't sure he understood the question. At the same time, since he'd forgotten her name, he couldn't politely reply, *Hello, Miss* whatever the name happened to be. He ended up saying nothing.

That tiny frown furrow appeared on the woman's brow,

adding to her beauty. "This waiting must be hard," she said.

Pirate shrugged. He was an expert at waiting.

"The hearing has been postponed," the woman said, "while they track down Napoleon Ferris."

"Nappy."

"Yes, Nappy. The liquor-store owner."

"I didn't like him."

"No?"

"He wanted nine ninety-nine for a pint of Popov."

"That's a kind of vodka?"

"Barely."

The woman laughed. He'd cracked a joke. It felt good, and seeing her laugh was even better. He remembered her name.

"Barely, Susannah," he said. "But I don't drink anymore."

Her eyes shifted slightly. He took that to mean *of course not, you're in prison,* and for a second or two—but no more—she wasn't quite so beautiful.

"Don't kid yourself," he said.

"I won't," she said, looking serious, and back to her old beautiful self. "In the meantime, we were wondering—"

"What meantime?"

Susannah blinked. "While the search goes on for Nappy."

"Nappy, Nappy, Nappy."

"Mr. DuPree?"

"Why all this talk about Nappy?"

"We need his testimony to fill in the gaps."

"Gaps?"

"In the whole story of the tape—when it was sent, why, why not pursued." Her answer led to confusion in Pirate's mind, but before he could speak she went on: "We'll have a much better chance with the judge."

"What judge?"

"We don't know who it will be yet, but I'm talking about the judge at your hearing," Susannah said. "The hearing to free you."

"Turn the captivity," said Pirate.

"I'm sorry?" she said.

Pirate bowed his head, remained silent.

"In the meantime," she said, "we wondered whether you've given any thought to what you might want to do if we're successful."

Pirate looked up. "Successful?"

"At the hearing."

"Oh," said Pirate. His mind was a blank.

"Have you kept in touch with any relatives or friends?"

In touch: Pirate thought of the slightly damp, surprisingly hard surface of Esteban Malvi's eye. He shook his head.

"Is there anyone on the outside you'd like us to contact?"

"Besides Nappy, you mean?"

Susannah paused for a moment, then laughed. He'd cracked another joke. "Yes," she said, "besides Nappy."

"Nope," said Pirate.

She gazed at him. "There'll be plenty of time to figure this all out later."

"Okay."

"Is there anything we can help you with for now?" she said. "Anything you need?"

"An earring of gold."

She laughed right away, catching on to his sense of humor. But this time he hadn't been joking. "It's good to see you holding up so well, Mr. DuPree—and I think you have every right to be cautiously optimistic."

Cautiously optimistic! What a great expression! That was him in a nutshell. "Okay," he said.

"I'll be in touch. Bye, Mr. DuPree." She hung up.

"I'm going to have twice what I had before," Pirate said.

She picked up the phone. "Sorry, what was that?"

"Drive safe," said Pirate.

CHAPTER 6

Lee Ann was on the phone. "Any chance of getting together today?" she said. "I've got a few things I'd like to go over with you."

"What kind of things?" Nell said. She was in the middle of writing an e-mail to Norah: *I've left a couple messages, sweetheart. Everything ok? If you've lost your phone again, don't wor—*

"Concerning Alvin DuPree," Lee Ann said.

"Lee Ann, please. I've got nothing to say. This is a mistake and it's going to get cleared up."

"Even if it is," Lee Ann said, "that's a story, too. How a mistake like this could happen, the role of Bernardine and the flood, what it says about the whole town."

"Maybe you're right," Nell said. "But I can't help you."

"Can't or won't?"

"I don't understand that question," Nell said; she heard her tone sharpening. "It's *can't* of course. This tape is a fake of some kind, but other than that, I have no information at all."

"Has it been definitely identified as a fake?"

"I don't know," Nell said. "Why don't you call Clay?"

"I did."

"And?"

"He had no comment."

"Then neither do I."

"But—"

In fact, this was sneaky: Lee Ann was trying to get her to talk behind Clay's back. "Sorry, Lee Ann, I've got to go."

"But there's—"

Nell hung up. She went back to her e-mail, fingers not quite steady. . . . *don't worry—just get another one and put it on the debit card. Talk to you soon, I hope. Love, Mom.*

The phone rang just as she deleted *I hope* and hit send. Nell let it ring. The answering machine took the call. Lee Ann said, "Nell? You there? I was about to mention something I probably should have figured out long ago but didn't. I've been going over the timeline, and there doesn't seem to be any way for Clay to have been Norah's father. Am I right on this? And if—"

Nell grabbed the phone. "What the hell are you doing?" she said.

"Working on a story."

"My private life has nothing to do with your story." Nell slammed down the phone.

Her first instinct was to pick it right back up and call Clay. But why add to his burden? Nell took a deep breath and called Lee Ann instead.

"Are you planning to put it in the paper?" she said. "About Clay?"

"No," Lee Ann said. "I have no plans to do that."

"Good," said Nell. "Because it's not a secret. Clay filed adoption papers." And had tried his best—and Clay's best meant a very high standard—to be a good father to Norah and even more than that, loved her as his own daughter; Nell left all that unsaid.

"Sorry," Lee Ann said. "I should have checked that."

"But why? Why are you doing any of this? This is my personal business."

"I'm only trying to understand," Lee Ann said, "to get all the pieces straight in my head before the hearing."

"But the hearing will be the end of it," Nell said. "The

tape is a fake. How many times do I have to say it? I saw the killing happen with my own eyes."

"I know," Lee Ann said, her tone softening. After a short pause, she said, "What if I picked you up and went over there, would you be willing to talk me through the whole thing?"

"Over where?" said Nell.

"Parish Street," Lee Ann said. "Down where the pier used to be. This is for background only, as I said, but also . . ."

"Also what?"

"I know we were never really close, but—also as a friend."

"That's very nice," Nell said, actually meaning it. "But no."

"Your call, no problem," said Lee Ann. "Just one last thing—I've got an idea or two about the tape."

"Go on."

"I'd prefer to do that in person," Lee Ann said.

Lee Ann picked Nell up about ten minutes later. She drove a small convertible, with the "service engine" light on, clutter everywhere but the passenger seat and the AC running full blast even though it was pleasant outside, the real heat still two or three months away.

"Got you a latte," Lee Ann said, handing her a paper cup. "Hey, nice ring." She gazed at the premature anniversary ring. "What is that—garnet?"

"Ruby," said Nell, sticking the latte in the drink holder and leaving it there. "What are your ideas about the tape?"

"We'll get to that," Lee Ann said, driving down Sandhill Way and taking a left turn at the bottom, a little too fast. "First, what can you tell me about your husband's relationship with Bobby Rice?"

"They had a great relationship."

Behind her strange glasses, Lee Ann's eyes narrowed. "Racial tension in the Belle Ville PD has been well documented."

"It never affected Clay and Bobby," Nell said. "They were friends. They coached Pop Warner together."

"How long were they partners?"

"For years, right up until when Clay first ran for chief."

"What was Bobby's reaction to that?"

"To Clay becoming chief? He was happy."

"No resentments?"

"He raised funds for Clay in the black community," Nell said. "What are you getting at?"

Lee Ann drove past the zoo, now open again, although one tiger and all the former inhabitants of the reptile house had still not been found, and turned onto North Sunshine Road. "There's a lot of anger in Lower Town about what went on after Bernardine."

Nell didn't say anything. The gates to Magnolia Glade went by on their left, a guard sitting in the booth, face blank.

"Anger directed at the town government in general," Lee Ann said, "and the police department in particular."

Nell knew that. She also knew how hard Clay had worked, forty-eight hours at a stretch, including a frenzied twenty-four straight on the Canal Street sandbag line before the gates, the pumps, everything, finally failed completely and the storm surge flooded in. "The police did their best," Nell said. "Everybody just got overwhelmed."

"Not everybody," said Lee Ann. "Not equally."

No arguing that. "But I don't see what this has to do with the tape," Nell said.

"Some of the anger comes from the fact that the only cop who died in the flood was black."

"You're losing me."

"I'm talking about the motive," Lee Ann said.

"For what?" said Nell. "Some . . . some conspirators to get together and rig up a tape making DuPree look innocent? How does that do anything for the black community? Bobby was black and DuPree is white."

Lee Ann came to Parish Street, headed toward the bayou. The old Creole elite had lived on Parish Street until thirty or forty years before, their pastel houses shaded by huge cypress trees, many overhung with Spanish moss. But Bernardine had swept the trees away, and now the houses looked shabby. "There are other interpretations," Lee Ann said.

Parish Street dead-ended at the bayou. Lee Ann parked by the side of the towpath.

"Like what?" said Nell as they got out of the car.

Lee Ann gazed at her over the roof, the sun glaring off her glasses. "How about making the whole department look bad?" she said.

"Seems a little far-fetched."

"Maybe to someone like you," Lee Ann said.

"What does that mean?"

"No offense," said Lee Ann. "Just the opposite. The world's full of people very unlike you, people with nasty imaginations and lots of misplaced energy."

They walked onto the towpath. Nell hadn't been here in twenty years, accompanied that last time by Clay, Bobby, and an evidence-gathering team. Her memory of that day—of so many days after the murder—was blurred and streaky, like images on a failing screen, but she didn't think much evidence had been found; certainly not the knife, which never turned up. She stared down into the bayou; the rickety pier was gone, as Lee Ann had said, but she saw other things in there: floating garbage, two or three cars submerged to their roofs, a refrigerator door, oil slicks, trees ripped out by the roots, dead birds, dead fish, a dog, dead and eyeless, his collar caught on a root on the far bank.

"This is terrible," she said.

"I'm sorry," said Lee Ann. "If it's too painful, we can—"

"It's not that," Nell said. "I'm talking about—" She gestured down at the bayou.

"It's worse lower down," Lee Ann said. She took a few steps along the towpath. "I can't quite make out the old levee from here," she said. "Is that where you were coming from?"

"Yes."

"And the assailant was waiting on the pier?"

"Yes."

"Then what happened?"

Nell told her story, the kind of story Lee Ann must have heard many times: a robbery gone bad.

"So you got a good look at him?"

"There was a full moon."

"And how long was it before you made the identification?"

"A couple weeks or so. I don't remember exactly."

"Was it a photo array or a lineup?"

"Both, I think."

"Both?"

"First came the photos."

"How many?"

Nell thought back. She'd sat at a desk, Clay on the other side, turning up photos and sliding them toward her, one at a time. "A lot."

"Like?"

"I'm not sure." Her clearest memory of the photo-array episode was Clay's calming presence, and the careful way his hands moved, sympathetic somehow.

"And then they brought DuPree in?"

"I'm not sure. He might have been in custody already, for something else."

"But you're certain you picked him out of a lineup as well."

"Yes." Nell closed her eyes, tried to summon the memory of standing before the one-way glass. All she could picture was the number card in DuPree's hands: 3.

"How hard was that?"

"In what way?"

"Did you have doubts, or did it seem like he was the one, right off?"

"He was the one," Nell said; there was no *seeming* about it.

Lee Ann gazed at her, eyes unreadable behind those intelligence-magnifying lenses.

"Where did you get the glasses?" Nell said.

"You like them?"

Before Nell could answer, a big black car came speeding down Parish Street, braking hard on the other side of the towpath. The car was still rocking on its suspension when a rear door opened and a big man jumped out, followed by a small man and a woman, all of them wearing business suits. Nell knew the big man: Kirk Bastien, Duke's younger brother, former all-SEC linebacker at Georgia Tech and now mayor of Belle Ville. He strode right past Nell and Lee Ann without a glance—the small man and the woman hurrying after him—and glared down from the edge of the bayou, sunshine glinting on his swept-back hair.

"God damn," he said, swinging around, "this is a disgrace. Why the hell didn't I know about it?"

The small man and the woman glanced at each other, said nothing.

"You're fired," Kirk Bastien said, voice rising. Nell had heard he had a bad temper, had never before seen a demonstration. "The both of you. Get out of my sight." At that moment, Kirk Bastien noticed her.

"Nell?" he said, lowering his voice and putting on his sunglasses. His face was bright red.

"Hi, Kirk."

"What are you doing here?" he said. He turned toward Lee Ann and frowned.

"Hello, Mayor," Lee Ann said. "We were just out for a spin."

"Oh, Christ," Kirk said. "You're doing a story on this?"

"Looks like a story to me," Lee Ann said.

"Aw, come on now," Kirk said. He approached Lee Ann, buttoning his jacket. Nell hadn't seen him in a while, noticed how much weight he'd put on; hurricane stress had had the opposite effect on Clay, dulling his appetite, reducing him. "How's that going to help morale?"

Lee Ann looked up at him. "That's not our job."

"I know that, Lee Ann. But everyone's so worn out. How about we make ourselves a deal?"

"What kind of deal?"

"This mess is all cleaned up by nightfall," Kirk said. "You write a nice story about something else."

He waited, towering over her. There was no threat or anything like that, but still Nell admired the way Lee Ann stood her ground and waited a long time before saying, "It's a deal, but I'll need some pictures just in case."

"Knock yourself out," Kirk said, stepping aside.

Lee Ann dug a small camera from her bag, moved closer to the bayou, took pictures from different angles. Then she turned to Nell. "All set?"

"Bye, Kirk," Nell said.

"That husband of yours is doing a fabulous job," Kirk said. "You say hi, now."

Nell and Lee Ann got in the car. They heard Kirk's voice rising again. "You two familiar with that expression?" he said; the jobless assistants hadn't moved. "Nightfall?"

"So they're not fired?" Nell said as Lee Ann did a U-turn and drove back down Parish Street.

"Not till tomorrow," Lee Ann said. "And tomorrow and tomorrow and tomorrow."

Nell laughed. She reached for her latte, took a sip. It was cold.

"That woman staffer has a law degree from Tulane," Lee Ann said. "What the hell she's doing—" Lee Ann's cell phone rang. She picked it up. "Hello?" Her hand tightened on the receiver; the knuckles went white, almost as though they were piercing her skin. "Got it," she said, and clicked off. All of a sudden Nell could smell her.

Lee Ann slowed down, glanced over. "I'm not sure what to do about you," she said.

"What do you mean?" Nell said.

"Drop you off or bring you along." Lee Ann bit her lip. "Bringing you along might be better, but . . ."

"Bringing me along where?" said Nell.

"To meet Nappy Ferris," Lee Ann said; then, after a little pause, she stepped on the gas.

CHAPTER 7

L ee Ann drove fast, hunched over the wheel. She swung north on Stonewall Road, passing the DK Industries yard, where Nell caught a glimpse of Duke Bastien striding somewhere in a hard hat. Then came strip malls, used-car lots, gun shops, the town line, and they crossed into Stonewall County, rural and piney, where all the faces were black.

"Aren't the police searching for him?" Nell said.

"Looks like I got there first," said Lee Ann.

"How?"

"Reporter's weapon numero uno," Lee Ann said. "Contacts." She slowed behind a pickup with farmworkers in the back; they gazed down through the windshield of the convertible, eyes expressionless. "Can I ask you something personal?"

"What if I said no?"

Lee Ann laughed. "Everyone likes you—did you know that?"

"Is that the question?"

Lee Ann laughed again. "No. The question is did Johnny Blanton know you were pregnant?"

No reason that question should have hit Nell so hard, but it did, the long-lost feeling of just starting out came welling up; the feeling of starting out on something new and grand.

Lee Ann's eyes shifted toward her, looked a little alarmed. "You don't have to answer."

"No," Nell said. "I'll answer. Johnny—" Nell wasn't a crier, but she felt tears building; and forced them back down. "Johnny knew," she said. At that moment, she pictured his face with the clarity found in life, not memory—his exact face, so young and happy—when she told him the news. "We were going to get married."

"So when he stepped in front of you," Lee Ann said, "he was actually protecting two people, you and Norah."

Nell had never considered that before. Lee Ann's take seemed a little maudlin to her, even sensationalizing, the way material might be hyped by a— "Lee Ann? Are you planning to write a book about this?"

Lee Ann's eyes shifted. "Let's not get ahead of ourselves."

"My God, you *are* planning a book." Then it hit her. "Do you know something I don't?"

"To answer that question, I'd have to know everything you know."

"Alvin DuPree murdered Johnny. Clay caught him and put him away. Now there's some crazy talk about a tape, but it won't add up to anything and DuPree will spend the rest of his life in jail. That's what I know. So I'll ask again—do you know more?"

"No," said Lee Ann.

"End of story," said Nell.

"One more thing," Lee Ann said. "When did the romance start?"

"With Johnny?"

Lee Ann shook her head. "With Clay."

"No precise date," Nell said. "He called me about a year after . . . after it was all over. We had coffee."

"So you hadn't met him before."

"Before when?"

"The murder."

"No, of course not."

"Did you know the Bastien brothers back then?"

"No. Why do you ask?"

Lee Ann shrugged. "Your husband's close to them, isn't he?"

"He's close to Duke," Nell said. "I wouldn't say he's close to Kirk. What are you getting at?"

"Just accumulating facts," Lee Ann said. She went by a fireworks stand and slowed down, peering at the woods to her left. After a few hundred yards a narrow road appeared. Lee Ann turned on to it. "This should be Pond Road," she said. "Did you catch a sign?"

"No."

Lee Ann kept going. The road was paved at first, soon full of potholes, and finally gravel. They went up a slope, then down a long curve, the trees—mostly pine and sycamore— growing denser, some pockmarked with bullet holes.

"Watch for a track on the right," Lee Ann said.

"That might have been one," said Nell.

"We're getting to be like a comedy team," said Lee Ann, backing up. Branches scraped the bodywork. The car bumped up onto the track, two reddish ruts with a strip of stunted brown grass in the middle. A few squashed beer cans passed under them, and then one that still hadn't been run over. "I think we're close," she said.

The track entered a hollow with a small pond in the middle, and came to an end at the edge of the water. Lee Ann looked around. "See anything?"

"What kind of anything?"

"A cabin, maybe. Some sign of people. I can't stand nature."

Nell saw trees, a pocket of yellow wildflowers, a sudden rippling in the pond.

"I'm thinking gators," said Lee Ann. "I'm thinking snakes."

"Come on," Nell said. She got out of the car and immediately smelled smoke. "We'll just follow the smell."

"What smell?" said Lee Ann.

Nell started walking around the pond, the earth moist and giving under her feet. More of those yellow flowers grew by the bank; a bullfrog croaked, but she couldn't spot it. The smoky smell seemed stronger. Not far ahead something glinted at the base of a tree. Nell walked over, picked it up: an empty pint of Knob Creek, an expensive bourbon she'd seen in the liquor cabinet on Little Parrot Cay, a surprising find in a place like this. Then she remembered that Nappy Ferris was—or had been until Bernardine—a liquor store owner. She looked down and saw a sneaker footprint, pointing into the woods.

"Over here," she said.

Lee Ann took a few steps, then stopped and said, "Christ almighty."

"What's wrong?"

"Goddamn mud took my shoe."

She bent forward, her bare foot sticking up in the air; for a moment she could have been some girlish character in a screwball comedy. Nell was starting to like her. Lee Ann rinsed her shoe in the pond and came over, a mud streak on her face.

"This way," Nell said.

"What way?"

Nell pushed a branch aside, revealing a faint path heading away from the pond.

"Natty Bumppo," said Lee Ann.

They took the path, Nell in the lead. The smoky smell was now stronger still and she found herself speeding up. Behind her, Lee Ann's breathing grew labored.

"You're in shape," Lee Ann said. "How come?"

"Because of—" Nell began, cutting herself off when a clearing came in sight, not far ahead. A small cabin stood at the back of the clearing, smoke drifting from a stovepipe that slanted at a forty-five-degree angle through the roof. A rusted-out car with running boards and tiny windows lay partly sunken in the ground, vines curling up through the grille.

"This must be it," said Lee Ann.

"Why are you whispering?"

"I'm not sure," Lee Ann whispered, and then repeated it at normal volume. "I'm not sure."

"Is he expecting you?"

"I'm not sure."

They were both laughing as they crossed the clearing. The cabin was weather-beaten and crooked, the two front windows grimy and cracked. A sticker on the door read: NO SOLICITORS, NO PEDDLERS, NO TRESPASSING. Lee Ann stepped up and knocked.

No response from inside. Lee Ann knocked again, harder this time. "Mr. Ferris? You there? It's Lee Ann Bonner, from the *Guardian*." She was about to knock again when a voice spoke behind them.

"What you want?"

Nell and Lee Ann whirled around. A man stood about fifteen feet away, somehow having come so close without making a sound. He was tall and thin, with big liquid eyes and a bony face: resembled an El Greco saint, except Nell didn't recall any with café au lait–colored skin. One other nonconforming detail: the snub-nosed handgun held loosely in his long, tapering fingers, not pointing at them but not really pointing away either. Nell felt no fear until she realized that this was the second time in her life she'd been confronted by an armed man. Then her heart began to pound.

"Mr. Ferris? I'm Lee Ann Bonner of the *Guardian*."

The man licked his lips; his tongue was cracked and yellow. "Prove it."

"I've got a card," Lee Ann said, taking her bag off her shoulder, starting to open it.

The gun came up, pointed right at the center of Lee Ann's forehead. "Uh-uh," said the man. "Toss it over."

"But the card's just inside the—"

The man made a dismissive gesture with the gun. "Don't wanna argue," he said.

Lee Ann tossed her bag to him. He caught it with his free

hand—the gun back in that loose grip, pointing nowhere special—raised the bag to his mouth and unzipped it with his teeth. Then he squatted down, laid the bag on the ground, and fished around in it, his eyes on Nell and Lee Ann.

"The card's in that compartment at the side," Lee Ann said. "With the Velcro snap."

The man's hand went still. "Well, well," he said, and withdrew his hand, now holding another handgun, the same silver color as his but smaller and with a pearly pink grip. "This what we're callin' a Velcro snap?"

Nell gazed at Lee Ann in surprise. Lee Ann ignored her. "The card's in the compartment," she said.

"Your reporter card?"

"Yes."

"Reporters in the habit of totin' these around?" he said, waving Lee Ann's little gun.

"In Belle Ville they are," Lee Ann said.

The man stared at her for a moment: soulful El Greco eyes, but bloodshot, too. Then he laughed, a light, musical laugh, close to a giggle. "Say the truth," he said. He tucked Lee Ann's gun in the pocket of his jeans—torn and grease-stained—fished around some more and came up with the card. "'Lee Ann Bonner,'" he read, rising. "'Reporter, *Belle Ville Guardian,* the True Voice of the Gulf.'" He smiled. "'True Voice of the Gulf'—so righteous. Tell me, Sister True Voice, how you're finding me?"

"It was mostly luck, Mr. Ferris," Lee Ann said.

"Yeah? You feelin' lucky today?" Before Lee Ann could answer, he swung his gun toward Nell. "Who we got here?"

"This is my friend," Lee Ann said. "Please don't point that at her."

He kept pointing it at Nell just the same. "Friend got a name?"

"Nell," Lee Ann said.

"She dumb or somethin'? Can't do no talkin' for herself?"

"Nell," Nell said.

"Nell," he said. "Nice name. And nice voice, beside. Nicer 'n hers." He checked the card. "Lee Ann's more kind of harsh, hear what I'm sayin'? Nell's more sweet." The gun shifted back to Lee Ann.

"Now that introductions are out of the way, Mr. Ferris," Lee Ann said, "maybe we could get down to business."

"Nobody call me Ferris," he said.

"No?"

He took a step closer, prodding Lee Ann's bag forward with his toe. He wore snakeskin boots, old and worn, the skin torn here and there. Nell smelled booze. "That Ferris—a slave name," he said. "Everybody call me Nappy."

"Okay, Nappy," Lee Ann said. "Maybe we can go inside and talk."

"Outside the best," Nappy said. "The great outside."

Lee Ann nodded. "I'd like to hear about the tape."

"Don't know about no tape."

"I'm talking about the tape you made twenty years ago at your liquor store on Bigard Street," Lee Ann said. "The tape that—"

"Flood took my store," Nappy said.

Nell had a thought. "Maybe—" she began, and then stopped; this was Lee Ann's show.

"Maybe what?" said Lee Ann.

Nell gazed at Nappy, saw what should have been obvious: he was drunk. "Maybe you don't know that people are looking for you."

He took a quick scan of the clearing. There was nothing to see but a blue butterfly hovering over one of those yellow flowers. Nappy's index finger slid off the trigger guard, onto the trigger.

"Not to harm you," Lee Ann said. "They've been looking in Houston, Atlanta, all the places the refugees went."

"I ain't no refugee."

"You're not?" Lee Ann said.

"Didn't flee no hurricane."

Lee Ann glanced around. "You're saying this is where you were living, even before the hurricane?"

"Not sayin' nothin'."

Nell had another thought. "Are you here for some other reason?"

His finger left the trigger, moved back to the guard. Was it just because he preferred the sound of her voice? "Like what reason?" he said.

Nell couldn't think of any. Lee Ann said, "Getting back to the tape, what was your motivation in sending it? Were you friends with Alvin DuPree? And who did you actually send it to, by the way?"

Nappy waved his free hand in front of his face, as though brushing away flies. "Lot of questions," he said.

"Why don't we go inside?" Lee Ann said. "Take them one at a time."

"Etiquette," Nappy said.

"Etiquette?" said Lee Ann.

"Etiquette is why," Nappy said. "Meanin' manners. My place, so my place to hand out invitations. Or not."

"My apologies," said Lee Ann.

The sarcasm was plain in her tone, but Nappy must have missed it, because he nodded in an apology-accepting way and said, "Manners don't cost nothin', but they worth many treasures." He took a bottle from his back pocket—Knob Creek—pulled the stopper with his teeth, spat it out, tilted the bottle to his lips. His Adam's apple bobbed. He held the bottle out to Nell. "Drink, Nellie?"

"Thanks, but it's a little earl—"

His voice rose. "Many treasures."

Nell took the bottle. She didn't like bourbon, not even premium bourbon, and it was too early for her, plus she hadn't drunk straight from the bottle since high school, and didn't much like the idea of putting her lips where his had been; but she drank.

Nappy watched closely. "Sweet," he said. "Now pass it around the circle."

Nell passed the bottle to Lee Ann. Lee Ann wiped the rim on her sleeve—*Why didn't I have the nerve to do that?* Nell thought—and took a real slug. That brought the little giggle from Nappy.

"We havin' fun?" he said. Lee Ann gave him the bottle. He did an elaborate imitation of how she'd wiped the rim, then took an even deeper slug. It made him shudder.

"Getting back to the tape," Lee Ann said.

"Somethin' else," said Nappy.

"It'll all come out anyway," Lee Ann said. "When you testify at the hearing."

"Don' know nothin' about no hearing."

"That's because they can't find you," Lee Ann said. "The hearing's to free Alvin DuPree, based on the security-camera tape and the note that went with it, the one that said they had the wrong man. The tape turned up in a file cabinet that belonged to Bobby Rice."

"That's fucked up."

"Why?" said Lee Ann.

"Why not?" Nappy said.

"Can you elaborate a little?" Lee Ann said. "Why is the tape turning up in Bobby Rice's file cabinet fucked up?"

"Whyn't you aks him?"

"Impossible," said Lee Ann. "Bobby Rice drowned in the flood."

Nappy shook his head, a little too hard, like a child warding off something he didn't want to hear. "Strong sober man like Bobby? No way."

"It's true," Lee Ann said.

Nappy's eyes seemed to get redder. "Make you think who the hell runnin' things."

"In Belle Ville?" Lee Ann said.

Nappy took a long, long drink, head way back, then raised his hands high, bottle in one hand, gun in the other, as if to indicate: *things everywhere.*

"Were you friends with Alvin DuPree?" Lee Ann said.

"Al DuPree? Thief, bully, coward, snake."

"Then why did you send the tape? Why did you write the note?"

Nappy gave Lee Ann a pitying look, arms still raised high. Nell wondered about the wisdom of making a grab for the gun, or maybe just asking him to put it away. "Ever heard of justice?" Nappy said.

"In the interest of justice," Lee Ann said. "I understand. But then, when nothing happened with the tape, why didn't you follow up?"

"Know what I don' like about you? You look so smart, but it turns out the other."

"Then walk me through it," Lee Ann said.

"Walk you through it," Nappy said, mimicking her. He started to lower his arms. "You still don' even realize the obvious fac'—I was inside of the store when Al was poundin' away on the—" At that moment, he was interrupted by a sonic boom, not very loud, that might have come from a distant plane. Nappy stopped speaking and toppled over.

"Christ," said Lee Ann, "he passed out."

Bourbon gurgled out of the bottle, onto the grass. Nell and Lee Ann knelt beside Nappy. Twenty or thirty seconds passed before they realized he'd been shot in the head. In fairness to them, the entry wound was small and partly hidden by his hair. Only when they turned him over, revealing the other side of his head with the exit-wound crater, was the truth plain.

CHAPTER 8

C lay hurried across the clearing, followed by his driver and, farther behind, Sergeant Bowman, oldest detective on the Belle Ville force. He saw Nell and picked up the pace, was almost running when he reached her. He put his hands on her shoulders, looked into her eyes.

"Are you all right?" he said.

"Yes."

He embraced her, just for a second, and squeezed. She squeezed back. Then he let her go and turned to Solomon Lanier, first black sheriff of Stonewall County.

"Big Sol," he said. "Thanks for calling."

"Don't even mention it, Chief," Lanier said.

They shook hands; not many men made Clay seem small, but Sheriff Lanier was one. Clay glanced around, took in the cops moving in the woods; the stretcher on the ground, a sheet covering the body, EMTs standing by; a spray-painted human form in front of the cabin with a small spray-painted circle a few yards away; and Lee Ann, writing in a notebook. She looked up, met his gaze, nodded. Clay turned to the sheriff, not acknowledging Lee Ann at all.

"What have we got, Sol?"

"Shooting victim," the sheriff said. "Makes five in the county so far since January, down a tick from last year."

They walked over to the stretcher. An EMT pulled back the sheet, down to Nappy Ferris's chin. From this angle, Nell couldn't see the exit wound, but the cliché that the dead man could have been sleeping did not apply: one of his eyes was open, the other closed. Nell wished someone would do something about that.

"Name of Napoleon Ferris," said the sheriff. "Subject of interest down your way?"

Clay nodded.

"There he is," said the sheriff.

The two men gazed at the body. Clay glanced over and saw Nell watching. She didn't say anything, just thought the thought. He bent over, closed the open eye, drew the sheet back up.

"Plus we got this," said the sheriff, taking a misshapen, lead-colored slug from his pocket and holding it up to the light. "Just the one so far," he said, "turned up over there." He pointed to the spray-painted circle. "Looks like a thirty-ought-six to me, but I'm no expert."

"Me either," said Clay.

"We'll let those good old lab boys worry about it."

"Belle Ville lab's at your disposal."

"Much obliged," said the sheriff. "We'll take a swing at it up here, all the same with you."

Clay gave a slight nod. "Where did the shot come from?" he said.

"Little bump in the road on that one," said the sheriff. "The ladies didn't hear a shot." The sheriff held his hand out toward Nell and Lee Ann, almost like an MC encouraging celebrities to take a bow. "But from where they all were standing, angle of entry, flat-out guesswork, we're—"

Someone whistled in the woods.

"That'll be L'il Truman," the sheriff said. "You know L'il Truman?"

"No," said Clay.

"Best tracker in the county. They say it's on account of he's one quarter Cherokee, but I don't buy that kind of thing." The sheriff's eyes were on Clay, maybe trying to see where he stood on the question of genetic predispositions, but Nell saw no sign on Clay's face, actually didn't know the answer herself.

Two minutes later, Clay and the sheriff were examining a brass cartridge.

"Thirty-ought-six it is," Clay said.

"Lucky guess," said the sheriff. "Pace that distance off, Truman?"

L'il Truman, dressed in T-shirt, shorts, and flip-flops, said, "Yes, boss. Two hundred and fifty-six yards."

Everyone gazed back into the woods. "Two hundred and fifty yards, possible silencer, southwest breeze, one shot," said Clay.

"Not a beginner," said the sheriff. "I'd estimate there's no more'n three or four thousand hunters in the county could have done it."

Lee Ann stepped forward. "Surely this wasn't some hunting accident."

The sheriff turned to her.

"You're aware that Ms. Bonner's a reporter, Sol?" Clay said.

"We touched on that—got no problem with the media," the sheriff said. "Not calling it a hunting accident, ma'am, just pointing out the level of shooting ability around these parts—kind of like at the Olympics."

"I get that," Lee Ann said. "But won't the motive help narrow things down?"

"We got a motive?" said the sheriff.

"Napoleon Ferris was supposed to testify in the Alvin DuPree hearing," Lee Ann said.

"Don't know much about that," said the sheriff. "But I do know something about this cabin." He took an envelope from an inside pocket. "Which is why I picked myself up a warrant on the way up."

A uniformed cop moved in with a battery-powered lock picker but they didn't need it; the door was unlocked, swung open when the sheriff gave a little push. "After you," he said.

They went inside—Clay, the sheriff, Nell, Lee Ann. A small cabin, no real space for hiding things, and no one had tried: bags of marijuana were stacked everywhere. Also out in the open were two shotguns, a handgun, and a long-bladed knife.

"What we've had in the county," the sheriff said, "past year or so, is what amounts to a war between these two drug gangs, one Mexican, one black. This here's black territory. Not saying your man was involved in the dealing. Might have just been in the wrong place at the wrong time, got caught in the switches."

"Ferris had two drug priors," Clay said. "One for possession, one for dealing, marijuana both times."

"Interesting," said the sheriff.

"But not as good a story," said Clay.

Lee Ann said nothing. A uniformed woman came in and started taking pictures.

Nell and Clay drove home in the back of the cruiser. The driver pressed the button that made the screen slide up, sealing off the front seat.

"Sure you're all right?" he said.

"Yes. Are you angry at me?"

"Why would I be?"

"I don't know," Nell said. "Going off with Lee Ann like that. I had no idea we'd end up where we did—she got a tip."

"Who from?"

"She didn't say."

"It doesn't matter," Clay said. "As long as you're unharmed."

Nell thought of the gentle way Clay had closed Nappy's eye. She leaned against him; she loved that gentleness, the gentleness of a strong man who kept his power in reserve. "All she wanted was to hear about how Johnny died. I haven't talked about that in a long time."

"And?"

"It's still awful, but far away now."

Clay kissed the top of her head. He did that sometimes, had done it on their second date. That was a year after the DuPree trial, dinner at one of the shrimp places at the beach, now wiped out by Bernardine. He hadn't tried to kiss her lips or her cheek; just that one kiss on the top of the head, quick and shy, after he'd walked her to her door.

"I saw it with my own eyes," Nell said.

"I know."

"Do you think Nappy Ferris made the fake tape?"

"Would have been nice to find out," Clay said.

"Will there still be a hearing?"

"Probably."

"But now he can't win, can he?"

"He never could," Clay said. She put her arms around him, kissed his lips.

They crossed the Belle Ville line. Almost right away, Nell smelled that Bernardine smell.

"It's all polluted in the bayou where the pier used to be," Nell said. "Kirk Bastien came for a look while we were there."

"He did?"

"With a couple assistants. He was furious with them."

Clay was silent for a moment. Then he said, "He should turn some of that anger on himself."

"What do you mean?"

Clay shrugged.

"Because he didn't handle the hurricane well?" Nell said.

"Yeah."

"But it was so huge, so out of scale with anything people can do."

Clay shook his head, didn't answer. The cruiser went by a car in the next lane. The driver glanced over, saw the roof lights, got an expression on his face Nell had seen many times, then hit the brakes and dropped back out of view.

* * *

The cruiser drove up Sandhill Way, swung into the cul-de-sac. Another cruiser was already sitting in front of the house. Clay parked in the driveway. A rookie patrolman Nell recognized from the Christmas party Clay gave every year jumped out of the cruiser and hurried over.

"What's up, Timmy?" Clay said.

Nell expected some reply about Nappy Ferris, but that wasn't it. Timmy's eyes went to Nell, back to Clay. His face pinkened.

"Minor accident, sir," he said. "Fender bender, all it was, nobody hurt."

"What accident?" Clay said.

"Southbound on Guyot, just past the Exxon, corner of National. I'd been tailin' her for half a mile or so, on account of some weaving, nothin' too too bad but—"

"Oh my God," Nell said. "Norah?"

"She's inside, ma'am," Timmy said. "Sleeping it—resting. That little Miata of hers, I had it towed to Yeller's Autobody. Yeller don't think—"

But Nell missed whatever Yeller did or didn't think. She was already in the house, running down the hall and upstairs to Norah's bedroom. At the same time, a woman was leaving a message on the kitchen answering machine. " . . . please call the dean's office at your earliest . . ."

Norah's bedroom sat over the garage, a big, bright space. Nell knocked on the door. "Norah?" No answer. Nell turned the knob, went inside.

It was dark and stuffy in Norah's bedroom, shades drawn, windows closed, AC off. In the shadows, Nell could see Norah in her bed, face to the wall, stuffed animals on a shelf above her. Higher up, three stuffed monkeys dangled from the ceiling, put up there by Clay long ago to look like they were swinging from branch to branch.

"Norah?"

Nell approached the bed. After just a step or two she

smelled booze, a smell that got mixed up with Nappy's, and made her feel sick. She sat on the edge of the bed, reached over to raise the shade an inch or two. A ribbon of light came slanting in, cutting across Norah's face. Her eyes were closed; in sleep, she looked so young, almost the way she'd been in eighth grade. And beautiful: seeing her own flesh and blood re-formed into something this lovely—even though the fair coloring and fine features were all Johnny—still often stunned Nell. Even now, the makeup smeared on Norah's face, the sweat dampening her blond hair, the bruise on her neck—all of that barely registered.

"Norah? Wake up, honey."

Norah didn't wake up. All at once, from Norah's stillness, and the heavy, dead air in the room, Nell got a bad feeling. She bent forward, held the backs of her fingers just under Norah's nose; and felt her breath.

"Norah." Nell laid her hand on Norah's shoulder. "Norah. Wake up."

Norah's eyes opened, or at least the one Nell could see. It shifted, took in Nell, filled with some deep, unhappy emotion, and closed.

"Norah. Sit up. We have to talk."

"Later. Gotta sleep." That eye stayed closed.

Nell shook Norah's shoulder, not hard. Norah groaned. "Why aren't you in school?" Nell said.

"Please."

"What's going on?"

"I said please."

Nell shook Norah's shoulder again, harder this time. Norah wrenched herself free, squirmed closer to the wall. "Fucking hell."

"Don't talk to me like that." Nell took hold of the covers and pulled them down. Norah was fully dressed, even had her red leather sneakers on, the ones Nell had given her for Christmas.

Norah sat up, grabbed at the covers.

"How much did you have to drink?"

"Nothing."

"I can smell it."

Norah was silent.

"What's wrong, Norah? What are you doing here?"

Norah looked Nell in the eye, if only for a brief moment. "This isn't home anymore?"

"Of course it's home." Nell heard her tone sharpen. "But you're supposed to be in school."

"Friday's classes got canceled. I decided to come home for the long weekend. I drove all night, Mom. I'm tired."

That sounded convincing except for one thing. "Today's Tuesday," Nell said. Her tone sharpened some more.

Norah got a faraway look in her eyes. "It is?"

"What's wrong?" Nell said. She repeated it, not so loud. "Tell me."

"Nothing."

"Is there some problem at school? More than the academic probation thing?"

"I just need a break, Mom. School's fine."

Clay spoke from the doorway. "Not according to the message on the machine," he said.

"Oh, great," Norah said. "The Man."

"Don't talk to your father like that."

"He's not my father."

Nell got off the bed. She felt disappointed in her daughter, real disappointment, and for the first time. "You sound so childish right now. No one ever deceived you about that, not for a second. But as you know very well, he's your real father in every way except biologically."

"The exception that proves the rule, Mom and Dad," Norah said.

"There's no excuse for this rudeness," Nell said. "What the hell is going on?"

"Nothing," Norah said. Her eyes closed. "Everything's hunkydory."

There was silence in the room. Light from the hall glinted in the eyes of the stuffed animals—bear, lions, tigers, elephants, a giraffe. Higher up, the monkeys began to move in a current of air.

"Let her sleep it off," Clay said, his voice quiet. "We can talk later."

Downstairs, Nell listened to the answering machine, called the dean. He'd expelled Norah for cutting all her history classes, thus violating the terms of her academic probation.

"History?" That made no sense at all. History had always been Norah's favorite subject; she'd won the history prize, a biography of Samuel Adams, in her senior year at Belle Ville Academy.

"She's actually been missing all classes in all subjects," the dean said. "The history professor's report happened to come in first."

"Is there any way she could get a second chance?" Nell said.

"This was her second chance," said the dean. "There was a similar violation last semester, not quite as pronounced. Didn't she tell you?"

Clay watched her across the counter. Nell didn't answer.

"Norah's eligible to apply for readmission in the fall," the dean said. "She's obviously very bright."

"What—" she began, stopped herself, then blurted it out: "What's happened to her?" A crazy question for the mom to ask the dean.

There was a long pause. The dean said, "Some kids, um, just need a little more time to find themselves."

Nell hung up. They got in the car—not the cruiser, but Clay's pickup, since this was personal business—and drove to Yeller's Autobody for a look at the Miata, Norah's high-school-graduation present, bought brand-new less than two years before.

"I wouldn't call it totaled," Yeller said. "Your daughter wasn't hurt?"

"No."

"Then no harm done, I always say. I'll get the adjuster over in the morning."

They drove home. "She hit a parked car before Timmy could pull her over," Clay said. "Then she tried to take off again. The kid would have cuffed her, been anyone else."

"Oh, God." And then Nell had a thought. "What are you saying?"

"Chargeable offenses," Clay said. "At least three, and that's not counting DUI."

"He gave her a Breathalyzer?"

Clay shook his head. "He didn't write her up at all." He glanced over. "I won't count it against him."

"What do you mean?"

"You know what's right."

"Oh, Clay—you saw her, how vulnerable she is right now. She couldn't take charges, going to court, anything like that."

"But if she was anybody else . . ."

"I know. And I know how . . . how upright you are—who knows better? But you've told me yourself, as a practical matter, there's always room for discretion."

"A very little bit, and only up to a point."

"She's never been in an accident before. And of course we'll take her license away ourselves, for as long as you say."

Clay was silent.

"And no one got hurt."

A vein throbbed in his neck.

"I'm worried about her, Clay." Her worry for Norah had a physical manifestation, an airlessness, as though she were drowning.

"So am I," Clay said. He took a deep breath, let it out slowly. "She's my daughter, too."

CHAPTER 9

Scuff, scuff, scuff. Pirate, on his bunk, picked up the sound, a sound he liked; it reminded him of a drummer he'd played with long ago. He knew the sound meant the Hispanic guard with the salt-and-pepper mustache was on the way, but his mind preferred to dwell on the drummer, whose name would not come although Pirate remembered the brass knuckles the drummer had sold him and the exact price: twenty-three dollars. The chords to "You Win Again" went E, B7, E, A.

Scuff, scuff. Then, from the other side of the bars, the voice of the Hispanic guard: "Hey, Pirate."

Pirate, face to the wall, fingering the gold tassel, made a little grunt, or thought about it.

"That hearing of yours? Forget it. Nappy Ferris got his head blowed off."

Pirate didn't speak. Wasn't he at peace? Yes. And peace in this situation meant silence.

"And guess what?" said the guard. "Word is the Ocho Cincos ain't too happy with you. How come is that?"

"I have no quarrels," Pirate said. But at the same time, he covered his good eye with his hand, couldn't help it.

"Wanna put in a request for the protective wing?" the guard said. "Just in case some of them boys got quarrels with you?"

Protective meant twenty-three hours of solitary every

day; much harder to be at peace in solitary. Pirate remained silent, exercising what he had finally learned was the most important right. He kept his good eye safe under the palm of his big strong hand.

"Yeah," said the guard. "Prob'ly wouldn't get it anyhow."

Nell swam in the lap pool: one of those days when she found her rhythm right away, didn't have to make herself feel the water or picture herself riding up high. Everything just happened, freeing her mind to wander, and it soon wandered to a painting at the museum, one of her favorites in the whole collection: *Fortune Teller,* by Caravaggio. A fortune-teller is reading a man's palm. You can see in her eyes that she has a big premonition about his future, but is it good or bad? Nell could never make up her mind about that, had gazed at the painting so often that her mental image of the fortune-teller's eyes exactly matched what was on canvas. Today, gliding along, uncounted laps piling up, she felt that the young man's future was good.

Nell took one last lap, going all out on the first length, lungs bursting, then ramping down on the second. She climbed out of the pool, still breathing hard, and saw Norah sitting on a chaise longue. Norah wore boxers, a man's shirt, sunglasses; she was reading the paper.

"I didn't know you were up," Nell said.

"I'm up."

Nell crossed the patio, toweling her hair.

"Feeling okay?"

"Uh-huh."

"The water's nice if you feel like a swim."

"No thanks."

"How about some breakfast?"

"Not hungry."

"We need to talk."

"I'm not talkative at the moment."

That wasn't good enough. Nell pulled up a chair, sat beside

her, but before she could begin, she noticed that Norah had the paper—the *Guardian*—open to a story with the headline DUPREE HEARING SCHEDULED. Nell leaned forward.

BY LEE ANN BONNER, *GUARDIAN* REPORTER
Despite the death of key witness Napoleon Ferris, the Alvin DuPree hearing is still scheduled to take place, according to the court clerk for presiding judge Earl Roman. To be sure, the absence of Ferris, shot in what Sheriff Solomon Lanier of Stonewall County has labeled "most likely a gang conflict," is seen as considerably reducing DuPree's chances. According to a veteran court observer who asked to remain anonymous, those chances are now "slim to none." Nevertheless, Susannah Upton, associate counsel to the Justice Project, said in response to a reporter's question that "we are going forward with every expectation that this innocent man who has suffered so unjustly will be freed at last." The hearing is scheduled for Monday at—

Norah's shadow fell across the page. "What's going on? Why didn't you tell me?"

"It's all so sudden," Nell said. She began the story, leading with Little Parrot Cay, scrapping that and starting all over with the hurricane.

Norah covered her mouth. "Are you saying he didn't do it after all?"

"I'm saying the opposite. He did it. This tape is some kind of mistake."

"What makes you so sure?"

"You know all this." Nell had told Norah everything over the years, but in pieces, adding the last one—how Johnny died—when Norah was nine or ten. "I saw it with my own eyes."

"But what if you were wrong?"

"I wasn't."

"Everybody makes mistakes," Norah said. "Because you wouldn't do something like that on purpose, would you, Mom?"

"Norah? What are you saying?"

"Nothing. Forget it." Norah's eyes were unreadable behind the sunglasses.

"You'll have to do better than that," Nell said. "Explain yourself."

"I'm a bastard child," said Norah. "That's the only explanation for such as I."

Nell felt strange—faint, angry, scared, all at once. "What is that supposed to mean? Are you saying I've done you harm?"

"I'm not saying anything," Norah said. Was that a tear leaking down from under her sunglasses?

"What's bothering you, Norah?" Nell said. "Did something happen at school? You weren't . . . " She took a wild guess. " . . . taken advantage of, or anything like that, were you?"

"Like raped, you mean?"

Nell felt sick. She nodded.

"Then say raped, instead of taken advantage of. That sounds so lame."

"Raped," Nell said. The word came out much too loud. She saw her own face reflected in the sunglasses, fear undisguised.

"No," Norah said. "I wasn't raped. Or date-raped or anything at all. Nothing bad happened—guys are pretty careful when they find out your stepfather's a cop."

"Why do you call him that—stepfather?"

"It's accurate."

"But you never used to—you've always called him Dad." Norah shrugged.

"And you've always been such a good student," Nell said. "You love history."

Norah did not explain.

Some kids just need a little more time to find themselves;

making them lost until they did. Nell had never thought of Norah that way, but she said, "I'm here to help."

"Great," said Norah.

Saturday night, Duke Bastien threw a party on the Bastiens' compound on Lake Versailles, a few miles northwest of town.

"Ooo," said Duke's latest girlfriend, Vicki something-or-other. "Don't you love pig roasts?"

A waiter appeared with champagne before Nell had to answer.

"And champagne!" said Vicki, sweeping two glasses off the tray. "You people sure know how to have fun."

"Us people?" Nell said.

"Southerners," said Vicki. "I'm from New Jersey, but you know something?"

"What?"

Vicki downed one of the glasses. "I feel so at home here. Like totally." She looked around, taking in the huge main houses—Kirk's the one with the observation tower—the guesthouses, the sloping lawns, tennis court, speedboats at the dock, and Duke coming toward them, a big smile on his face.

"Hi, darlin'," he said.

"Hi," said Vicki.

But he was talking to Nell. "Hear you ran into my brother, Kirk, the other day. He's embarrassed, big-time."

"Why?" Nell said.

Duke spotted Kirk not far away, talking to a fat man with white hair in a George Jones–style cut. He waved Kirk over. The fat man followed, drink in one hand, cigar in the other.

Duke grabbed his brother's shoulder, pulled him close. They looked a lot alike, big, blond, blue-eyed; Duke the original, Kirk an imperfect copy, features a little bloated, hair and eyes lighter, almost unpigmented.

"Bro," said Duke. "Let's hear a nice apology to Nellie, here."

Kirk blinked. "Apology to Nellie?"

"For the Parish Street mess."

Kirk gazed at his brother, mouth open, even paling a little.

"Come on, bro," Duke said. "You're the mayor."

"Oh, right," said Kirk. He turned to Nell. "It's all cleaned up now. I feel just . . . mortified you had to see something like that."

"You don't have to apologize to me."

"Very nice of you to say that, but the buck stops here," Kirk said. "I reamed out the DPW guys pretty good, I can tell you. The good news is I had the health inspector down there and the bayou water tested fine—actually better'n before the hurricane. Flushed out all the toxins, he said."

Then what about the dead fish? Nell left that thought unspoken. This was a party, after all, and she had been raised a certain way.

The fat man stepped forward. He wore a red blazer and a yellow tie with a scales-of-justice motif in green. "Aren't you boys going to introduce me to these lovely young ladies?"

"Only if you promise to behave," Duke said.

The fat man laughed; rather uproariously considering the slightness of the joke, unless Nell was missing something. His drink sloshed over the rim of his glass, golden-brown whiskey. He licked it off his hand.

"This is Vicki," Duke said.

"Duke's girlfriend," said Kirk, "so don't you be getting any ideas."

"Fiancée," said Vicki.

"And this is Nell Jarreau."

"Chief's wife?" said the fat man.

Duke nodded.

"Damn," the fat man said. "Both taken."

"Not your lucky day," Duke said. "Ladies, meet Judge Earl Roman."

Nell got a little dizzy, although she'd had no more than two or three sips of champagne. Was there something wrong with this, meeting the man who was going to handle the DuPree hearing? If so, she couldn't identify it logically, and so was left with just the untethered feeling of something wrong.

The judge stuck his cigar in his mouth, offered his free hand for shaking; the unlicked hand, so it could have been worse.

"A real live judge?" said Vicki. "Nice to meet you."

"Liveliest judge in the state," said the judge, shaking Nell's hand, and holding on much too long. His skin was hot, almost feverish. "May I say, ma'am, what a fine fine job your husband is doing."

"Thank you."

"Not to mention his good fortune in matrimony." The cigar bobbed up and down between his lips, smoke drifting onto Nell's face.

She pulled her hand free. "He's tied up at the office," she said. "Should be along any minute."

"One hardworking SOB," said the judge. "Need more like him around these parts, am I right, Duke?"

"Always," said Duke. "That's why you're a judge."

Everybody laughed, the judge most of all. His round face went bright red; for a moment, as he gasped for air, Nell thought he might have a heart attack.

"But that's not why I'm a judge," he said, wiping his mouth on the sleeve of his red blazer. "Y'all want to know the real reason I'm a judge?"

"More than anything, your honor," said Kirk.

Nell heard sarcasm in Kirk's tone; so did his brother, who shot him a quick look. But the judge showed no sign of having caught it.

"Goes way back to my early days in the practice of law," he said, "during the time I spent as a PD."

"You?" said Kirk. "A public defender?"

The judge's eyes, narrow to begin with, narrowed more. "Do I detect a little surprise there, Mr. Mayor?"

"Forgive the gaps in my brother's knowledge of local history, judge," Duke said. "A lot of people in town, myself included, remember your work back then."

"Why, thank you, Duke," said the judge. He drained the rest of his whiskey in one gulp, licked his lips. "Had me a client—now don't forget I'm fresh out of law school, still a baby—client name of Tatiana LaRue." His eyes, very watery all of a sudden, shifted to Vicki, settled on Nell. "Lady of the night, was Miss LaRue, of the higher type. Normally the soul of discretion, but on this particular occasion, she'd approached a judge—whose name won't pass my lips although he's acceded to the great bench in the sky." The judge chuckled. "Great bench in the sky," he repeated.

"A good one, judge," said Duke.

"Now, this judge was only human, like the rest of us, and he fell for temptation. Fell twice on the evening in question, if I can put it that way, but insisted on paying only for the once. In short, a contractual dispute. A contractual dispute that spilled out onto the street in front of Miss LaRue's abode, Miss LaRue buck naked at the time. At that very moment, wouldn't you know, of all people on God's green earth, along comes Reverend—"

A waiter went by carrying a tray of drinks. The judge twisted around to grab one, but missed, his momentum spinning him in a half circle. He reached for the back of a chair to steady himself, missed that, too, lost his balance and fell headfirst against the edge of a glass tabletop, his cigar pinwheeling into the night. There was a horrible cracking sound and then the judge lay still, blood spreading on the flagstones overlooking Duke's barbecue pit.

Vicki covered her mouth.

Nell knelt beside the judge, heard him breathing.

Kirk said, "What a useless fuck."

Duke's voice rose. "Kirk. Dr. Hirsch is here somewhere."

"Want me to find him?"

Nell looked up in time to catch Duke glaring at his brother.

* * *

Later that night, Nell felt Clay's hand on her back. She rolled over, said, "Mmm."

His voice was quiet. "Am I disturbing you?"

"Always."

He kissed her mouth, her neck, moved down. Then came a few timeless minutes she spent in a place without thought, rationality, cognition or anything else but pleasure, growing more focused and expanding simultaneously.

After, he said, "I love you."

"I love you, too."

"Everything's going to be all right."

"Norah?"

"We'll have a nice long talk. She'll come around."

They lay like spoons, intimate in every way. Nell heard water running in the pipes, thought: *she's up.* She checked the time on the bedside clock. The eyes of Caravaggio's *Fortune Teller* came to her mind, unbidden and unreadable.

irate dreamed about God. God thundereth marvellously with his voice. Pirate heard God's thundering in his dreams and was not afraid. Why? Because great things doeth he, which we cannot comprehend. For he saith to the snow, Be thou on earth; likewise to the small rain, and to the great rain of his strength. The great rain of his strength: Pirate slept to the sound of the great rain, God driving the deluge on and on. Picturing God was easy—a whirlwind with an unseen face inside. It poured and poured but Pirate was warm and dry on his bunk.

"Hey, you alive in there? Wake fuckin' up."

Pirate rolled over, sat up, saw the big guard with the modified dreads, whose normal voice was soft, but not today.

"And put that goddamn patch on. No one wants to look at you like that."

Pirate felt around on the bunk, found the patch. Sometimes it slipped off in the night; that had never been a problem with anyone before.

"Come on, shake a leg," said the guard, still sounding angry, maybe even angrier.

Pirate got his patch in place. "I didn't put in for it," he said.

"What you talkin' about?"

"Protective custody. I don't want it."

"Protective custody? Shit. Get a move on."

"Where?" said Pirate. "Where am I going?"

"Court. Forgot your own hearing?"

"I didn't, uh—"

"Move, for Christ's sake. It's a long drive."

"Where, um—"

"Belle Ville—where d'you think?"

"Leaving the . . . the building?"

"Goin' senile or something?"

Leaving the building: this was bad. Pirate didn't even like leaving his cell without the tiny weapon. "Need a minute," he said.

"Huh?"

"Just to, uh, clean up a little."

"Clean up? Ain't no job interview."

Pirate's hands got unsteady. This was bad. All he wanted was to be at peace. Then he had a thought. "Respect for the court," he said.

The guard gazed at him. This wasn't one of the hard-ass guards, but his gaze today was hard-ass as the most hard-ass. "One minute," he said, and moved down the block.

Pirate took less than half of that to get the tiny weapon from the secret hideout and stick it in place; cutting himself just the littlest bit on account of that unsteadiness in his hands. He was at the soup-bowl-size sink, splashing cold water on his face—there was no hot—when the guard returned. The door slid open.

"Raise 'em up," said the guard.

Pirate raised his arms, spread his legs, exposed his anus, went through the whole routine.

"Move."

Pirate picked up his Bible.

"Who said anything about that?"

"Just my Bible."

The guard made a move to grab it, a move that slowed down, became a more respectful taking. He held Pirate's Bible by the spine, gave a shake. Nothing fell out; the gold tassel looped free, that was all. The guard handed back the Bible.

They walked down the block, past the rat cages.

"Adios," said one of the rats.

Adiós meant good-bye; also had God in it. Pirate was still thinking about that—the guard on his blind side, but there was nothing Pirate could do—when they left the block, crossed a patch of dirt near the kitchens and entered a room Pirate had never seen.

More guards. Some Pirate knew and some he didn't, but all were at their meanest. Why?

"What's he's got there?"

"Bible."

"Who said he gets to take that?"

The guards looked at one another. A phone call went out somewhere; Pirate thought he heard the words "warden's office." His Bible must have been important if the warden was getting involved. Word came back.

"Bible okay, but it can't be in his possession until transfer to court custody."

A guard took the Bible. Then they handcuffed him, hooked the cuffs to a waist chain, shackled his ankles.

"See you soon, Pirate," a guard said.

Pirate shuffled out a door, across another dirt patch, into the back of a white van with DEPARTMENT OF CORRECTIONS on the side. The double doors closed. Bolts clicked into place. The van started rolling, the driver and two guards, one with the Bible, in front, Pirate alone in back. There were two small windows and soon Pirate caught a glimpse of countryside going by, his first glimpse of countryside since . . . since the only other time he'd been outside the walls, the brief hospital visit after Esteban Malvi scooped out his eye. Pirate watched the countryside through the small windows. Once he spotted a woman in shorts and a T-shirt, walking by the side of the road. He kept a lookout for more to appear, but none did. After a while, he fell asleep. The sound of great rain rose up all around.

*   *   *

"Hey. Wake up."

Pirate opened his eye. The van wasn't moving. One of the guards stood before him.

"On your feet."

Pirate rose, checking that his patch was in place. He shuffled to the open doors, sat on the edge of the steel floor, bumping down awkwardly—he felt a tiny stab in his non-eye—swung his feet outside and slid down, stumbling, but not falling, as he landed on the pavement of a parking lot.

"Move."

Pirate walked across the parking lot, a guard on either side. They went down some steps, through a basement doorway, into a room with two cells at the back, both empty.

"Inside."

Pirate went into one of the cells. The door closed. Keys jingled, locking him in. The guards left the room. Pirate sat on a bunk, much like his own. He smelled coffee, real brewed coffee, not far away. Pirate hadn't drunk real brewed coffee in twenty years. He took a deep deep breath.

A door opened. People came in: his two guards in their tan uniforms, some others in blue; and behind them someone he knew—the woman with the amazing skin. Susannah, her last name almost coming to him. She walked right over to his cell.

"Hello Mr. DuPrce. Everything all right?"

"Hi, Miss, uh, Susannah."

All at once her eyes narrowed. She whirled around, faced those guards and cops. "Why is he shackled?" she said.

A man in blue, three yellow stripes on his sleeve, said, "Standard procedure."

"It may be standard procedure here, Sergeant, but it's also entirely discretionary, according to state code. I want them off—cuffs, shackles, chain."

"Can't do that," said the sergeant.

"Plus we have some normal clothes for him. My client is not appearing in court attired in this prejudicial way."

Pirate didn't know what that last sentence meant, but he liked the effect she was having on all these officers of the law. They were frowning, turning red, puffing out their chests; he almost laughed out loud. And maybe he did, just a little, because an officer of the law or two shot him a look, quick and nasty.

Then came a long silence. Pirate was familiar with silences like this, had witnessed plenty in the last twenty years: whoever spoke first lost.

The sergeant said, "Someone go get the chief."

A minute or two later, the chief appeared. Pirate wouldn't have guessed that, expected a chief to be dressed in a fancy uniform, while this man wore a gray business suit; but everyone called him chief, so Pirate knew. The chief was trim and broad-shouldered, not as big as Pirate; one of those handsome types with some Cajun blood, dark-haired and dark-eyed. People were explaining things to him. The chief listened, his eyes on Pirate. All at once Pirate remembered that brown-eyed gaze, seemingly sympathetic, remembered who this was, remembered a detective named Jarreau. And now: the chief?

The room went quiet. The chief spoke. "No shackles," he said. "No cuffs. He can wear street clothes, but go through them first. Two court officers behind him at all times." The chief turned to Susannah. "Good enough?" he said.

"Thanks," Susannah said.

"It's discretionary, as you say," the chief said. "Anything else?"

"I'd like a few minutes alone with my client."

"Stay as long as you want," the chief said, "but a court officer is here at all times."

Susannah gave the chief a long look but didn't argue. Everyone except one uniformed man went away. The uniformed man sat on a stool in the corner. Susannah approached the cell.

"Can't be in contact range with the prisoner," the guard said.

Susannah stopped about three feet from the bars.

"How are you, Mr. DuPree?"

"Um," said Pirate. "You know."

"You must have a lot of questions."

There was always that one question: Why did God pick on Job in the first place? But other than that, Pirate couldn't think of any.

"About the hearing, for example?" Susannah said.

"Yeah, the hearing," said Pirate.

"First, I don't want you to be nervous."

"I'm not," Pirate said, which wasn't true: thoughts about Esteban Malvi and the Ocho Cincos kept coming, unstoppable.

"Good," she said. "You won't be required to say a word. I'll be sitting with you the whole time. As for what to expect, there's no telling. My customary advice in these situations is to expect the worst."

"No problem," said Pirate.

Susannah gazed at him for a moment, then went on, but suddenly distracted again by the beauty of her skin, so soft and glowing, he missed most of what she said, just catching the last few words: " . . . haven't been able to find out what it means, if anything."

"What what means?" said Pirate.

"This last-minute change in judges," Susannah said. "That I've been explaining."

"How many judges are there?" Pirate said, a little embarrassed, wanting her to know he was interested in what she had to say.

"How many judges?"

"Like nine or something?"

"Nine?" Susannah laughed. "Are you talking about the Supreme Court?"

Pirate didn't like that laugh. All of a sudden he was seeing flaws in her skin, or flaws that could be there with a little help. He said nothing.

The laughter left her face. "There's just one judge," she said. "The judge on the schedule—a good ol' boy apparently, but with a decent reputation—got pulled for some reason and we don't know much about the replacement."

"Never got along with good ol' boys," Pirate said.

"Then maybe this is a lucky break," Susannah said. "The replacement's certainly no good ol' boy—she's black, for starters."

That wasn't good either.

And young, besides. That was the first thing Pirate noticed when they led him into the courtroom. Pirate found himself blinking, even though it wasn't very bright. Then, as the blurriness cleared, he saw the judge, sitting up high with that hammer thing—name escaping him at the moment—beside her. The judge looked about Susannah's age, but not so friendly. She saw Pirate following Susannah to one of the two long tables in front, Bible in hand, and frowned. Pirate began to change his mind about protective custody.

He sat down, feeling strange in regular clothes: a suit, in fact, brown, with a white shirt and a beige tie. Pirate had never actually owned a suit, not if a suit meant the pants matching the jacket. He'd once had a purple jacket with silver buttons; in fact, it hit him at that moment, he'd been wearing that purple jacket the last time he was arrested.

"You all right?" said Susannah.

"Uh-huh."

"I want you to meet," she began, and then introduced the man sitting on Pirate's other side, a Jewish-sounding name that Pirate didn't quite catch.

"Hold on tight," said the man.

Did he mean the Bible? Pirate had it in his usual grip, loose, fingering the gold tassel. He glanced around, saw lots of people sitting in back, a few still coming in. And one of those—a tanned, in-shape-looking woman, older than Susannah but just as pretty, in a softer, better way—he recognized. Pirate had seen her only once, and that was twenty years ago, but he would never forget that face, not so soft, on second thought. Oh, no. She was the woman who'd sat in the witness chair—in this very courtroom?—pointed right at him and said he was the one. But he wasn't the one; and the whole thing came flooding back: how he'd been down in a holding cell, still in that purple jacket, waiting to get bailed out on an everyday B&E he'd done, maybe unwisely, on the spur of the moment, when the next thing he knew he was upstairs getting asked about the Parish Street Pier, where he'd never been, and somebody named Johnny Blanton, who he'd never heard of. He didn't do it, didn't kill Johnny Blanton, had still to this day not yet killed anyone in his life. The woman—he'd forgotten her name—met his gaze, then quickly looked away. Oh, yes. At that moment, starting to get wound up like he hadn't been for a long time, Pirate remembered how hard he'd worked to be at peace. He turned around, opened the Bible in his lap.

For he saith to the snow, Be thou on earth; likewise to the small rain, and to the great rain of his strength.

"Are you all right?" Susannah said.

Pirate nodded, kept reading.

"This court is now in session. All rise."

Pirate rose with the others, sat down when they sat down. Things started happening, but Pirate's mind was elsewhere. He could tell from the tones of all the voices that a big argument was going on. A little guy with a mustache who kept stabbing with his finger wanted to keep him in prison. Susannah's Jewish buddy wanted to get him out. They fought about the tape. They fought about Napoleon Ferris. Someone from FEMA, whatever that was, took the stand. A fight broke out about how the tape got found, then about whether this FEMA guy knew someone at the Justice Project. And had he also once been busted by a cop named Bobby Rice?

So was this all about getting revenge on Bobby Rice? But what sense would that make? said the Jew, real sarcastic: Bobby Rice was already dead before the tape got found. Did you ever consider it might be a plot against the whole department? said the finger stabber, even more sarcastic. The fighting moved on. Someone else took the stand. Was it true that there was tension in the department between the chief and his deputy? Voices rose. Pirate lost interest.

Time passed—a loud and angry blur of sound. Pirate found himself reading and rereading the part about the great rain. God, a whirlwind, made the great rain. He suddenly got it. Great rain plus whirlwind: hurricane. The great thing about the Book of Job was—

All at once Susannah gripped his knee. It shocked him. He jerked upright, stared at her. She pointed to the judge. The judge was speaking.

" . . . and in terms of establishment of reasonable doubt, if this tape had been produced at the original trial, it is the opinion of this court that despite . . ."

A minute or so later, she banged that hammer thing.

"Oh my God," said Susannah. "You're a free man."

Then came all sorts of turmoil. Pirate's tongue got thick, making coherent speech impossible. Susannah turned him toward a door. Pirate saw the tanned, fit woman again, the one who'd ID'd him. He got that weird, squinting feeling in his non-eye, a little painful this time, because of the tiny weapon. The soft skin on the woman's face dissolved and he saw underneath, glimpsed something all twisted up. She might not have long to live.

CHAPTER 11

"Y ou went to the hearing?" Clay said. "I don't understand."

They sat in a coffee shop across the street from the museum. A DK Industries grader went back and forth over the spot where the *Cloud Nine* had stood, its attenuated arches making the stolen sculpture seem much taller than it really was. "Is that what matters—that I went?" Nell said. "What about the result?"

"Anything can happen in court," Clay said.

"Was it because of that judge? Would the other one, Earl Roman—"

"No telling," Clay said; but didn't she hear doubt in his voice? And hadn't she caught a flash of anger in his eyes, merely at the mention of Earl Roman's name? "But tell me why you went to the hearing," he said.

"What's wrong with me going?" Nell said.

The coffee came: an espresso for Clay, a latte for Nell. The cup looked tiny in his hand. He had beautiful dark hands, powerful and finely shaped at the same time, two perfect incarnations of him. "What's wrong?" he said. "For starters, why would you want to subject yourself to it?" He sipped his espresso, watching her over the rim of his cup. She almost thought there was something professional in his look.

"I just had to see him."

"Why?"

"To see what he looked like."

"Doesn't matter what he looks like now," Clay said. "People change in twenty years."

"I know." Other than his size, Alvin DuPree had looked nothing like he had back then, either in her memories of him in court or on the Parish Street Pier; so much older, much more than twenty years' worth, so scarred, so worn; all of him so different, except for one small similarity—that remaining pale blue eye.

"So why, Nell?"

"I told you."

"Why didn't you bring it up before?" Clay said.

"You'd gone to work. It was spur-of-the-moment."

"Spur-of-the-moment."

"Yes."

"You hadn't been thinking about it?"

"No. Not really."

"Not really."

"No."

"So what provoked this spur-of-the-moment decision?"

"Clay? I feel like I'm being questioned."

A pained look rose in his eyes. "Sorry, baby," he said. He reached across the table, laid his hand on hers. She felt a little better right away. "There was no call from Lee Ann Bonner, or anything like that?" he said.

"A call from Lee Ann?"

"Before you jumped in the car and rode down to the courthouse."

Nell withdrew her hand. "There was no call from Lee Ann," she said. "I can think for myself."

"Hell, I know that," Clay said. "You're the smartest person in my life, always have been, always will be. I just can't get the reasoning behind—"

She interrupted. "Don't you see? What if I put the wrong man behind bars? Destroying a whole life, Clay—he's old now, he lost an eye, God knows what else happ—"

"Stop," said Clay. "Stop right there. "You didn't put—"

The waitress came by. "You folks all set? We've got some nice almond cake today, baked fresh. On the house, Chief."

"We're fine," Clay said. "And we'll be wanting a check when it's time to settle up, please." She went away. He leaned forward, lowered his voice. "You didn't put anyone behind bars. A jury did that. And it wasn't just your testimony. DuPree was a known thief, with a record—a record that included a very similar nighttime attack where he showed a knife, and that could easily have had a similar ending if a cruiser hadn't by chance—"

"And that bothers me, too," Nell said. "That the knife never got found."

"No case," Clay said, "not one, ever gets resolved without a loose end or two. It doesn't mean things don't add up. Forget your sighting of the knife. We had the knife wound. We had his previous knife history. That adds up."

"But what happened to the knife?"

Clay raised his hands. "He threw it in the bayou."

"But divers went in there and they didn't—"

"Or in the bushes somewhere, or down a drain, or in a trash can. Doesn't matter. He did it."

She gazed at him. To know someone so well, to know exactly what he was thinking, but to disagree, or at least be in doubt: Nell felt the first twinge of a special kind of pain restricted to good marriages alone.

"But what about the tape?" she said.

He gazed back at her. "This is going to be hard for you, Nell, but—we may never know."

"Never know?"

"The story of the tape, who fabricated it, why, all those other questions someone with a mind like yours—a conscience like yours—needs answers to. I was downstairs, watching on the closed-circuit hookup, and that's the feeling I got, a real bad feeling—we may never know."

Never knowing? At the moment, that struck her as intolerable. Would time change that, bring acceptance? She knew time had the power when it came to some things, but that didn't make it right, was more a sign of human weakness.

"I don't understand about the FEMA guy maybe having some grudge against Bobby Rice," she said. "And what was all that about tension between you and Darryll?" Darryll Pines was the deputy chief, had been deputy chief back when Clay was still a detective.

"He wants my job, has always wanted it—that's no secret," Clay said. "But that can happen in any organization—we work together fine."

Nell had a sudden thought. "How did Darryll and Bobby get along?"

Clay took another sip of his espresso, again gazed at her over the rim of the cup, again a gaze that reminded her of his profession. "Where are you going with that?"

"Nowhere," she said. "I'm just trying to understand." She reached across the table, now laid her hand on his. Clay had thick veins on the back of his hand; she could feel blood pulsing inside. "Is this about protecting Bobby's memory?" she said. "Is that what you're doing?"

"Bobby's memory doesn't need my help," Clay said. His cell phone went off. He answered, listened, clicked off. "Got to go."

"Is it about this?"

"No," Clay said, rising. "Bank robbery in progress, out in Riverbend." He laid some money on the table.

"Be careful."

"Always," he said, leaning down and kissing her. Then, his face very close, he added softly, "We may never get to the bottom of this. Don't let it ruin anything."

Their eyes met. There was nothing professional in his gaze now, she thought: just him and her. "I would never do that," she said. "But whatever happens, DuPree is guilty, right?"

His mouth opened, closed, opened again. She could smell his breath, always fresh and sweet, now with an espresso overlay. "I just don't know, baby."

Nell felt blood rushing from her head, a flood, almost faint-inducing, as though a plug had been pulled inside her. "You don't know?"

He put his finger over her lips. "One way or another," he said, "we have to put this behind us, move on. Okay?"

She tried to nod like it was okay, maybe shifted her head a little. He smiled at her, turned, and walked toward the door; then stopped suddenly and came back. "That Norah matter?" he said, glancing around; the waitress was busy behind the counter, the only other customers sat across the room. "It's all straightened out."

"Thanks."

"There's her to think of, too," he said. "We'll get through this. All of it."

They were a team; yes, intimates in every way. The feeling of his finger on her lips lingered even after he'd left the coffee shop and driven away, siren on. The sound faded. Nell called the house, got no answer. She tried Norah's cell. Same.

Nell drove out to Parish Street, parked at the towpath, stood on the edge of the bayou, where the pier had been. The bayou was all cleaned up, as Kirk Bastien had said: garbage, wrecked cars, and all the dead things—trees, birds, fish, the dog—gone. There was even a little current flowing downstream toward the Gulf, and a crab scuttled through weeds on the far bank. Had Kirk really fired those two assistants? Was that somehow part of the cleanup, a ritual sacrifice to nature? If so, what kind of sacrifice would be necessary to make up for all that Bernardine had done?

Nell closed her eyes, tried to imagine darkness, a full moon, Johnny. She remembered Johnny talking about the contours of the sea bottom and a giant funnel; she could picture the big man stepping out from behind the support post, and how the bandanna had fooled her into thinking his face was deformed—as DuPree's face later became. Was there meaning behind that? Nell wrestled and wrestled with the idea, got nowhere.

She sat down on the edge of the bank, feet dangling, watching the current. Cloud reflections drifted on the water;

when viewed from a bit of an angle, they could have been shadowy things far far down. Johnny had shielded her. The man had spoken behind the bandanna, just the single word—"money"—not enough to have left her with a trace of the sound of his voice even back then. Then had come the long blade and the sound of steel on bone, in bone, through bone, a sound still clear in her mind even now, sitting by the cleaned-up bayou. The knife had slipped out of Johnny; the curve of the blade visible in the moonlight and like the sound of the stabbing, still clear. Then, too late, she'd resisted, kicking out, and caught that one glimpse of his face. Nell closed her eyes again, tried and tried to see that face. Her mind offered up the paltriest of visions, no more than an oval, blank and white, all except for the pale blue eyes, which she pictured vividly for a moment before they got all mixed up with the eyes of the *Fortune Teller*. She regretted sitting in the last row in court; up front, she might have gotten a better look at DuPree's eye, those two moments when he'd turned around. Had he recognized her? He hadn't shown the slightest sign, in fact, had seemed barely there the second time, as though on some sedative. Were his lawyers allowed to—

What was that? Nell thought she caught a flash under the water, a quick gleam down deep, there and gone. She leaned forward, peered into the water, didn't see the gleam. That didn't mean she'd imagined it, didn't mean the knife wasn't somewhere on the bottom. True, divers had searched without success back then, but why couldn't they have simply missed the knife, maybe buried in the mud? And now, so long after, comes Bernardine, stirring things up. Why not? The Justice Project was making the exact same claim for the tape.

Nell rose, kicked off her shoes. She glanced around, saw no one. A minute later, in bra and panties, she slid down the bank and into the bayou.

Nell had played in this very bayou as a kid, farther upstream where it cut across a corner of Magnolia Glade. The water had always been warm, close to bathtub temperature,

but now it was cold enough to make her gasp. Had Bernardine uncovered a previously hidden spring, or something like
that? Johnny would have known. She took a deep breath, cut
through the surface in a quick duck dive, kicked her way
down.

The bayou was only ten or twelve feet deep, clarity nothing like the water around Little Parrot Cay, but good enough.
Nell glided along the bottom, eyesight distorted by the lack
of a mask, but able to pick things out: soft green algae, shells
lying on the bottom, yellow and pink, a fat brown catfish
with long white whiskers swimming by. Had Bernardine
brought the catfish back? Nell remembered what should
have been second nature—that gators lived in the bayous,
too, making it a good idea to check before diving in—got
the sudden feeling of something behind her, glanced back.
No gators, but she saw a dull gleam in the mud at the base of
the far bank. Two or three strokes and it was in her hand. A
mirror, not a knife: a small round mirror in a chrome frame,
the kind found on car doors.

Nell kicked up to the surface, breathed, examined the
mirror. A cracked mirror: she saw her face split down the
middle. Nell swam to the towpath-side bank, found a foot-
hold, climbed to the top.

A Belle Ville cruiser sat beside her car, the words DEPUTY
CHIEF on the side. Nell had left her clothes on a rock by the
towpath. She put down the mirror, slid into the blouse she'd
worn to court and was buttoning it up when the driver's-side
door of the cruiser opened and Darryll Pines stepped out.
He was in uniform, cap bill pulled low over his eyes, belly
sticking out over his belt. Nell reached for her skirt.

"Hold it right there," said Darryll Pines; his hand was on
the butt of his gun.

"Darryll."

"Huh?"

"It's me. Nell Jarreau."

His hand left the gun butt. "Were you in the bayou or
somethin'?" His head moved in a way that suggested he was

looking her up and down; impossible to tell, the way he had his hat.

"Yes." She wrapped her skirt around her, zipped it up.

Darryll crossed the street, stepped onto the towpath. "Din't recognize you there for a secont," he said.

Nell slid into her shoes. "It's been a while," she said.

"What has?"

"Since we've seen each other. The charity basketball game, I think it was."

"Yeah, must of been." He came closer. Now she could make out his eyes; they were focusing down her blouse. She buttoned it to the top, picked up the mirror. "What's that?" he said.

"An old car mirror."

"Got that out of the bayou?"

"Yes."

"C'n I see?"

She handed him the mirror. He turned it over in his hands, stared at it, then into it. His hair, which she remembered as light brown, was now a yellowish white, kind of greasy, and too long; and his eyes, which she'd never taken note of before, were blue.

"What's important about it?" he said.

"Nothing."

"Then how come you—" He cut himself off, glanced around. "This here's where it went down, huh? The murder and all."

"That's right."

"Was there an automobile around? I'm not remembering that."

"There wasn't."

"So why'd you—" He waved the mirror in a short arc.

"Cleaning up debris," Nell said.

"That's nice," Darryll said. "Lemme ask you—what's your take on all this, DuPree and such?"

"My take's on the record, Darryll, and hasn't changed. I'd be interested in yours."

"Don't get too concerned with such matters, down at my level," he said. "Justice prevails, nine times out of ten."

"That doesn't strike me as a great percentage," Nell said.

"Sorry, ma'am," he said. "We'll just have to try harder." He handed her the mirror. "Nice seein' you."

"Good-bye, Darryll." Nell walked over to Parish Street. A wire-mesh trash barrel stood on the corner. She dropped the mirror inside, got in her car, drove home; wet and clammy under her clothes.

CHAPTER 12

N orah?"
     Nell walked through the house, checked out back.
No sign of Norah, but a tree branch, probably weak-
ened by Bernardine, had fallen, and now floated in the lap
pool; a long bare tree branch with a head of trailing brown
leaves, like a crude rendering of a person. Nell went upstairs,
knocked on Norah's door. No answer. She opened the door.
Norah lay in bed, watching television.

"Norah? You didn't hear me?"

"Nope."

"Are you all right?"

"Great."

Norah's gaze had remained on the screen. A reporter was
doing an interview outside the courthouse.

"With me now is Susan Upton of the Justice Project.
Susan, first of all—"

"It's Susannah," said a woman who didn't look much older
than Norah; Nell had noticed her in court, attractive in a
strong-featured way, Northern and big-city.

"Sorry, Susannah," said the reporter. "First, what's your
reaction to today's decision?"

"We're elated," Susannah said. "At the same time, a terrible wrong has been done, a wrong that can never be put
right."

"You're referring to the imprisonment of Alvin DuPree?" the reporter said.

Susannah gave the reporter a look. "Exactly," she said. "How does he get those twenty years back?"

"No doubt a big question," said the reporter. "Any indication at this time of Mr. DuPree's future plans?"

"Right now he's just going to take a few days to absorb all this."

"There you have it—Susannah Upton of the Justice Project. Back to you in the studio, Matt."

"Judy? Matt in the studio. Do you happen to know if DuPree himself is talking?"

"Negative, Matt—he's giving no interviews at this time."

The words *Up Next* appeared on the TV. Norah switched it off, but her eyes stayed on the blank screen. "I thought you said he did it. You saw with your own eyes."

"I did."

"So they just let my dad's killer go? Is that what you're saying?"

"*I'm* not saying anything."

Norah turned to her, voice rising. "Why not? You loved him, didn't you?"

"Yes."

"Then how come you're not upset?"

"I am upset."

"You don't show it," Norah said. "How much did you love him?"

Now Nell's voice rose, too. "What the hell kind of question is that?"

Norah shrugged. Nell got a grip on her anger, sat on the edge of the bed. She could smell her daughter; Norah needed a shower, needed to brush her teeth. "What's happened to you this year?" Nell said. "What's wrong?"

"Maybe it's genetic," Norah said, "handed down from my real dad, just kicking in now."

"Clay—Dad—is your real dad. He raised you from the age of two. He loves you. Don't you realize you could have faced criminal charges for what you did? He made that all go away."

"He's the Man."

Nell rose. "And you also don't understand how it tears him up to do something like that, to play favorites." All of a sudden Nell was in tears. They took her by surprise. She grabbed a framed photograph, almost at random, off Norah's bookshelf. It showed Clay carrying Norah—about ten, in her soccer uniform—on his shoulder, her little hands curled in his hair, big grins on both their faces. Nell thrust it in Norah's face. "Look," she said. "Just look." She let go of the photo, hurried downstairs, splashed water on her face.

Toweling off, Nell saw her face in the mirror. "Pull yourself together," she said. She went outside, got hold of the branch in the lap pool, dragged it across the yard to the brush pile by the shed. After that, she picked up the skimmer, skimmed the surface of the water, got rid of those dead brown leaves. Then she fetched the pool vacuum from the shed, vacuumed the bottom. She was just finishing when Norah came out, freshly showered, wearing jeans and a Vanderbilt T-shirt, looking like what she was, a beautiful young woman with a golden future. They could get through this. Everything was going to be all right. The sun came out and the pool sparkled.

"Mom?"

"Yes?"

"I'd like to see the pictures."

"What pictures?" Nell said, thinking: *More of her and Clay?*

"Of my . . . biological father."

"Oh, Norah. You've seen them before."

"Not in years. Where are they?"

"This isn't a good time."

"Why not?"

"We have to move on, return to normal life, get you back in school."

"School? That's what started all this."

"All what?"

"Nothing."

"What do you mean—school started all this?"

"Nothing. I don't mean anything. All this . . . confusion."
Norah made a gesture, taking in the pool, the yard, points
beyond.

Confusion inside her head? Is that what Norah meant?
"Norah? How about the idea of seeing someone, some kind
of a therapist?"

"I don't need to see a therapist," Norah said. "I need to see
the pictures."

Nell gazed at her daughter: freshly scrubbed, damp hair
combed back and gleaming. But the look in her eyes was
wrong. Therapist: a good idea, although Nell didn't know
any. The goal would be to nudge Norah into wanting to see
one; meanwhile, what harm could there be in looking at the
pictures? Pain, maybe, but not harm.

"They're in the office," Nell said.

They went upstairs where Nell had a small office, formerly
the guest bedroom. She opened a closet, began unstacking
boxes. The one lettered UNC in felt pen lay on the bottom.
She put it on her desk, blew off the dust. Norah handed her
scissors. Nell sliced through the packing tape, opened the
box. She caught a whiff of that Bernardine smell, got a bad
feeling at once.

Nell removed a layer of bubble wrap. Underneath lay
old art-history notebooks, a file bulging with research for
her master's thesis, never written, an introductory geology
textbook bought in the hope she wouldn't be so ignorant of
Johnny's work, some souvenirs, including postcards from
Cape Cod, where they'd gone for a Labor Day weekend, and
a coaster from the Chapel Hill restaurant where they'd had
their first date. And at the bottom: a photo album.

Nell took it out of the box. The Bernardine smell got
stronger. She opened the album. On the first page was a picture of Johnny standing by a pool with a big smile on his
face and a trophy in his hand. But none of it—trophy, smile,

pool, Johnny—was visible, unless you knew what to look for, could fill in the blanks from memory. Mildew, mold, humidity, had ruined the picture, blurring and fading all that had been, leaving no more than suggestive patches of light and dark.

"Mom?"

Nell turned the pages of the album, faster and faster. All the photos were like that first one, or worse; all ruined.

"I don't understand," Norah said, wringing her hands. "There wasn't any flooding in the Heights."

But there'd been no electricity for a month, meaning no AC. "Oh, God," Nell said. "The power went—"

"Everything is so fucked up," Norah said, and hurried from the room. Nell was about to follow when the phone rang. She thought: *Clay;* and picked it up.

But not Clay. "Hope this isn't a bad time," Lee Ann said.

"Of course it's a bad time," Nell said. "And I've got nothing to say."

"You don't have to say anything," said Lee Ann. "I just want you to listen."

"To what?"

"My interview with Alvin DuPree. It's running tomorrow."

"But he's not giving interviews."

Lee Ann laughed—quick, low, pleased. "Making it what we in the biz call a scoop," she said. "I left him less than half an hour ago."

"Where?"

"Where did we meet?"

"Yes."

"They've got him at the Ambassador Suites for now," Lee Ann said. A phone rang in the background, then another. "Ready? '"I've got no quarrels," said Alvin Mack DuPree within minutes of walking out of the downtown Belle Ville courthouse as a free man, a decision that stunned many longtime court observers.'" Lee Ann paused. "Damn. Needs tightening. 'Mr. DuPree spent twenty years in Central State Prison on a murder conviction thrown out today by Judge

Ella Thomas. "I'm at peace with the world," Mr. DuPree told this reporter in an exclusive interview conducted in a downtown restaurant. For his first meal on the outside, Mr. DuPree ordered a cheeseburger with fries and coffee, heavily sweetened. Asked about losing an eye in prison, for which he wears a patch that evidently inspired the jailhouse nickname "Pirate," he commented that "it could be worse." Had he ever given up hope? "Got to have hope," Mr. DuPree said. Did he have any thoughts on why the exculpatory evidence appears to have been moldering away inside police headquarters at One Marigot Street all these years? "Don't know about any of that," Mr. DuPree replied. Mr. DuPree's conviction for the stabbing murder of a young scientist named Johnny Blanton was based partly on the eyewitness testimony of Nell Jarreau, Mr. Blanton's girlfriend at the time, and now assistant curator of the Belle Ville Museum of Art, and wife of Belle Ville police chief Clay Jarreau. Asked about his present thoughts concerning Ms. Jarreau, who was spotted in court today, Mr. DuPree repeated, "I have no quarrels. Folks make mistakes. I just want to move on.""

"Wait a minute," Nell said. "Do you need to put that in?"

"Put what in?"

"My being there."

"You're not disputing the fact?"

"The fact that I was there? Of course not. But does it have to be in the story?"

"If true, why shouldn't it be?"

Nell almost said, *Whose side are you on?*—stopping herself at the last instant. "How is it important?"

"Human interest," Lee Ann said.

"But what about my privacy?" Nell said. "I was there as a private citizen."

"This is a public matter, Nell—couldn't be more public. And speaking of human interest, have you got any reaction I could quote?"

"No."

There was a pause. When Lee Ann spoke again, her tone was perhaps more that of a friend than a reporter. "I hope you're not beating yourself up about this."

Not beating herself up about it? A friend who didn't know her very well: Nell almost laughed out loud, a laugh that would have sounded ugly and that she kept inside. She said nothing.

"I've been talking to this expert in mistaken eyewitness testimony," Lee Ann said; paper crinkled in the background. "Professor Urbana at Tulane. He told me, quote: 'Memory of a crime event is just like the crime scene itself—ambiguous and prone to contamination.'"

That didn't make Nell feel any better.

Another pause, more phones ringing wherever Lee Ann was. "If I could just clarify one last thing," Lee Ann said, tone reportorial again.

"What's that?"

"Did you know Clay before the murder?"

"You already asked me that," Nell said. "I don't know why you keep coming back to it." And maybe she didn't, not in the reasoning part of her mind, but it gave her a sick feeling.

"Just trying to nail down the timeline."

"As I think I told you, the first time I ever saw Clay was at my parents' house, a few hours after the murder." *I had his blood all over me.*

More riffling paper. "I don't have that in my notes."

"Then put it in now." Nell was conscious of her tone, sharp and unpleasant.

"My mistake, I'm sure," Lee Ann said. "I'm sorry you're going through this."

"I don't want sympathy." And why should she? She hadn't spent twenty years behind bars; in fact, if there was some opposite to incarceration, better-than-normal unimprisoned life, many of those years belonged in that category for her.

"That's one of the things I like about you," Lee Ann said. "But I'm not sure you get it—this is not going away."

"Why not?" Alvin DuPree and Clay: both had said the same thing—they wanted to move on.

"For one thing," Lee Ann said, "there's no statute of limitations on murder. If the judge was right and DuPree is innocent—and that sure is the way it's starting to look to most everybody, I'd be lying if I told you otherwise—then the real killer is still out there. Unless he's dead, of course. Which reminds me—did Johnny Blanton have any enemies, anyone who might have borne him a grudge or had it in for—"

"I'm hanging up."

"Don't, I—"

Nell hung up, and, as she did, heard the little click of someone else hanging up, too. She turned, strode upstairs. The phone rang. She let it.

Nell didn't knock, burst right into Norah's room. Norah sat at her desk, the phone inches from her hand.

"Yeah," she said. "I listened in. So what?"

"So what? That was a private phone call."

"You heard her—'this is a public matter, couldn't be more public.'"

"That has nothing to do with you—"

"Everything," Norah said. "Everything, everything, everything. He was my father."

"I know that, but—"

"And you couldn't even take care of the fucking pictures."

"Don't speak to me like that," Nell said, shouting now. "Say it again."

"Huh?"

"Without the 'fucking.'"

Norah gave her a strange look, as though trying to see from a new angle. "You couldn't even take care of the pictures," she said, her voice suddenly almost punchless. "And where's his computer?"

"What computer?"

"He was a scientist, wasn't he? He must have had a computer."

The phone rang before Nell could answer. Norah snatched the receiver. She listened, handed it to Nell, walked out of the room.

"Hello?" Nell said.

"Solomon Lanier, ma'am. Up in Stonewall County."

"Yes, Sheriff?"

"Just wantin' you to know we arrested a suspect in the Nappy Ferris killing. One of those Mexican drug dealers, like I thought."

"So there's no connection to . . . to anything down here?"

"Not so far as I can tell."

"Thank you, Sheriff."

"Don't mention it, ma'am. Just wanted to give you a heads-up—D.A.'ll probably be needin' you to testify if it comes to trial."

CHAPTER 13

That night Nell fixed a nice dinner—roast pork with orange and honey sauce, a salad of lettuce and cucumber, with red pepper from her own garden, and corn bread, made from a recipe handed down by Clay's grandmother. She set three places in the dining room, using her best silver and plates, and was opening a bottle of wine when she heard the pickup turning into the driveway.

Nell paused, corkscrew sunk in the cork, waiting for the sound of the side door opening. It didn't come. She went into the living room, looked out the window. The pickup was parked in the driveway; Clay sat behind the wheel. He didn't seem to be on the phone or anything, was just sitting there.

Nell walked back to the dining room, drew the cork, poured two glasses of wine. She carried them outside, climbed into the pickup, sat beside him.

"Here."

He took the glass, gave her a little smile.

"You okay?" she said.

"A long day, that's all."

"I've been thinking about our second date," she said. The first date, in a coffee shop, had come a few days before—a year after the DuPree trial—mostly just setting up the second.

"Yeah?" Clay's skin, normally so healthy-looking, seemed pale, almost a white line where it overlaid his cheekbone. At that moment, Nell realized she hadn't been thinking about their date at all, but, reminded by the restaurant coaster, of hers and Johnny's; she'd gotten all mixed up. "Hey," he said, "what's wrong?"

"Nothing."

He drank some wine. "I can still see the look on your face," he said.

Their second date: Clay had taken her a few miles down the coast to Cotton Beach, with two eight-foot rods and a bait can. They'd waded out and he'd gone over the basics of surf fishing. On her very first cast, she'd hooked a three-foot sand shark, then jumped straight up out of the water. After, they'd eaten at a shrimp shack, not speaking much, and never about the case, the trial, Johnny, or the past at all; their salty bare legs touching once under the table, by accident.

Nell shifted closer to him, put her arm over his shoulders. "At least there was some good news," she said.

"Like what?"

"Didn't Sheriff Lanier get in touch with you?"

"Oh, that."

"Come on, Clay. One of the Mexicans did it—so there's no connection to the tape or anything like that."

Clay took another drink, almost emptying the glass.

"That's true, isn't it?" Nell said.

Clay stared straight ahead.

"It isn't? I'm missing something?"

He turned to her. "No," he said. "It's true." He leaned forward, kissed her cheek.

"He said I'll probably have to testify."

"Maybe we can get you out of it," Clay said, his lips moving against her skin.

"No, I'll do it," Nell said. She patted his face. "Corn bread's waiting."

Clay gave her another little smile. They got out of the car. A big wrecker was coming up the street, followed by the Miata, brand-new paint job glowing in the evening sun. The wrecker, YELLER'S AUTOBODY written on the side in flaming letters, parked on the street; the Miata swung into the driveway and Yeller got out.

"Hey, Chief, ma'am. All set. How's she look?"

"Great," said Clay. "But we could have come gotten it."

"No problem, Chief."

The three of them walked around the car. "Looks better than new," Nell said. It really did; the thought cheered her.

"Did the insurance check come yet?" Clay said.

"All taken care of," Yeller said. He winked. "Plus a couple l'il extras the insurance won't be mindin'."

"Extras?" Clay said, frowning.

"Brake job, new plu—"

Norah came out of the house.

"Hey, miss," said Yeller. "How's she look?"

Norah walked over. Her eyes widened. For a moment, she was so young, young and happy. "Wow," she said.

Yeller grinned. He turned to the truck. "Hey," he called, motioning for the driver to come out. The driver climbed down from the cab, approached. He was tall and lean, wore jeans and a sleeveless T-shirt, had a smiling red devil tattooed on one of his biceps. "Joe Don, meet Chief Jarreau and his lovely fam'ly," Yeller said. "Chief, ma'am, miss—this here's my son, Joe Don."

Joe Don looked at them shyly. "Pleased to, uh, pleased to meet y'all." He had a soft voice, a graceful way of standing; in fact, was beautiful, and Nell wasn't surprised when Yeller said, "Joe Don plays a mean guitar—you c'n hear him down at the Red Rooster Sadiday nights."

Nell glanced at Norah; Norah appeared to be gazing at her reflection in the new paintwork.

"What kind of music?" Nell said.

"Uh," said Joe Don, "guess you could call it like that alt country."

"Sings a bit, too," said Yeller.

Joe Don shuffled his feet; he wore black cowboy boots with silver stars.

"We'll have to catch your act sometime," Nell said.

"That's not really, you know," Joe Don said, his voice getting low, almost as though the next sound out of him would be the opening of "Are You Lonesome Tonight?" or some song like that.

"If you do, give me a buzz," said Yeller. "Drinks on me." He made a clucking sound, the way you'd summon a horse; he and Joe Don got in the wrecker and drove off.

"I hate country," Norah said, her eyes on the departing wrecker; Joe Don behind the wheel, window open, lean left arm resting on the door frame.

"Can't hate Willie Nelson," Clay said.

Nell laughed; and Norah laughed, too. All at once they were all laughing.

"Remember the potato chip factory?" Clay said.

Norah threw back her head and laughed some more. The potato chip factory—culmination of a misadventurous road trip, hilarious in a small, family way, and of course the man who'd finally burst free from the giant potato chip bag had looked a lot like Willie Nelson.

They went in and sat at the dining room table. Clay passed the corn bread around. They all loved the corn bread, one of those unifying dishes.

"Butter on that?" Clay said.

"Thanks," said Norah.

He passed the butter. Norah started buttering her corn bread. "Whatever's going on," Clay said, "your mom and I are here for you."

Norah put down her knife; dropped it, really. It clattered on her plate, fell to the floor. "And my father?" she said. "Where's he?"

Clay turned pale.

"Enough of that," Nell said. "This is your father, right here." Norah gazed at her, eyes blank, the effect infuriating. Suddenly Nell was on her feet. "Did you ever stop and think that a man in his position might have wanted another child, one of his own, so-called?"

"Don't," Clay said.

But Nell kept going. "You know what he said about that?" Was Norah actually looking bored? "He said, 'I don't want another kid—this one's perfect.'"

Silence. Then Norah said, "Pressing my guilt button?"

"No," Nell said. "I'm just trying to get you to see straight."

"Yeah?" said Norah. "You know what I don't see?"

"No," Nell said.

"Your guilt button." She looked at Clay. "Or yours." He went a little paler.

"What does that mean?" Nell said.

"Figure it out." Norah rose and walked out of the room. Nell heard her footsteps on the stairs; then a door slammed.

"What is she talking about?"

Clay shook his head.

Dinner was over. Nell wrapped it in foil, put it in the fridge. All that laughter, Willie Nelson: what did it amount to? The truth of what they were really about? Or nothing more than the little high that came from seeing the better-than-new Miata back safe in the driveway?

Nell woke up in the middle of the night. Clay's breathing was slow and regular. She slipped out from under his hand, resting on her hip, and went upstairs, pulling on her robe. Norah's door was closed, no light showing at the bottom, no sound. Nell went into her office, closed the door, switched on the computer. She started searching for information on Professor Urbana at Tulane. A frog croaked out back, maybe in the pool. She made a mental note to clean it again in the morning.

Nell found him in less than a minute: Victor Urbana, associate professor of psychology, author of an article in *Contemporary Issues in Psychology* entitled "Can You Point Him Out for the Jury?: Problems in Eyewitness Testimony."

Abstract:
Weaknesses in eyewitness testimony can arise in three

different areas. First, visibility may have been poor.
Second, recent studies undermine traditional belief that
people are good at facial identification. Three, police
procedures may be deliberately or accidentally biased.

Nell read the article. She skimmed the obvious paragraphs
on the effects of low light, bad weather, differences in rela-
tive motion, as when the eyewitness was in a moving ve-
hicle and the suspect was not. Yes, nighttime in her case, but
there'd been a full moon, *the little ghost brother.* She slowed
down as she went through part two, problems in facial identification.

Many laymen assume memory works like a video recorder.
This is false, especially in times of stress or trauma, such
as during a criminal attack. In fact, only experiential bits
and pieces are stored, not necessarily in chronological
or any other order. It is in the telling of the event, very
often the first or other early tellings, that a "narrative"
or "story" takes shape. Furthermore, eyewitnesses often
perceive time to be slowing down during a traumatic
event, leading them to falsely exaggerate the time
available for absorbing data. Another factor, limited to
cases involving a weapon, is a phenomenon labeled
"weapon focus," describing a tendency of eyewitnesses
to be so distracted by the presence of a weapon that all
other memories are distorted.

Stress and trauma, oh yes, and a weapon. But had all that
distorted her memory? Nell sat back, closed her eyes, forced
herself to go back twenty years and remember again. And
right away got tripped up:

Nell: *Maybe painters didn't want to do landscapes at
night.*
Johnny: *Because it's hard to see?*

Almost as though Johnny was feeling his way toward questions that were only arising now, long after his death; like . . . like a fortune-teller. The sick feeling in her stomach she'd been getting lately came back. But despite the sick feeling, despite the retrospective eeriness of Johnny's remark, she could still bring it all back: the man stepping out from behind the post at the Parish Street Pier; the strange deformity of his face, due to the bandanna; that single spoken word, "money"; the long blade in the moonlight; the face of the attacker—white, tending toward fleshiness, and those blue eyes, almost colorless. These memories were all still very clear; would probably be clear on her dying day.

Had she been distracted by the sight of the weapon? Nell didn't think so; in fact, the sound of the stabbing, the collision of steel and bone, had made a deeper impact. And therefore?

She scrolled down to the last section:

Police procedures may be deliberately or accidentally biased. An eyewitness to a serious crime and a police investigator often share a common goal, namely the solving of the case and the bringing to justice of the perpetrator. A motivated witness may be vulnerable to feedback, witting or un—

Nell heard footsteps in the hall.

"Nell?"

Her right hand shifted the mouse, clicked on the red *X* in the top right-hand corner of the screen, almost acting on its own. Professor Urbana's paper vanished, leaving behind Nell's browser page, a waterfall by Courbet.

The door opened and Clay walked in.

"Nell? What are you doing?"

"Just I . . . couldn't sleep," she said, turning to him. He wore only a pair of boxers. "Thought I'd catch up on some work."

"Work?" He came closer, glanced at the screen. "But the museum's still closed."

"I know. It's a chance to rethink a few things."

He squinted at Courbet's waterfall, a modest waterfall in a quiet forest dominated by blocks of yellow and green. "Rethink things?"

"Like the Web site," Nell said, angry with herself for lying, not even sure why she was doing it. And then added another, although the statement itself was true: "And some of the wall labeling needs revision."

Clay touched her shoulder. "It's late."

She shut down the computer, a good reason for lying coming to her at the same time: the truth, that she was rooting around for information on the science of messed-up eyewitness testimony, would only upset him.

They went back to bed. Clay turned off the light. Then his hand was on her breast. She began to say something she'd hardly ever said in their whole marriage, maybe never: "Clay, I'm not—"

"Sorry," he said, taking his hand away at once.

"There's nothing to be . . ." She let the sentence die.

They lay side by side; the house, the whole world, quiet. Somehow the touch of his hand stayed on her breast, like magic, and her body began to change her mind. For a while, she resisted. But why? Just for the sake of consistency? What kind of marriage was that? She reached for him.

He was awake. "But I thought . . ." he said.

"Let's not think."

After, as they lay together in a hot, shared dampness, he said, "What else?"

"What else?" she said.

"I can do. Anything you want."

"That was more than enough."

He laughed softly. She fell asleep in seconds.

But in the morning—Clay gone to work, Norah still asleep— Nell was back at the computer. She found more information about Professor Victor Urbana, including his office phone number. For five or ten minutes, she searched for some way to talk to him without revealing her name or true motivation. The best she could come up with was a silly little scheme in which she played a college student's mother helping her daughter with a research paper; Nell's mind didn't work well in areas like this. So, that was that, no?

She rose, looked out the window, saw a bullfrog sitting by the lap pool. The problem—this horrible possibility, maybe even a probability now, and a certainty in the eyes of the law—that she'd sent an innocent man to jail was not going away. Did that mean this sick feeling would be inside her forever? Nell went back to her office and dialed Professor Urbana's number.

He answered halfway through the first ring. "Vic Urbana."

Nell wasn't ready. "Hello. Um, I read what you said— about eyewitness testimony being like crime scenes."

"Where was this?"

"In the *Belle Ville Guardian*."

"Oh, yes."

"And, uh, I've got some questions."

She expected a question from him—who she was, her interest. Instead, he just said, "Like?"

"Well," she said. And then out popped: "I've got a good eye."

"I'm sorry?"

"My field's art history," she said. "I'm trained to spot details, to have a sharp visual memory."

"Yes?"

"So I don't think I could make a mistake like that, misidentifying someone."

Pause. "Were you involved in such a case?" said the professor.

"Yes."

"Where exonerating evidence of a physical nature disproved your testimony?"

"Something like that." Nell was not about to give a flat-out yes to "disproved."

"And it offends your common sense," said Professor Urbana.

"Yes."

"Tell you what," said the professor. "I'm kind of a proselytizer when it comes to this subject. If you're ever around, I've got a little video I could show you."

"How's today?" Nell said.

He laughed. "Eleven-thirty, my office?"

"Perfect."

"And your name?"

"Nell. Nell Jarreau."

The name didn't appear to mean anything to him. "See you then," he said.

Nell left a note for Norah, one of those simple family notes, but she went through three versions before getting it right: *Back soon. There's a nice sandwich in the fridge. Remember—Dad says no driving till we find out about the new premium. Love, Mom.*

Then she drove south to the I–10 interchange and headed for New Orleans.

Nell parked on the Tulane side of St. Charles, walked onto the campus. Professor Urbana's office was on the top floor of a stone building on the main quad, door open. He saw her and said, "Come in." Professor Urbana was about her own age, bearded and chubby. He came out from behind his desk and shook her hand. "I looked you up," he said. "Hope you don't mind."

"No, I guess—"

"Don't know anything about the actual case," the professor said. "The personalities and so on. My interest is scientific, and I assume you're looking for a quick synopsis in that area."

"Ye—"

"And I also assume you'd prefer this conversation to remain private."

"Yes."

"No problem."

Through the window, Nell saw a Frisbee soaring by. "You mentioned a video," she said.

"Good place to start," said the professor. He sat her in front of a TV, pressed a button.

Night. A car appeared on the screen. It drove into a parking lot, stopped in an empty space. A man got out, stood for a moment under a lamppost. He wore a leather jacket and a baseball cap, hadn't shaved in two or three days. For a moment, he looked right into the camera. Then he took a small black box from his pocket, knelt and stuck it up underneath the engine of the next car over. After that he turned his back, got into his own car and drove away. The screen went blank.

Nell turned to the professor. He was writing in a notebook.

"Coffee?" he said, looking up. "I'm having some." He went to the coffeemaker on the window sill, poured coffee into two mugs with green-wave logos. "Organic Sumatran, plus a hint of chicory."

"Delicious," said Nell.

He sat at his desk, motioned her into the visitor's chair. "Where did you study art history?" he said.

She told him.

"Any special period?"

"Early Baroque, but lately, before the hurricane, I was getting interested in Southern landscape painting."

"Early Baroque was when?"

"Beginning of the seventeenth century."

"Any painters I might have heard of?"

"Caravaggio?"

The professor shook his head. "Don't know much about art, sorry to say." He took a folder from his top drawer, slid it across the desk. "Please open it," he said.

Nell opened the folder. Inside were six photographs, three-by-five, head-and-shoulder shots, all men.

"Which one planted the car bomb?" said Professor Urbana.

Nell laughed, slightly embarrassed, slightly annoyed. She didn't like being manipulated; on the other hand, his attempt to distract her had been so crude and transparent, in retrospect. And what he hadn't factored in was the dual reality of her fine eye for detail and excellent visual memory. This would not be hard.

Nell examined the photos, numbered one through six. She eliminated two and four immediately—a black man and a Hispanic. The car bomber had been white. And also much younger than number one; she pushed him aside. These prominent eyebrows on number six, almost meeting in the middle—she would have remembered a feature like that.

Leaving three and five. Both had weak chins, as the car bomber had, and five also had the same kind of stubbly beard. But stubbly beards could be shaved off, and number five's lips seemed too thin. The car bomber's lips had been puffy, pretty much identical to the lips of the man in photo three. That was the one Nell put her finger on, neatly avoiding the stubbly beard trap.

"Him," she said.

"The answer," said the professor, "is none of the above." He took out a seventh photo: the car bomber. At best, the real car bomber bore a casual resemblance to number three, but no more so than to number five; and an argument could be made that he didn't look at all like either of them. Nell fought the urge to hang her head.

"Don't worry," Professor Urbana said. "No one ever gets it—just proves you're human. The point of all this is we need better police techniques."

"Such as?"

"We'll skip over the obvious—out-and-out prompting by the investigator," the professor said. "First, in photo arrays, the pictures should be shown sequentially, not all at once. Second, in both arrays and live lineups, the witness should be told that the perpetrator or his image might not be there. Third, the distractors, the fillers, should be chosen fairly—to use an extreme example, suppose the witness has already described a light-skinned man, and five of the six in the lineup are dark—not fair." Professor Urbana put the folder away. "But the most important reform would be to impose double-blind procedures."

"Meaning?"

"The officer conducting the lineup would have no knowledge of the identity of the suspect. This would eliminate all possibility of suggestion, blatant, subtle, or even unconscious. I happen to be working on a paper right now on the subject of subtle signals—changes in posture like a leaning forward or a relaxation of the shoulders, changes in tone, sidelong glances, throat clearing, the well-timed sniff." The Frisbee went by again, behind the professor's back. He glanced at his watch. "Class time, I'm afraid. Any questions?"

Nell had many, but not for him.

She headed for the freeway. Her route, west on St. Charles, took her past the house Johnny had grown up in, a beautiful Uptown mansion. Contact with his parents, whom she'd hardly known and had never really warmed to, had ended not long after the funeral, except for a gift when Norah was born, and cards for a few Christmases. Nell had caught Johnny's mother's obituary eight or nine years later. Was it possible his father still lived in the house? Nell slowed down as she passed it. She remembered the house being white with black trim; now it was cream-colored with green. And a fence had been added, one of those tall, spear-tipped wrought-iron fences. A paperboy stood by it. On the other side, an old man in a straw hat—yes, Johnny's father, shrunken and stooped—was making angry gestures at him. Nell kept going.

CHAPTER 14

Pirate unlocked the minibar. "Just lookin'," he said aloud. Nice to be able to say things out loud, do what he felt like, no one to see, no one to tell him no. Lots of cool shit in the minibar—peanuts, Twizzlers, Mars bar, Jujubes, Coke, OJ, beer, wine, whiskey, vodka, gin, Kahlúa. First minibar in his life. *The Lord gave Job twice as much as he had before.* Pirate didn't know where to begin. Was he hungry or thirsty? Both. A lot of both. Lots and lots of both.

He started with the peanuts. Then he polished off the Twizzlers, Mars bar and Jujubes, washing them down with Coke, and when the Coke was gone, OJ. It all went down good, real good. He felt refreshed, like a new man.

Knock knock. Pirate went to the door, had a little trouble with all the locks, bolts, chains; and opened up. Susannah, and behind her a man in one of those pastor collars.

"Hey, Susannah."

"Hi, Alvin. Bet that juice tastes good."

"Juice?"

She glanced at the Tropicana carton in his hand.

"Oh, yeah, real good."

"This is Reverend Proctor of the Chessman Society," Susannah said.

"What's that?" Pirate didn't like pastors, reverends, priests, didn't need them for his religion.

Reverend whatever-his-name-was cleared his throat, spoke in a mellow reverend voice. "We help reintegrate former inmates into the community."

"Yeah?" Reintegrate? Was this guy trying to get him to move to the ghetto? How was that going to work?

"May we come in?" Susannah said.

"Be my guest," Pirate said. That gave him such a kick he said it again.

They sat in the living room of Pirate's suite. A suite, not bad. He'd stayed in a couple Motel 6s back in his bar-band days, but they didn't have suites.

"I'm leaving town soon," Susannah said, "so Reverend Proctor will be your contact."

"Where you going?" Pirate said.

"Back to Chicago."

"That's where you live?"

After a moment of hesitation—maybe Susannah hadn't quite heard him—she said, "Yes." Her skin was particularly lovely today.

"The Windy City," Pirate said. "Never been, myself."

"You'd probably find it too cold," Susannah said.

"Might make a nice change." He smiled at her in a friendly way. Her smile back was a little weak—Susannah didn't seem her normal self today. Pirate understood: she was riding one of those downs that follow a big effort. He knew the feeling from his one audition for a real producer, up in Atlanta; didn't remember the name of the producer, just the down feeling after the audition, even though he'd played great and the producer's assistant said they'd be in touch. "Want to thank you," Pirate said. "For everything you, uh . . ."

"Seeing you free is thanks enough," Susannah said.

"Yeah," Pirate said. "I'm free. Anyone want a drink or something?" He found he still had the Tropicana carton, held it up.

"No tha—" said Susannah.

"That might be—" said the reverend.

Pirate went to the minibar, poured two glasses of juice, handed them out. "How about a toast?" he said.

"Wonderful idea," the reverend said.

He raised his glass. Susannah raised hers. "Yo," said Pirate. He drank his from the carton. Maybe Susannah wasn't thirsty, because although she raised her glass, she didn't actually drink. But the reverend did.

"To your future," he said.

"Yeah," said Pirate. "Twice as . . ." He left the rest unsaid.

"What was that?" asked the reverend.

"Nothin'."

The reverend rubbed his hands together, like he was trying to warm things up. Pirate could see he was the enthusiastic type, like volunteers he'd run across on the inside. "While we're on that topic," the reverend said, "what's your thinking at this point?"

On that topic? Thinking at this point?

"About your future," Susannah said.

Pirate took in a deep breath. It felt good, freedom air. "Take it slow," he said. "Slow and easy."

Susannah and the reverend glanced at each other. "Are there any people from the past we could help you connect with?" the reverend said. "Family? Friends?"

"Nope."

The reverend nodded. "What do you see yourself doing two or three years from now?"

Pirate drew a blank on that one. Had he spotted the Jim Beam label on one of those little whiskey bottles? All at once, he remembered the Jim Beam taste, real fine.

"Should we go over the financial situation again?" Susannah said.

"Sure," said Pirate. Had they been over it before? He put down the OJ carton, got ready to listen.

"As you know," Susannah said, "we're suing the state on your behalf. We're in settlement talks now, but there are no guarantees. Meanwhile, you're being financed by a short-term loan from the Justice Project, to be repaid from the eventual settlement, if successful." She paused. "Any questions?"

"Yeah," said Pirate. "This settlement talking thing—is the Jew—that other lawyer, handling it?"

Susannah blinked. "No," she said. "We have a monetary specialist for these negotiations. She's very good."

That sounded all right to Pirate. A Jew would have been better, of course, as everyone knew. But, hey! No reason this specialist woman couldn't be a Jew. He almost asked.

"Anything else?" Susannah said.

"How much?" said Pirate.

"How much?"

"The settlement."

Susannah sat back in her chair. Maybe she wasn't as beautiful as he'd thought. It was also possible that his eye was tired; that happened, with just the one doing all the work. He closed it for a moment, massaged it with the base of his palm.

"Mr. DuPree?" the reverend said. "Are you okay?"

Pirate stopped massaging his eye, opened it, saw Susannah and the reverend, both blurry now, streaked, like the reception was bad.

"Susannah," said the reverend, "is there any figure at all, however conservative, you might venture?"

"Not really," she said. "We're not quite in uncharted territory here, but it is pretty new."

"Is there possibly a comparable case you could cite, just to give some idea?" the reverend said.

Susannah shot the reverend a quick glance, eyes narrowed. Was she pissed at him or something? This was hard to follow. "There was a case in Oklahoma last year, quite different—less time served, a college degree, some corporate experience."

"So we would expect somewhat less for Mr. DuPree."

"Correct."

"Less than what?" said Pirate.

"The Oklahoma settlement came to a shade under

five hundred thousand dollars," Susannah said. "Before taxes."

"Five hundred grand?" Pirate said; and now, at last, understood the end of Job, where people shower him with things—money, gold earrings, fourteen thousand sheep, all those camels, oxes and she asses. She asses—oh, yes, she anything with five hundred grand. He could do the math: five hundred grand was half a million dollars. Pirate's vision cleared.

"As I mentioned," Susannah said, "we're expecting considerably less, right down to the possibility of nothing at all."

Pirate barely heard that. These Justice people were winners; wasn't that obvious by now? Look at him: free, in the suite.

"All very promising," said the reverend, rubbing his hands again. "But in the meantime, you're going to need some money."

"Yeah?" said Pirate.

"For food, rent, routine living expenses," the reverend said.

"Rent?" Why would he need rent? "I'll just stay here," Pirate said.

Susannah and the reverend shared another one of those private looks. Pirate was getting tired of that. Wasn't five hundred grand worth more respect?

"Mr. DuPree?" said the reverend. "It's my understanding that Susannah's organization won't be able to keep you in the hotel much longer."

So I'll just buy the fuckin' place! Pirate kept that thought to himself. These were nice people, no doubt about it, but would he be spending time with them by choice? No way.

"To defray living expenses," the reverend said, "we've been thinking of a fund-raiser."

"Uh-huh."

"Which also allows the community to give a little something back."

"Back where?"

"Why, to you, Mr. DuPree."

"Okeydoke," said Pirate.

"Any thoughts on the fund-raiser?"

"I said okay."

"Meaning where you'd like to have it, that kind of thing. A picnic, say, or a celebrity basketball game?"

"Celebrities?"

"Local celebrities."

Local celebrities? Picnic? "How about some music?"

"Music?"

"I used to play."

"Oh? What instrument?"

"Guitar."

"Love the guitar," said the reverend. "Were you able to keep it up?"

"Inside?"

The reverend nodded.

"No guitars inside."

"That's a shame," the reverend said, maybe not getting what could be done with guitar strings.

"Yeah," said Pirate. "Red Rooster still around?"

"The club?" said the reverend. "I believe so."

One of his best gigs, backing up a dude who was going to be the next Delbert McClinton. "Let's have it there," Pirate said.

"I'll see what I can do," said the reverend.

He and Susannah rose. Susannah approached Pirate's chair. "I'll be saying good-bye," she said.

Pirate got up; he had manners. Were they going to hug or something? Maybe he'd give her back a friendly pat. Susannah held out her hand. He shook it, such a tiny hand.

"I'll be in touch about the settlement," she said. "Good luck."

"You, too," said Pirate. "And, you know, mucho gracias."

* * *

Pirate felt tired after they left; they'd sapped his energy somehow, even though nothing had happened but blah blah blah. He opened the minibar and looked in: nothing left but the booze—beer, wine, whiskey—yes, Jim Beam—vodka, gin, Kahlúa. And booze was out; he'd given it up, had learned self-control. What exactly was Kahlúa? Some coffee thing? Did it actually count as booze? Pirate was wondering about that when the phone rang. Hey! His first phone call.

He picked it up. "Yeah?"

"Alvin? Lee Ann Bonner here." A little pause. "The reporter."

"With the glasses?"

She laughed; a nice sound—nice, in fact, to hear a woman laugh. He tried to think of some joke, make her do it again.

"Did you get to see the piece?"

Whoa. Piece? What the hell was she talking about?

"The article I wrote—based on our interview."

"Nope."

"It's getting a lot of comment."

"Yeah?"

"All favorable."

"Uh-huh." This was one of those cordless phones, where you could walk around. Pirate walked over to the minibar, took out the Kahlúa bottle, tried to read the label. The writing was tiny; his vision blurred.

"What are you up to?" the reporter said. Pirate put the bottle back, real quick. "I was hoping I could take you out to lunch, if you're free."

Was it lunchtime? He was hungry, no doubt about that. "Yeah," said Pirate. "I'm free."

"Cool car," Pirate said. He'd owned a convertible himself once, till it got repossessed. "Any chance of like putting the top down, Miss, ah?"

"Call me Lee Ann," the reporter said. "Sure it won't be too hot?"

"Nah."

She put the top down, letting out a blast of cold air. Pirate got in.

"Seat belt, please," she said.

He fastened his seat belt.

"How does Mexican sound?" she said, zooming off fast enough to sink him back in his seat.

"Mexican?

"For lunch. There's a real nice place, Café Feliz, just opened up."

"Well . . ."

"Don't like Mexican? How about Italian?"

"Yeah. Italian."

"There's Vito's on the west side."

"Sounds good."

"But on the way, we're going to play a little game."

"What kind of game?" Pirate didn't like car games—license plates from different states, spotting the most cows, all that shit. Did he look like a kid?

The reporter dug around in the compartment between the seats, handed him a strip of cloth.

"What's this?"

"A blindfold," she said. "Put it on."

"Huh?"

"Just trust me."

"Trust you?"

She touched his knee. "Come on, Alvin, you're free now. Relax."

A little touch on the knee, but it had a double effect on him: first, he missed what she said after that; second, he put on the blindfold.

"It's just for a minute or two," she said. "How about some music in the meantime?"

"Okay."

"I hear you like country." Then came George Jones: "Things Have Gone to Pieces." Pirate felt the wind on his face. This was freedom, America, being young on the road.

Only he wasn't young anymore. Pirate tried to figure out the chord progression, could not. He stopped listening, stopped feeling the wind, waited for whatever was coming next.

The car stopped.

"You can take off the blindfold."

Pirate took off the blindfold.

"Notice the changes?" the reporter said.

Pirate looked around. They were parked at the end of a street, facing a path, and maybe a canal or something beyond it. "Changes?" He didn't get it.

"You don't notice something missing?"

Pirate thought for a moment. "No people around, you mean?"

"The pier's gone," the reporter said.

"What pier?" said Pirate, starting to get annoyed. What the hell was she talking about? They climbed out of the car.

"Sure you don't recognize the place?" the reporter said.

"Is this part of the game?" he said. "I don't think we're in Belle Ville anymore. Besides that, I couldn't tell you."

The reporter laughed. "You win," she said.

"How come?"

"Because this is where the old Parish Street Pier stood, where Johnny Blanton got killed. Now I know for absolute one hundred percent sure you didn't do it."

"This was a test?"

"Which you passed with flying colors. Let's go eat."

For a moment, Pirate felt even more annoyed, close to anger. He took a deep breath. *A test, only a test.* "Okey-doke."

They got back in the car. The reporter turned the key. "Any idea who did kill him?" she said.

"Nope."

"Because unless he's dead, the real killer's still out there."

Pirate shrugged.

"Wouldn't it be something to find out who?"

He started thinking about that.

* * *

They sat in a booth at Vito's, the fanciest restaurant Pirate had ever been in. He ordered what she ordered, the menu turning out to have so many Italian words, but not any he knew, like pizza and spaghetti.

"Feel like talking some business?" the reporter said while they waited for the food.

"What kind of business?"

She leaned forward. Not as good-looking as Susannah, none of that glowingness to her skin, maybe not good-looking at all, but there was something about her, like . . . hey! He got it: maybe she was available. Uh-oh. Her lips were moving, but he'd missed whatever she'd said.

"Uh, Lee Ann, right?"

"Right."

"Can you say that again?"

Behind those weird glasses, her eyes were looking at him a little funny; just a little, not enough to mean she wasn't available.

"I'm thinking of writing a book," she said.

"Yeah?"

"About you."

"Me?"

"You, your case, what you've been through, your whole story."

"Yeah?"

She nodded. "What's your reaction?"

"How long?"

"How long a book?"

"Yeah."

"Two or three hundred pages."

"Sounds like a lot of work."

"I can't tell you how much I'm looking forward to it."

"What's the title?"

"Haven't got one yet. Any ideas?"

He said nothing. She was watching him closely.

"I do believe you have a title," she said. "Spit it out."

"*This Is a Test, Only a Test.*"

Lee Ann sat back. "Wow." She opened her mouth to say something more, but at that moment the headwaiter went by, followed by three or four customers. The last one, a big, blond guy in a dark suit, saw Lee Ann.

"Well, well," he said. "The voice of the *Guardian*."

Lee Ann smiled up at the blond man. "The *Guardian* has many voices, Mayor," she said. Her eyes shifted to Pirate, back to the man, her smile spreading. Mayor? Was that his name, or was he maybe—

"Mayor?" she said. "Have you met Mr. DuPree? Alvin DuPree, meet Mr. Kirk Bastien, mayor of Belle Ville."

The mayor stuck out his hand. "Hi, there, Mr.—" His gaze went to the patch. Words stopped coming but the mayor's mouth stayed open and his color went bad, like he was turning into black-and-white. By that time Pirate was shaking his hand, not too hard, not too soft, just right. Pirate's hand was probably bigger, but hard to tell, the way the mayor's hand withdrew so fast.

"Nice meetin' you," Pirate said.

"Beg pardon for my slowness on the uptake," the mayor said, his color coming back. He shot Lee Ann a quick glance, not especially friendly. "Word is you're on a bit of a roll, Mr. DuPree. Enjoy your stay in Belle Ville."

"I'm *from* Belle Ville," Pirate said. "But, hey, thanks." He started to get that strange squinting feeling in his non-eye, but before he got a look beneath the man's skin, the mayor had moved away toward his table.

CHAPTER 15

The *Guardian* landed with a thump in the driveway. Nell, on the phone in her office with an insurance agent who refused to accept that the *Cloud Nine* sculpture was gone for good, heard the sound through the open window.

"From what you're telling me," said the insurance agent, "the thing's indestructible."

"I never said that. I only said it was made of bronze. Some parts, especially at the top, are actually quite delicate, and—"

"We're going to give it more time, ma'am. That's straight from Houston."

Houston, as Nell well knew by now, was headquarters, obdurate and dictatorial. She hung up, went outside and picked up the *Guardian*. The lead story was about bad things in the Middle East. It gave her a weird feeling of relief, a dishonorable feeling that ended up lasting only a few seconds. Page two, below the fold:

WHO KILLED JOHNNY BLANTON?
BY LEE ANN BONNER, *GUARDIAN* REPORTER

The recent exoneration of Alvin Mack DuPree, who spent twenty years in Central State Prison wrongly incarcerated for the murder of Johnny Blanton, leaves the identity of the young scientist's murderer still unknown. When asked if the case is still open, Belle Ville police chief Clay Jarreau replied, "There is no statute of limitations for murder." To a reporter's question regarding the difference between an open case and an active investigation, the chief responded, "The investigation is ongoing." The chief added that there were no current suspects and no leads. Although no public tip-line has been set up, the chief didn't rule it out. "Anyone with information is asked to come forward." Chief Jarreau, while still a detective at the time, was responsible for the original arrest of Mr. DuPree, an arrest at least partially responsible for his promotion to chief of detectives the next year, according to contemporary news accounts.

After dinner that night, Clay went into the family room. He liked watching sports on TV, just about his only indulgence. Clay had been a fine athlete all his life: there was a whole drawerful of photos going back to his early childhood, showing him on diamonds, courts, football fields. Duke Bastien was in many of them. At Belle Ville West High School—neither family had the money for Belle Ville Academy—state champions their senior year, they'd played together in the backfield, one of those Mr. Inside/Mr. Outside combinations, with Duke, bigger, not quite as fast, as Mr. Inside.

Nell walked into the family room, found Clay feet up, a drink in his hand, basketball on the screen.

"Good game?" she said.

"Not if you like defense."

He patted the cushion beside him. She sat down.

"You look tired," she said.

"I'm not."

On the screen a player in red went end to end, dunked with two hands, hung on the rim. Clay made a face.

"Clay?"

"Yeah?"

"I've got a question, maybe a bit strange."

"Oh?" His eyes were still on the screen.

"What happens to old photo arrays?" Nell said.

"Photo arrays?" His eyes shifted toward her, then back to the game. The ref blew his whistle, calling a foul.

"Those photo spreads," Nell said. "For identifying criminals."

"We make them up from our collection—suspects, cons, street people. When we're done they go back in the file."

"Are they numbered?"

"The photos?" He nodded.

"So you could recompose the arrays for a specific case?" Nell said.

"Why would we want to do that?"

"Suppose you had to go over an investigation, start fresh?"

Clay switched off the TV, turned to her.

"What are you saying?" he said.

"I'd like to see the photo array from the DuPree case," Nell said, "the same ones I looked at back then."

The prominent vein in the side of his neck throbbed. "Why?" he said.

"Because something's gone wrong, horribly wrong. Don't we have to start facing that?"

"Nothing went wrong back then," Clay said. "He did it."

"No, Clay. I think I made a mistake. And the other day you admitted you weren't sure anymore."

Liquid slopped over the side of his glass; he laid it on the table. "You didn't make a mistake."

"But I must have."

"This has nothing to do with you," Clay said. "He had a fair trial. The jury decided."

"Would they have made the same decision without me?" Her memories of the time after the murder were so blurry, but the long-ago courtroom moment was suddenly clear, how from the witness chair she'd pointed her finger at Alvin

DuPree, wearing a shirt much too tight for him and a badly knotted tie, and said: "Him."

"You never know what's in the mind of a jury," Clay said. "Maybe you actually made a bad impression on them, almost tipped the scales the other way."

That answer surprised her. "You think?"

"It's possible—that's all I'm saying. The system isn't perfect, isn't even designed to be. That's the difference between guilt beyond a reasonable doubt and guilt beyond a shadow of a doubt."

That made sense, but didn't help her at all. She gazed at him. Those eyes of his, so expressive, at least to her, were now somehow watchful and pained at the same time, a look she'd never seen in them.

"Maybe that's true," she said, "but I'd still like to go over the old photo spread."

He sat back, very quickly, almost as though he'd been slapped. "Impossible. Even if we kept track of the individual spreads, all those pictures are long gone by now."

"What about the original picture of DuPree?"

"I don't understand."

"The one from the array." She remembered Clay's hand, sliding it across a steel desk, even remembered the position of his fingers.

He gave her a long look, another one of those looks with his professional side mixed in. "That might be in his file."

"I'd like to see it."

Clay rose, put on his jacket.

"Not now," she said, rising, too, putting her hand on his sleeve. "I didn't mean now. Don't go."

But he did, shrugging out of her grasp and leaving without another word, closing the front door hard enough to send a low-level tremor through the house. Nell went into the kitchen, found the paper, reread the last sentence of Lee Ann's article: *Chief Jarreau, while still a detective at the time, was responsible for the original arrest of Mr. DuPree, an arrest at least partially responsible for his*

*promotion to chief of detectives the next year, according to
contemporary news accounts.* Now Nell saw that sentence
for what it was, an attack on her husband. And if she had
really blown the identification, really sent the wrong man
to prison, then she'd given Lee Ann the ammunition. Nell
tossed the paper into the trash.

She heard the front door close, softly this time. Looking
out the window, she saw Norah walking across the lawn and
the big wrecker from Yeller's Autobody idling on the street.
Nell went outside, couldn't stop herself.

"Norah?"

Norah was standing by the driver's-side door of the truck.
She turned, too far away for Nell to read her face, but the
way she turned had said enough. Nell took a step or two
closer anyway. The truck's engine cut off and the driver's
door opened. Joe Don got out, came toward the house, Norah
trailing after him.

"Hello, ma'am," he said. He wore a cowboy hat, tight
jeans, in no way resembled the kind of boys Nell had seen on
parents' weekend at Vanderbilt. "I was thinkin' we'd maybe
go on out for pizza," he said.

"I've eaten," Nell said.

Norah made a grim face, but Joe Don laughed, a delighted,
unselfconscious laugh, easy to listen to. "You'd be real welcome to come along," he said.

"That's okay," Nell said. "You two have fun." She shot
Norah a quick glance, meaning *not too much fun, not too
late, be careful* and other motherly messages. But couldn't
this—going out for pizza, hanging out with someone her
own age—be a good thing? Norah gazed back blankly and
climbed in the wrecker.

The phone rang as she went back in the house. Nell answered.

"Is Norah there?" said a woman; she sounded young.

"She just left."

"Oh," said the woman. "Um. I was just calling to say hi."

"I'll pass that along. Who should I . . . ?"

"Is this her mom?"

"Yes."

"Hi."

"Hi."

"My name's Ines. I live down the hall—at school. Vanderbilt? Down the hall from Norah."

"I'll tell her you called, Ines."

"Thanks," Ines said. Pause. "Mrs. Jarreau?"

"Yes?"

"How's she doing?"

"All right," Nell said; she found herself squeezing the phone. "I think."

"Yeah?" said Ines. "I was a little . . ." Her voice trailed off.

"A little what?"

"Nothing." Another pause, this one longer. "Just glad to hear she's doing bet—doing okay."

"Does she have your number?" Nell said.

"Should," said Ines. "But here it is, just in case." Nell wrote it down.

Nell was loading the dishwasher when Clay came home. He sat at a stool by the small butcher-block island in the center of the kitchen, laid down an envelope.

"You wanted to see this?" he said.

"Yes, but I didn't mean for you to—"

"Here it is." Clay opened the envelope.

Nell moved closer to the island, stood on the other side. All at once she realized they were replaying that scene from twenty years before, some things changed—a custom-made butcher block instead of a steel table—and some things not, such as Clay's strong, fine hands and the fear and uncertainty in her mind.

Clay slid the photo out of the envelope. It had a faded

number on the back: D964. Clay turned it over. Alvin Mack DuPree, but the only reason Nell knew that was because of the resemblance to the face in the still from Nappy Ferris's surveillance camera. She could see nothing of the present-day Alvin Mack DuPree in these features, unlined and un-marked. He gazed unsmiling at the camera, the light harsh, but the man himself not bad-looking, if not in Joe Don's league. She realized he would have been about Joe Don's age. The thought unsettled her some more, and so did the fact that she had no memory at all of this photograph.

The tip of Clay's index finger rose. Then he tapped the photo, a half inch or so above DuPree's head, lightly and just once. "Well?" he said.

She stared at the picture, tried to somehow Photoshop it in her mind, sliding it over her memory of the face of the killer on the pier, blending them together. They wouldn't blend. "I don't remember this picture at all," Nell said.

"Why would you?"

His tone—so impatient, so unlike him—made her glance up. She caught the expression on his face, professional, even cold for a moment, almost like another person, a look-alike ignorant of the character he was supposed to play.

"Because it's so important," Nell said. "I must have examined it carefully."

"You did."

"You remember that?"

"Of course," Clay said. His face softened. "I also remember telling you—this was at your parents' place—that you couldn't blame yourself for anything, then or ever."

And then Bobby Rice had said: *You survived. Survive something like that, you're a hero, plain and simple.* She had no trouble remembering that, or how she'd gone on and on about Johnny's swimming and everything about him, and the solemn way the two detectives had listened to every word.

Nell's eyes returned to the picture, as if drawn by an invisible force. She just couldn't blend those faces.

"Why are you shaking your head like that?" Clay said.

Nell looked up, unaware that she'd shaken her head. She met Clay's gaze. "I got it wrong," she said.

"I don't think so," Clay said. "But we'll never know."

"We know," Nell said. "I can't tell you how I feel, getting it wrong for you, but we have to face it."

Clay grabbed the photograph, ripped it into tiny bits, tossed them away.

It shocked her, like an act of violence. "Clay! What are you doing? That's evidence."

He rose, the pulse pounding in his neck. "There's nothing to face. It's over." He strode out of the room.

Nell bent down, gathered all the pieces of the DuPree photo. She placed them on the butcher block, tried for a moment or two to fit them back together. Then she dropped them in the trash.

Clay was already asleep when Nell went to bed; she could tell from the sound of his breathing. She knew his breathing, his gait, his facial expressions, the songs he sang in the shower, how he brushed his teeth too hard—everything about him.

She lay down, not touching him, but feeling the presence of his body. Nell had slept with three men in her life: the first, her boyfriend junior year in college; Johnny; and Clay. Sex with the college boyfriend she hardly remembered: clumsy and unsatisfying, as though they'd been sent the wrong manual; sex with Johnny had been better—even much better—but sex with Clay had obliterated it, wiping out actual memories of Johnny in bed, leaving only summary impressions. The obliterating had not merely begun but had happened in total that very first time—about two months after the surf-casting date—when he'd taken her out on a little powerboat of Duke's; rocking at anchor under a hot sun, the rhythm of the sea beneath them.

At that moment, in bed with Clay, she remembered something Johnny had told her, explaining the forces that ran the universe. There were four, but the one that stuck in her mind was the strong force, the attraction that kept the nucleus of the atom together. She and Clay were subject to a strong force, too, a strong force with the power to see them through anything.

Nell reached across the small space between them, touched his thigh. He shifted away.

A first.

She lay still, first not believing, then believing, then wide-awake. After a while, she heard the wrecker drive up outside, heard the front door open, and then Norah on the stairs; didn't hear anything bad, like soft crying or a stumbling footstep.

Nell closed her eyes. Right away, she had a mental image of Clay's index finger, rising up and tapping down, a half inch above DuPree's pictured head. Was it a memory or something else, rising from unknown and self-destructive depths? In this image, the photo lay not on the butcher block in her kitchen, but on a steel table.

She sat up, went into the bathroom, splashed cold water on her face. The Bernardine smell was in the air. Nell closed all the windows and switched on the AC.

CHAPTER 16

P irate awoke. For a moment, he didn't know where he was. Then he saw the foil-wrapped mint lying on the pillow beside him. He took off the foil and ate the mint, right there in bed, as free as it gets, in his suite at the Ambassador. A real good feeling, till he thought of his age.

Knock on the door.

Pirate rose, put on jeans and a T-shirt, both brand-new, and opened the door, remembering too late he wasn't wearing the patch; he didn't want his reporter-buddy slash other-possibilities to see him like this. But not Lee Ann, not a female of any kind: this was a big-bellied guy in a suit, and everything about him said *cop*.

"Got a moment?" the cop said. His gaze flicked over to Pirate's non-eye. Pirate remembered the tiny weapon, in the bathroom toothbrush holder. Then he had an amazing thought: the non-eye was a weapon all by itself.

Pirate smiled and said, "Nope."

The cop smiled back. Kind of: the corners of his mouth turned up; his pale eyes stayed the same. "Might be worth your while," he said.

"Nothin' with cops ever been worth my while."

The cop nodded. "That's my point."

"You made it," Pirate said. "Adios."

The cop kept smiling, like something funny was going on. "Always this hasty?" he said.

Pirate thought about that. Long ago he'd been plenty hasty, oh yeah. Now was different—he'd learned to slow things down, way down. That was a big part of being at peace. "Say what you got to say," he told the cop.

"From out here?"

"Yeah."

The cop glanced around. A maid was coming down the hall with a stack of fluffy towels, towels Pirate loved.

"Thanks for the mint," he said as she went by.

"The? . . . oh, yes, you're welcome sir. Enjoy."

The cop watched till she went around a corner. Pirate, with his hearing, could still pick up something jingling in her pocket. The cop lowered his voice. "You were away for a while."

"That's what you come to tell me?"

"Yeah," said the cop. "What you're maybe missing is developments out here. On this side of the wall, so to speak."

"Like?" said Pirate.

"Want an example?" said the cop. He leaned a little closer. His breath was foul, as bad as any inmate breath Pirate had smelled in twenty years. "Remember the detective who put you away?"

Pirate nodded.

"Now he's chief of police."

Pirate had already figured that out, down in the holding pen under the courthouse. "Tell me something I don't know."

Now the smile on the cop's face had nothing to do with fun, was just so many face muscles at work. Pirate started getting the squinting feeling in his non-eye, came close to actually seeing those face muscles strain under his skin. "How about the eyewitness who pointed you out?" the cop said. "Killer bod—remember her?"

"What if I do?"

"Do or don't, maybe you want to chew on the fact that she married the detective not long after they put you away. Got a regular little model family for theirselves."

"So?" Pirate said; but something slipped inside.

"Should be obvious," the cop said. "How about I leave you with two words? Frame job." The cop turned, started walking away, looked back over his shoulder. "Or maybe it's just the one, with a whatchamacallit in between."

Pirate unlocked the minibar. Everything was back in place: peanuts, Twizzlers, Mars bar, Jujubes, Coke, OJ, plus the original supply of booze—beer, wine, whiskey, vodka, gin, Kahlúa. Every day he ate the snacks, drank the Coke and OJ, and every next day the minibar was full up again. How good was that? Even better than getting twice what he had before.

At peace; at peace in the Ambassador Suites Hotel, except for this one disturbing visit: *frame job.* Pirate reached into the minibar, fished out the Kahlúa. He tried to read the label. Was it booze or not? He thought he made out the word *alcohol,* but was that enough to make it booze? He needed one of his lawyers to figure this out; the Jew would be best. Pirate unscrewed the cap, took a sniff. Booze? He didn't think so; more like a liquid dessert. Pirate tipped the little bottle to his lips and drank it down.

A pleasant coffee taste, sweet and syrupy, and as a bonus it had no effect at all, no high, nothing that would knock him off the rails. Pirate went to his desk, found Lee Ann's card, gave her a call.

"Hey," she said, "I was just going to phone you."

"Yeah? What about?"

"Thought maybe we'd go for a little outing. There's a wake you might be interested in."

"Whose?"

"Nappy Ferris's. How does that sound?"

How did that sound? Wakes were peaceful, right? That was the whole point—seeing one more guy off to his last reward. But even more important: he owed Nappy. "Big-time."

"What was that?"

"Sounds okay," Pirate said.

He brushed his teeth, shaved and showered, put on the patch. The tiny weapon? Did he need it? No. He wrapped it in toilet paper and stuck it under the mattress.

"Beignet?" said Lee Ann.

Pirate ate the sugar-dusted beignet, licked the sweetness off his lips. "What's the name of that little line?"

"What little line?" Lee Ann said, pulling out of her parking space without looking.

"Between two words sometimes." Someone honked nearby. Pirate had been in a noncar world for a long time, long enough to have made him slow to see the obvious: Lee Ann was a bad driver. He buckled his seat belt tight.

"Like in All-American?" she said.

"Yeah."

"Hyphen. Why?"

"Catching up on my education," Pirate said.

Lee Ann laughed. "I spoke to an editor in New York. She really likes the idea."

"*Only a Test*?"

She stopped laughing, gave him a look he'd never seen from anyone before, so serious. "And the title—she positively loves it."

"Uh-huh."

"You're probably wondering what happens next."

Pirate wasn't, not at all.

"First thing," she said, "I write an outline and a couple chapters."

Pirate noticed they were on Princess Street, wondered whether the Pink Passion Club was still there.

"And somewhere along the way you and I are going to get something on paper."

On paper? What was she talking about? Now he was supposed to write books? "You want me to write the fuckin' thing?"

She glanced at him and laughed. Pirate joined in for a few moments. Then he decided he didn't like the sound of them laughing together, especially if he himself was on the receiving end, and clamped his mouth shut. Outside, the Pink Passion Club went by. A sign on the door read: grand reopening tonight!!! A good sign, right? Hey! Double meaning! Pirate started laughing again. Lee Ann was still sort of chuckling from before.

"You've got a good sense of humor," she said. "Anyone ever tell you that?"

Sure. All the COs, the Ocho Cincos, Esteban Malvi, all the rats in all the rat cages. This time Pirate just let the laughter die away.

Red light. Lee Ann stopped. A Belle Ville cruiser pulled up beside them. "You don't have to write a thing," she said, "except for—"

Pirate, taking a sidelong look at the cruiser, missed whatever that was all about. A uniformed cop was at the wheel; he glanced over—a real young kid—showed no reaction, drove off the moment the light turned green.

"So how does that grab you?" Lee Ann said.

Grab him? "Um, I didn't . . ."

"And of course you should have a lawyer check it over—in fact, I insist."

"Lawyer?" Wasn't he all done with lawyers?

"Maybe the Justice Project people can suggest someone."

"For what?"

Behind those strange glasses, her eyes shifted toward him, smart eyes he didn't like the look of all of a sudden. "To vet the contract—what I've just been telling you about."

The way he'd pried up Esteban Malvi's eyelid and gently rubbed his eyeball? Now the thought of doing the same thing to Lee Ann appeared in the back of his mind, or maybe it had been lurking there the whole time.

"Sorry," he said. "A little slow today."

She laughed, patted his knee. "It's routine with book proposals like this. We need a contract that gives me permission from you for exclusive rights to your story. In return you get a percentage of the royalties."

Royalties? That sounded good. So did *settlement*. When Pirate was a kid, he'd wanted a Mustang, one of those cool old ones, a rag-top pony. And now: why not? His knee tingled.

"How much?" he said.

"The royalties?" said Lee Ann. "Depends on how well the book does. But first there'll be an advance to split—if they go for the proposal, that is."

"And I get a percentage?"

"Exactly."

"Like what?"

"I was thinking of ten."

"Twenty."

"Split the difference? Fifteen?"

"Sixteen."

"Deal."

They were both laughing again. Freedom, money, rag-top ponies: pretty good. Then, from out of nowhere, came the worry that a one-eyed man might not qualify for a driver's license. In Pirate's mind, the rag-top pony went up in flames.

Those eyes, real smart, were on him again. "You all right?" she said.

He nodded. "Light's turning red."

Lee Ann hit the brakes.

A string of Mardi Gras beads hung over a sign reading: DE SOTO CAMPGROUND—all visitors report to office. Lee Ann turned into the entrance, fishtailing on the dirt track; Pirate felt weightless for a moment, like an astronaut, and didn't like it.

"Whee," said Lee Ann.

Pirate got a coffee-and-syrup buzz in his head, wanted to give her a smack, not hard. Instead he took a deep breath and tried to settle back into his peaceful groove. His fingers moved the way they did when feeling the gold tassel.

Lee Ann drove past the office, a few cabins and trailers, and parked beside other cars. Through some trees, Pirate saw a pond and picnic tables with twenty or thirty people standing around, all black. Was this a good idea? Pirate looked at Lee Ann. She was sticking two twenty-dollar bills and her card into an envelope. On the front she wrote *In Memory of Napoleon Ferris.*

"All set?" she said. "You can pay me back your sixteen percent later."

Sixteen percent? Of the forty? Is that what she meant? Was it a joke? Pirate didn't know. They got out of the car, walked through trees, lots with snapped-off trunks. Pirate felt Lee Ann's presence beside him, real small. He realized they were partners. He'd never had a partner before, had never even thought about having one. Pirate tried to calculate sixteen percent of forty but didn't know how.

All the black people heard them coming—or maybe sensed it—and turned at the same time. Lee Ann went right up to the nearest table and laid her envelope in a basket with some others. An old man sitting at the table nodded and said, "Bless." Everyone else went back to what they'd been doing—cooking on a charcoal grill, eating, drinking. Beyond them lay a pond with scummy water; a skinny kid was skimming rocks across it. He was a real good rock skipper—one or two skipped clear across to the other side. Or maybe not: Pirate's eye was tiring and things were starting to blur.

A woman came toward them, dressed in black. She was thin, like the rock-skipping kid, with white hair and an unlined face.

"Thank you folks for coming," she said. "I'm Napoleon's momma, Dinah Ferris."

"Condolences, ma'am," said Lee Ann. "I'm Lee Ann Bonner of the *Guardian.* I was with—"

"I know who you are," said Dinah Ferris.

"Very sorry," said Lee Ann. "Sorry for your loss."

"Thank you," said Dinah Ferris.

"And this is Alvin DuPree," Lee Ann said.

Dinah Ferris turned to him. She had small dark eyes, somehow hard and sad at the same time.

Pirate thought of sticking out his hand; but maybe not. "Big-time," he said. "I owe him big-time."

Dinah Ferris nodded. "We have refreshments."

"You're very kind," Lee Ann said. "I have one quick question."

Dinah watched her, showed no reaction.

"Did your son ever discuss the tape with you?"

"No."

"Do you know if he followed up in any way after he sent that tape in?"

Dinah shook her head.

"You don't know or he didn't follow up?"

"We never discussed nothin' about the tape," Dinah said. "No sense talkin' 'bout it now—Napoleon was in the wrong place at the wrong time, is all."

"Do you mean back then or—"

Dinah frowned; lines appeared all over her smooth face. "The wrong place at the wrong time. The sheriff told me himself."

"Solomon Lanier?"

"That's right. The sheriff."

Pirate caught the pride in her tone when she said that. He was ready to grab some of the refreshments and go. But not Lee Ann.

"The sheriff has a good reputation," she said.

Dinah nodded.

"So I was just wondering whether he asked why Nappy— why Napoleon—had been laying low the past while."

"Laying low?" said Dinah.

"They were looking for him—Houston, Atlanta, everywhere. To verify the tape."

"There was a hurricane," Dinah said, her voice soft.

"Right—the refugees," Lee Ann said. "But what about after—when the tape turned up?"

"Don't know about the tape," Dinah said. "And no laying

low, neither. Napoleon was livin' right here, on the camp-ground, ever since the storm come. Campground belongs to my cousin."

"So why did he leave, go up to Stonewall County?"

"Wrong place, wrong time," said Dinah.

Lee Ann nodded. Her eyes shifted, like she had some thought, but all she said was, "Thank you, ma'am. Thank you for your time."

"Refreshments," Dinah said. She waved them toward the grill.

Pirate backed away. Smoke curled across the campground, bringing smells of chicken and shrimp. He was ready to eat.

Lee Ann handed Dinah her card. "If you ever need me for anything," she said.

Dinah took the card, face showing nothing.

"One last thing," Lee Ann said. Dinah closed her eyes slowly, slowly opened them back up. Now the lines on her face were deep. Lee Ann was tough, or was that just part of being a reporter, putting lines on people's faces? "How well did Napoleon know Bobby Rice?" she said.

"Not too well. He knew the other one better."

"The other one?"

"The other detective."

"Clay Jarreau?"

"Him."

CHAPTER 17

And what about the live lineup, the one that came a day or two after the photo spread: Was it possible there'd been no blue-eyed men standing behind the one-way glass, other than Alvin DuPree? Nell sat up in the night, her pulse racing. Clay was sleeping on his side, facing the other way. Moonlight came through the window, shone on his profile. For a moment, Nell saw how he would look as an old man.

She got up, walked out on the balcony. The moon hung high in the sky, only a half-moon but very bright. Her mind formed some connection between the half-moon and Clay's profile, wanted her to take it further, but she couldn't.

Something was floating in the pool. Nell put on her robe, went outside, found the skimmer and skimmed in what turned out to be a page from the *Guardian,* the print all blurred. Water ran down the pole of the skimmer and dripped on her arm. It felt warm. She took off her robe, slipped into the pool, started swimming, not fast, but on and on. The moon sank, lower and lower, was hidden behind the treetops by the time Nell climbed out, water dripping off her body the only sound. She wrapped herself in her robe and lay on one of the chaises. Now, with the moon so low, the stars seemed brighter. So many, yet all those she saw were in just the one galaxy, the Milky Way—Johnny had taught her that. And how many galaxies were there?

Not just billions and billions, Nellie, but billions times billions. You see what this means?

That we're next to nothing?

No, no—the opposite. The fact that we're figuring it all out makes us important, gives us meaning.

And what's the meaning—they'd been in bed at the time and she'd reached down under the covers—*of this?*

Must be the strong force, Johnny had said.

And she'd said: *We'll see about that.*

Nell opened her eyes. The stars were gone and pale light was showing in the east. A breeze blew, hard enough to ripple the water in the pool. Nell shivered, got up, went inside. She had coffee brewing and was making toast when Clay walked into the kitchen, knotting his tie.

"You're up early," he said.

"Lots to do," Nell said, taking a quick glance at him; did he really not know she'd left their bed in the middle of the night? She poured a cup of coffee, set it before him on the butcher block.

"Like what?" he said; he raised the cup and made a little motion with it, thanking her.

"At work," Nell said. "We're going to put all the Civil War material in the atrium. Toast?"

"Please."

She served him toast, with butter and peach jam, his favorite. Nell could smell his shampoo and aftershave, and beneath them his own smell, fresh and healthy, a smell she loved.

"Aren't you having any?" he said.

"Maybe later," said Nell. "Clay?"

"Yeah?"

"I've had this idea, kind of strange."

"Oh?" He buttered his toast, not looking up.

"It's about Darryll Pines."

"Go on."

"Have you ever noticed his eyes?"

Now Clay looked up, his own eyes wary. "What about them?"

"They're blue. Very light blue."

"So?"

"The killer had eyes like that, very light blue—that's one thing I'm sure of."

Clay put down the butter knife. "You're saying Darryll did it?"

"I'm just asking."

"Asking what?"

"Where he was that night, for starters."

Clay pushed his plate away. "Did Darryll know Johnny?" he said.

"Not to my knowledge."

"Did he know you?"

"No."

"Ever heard of Darryll getting involved in a robbery, or any crime at all?"

"No."

"So he just up and murdered a man, a complete stranger, for no reason."

Nell said nothing.

"Making him a psycho," Clay said. "You think Darryll's a psycho?"

"I know there's tension between the two of you—it even came out at—"

Clay banged his fist on the butcher block, hard and sudden. She jumped, maybe even let out a little cry: she'd never seen him do anything like that before. The butter knife spun through the air and clinked across the tiles. "There is no tension," he said, his voice rising. He pointed his finger at her—another first. "This has got to stop. You're going to do damage."

Nell was stunned, almost frozen in place, her eyes on his pointing finger. It was partly the aggressiveness of the gesture, so alien to him, and partly the reminder of the little finger tap over the pictured head of Alvin DuPree. Not the recent finger tap, here in their own kitchen, but twenty years before down at One Marigot: Had that really happened, or was it some kind of false or invented memory? Clay followed her gaze, lowered his hand, a pained expression crossing his face.

"Please, Nell, enough," he said, his voice now soft. "If there was a mistake, I feel bad about it . . ." He paused for a moment, as though his throat had thickened inside, choking off whatever was coming next. ". . . but there's no reason you should."

"But I do."

"We've been through this. The system isn't perfect. People aren't perfect. But everybody"—he paused again, took a deep breath—"did their best."

"I didn't," Nell said.

"Stop."

But she couldn't. Tears came, and she couldn't stop them either. Twenty years: there was no fixing something like that, no making it go away, not even a silver lining, so what would ever make this stop, her guilt, her doubt? Clay came around the butcher block, held her, patted her back. She calmed down.

"I want you to do something for me," she said, her face against his shoulder, "even if you think it's crazy."

"What's that?"

"Look into the old records. See if Darryll was working that night."

Clay's hands tightened on her back. "Those records are all gone—Bernardine," he said. "But I don't need them. He was working."

"How do you know?"

"Darryll was on the desk that night," Clay said, "took the first call. Easy to remember."

That should have wiped the Darryll idea from her mind; why didn't it? Nell had another thought. "Are the lineup records gone, too?"

"Lineup records?"

"The names of the men I saw," Nell said. "Pictures of their faces." He was silent. She felt him go still inside. "Did Bernardine get them, too?" she said.

"Nothing to get," Clay said. "We don't keep records of who the fillers were. There's only one real suspect in a lineup—I thought you knew that."

She knew it now, from her conversation with Professor Urbana. Nell might have told him about Professor Urbana right then, but something about that stillness deep inside him stopped her. "I just have this worry," she said.

"What worry?"

"That maybe, somehow . . ."

"Go on."

"That DuPree was the only blue-eyed man in the lineup."

Clay let her go, fast, reflexively, almost as though he'd been hit with an electric shock. He stared down at her. "Go on," he said again.

"Go on?"

"You're driving at something."

"I'm not. I'm not driving at anything."

"Then who is?"

"I don't understand."

"Has someone—Lee Ann, maybe—been putting ide—been influencing you?"

"Putting ideas in my head? Is that the way you see me?"

"I didn't say putting ideas in your head. I said—"

"You did. Don't lie to me."

"What did you just say? You think I lie to you?"

"You just did. You—"

Norah walked in, her face still rumpled from sleep. The room went silent. Nell realized she and Clay had been out of control, totally.

"What's going on?" Norah said. "What's wrong?"

"Nothing," Nell said.

"Nothing? You're screaming at each other. What happened?"

"Your mom and I were having a slight disagreement," Clay said. "Nothing to worry about."

Norah looked from one to the other. Nell could read her mind: *But you never fight like this.* "A slight disagreement about what?" Norah said.

"Nothing," Nell said again. "Nothing important. Nothing to worry about."

"About me?" Norah said. "It's about me, isn't it?"

"No," Clay said. "It's got nothing to do with you." He walked up to Norah, moved to kiss her on the forehead. She backed away. His face tightened. "Everything's all right," he said. He checked his watch. "Got to run." Clay walked over to Nell, kissed her forehead, barely touching. "See you tonight."

"It really wasn't about me?" Norah said.

"No," said Nell.

"Then what?"

"How about some breakfast?"

"What's it about? What's the problem?"

Nell poured coffee for Norah. Her hand wasn't quite steady; some coffee splashed into the saucer. She took it to the sink, fetched another from the cupboard.

"Something to eat?"

"I want to know, Mom."

"It's just this case, honey, the tape and everything. It's all very . . ." Nell felt tears coming again, forced them back down; this, the loss of control, was unbearable to her, had to end. ". . . stressful, that's all."

"You and Dad disagree about it?"

Was Norah back to calling him Dad, as she had all her life, or was it just a slip? Had pizza with Joe Don improved her mood? The darkness in Nell's mind started to recede. "Not really," she said.

"Then what?"

"Everything's going to be all right. Don't worry."

Norah sat down, sipped her coffee. Nell made an omelet, split it with Norah. Nell took one bite before her stomach closed up, but the sight of Norah eating lightened her mood a little more.

"Ines called yesterday," Nell said.

"Yeah?"

"To see how you're doing."

Norah chewed slowly on her omelet.

"She wants you to call."

"Uh-huh."

Nell sipped her coffee. It tasted bitter. "Coffee all right?" she said.

"Yeah," Norah said.

"I don't think you ever mentioned Ines."

"No?"

"What's she like?"

"Nice."

"I gather she lives in your old . . . your dorm?"

"Uh-huh."

"Where's she from?"

Norah, gazing down at the remains of her omelet, said, "That's enough questions." Those words—their unexpectedness, the quiet delivery—gave Nell a sudden chill.

"What . . . what did you say?"

Norah looked up, anger in her eyes; her mood had changed completely. "You heard me."

"Norah! What's going on with you? What's wrong?"

Norah laughed, a derisive laugh that scared Nell. Then she rose and ran from the room, slamming the door behind her. Nell heard a muffled smash from the cupboard where she kept the good china.

Ten minutes later—Nell in her bathroom, putting on her pearl earrings, almost ready for work—the wrecker drove up Sandhill Way. Through the window, Nell saw Norah hurrying toward it across the lawn. She raised the window.

"Norah, where are you going?"

Norah turned. "Out."

"But where?"

"I'm nineteen years old."

"I know, but—"

Joe Don stuck his head out the window of the cab. "Just goin' out for a little breakfast, ma'am," he said.

But she just ate. Nell somehow kept that reply, so idiotic, inside. She gave them a little wave. Joe Don waved back.

Nell left the museum at five, picked up three small New York strip steaks—Clay's favorite cut—on sale. Driving up Sandhill Way, she checked the rearview mirror, saw Duke's Porsche coming up fast. She parked in the driveway. Duke pulled in behind her, jumped out of his car, a bottle of champagne in hand.

"Hi, darlin'," he said. "Clay home yet?"

"Any minute now," Nell said.

"Mind if I wait?"

"'Course not—come on in."

They went into the house. Duke set the bottle on the counter. He was practically jumping up and down.

"Something up?" Nell said.

"What makes you say that?" He laughed. "Can you keep a secret—just till the news hits?"

"What news?"

"We're going to come out clean. Absolutely spotless."

"Come out of what?" said Nell. "Who?"

Duke laughed again. "The company. DK Industries. The Corps of Engineers' report's out tomorrow and we're cleared, one hundred percent."

Had Lee Ann said something about this? Nell couldn't remember. "Cleared of what?"

"Cleared of what? My God—hasn't Clay discussed this with you?"

"Discussed what?"

"We could have been ruined," Duke said. "Lost everything."

"Why?"

"Why? Because we built the ship canal—the beginning of everything, our first big project."

"Where the flooding started?"

For a moment, Duke didn't look so cheery. "*One* of the places the flooding started," he said. "But I don't deny if we had known certain things, the dikes would have been higher and the Canal Street gates stronger. The opposite—I guarantee it."

"What things?"

"Technical things." He waved them aside. "All kinds of geologic data we didn't have and—this is the whole point—couldn't have been expected to have had by any regulating agency. Not back then, twenty years ago. We built, quote, according to acceptable, customary and legal standards of the time, end quote. Meaning it was an act of God, end of story."

"That . . . that's great, Duke."

"Thanks, Nell. Can't tell you how good it feels. Calls for a celebration—one of the reasons I'm here, in fact. I was hoping we could fly over to Little Parrot tomorrow for a day or two, just the four of us, take a quick break."

"That's very nice, Duke, but I don't—"

She heard the front door open. Clay walked in, holding a big bouquet of roses.

Duke shook his head. "You two lovebirds," he said.

Nell felt herself turning red; Clay's face was reddening, too.

CHAPTER **18**

N ell wasn't a gambler, had never made any kind of bet in her life, but she would have put almost anything on Clay turning down the trip to Little Parrot Cay.

"Sounds good," he told Duke.

Duke popped the cork. They finished off the bottle in a minute or two, all of them drinking fast, as though they'd been living through a drought.

"See you at the strip," Duke said on his way out. "Seven sharp."

"What about Norah?" Nell said when he'd gone.

"It's only a day or two," said Clay. "She'll be fine."

"I don't like leaving her."

"Then we'll bring her along."

Norah was in the family room, talking on the phone. "Oh, I'd never do something like that," she said, then saw Nell. "Call you back." She hung up.

Never do something like what? Who was on the phone? Nell swallowed both questions. "We're going to Little Parrot for a day or two."

"Have fun."

"We were hoping you'd like to come."

"No thanks."

"But you loved it there—remember when we went, that

Easter?" Nell could picture Norah, bursting through the surface of the water, a conch held high.

"It was all right."

"You could . . . bring a friend, if you want."

"I'll just hang out here."

"I don't know, Norah. It just seems to me—"

"Mom. I'm nineteen."

"I know, but—"

"Say it—you don't trust me."

"It's not that. But you've been through a bit of a rough time and—"

"Take the keys."

"The keys?"

"To the Miata. To all the cars. I'll be safe and sound, watering the plants."

At that moment, Nell came close to canceling the trip, or trying to persuade Clay to go without her. Norah was watching her; Nell could almost feel her daughter reading her mind.

"Do I live here or not?" Norah said.

"Okay," Nell said. "But don't screen my calls out."

Norah said nothing.

"I mean it."

Norah nodded, just barely.

"Say you won't screen me out."

"I won't screen you out."

"Promise?"

"Promise."

Clay sat in the cockpit with Duke; Nell and Vicki in back. Vicki's perfume smelled of orange blossoms, orchards and orchards of them.

"I'm so excited," Vicki said.

Nell smiled at her. Vicki was wearing a tiny dress, high heels, lots of makeup.

Vicki lowered her voice, said something that was drowned

out by engine noise. Nell leaned forward, put her hand to her ear.

"This is my first time," Vicki said.

First time? In a plane? In a small plane? Nell waited for more.

"Going to this Parrot place. How come everybody says key when it's spelled cay?"

"I'm not sure."

"Are there parrots?"

"I've never seen one."

Vicki shrugged, her breasts almost spilling free. "Don't like birds anyway," she said. "I'm so excited. He's never taken me there before. And look." She held out her hand, displaying a small emerald ring.

"Beautiful," Nell said.

"He gave it to me last night. He's in such a good mood—this engineering report or whatever put him over the moon. You hear about it?"

"Yes."

Vicki opened her tiny purse, took out some mints, offered one to Nell. "It's such a great story," she said. "So, you know, American."

"The report?"

"Nah. Duke and Kirk, the whole ball of wax. Two brothers starting from zilch, mortgaged up to their eyeballs for that first big deal. And now all this." She waved her hand. Outside the round window lay nothing but empty blue.

Vicki sat quietly for a few moments, sucking on her mint, looking thoughtful. Nell closed her eyes, started worrying about Norah right away. After a while, Vicki spoke, Nell missing whatever she'd said. She opened her eyes.

"Sorry?"

"I was just wondering if you were around. Like back then, when they started. DK Industries."

"I was still in grad school."

"The art thing?"

"Yes."

"Art is cool," Vicki said.

"You should come to the museum when we reopen."

"Count on it," Vicki said.

Nell gazed out the window. Far below, the ocean looked like solid blue steel, a false image—at least for her—hard and uninviting.

"They worked so hard," Vicki said, offering more mints. "He'd make a great governor."

"Who?"

"Kirk. Mayors sometimes go on to be governors."

"Kirk wants to be governor?"

Vicki glanced at the cockpit. "Maybe it's supposed to be a secret."

"Safe with me."

Vicki thought that was very funny, exploded with laughter. Up front, both men turned to look. Vicki gave them a little wave, pinkie raised high. "I'm so excited," she said. Both men tapped their earphones, meaning they couldn't hear. Vicki said it louder.

Bahamian air: Nell's favorite smell on earth. She lay under a palm tree on the beach at Little Parrot Cay, tiny waves sliding up the sand and sliding back down with a sound like a sigh; out on the reef bigger waves made sounds more like shushing. Duke and Vicki had disappeared into the master bedroom a minute or two after arrival; Clay was in the kayak, on an exercise paddle to the nearest cay, Big Parrot, and back, about three miles; Nell was alone, almost at peace. An electric-blue dragonfly darted by. An idea came, out of nowhere but somehow obvious at the same time: Why not meet with Alvin DuPree?

She began to plan her part in a conversation with Alvin DuPree. A plane appeared in the sky: the daily flight from Nassau to North Eleuthera. It droned slowly by, disappeared from her field of vision. How to begin? With an apology? What words could ever—

Something scraped on the sand. Nell sat up, fastening the top of her bathing suit, saw the kayak on the beach, Clay climbing out. He pulled the kayak across seaweed marking the high-tide line and came over, a drop of sweat rolling down his chest.

"How was it?" she said.

"Great." He gazed down at her. "You look nice."

"You, too."

He sat down beside her. "Anything going on in the house?"

"Probably."

Clay laughed. Then he grew quiet. He put his hand on her leg; her mouth went dry, as though whatever was going on in the house had spread. A look of desire that had passed between them many times was exchanged once more.

"Not here," Nell said.

But here turned out to be good, much better than good. Something exotic and tropical was going on, and the knowledge that it was going on up in the house at the same time heightened everything, as though at an orgy; and this was the closest someone like Nell would ever come to attending one. How long it lasted, up and up, she didn't know, but somewhere in there she caught a strange expression in his eyes, one she'd never seen before. It only rammed her up even higher, lust feeding on mixed-up emotions good and bad, love and doubt. Was she becoming perverse? She cried out, very loud, and didn't care. Somewhere down the beach a bird answered.

"Oh my God," said Clay, sliding out from under her. "That was incredible."

Nell rose, caked here and there with fine white sand. She walked into the water, spread her arms and legs, sank to the bottom, hard and ripply. An orange starfish lay inches from her face. She flipped the starfish over and a crab scuttled out of its dead insides.

A buzzing started up in the ocean. Nell rose, saw a boat coming around the point at the end of the beach.

"Water taxi," Clay said, trunks back on. He brought her bathing suit. "Glad we're here, baby?"

All at once Nell wanted to get right home, but she said yes.

The water taxi—an old wooden Abaco boat with a broad stern that took passengers landing at the North Eleuthera strip to the nearby cays—headed for the dock. The boatman wore a red ski hat; the face of the only passenger, standing in the bow, seemed to be covered with something, maybe a handkerchief. Then Nell saw it was just his unbuttoned tropical shirt flapping up in the breeze.

"Funny," Clay said. "Duke didn't mention it."

"Didn't mention what?"

"That Kirk was coming."

Nell looked again: yes, Kirk, with his distinctive swept-back blond hair, swept back more by the breeze. She hadn't recognized him.

Kirk came ashore. He seemed excited about something. "Sorry to bust in," he said, and hurried up to the house. Clay and Nell followed, found the brothers already talking on the terrace. Now Duke seemed excited, too.

Nell took a shower. No hot water in the house, but what ran from the well out back was always warm enough. And there, under that warm flow, all soapy, relaxed for the first time in many days, she was struck by a fresh idea, coming out of nowhere.

"Clay?" she said, stepping out of the shower, wrapping her hair in a towel. He was shaving at the sink, back to her but foamy face visible in the mirror. "What do you know about hypnotism?"

"Not much."

"Think it works?"

"Didn't work for Bobby."

"Bobby Rice?" Nell started feeling less relaxed.

Clay nodded. "He gave it a try, to quit smoking."

That should have stopped the ebbing away of the relaxed feeling, but for some reason it did not. "I was thinking more along the lines of recovering memories."

"Yeah?" In the mirror his eyes shifted, found her.

"Haven't you ever used it—hypnotism, I mean—to help a witness remember?"

"Almost never admissible in court," Clay said.

"But what about just to sharpen the memory, even if the result can't be used directly?"

Clay tilted his head back, ran the razor under his chin. "What are you saying?"

The brothers' voices drifted up from the terrace; Duke said something about percentages that made Kirk laugh. Nell reached for her bra, hanging on a towel rack. "Do you think it's true that all our experience stays in the mind somewhere?" she said.

"No idea."

"Because if it does, then maybe I could really see his face."

"Who are we talking about?" Clay said.

"The killer," Nell said. "His bandanna slipped—I'm sure of that—meaning I got a good look at his face. I must have. Don't you see? If that's imprinted somewhere in my—"

Clay made a little grunt of pain, set down the razor and turned to her, a cut under his chin. "Enough," he said.

"What do you mean?"

Clay's voice rose. Blood seeped into the shaving foam, sending a pink trickle down his neck. "We've been through this and through this. It's over, finished, done."

"You're closing the case?"

"God damn it," he said. "Do you really think that's what I meant?"

"But are you?"

He took a deep breath, spoke more softly. "We don't close unsolved murder cases, if that's what this is, but there's no way—"

"If that's what this is?"

"You heard me."

"Meaning you still think DuPree is guilty, that the tape is a fake?" He didn't answer, just gazed at her, foam reddening under his chin. She pressed on. "How would that have been done? Is there any evidence to back it up? Have you had the tape analyzed?"

"Of course."

"And?"

He turned back to the mirror, saw the blood. "Christ. Why didn't you tell me I was bleeding?" He patted his chin with a towel.

"And?"

Clay put his hands on the edge of the sink, as though holding himself up. "According to the serial number on the cassette, it's from a surveillance system that went out of business soon after the killing."

"So that's that," Nell said. "The tape is authentic."

Clay didn't answer, just stood there slumped, blood still seeping from his cut.

"What am I missing?" Nell said.

"I've tried to tell you but I can't get through. If it's true that DuPree is innocent—"

"If?"

He talked over her. "—then you—we—are probably going to have to live with never knowing. Cold cases are hard enough, but with no forensics, no DNA, the only way they get solved is if someone who knows comes forward. And if that hasn't happened in all this time, what are the chances now?"

"That's why it has to be me."

"What are you talking about?"

"I'm the witness," Nell said. "The only one."

Clay spoke, so softly she almost didn't hear.

"What did you say?" she said, wanting to be sure.

"I said maybe you should see someone."

Rock bottom. Nell walked out of the room.

* * *

She went onto the dock. Vicki lay on a towel, wearing a thong, gleaming with sunblock, reading a magazine.

"Hey," she said, rolling over. "I tried the beach, but those little bugs came."

Nell sat down, dangled her feet. A needlefish swam by, just under the surface. She watched it, a beautiful creature that seemed at ease, and felt a little more at ease herself. "The water's the same color as your ring," she said.

"Huh?"

"Emerald."

"Oh, right," Vicki said. "Funny how the ocean, you know, changes." She came over and sat beside Nell, dangling her feet, too. They were short and square, the nails painted purple. The tide was high now, waves no longer breaking over the reef; just beyond it, a gull swooped down, splashed into the sea, came up with something silvery wriggling in its beak.

"Feel like lobster for dinner?" Nell said.

"My absolute fave," Vicki said. "Did you bring some?"

Nell turned and smiled. She was starting to like Vicki. "I was thinking we'd take the Zodiac out to the reef and jook a few."

"Jook?"

"That's how you say spear in these parts."

"Spear? You want to go spear actual lobsters?"

"There's a ledge on the far side of the reef they like. I'll do the diving. You handle the boat."

"Me?" Vicki glanced around, a little wildly, saw Kirk walking on the beach, a beer in his hand. "Kirk! Kirk!" She waved, her pinkie pointed high.

Kirk drove the Zodiac. Nell sat in the bow. They took masks, fins and snorkels, plus Hawaiian slings, spring steel spears and a big pail for the lobsters.

"Take it just past the cut," Nell said, "on the north side."

"Aye aye," said Kirk. He wore sunglasses and a bathing suit, a big guy, bigger than his brother, but way past being in shape. He opened the throttle and the Zodiac roared across the water, curved through the narrow gap in the reef—Nell could see staghorn coral on both sides, a few feet below the surface. Kirk killed the engine and the Zodiac rose on its bow wave and stopped, then slid back in the swell.

"Here?" he said.

"Here." She tossed the anchor over the side, the water so clear she could follow it all the way to the bottom. It settled on the sand. The current started taking them south. Down below, the flukes of the anchor dug in and the line tightened. They rocked gently on the water.

"Didn't mean to be all mysterious, swoopin' in like this," Kirk said. "Business."

"No problem."

"Keep a secret?"

Nell nodded, dipping her mask in the water.

"We, meaning DK—my share's in trust for as long as I'm in politics—maybe got ourselves a buyer."

"Someone wants to buy the company?"

"Keeping current management in place, plus a capital infusion. Can I ask you something?"

"Sure."

"This extra capital means we—Duke—will be needin' some new people. Executive-type people. Think Clay'd be interested?"

"He'd have to retire from the force?"

"Oh, yeah—this would be full-time, but the compensation package would be real good."

Nell almost said: *No way he's ready to leave the force.* But was that right? She no longer knew. "I'm not sure," she said. "Why don't you ask him?"

"Clay's probably doing it as we speak," Kirk said. "This is just another one of my feeble attempts to see the future before it happens."

Nell laughed, surprised. She didn't know Kirk well, had never heard him say anything like that. Kirk laughed, too, and then his face went serious.

"How're you doin' with all this?" he said. "Must be tough."

"I'm okay," Nell said.

He shook his head in an admiring way. "I believe it," he said. "But if there's ever anything I can do, just say the word."

"Know any hypnotists?" The question just popped out.

"Matter of fact, I do," Kirk said. "Guy cured tendonitis in my elbow in two sessions, got me back on the golf course. But I don't think he performs."

"Performs?"

"At parties. That what you want him for, set the guests to crawling around, barking like dogs and stuff?"

Nell laughed again. "I'm looking for help with my memory."

"For remembering all the paintings?"

"No," Nell said. "It's more about the case."

"The case?" Kirk said. "Where does a hypnotist come in?"

"You know I was the eyewitness."

"The only one?" Kirk said. "I'm a little hazy on the details."

"The only one," Nell said. "And the thing is, Kirk, I know I got a good look at the killer. I just can't call it up. So I was thinking that maybe a hypnotist . . ."

"How good a look?" said Kirk.

Nell described the scene on the Parish Street Pier.

"The bandanna slipped?" Kirk said.

"Just for a second, and only partially. But if it's true that the mind remembers everything somewhere, then—"

"Gotcha," Kirk said. "I can set you up."

Nell saw her grateful self reflected in Kirk's sunglasses. "Thanks," she said.

"Don't mention it," said Kirk. "We all ready?"

"Yup." Nell spat in her mask, swished it in the sea, put it on, slipped into her fins.

Kirk handed her a sling and spear. "What's the depth?"

"About forty-five feet right at the bottom," Nell said, sticking the snorkel mouthpiece between her teeth.

"Oh, boy," said Kirk. He sighed, reached for his own mask. Nell flashed him the okay sign and rolled backward into the sea.

She swam along the outside edge of the reef until she spotted a familiar coral head, a huge brain coral topped by a purple sea fan, then took three deep breaths, jackknifed into a smooth duck dive and kicked her way down, strong easy kicks, upper body still. Normally she noticed all kinds of things on the reef, but with a spear in her hand it was all a blur, her eyes on the lookout for just one sight, in this case the dark orange, knobby antennae of the spiny lobster.

Nell reached bottom. The anchor lay dug into the sand, just a few feet from the base of the reef, the line angling toward the surface. She glanced up, saw Kirk on his way, legs spread too wide, arms not at his sides, back bent, chest and gut sticking out: a perfect how-not-to demonstration. He came to a stop about ten feet above her, paddled his hands around for a moment, pale eyes bulging behind his mask, then shook his head and started back up.

Nell turned to the reef. A sharp ledge jutted out two or three feet from the bottom, with a dark crevice underneath, the kind of place lobsters liked to spend the daylight hours. Nell gave one little kick, careful not to stir up the bottom, and stuck her head in. For a moment or two, she could see nothing. Then her eyes adjusted to the dimness, and yes, deep in the crevice: two antennae, dark orange and knobby, already raised at a wary angle; huge, thick, maybe the biggest she'd ever seen. Nell already had the spear set in the wooden shaft and nocked. She held the shaft out front, drew back on the thick rubber tubing with her right hand as far as she could, then sighted and released.

The spear shot forward, pierced the carapace of the lobster with a cracking sound, very clear in the enclosed space.

After that, a lot of commotion: stirred-up sand, clanging steel, the near end of the spear waving around; not a kill shot, but good enough as long as the barb had stuck. Nell swam in deeper, got one hand on the end of the spear and pulled. Nothing; meaning that the lobster had gotten into a hole somewhere. She felt a little pressure deep in her throat, first sign of the carbon dioxide buildup that would trigger the need to breathe. The lobster wasn't going anywhere; she could swim up for air, come back down. But first, one more yank on the spear, this time harder. Nell yanked on the spear.

She heard another metallic clang, this one seeming to come from the core of the reef itself. Then came a dull, watery crash, and with it an enormous weight fell on the backs of her legs, pinning her to the bottom, and everything went dark. The roof had fallen in.

Nell squirmed around, her heart pounding so loud it might have been a separate object nearby, outside her body. Her legs were stuck. She reached for a handhold, grabbed something rocky and sharp, tried again, this time digging her fingers into the sand. Nell twisted, pulled, tried with all her might to get loose, and then, with a tearing of skin she registered as pain but did not feel, her right leg slid out from under the rubble. Now she had more range, could double back on herself, use her hands to push aside all the debris. She heaved at the chunks of coral, massive and heavy, pressure building and building in her lungs. Her left leg came free. She rolled over, exploded off the bottom and into the light, kicking and kicking, not long, controlled kicks, but frantic, up toward the shining surface; and so slow with both fins gone. Then she could no longer hold in the air and it burst from her lungs; she saw nothing but flashes, black and gold.

"Nell? Nell?"

Black-and-gold flashes receded, dimmed, vanished. She floated in the warm water, facedown, breathing air—so fresh—through her snorkel.

"Nell? You all right?"

She turned her head, saw Kirk leaning toward her over the side of the Zodiac. Nell raised her hand, started coughing.

"Christ. You're bleeding." He helped her into the boat.

Everybody made a big fuss—Vicki's eyes so wide the whites showed all around her irises—but it was really nothing, just scrapes, cuts, a few sea-urchin needles. She didn't even need stitches. While there was still enough daylight, Clay went out to the reef with scuba gear and had a look.

"Front part of the ledge just caved in," he reported. He found Nell's spear, the lobster, an eight-pounder, the biggest Nell had ever seen, still on it; and delicious under the stars that night. The anchor had come loose somewhere along the way. Clay brought that back, too, except for one of the flukes, broken off.

CHAPTER 19

"Am I disturbing you?"

Susannah. Yeah, kind of disturbing him. Pirate was standing at his window at the Ambassador Suites, watching a woman at a bus stop. She wore a tank top, had big breasts, mostly exposed from this angle. Pirate tried to imagine what they would feel like and couldn't. That part of him had gone—what was the word? like the bears?—dormant. But maybe it was starting to wake up. An important development, right? Springtime. So yes, Susannah was disturbing him. Still, Pirate wanted to be polite.

"Nah," he said.

"I have some news," she said.

"Yeah?" She didn't sound the same as normal, not so warm and friendly, so Pirate got ready for something bad. But what could that be? Bad was over; he was free.

"It's about the settlement," Susannah said.

"The . . . uh, oh, yeah."

"We've had an offer. It's a good offer, and while there's always the option of taking a hard-line stance and holding out for more, our impression is that they won't go much higher, resulting in any extra payment merely being lost to legal fees."

Pirate tried to follow all that but got lost along the way. "Settlement," he said. A strange word—didn't it mean a village or something, like an Indian settlement? The woman at the bus stop had a kind of dark reddish skin; maybe she was Indian, although her breasts seemed a little lighter. Were the breasts of Indian women lighter than the rest of them? There were lots of facts he didn't know. The bus came and she climbed on and went away.

"Settlement?" Susannah was saying. "Is that what you just said? Meaning you want to settle? Shouldn't you hear the amount first?"

"Probably," said Pirate.

"As I explained, we think this is a good offer, although no monetary compensation can ever be adequate in a case like yours. Understanding that should help to keep emotions in check. This is really about going forward in a practical way."

Going forward? Sure, why not? "Hundred percent," he said.

"I'm sorry?"

"On going forward."

"Oh, good," said Susannah. "The offer is four hundred thirty-two thousand seventy-one dollars and sixty-three cents."

"Sixty-three cents?" The rest hadn't stuck.

"Crazy, I know," said Susannah. "The result of the metrics they use. I can forward you the work sheets—have you got e-mail yet?"

"Say it again."

"Have you got e-mail yet?"

"The fuckin' money."

There was a long silence. Why? What was going on? Hard to understand Susannah sometimes, frustrating even, made him want to smack her. Not actually smack her, of course, not after all she'd done for him, to say nothing of the fact that he'd advanced to a point way way beyond violence of any kind. At last she spoke, saying the number in a strange voice, like she was handing over something smelly. This time he wrote it down.

$432,071.63.

"Four three two zero seven one point six three?" he said.

"Correct."

Emotions aside? What was that about? He circled and circled the number with his pen until it dug right through that paper and scraped the desk. *Scrape, scrape, scrape*—he could buy a new desk, buy a hundred, a thousand, a million. Well, maybe not a million. He laughed out loud.

"Mr. DuPree?"

"What happened to Alvin?" he said

She cleared her throat. "Alvin," she said, "is the amount acceptable?"

Four hundred and thirty-two grand? Was she nuts? Supposing he'd been free all this time, would he have accumulated a chunk like that? Only if he'd hit the big time in Nashville, or made some huge drug score, and what were the chances of either of those? Had to be realistic. "Yes, Susannah, the amount is acceptable." So cool, the way he said that.

"Very good," Susannah said. "Reverend Proctor will be in touch regarding the paperwork and details of the transaction."

Pirate remembered Reverend Proctor, with his mellow reverend voice. He didn't like Reverend Proctor, didn't need any middlemen for his religion. Twice as much as before? Way way better than that. He tried to think up a joke about she asses but it got too complicated, and besides, there was the chance she might not get it.

"Alvin? Did you understand that about the reverend?"

"Yup."

"Any questions?"

He had questions: Why Job? Were the breasts of Indian women lighter than the rest of them? Was Kahlúa booze or not? By now he knew she wasn't the one for those kinds of questions. But Pirate had another.

"Does the reverend want a cut?"

"A cut?"

"A piece," said Pirate. "Of the four three two."

"Of course not," said Susannah. "Anything else?"

"Nope."

"Then I'll say good-bye."

"Okeydoke," Pirate said, then added, "And mucho gracias." But too late: she was gone.

After that, Pirate got restless. He switched on the TV and flicked through the channels, but nothing held his attention except a commercial for a real sharp knife, and that was over pretty quick. Pirate went into the bathroom, made himself look nice. Then he put on spotless new khakis and a T-shirt that said ROLL TIDE on the front. He left the tags on the T-shirt, also left behind the tiny weapon—did he really need it anymore?—and took the elevator down.

A bar stood in one corner of the lobby—a few stools, all empty, no bartender—but there was something inviting about it. Pirate strolled over, scanned the shelves for Kahlúa. He spotted a single bottle, a big one. A big one meant big writing, maybe big enough for his eye to deal with the lettering, solve the booze-or-not mystery. He moved behind the bar, reached for the bottle, already able to read: product of mexico. Pirate had never been to Mexico, but why not? Mexico was supposed to be cheap—and cheap wasn't even anything he had to worry about! Far from it, in—

A door opened behind the bar and a man in a red vest and red bow tie came out, wiping his hands on a cloth. "Sir?" he said.

"Hi," said Pirate, taking his hand off the bottle.

"Would you like a drink, s—" Maybe about to say sir again, but now he'd noticed the patch, or something else about Pirate, that made him cut off the last part.

Did rich men take offense at things like that? Pirate didn't think so. "Depends," he said.

"On what?"

The bartender's tone was slipping now, toward downright

rude. That ruled out any easygoing back-and-forth about the booze question. Pirate turned his head, giving the bartender a real good angle on the patch. Then he went back around the bar and sat on a stool.

"Kahlúa," he said.

"Depends on Kahlúa?"

"Serve," said Pirate.

The bartender went all tight-lipped. Pirate thought of the tiny weapon, under the mattress in his room.

"On the rocks or straight up?" the bartender said, now looking over Pirate's shoulder.

Pirate smiled. "Rocks."

The bartender got to work. When was the last time Pirate had bellied up to a bar? He had a vague memory of a pitcher of beer in midair and bar stools reduced to kindling; but that was then. He unfolded the cocktail napkin and put it on his lap. Behind him a woman said, "Alvin?"

Pirate turned. "Hey." And almost right away her name came. "Lee Ann." He was—what was the word?—adjusting. He was adjusting to life on the outside, real good.

"I was just about to call up to your room," Lee Ann said.

"Yeah?" What would she look like without those glasses?

She reached into her bag, took out some papers, sat beside him. "I've got the contract."

The waiter slid his drink across the bar. That gave Pirate a chance to piece things together. "*Only a Test*?" he said.

"Exactly," Lee Ann said. "This is the agreement between you and me, the sixteen percent, what we talked about earlier."

"Where do I sign?" Pirate said.

"Something for you, ma'am?" said the waiter.

Lee Ann glanced at Pirate's drink. "What's that?"

"Kahlúa," said the waiter.

For some reason, Lee Ann looked surprised. "Chardonnay," she said.

Chardonnay came. Lee Ann raised her glass. "Clink," she said. They clinked glasses. "Here's to *Only a Test*," she said. They drank. Coffee, sugar, something else, something nice: the taste of Mexico. "But there's no signing till a lawyer's been over it, remember?" Lee Ann said.

"Had enough of lawyers for now," Pirate said. He pulled the papers closer, leafed through. Lots and lots of print, big enough to see but hard to understand. Pirate came to the last page, saw the line where he was supposed to sign. "Pen?" he said.

"I really can't let you."

"No?" Pirate said. What did it matter, the details of some piddly little book deal? "So happens I got other resources."

"I heard about that. How does it feel?"

How could she have already heard about the settlement?

Lee Ann grinned. "I've got resources, too," she said, as though reading his mind. Lee Ann was okay, plus they were partners, but wiping that grin off her face would have been nice.

Pirate shrugged. "Feels all right," he said. He turned to the bartender. "Borrow your pen?"

"Yes, sir," said the bartender. Back to sir: resources did the trick.

Pirate took the pen and signed: Alvin Mack DuPree. He underlined his name three times, handed the pen to Lee Ann. She signed on the line below. "Partner," she said, extending her hand. They shook.

"This goes on my tab," Pirate told the bartender, and added his room number. But just before Lee Ann left, he remembered he was down to about eighty bucks in actual walking-around money, so he hit her up for sixty more, strictly as a loan. "Trust me for it?" he said.

Lee Ann laughed. She was okay. He came close to asking her to take off her glasses.

"And here's something else I'd like you to have," she said.

"What's this?"

"A digital recorder."

"What am I supposed to record?"

"Details that might help the book," Lee Ann said. "Ideas, memories, what you ate in prison, anything that fleshes out the story."

Pirate pressed the record button. "Flesh," he said. He pressed play. "Flesh." Was that him? He hadn't heard his recorded voice in over twenty years. It had changed, now sounded—what was the word?—menacing. But maybe not, because when he glanced up at Lee Ann she was smiling and didn't seem scared at all.

Pirate went outside. The sun felt good. He took a walk, no place particular, soon found himself in Lower Town. After a while, he came to a pawnshop, saw a cool guitar in the window, an old Rickenbacker. He'd never actually played a Rickenbacker, but he'd once played with a guy who was playing one. Pirate checked the price: $995. No way for now, but soon. He was turning away from the window when something else caught his eye: a gold earring. Just a simple little hoop of gold, price $135. *Every man also gave him a piece of money, and every one an earring of gold.* Pirate opened the door and went inside. A bell tinkled, a nice, quiet sound. It was nice and quiet out in the world. He was at peace.

"Help you?" said a man behind the counter. His gaze slid over to the patch; Pirate was tiring of that. And this was a tiny old guy with hairy ears, disgusting and weak; Pirate could almost hear the sound of brittle bones breaking.

"The gold earring in the window," he said.

"One thirty-five for the pair."

"Don't want the pair," said Pirate. "Just the one."

"Eighty-five," said the old guy.

That didn't sound right. Eighty-five had to be more than

half of one thirty-five, but how much more? "Seventy-five," he said.

"Split the difference. Eighty."

"Deal," said Pirate; he was a good bargainer—first getting Lee Ann to go up, now getting this old guy to go down.

The old guy went to the window, got the earring. Pirate paid.

"Wrap it for you?" said the old guy.

"Nope," said Pirate. "Gonna wear it."

The old guy had pea-size eyes. They shifted to one of Pirate's ears, then the other. "How?" he said. "Ears ain't pierced."

Pirate hadn't thought of that. "You do that kind of work?" he said.

"See that sign? Says pawnshop, not beauty parlor."

"Got a pin?" Pirate said.

"Pin?"

"Pin, needle, whatever."

The old guy rooted around in a drawer, came up with a long, thick pin.

"Match," said Pirate.

The old man handed over a book of matches. Pirate blackened the end of the pin; couldn't be too careful about this kind of thing. Then he moved a few feet along the counter so he faced a wall mirror and stuck the needle through his earlobe; left earlobe, to balance the patch—a nice touch, he thought. Maybe this was a beauty parlor, after all. He inserted the hoop, fastened it, blotted up the few drops of blood on the shoulder of his T-shirt.

"Learn something every day," said the old guy.

Pirate walked down Princess Street, came to the Pink Passion Club. A sign flashed: open. And on a chalkboard: NOW DANCING—AURORA, MYSTIQUE, CHOCOLATE. There'd been an Aurora back in his bouncer days—she'd always had a smile for him. Was this possibly the same one? Interesting thought; but Pirate, now a man at peace, kept walking. A path of righteousness existed—no doubt about that—and women and booze weren't on it.

Pirate turned the corner onto Rideau Street. There were bars and clubs on Rideau Street—Boom-Boom, Lot 49, Screaming Meemy's; and hey: the Red Rooster. Still looked the same: neon beer signs in the windows and a giant wooden red rooster looming over the door. That fund-raiser: a man in his position didn't need fund-raisers; in fact, the idea annoyed him now. Pirate heard music. He opened the door and went in.

He kind of remembered the place, or places like it: dark, with tables in the middle, all empty except for one up front with a lone woman, a bar along the side, no customers there either, and a band onstage: guitar, bass, drums, fiddle, Dobro. They stopped halfway through a song he didn't know, started up again. Pirate noticed that they were all lounging around or sitting on stools, and was starting to wonder if this was a rehearsal, when a woman in a cowboy hat stepped out of the shadows and said, "Sorry, we're closed."

"Rehearsal," said Pirate.

Her gaze slid over to the patch. "That's right. We open at five."

"I'd like to see the manager," Pirate said.

"That's me."

"Cancel the fund-raiser."

"I'm sor—" The manager raised her hands to her mouth. "Oh my God, are you Alvin DuPree?"

Pirate nodded. Was this bad or good?

"I recognize you from the paper."

"Yeah?"

"You're a celebrity," said the manager. She held out her hand, another one of those tiny female hands, lost in his. "Did you say cancel the fund-raiser?"

"Won't be needin' it," said Pirate. Then he added: "But thanks and everything." Celebrities had to be polite.

"We were all looking forward to it," the manager said. "Gearbox was going to play."

"Gearbox?"

The manager tilted her pointy chin at the stage. They were playing something he knew, maybe "There Stands the Glass," but very fast; and what was that in the guitarist's hands? A Rickenbacker. He took a solo—a lean kid with a smooth face, almost like he hadn't started shaving yet—and lost Pirate right away; he was real good.

"That's Joe Don on guitar," the manager said. "Isn't he something? You can listen in if you like."

"Yeah," said Pirate. "I'd like."

"Sit anywhere," she said, waving at the empty tables. "How about a drink? On the house."

"I don't drink."

"A Coke, maybe? Club soda?"

"Kahlúa on the rocks," said Pirate.

The manager blinked. "Kahlúa on the rocks it is."

Pirate sat at a table up front. "There Stands the Glass," "More and More," "Backstreet Affair," but all speeded up, all different, plus songs he'd never heard, just rocking, with the Dobro player—a woman!—wailing away, and the boy on guitar, even better, driving the music higher and higher; they were great. But after a while, Pirate's attention began wandering to the next table, where the only other spectator sat, a woman, young, possibly a teenager. Was she just about the most beautiful woman Pirate had ever seen, live, in magazines, on TV, anywhere? Yes. Everything about her, so fine: soft skin, clear green eyes, glowing hair, delicate features, all finely formed.

Oops. She caught him looking, maybe even staring. That was bad. He turned his eye toward the stage. At that moment, a note or two went wrong, drumsticks clacked together and the music petered out. The guitar player—Joe Don?—said something that made the others laugh. Straining to catch the joke, Pirate, despite his acute hearing, failed to pick up the sound of the young woman approaching on his blind side.

"Alvin DuPree?" she said.

He whipped around, almost knocking his Kahlúa off the table. "Yeah?" he said, then added, "Miss?"

She gazed down at him, not at the patch, but him. "My father was Johnny Blanton."

Big surprise, but the right response came. "Sorry for your loss," Pirate said.

C lay and Nell drove home from the airstrip east of Belle
Ville, the sun in their eyes. The brightness gave Nell a
headache; she hadn't had one in years.

Clay glanced over. "You all right?"

"Yes."

He took her hand. "Don't scare me like that again."

"I'll try not."

He seemed about to laugh but didn't. "You're so composed
about it all."

"I wasn't at the time," Nell said.

The muscles in his jaw hardened. "I still don't understand
why you were diving alone. Kirk's got a lot of experience."

"I told you—he couldn't pull the depth. Just look at him."

"But he should have stayed in the water, kept an eye out."

"Why? What could he have done?"

Clay had no answer, but his expression didn't change.

"There's no point being angry at Kirk," Nell said. "If
anyone made a mistake in judgment, it was me."

Clay shook his head. "He should have told you it was too
deep for him."

"What man does that?" Nell said.

"Why are you defending him?" Clay let go of her hand.

"I'm not—" Nell cut herself off. Were they sliding into
another fight? How easily that was starting to happen, suddenly almost a default position in their marriage. "Let's not

fight," she said, clamping down on what tried to come next, the pitiful headache defense.

"I'm not fighting," he said. "I just . . ."

Clay took the Lower Town cutoff. The windows were up and the AC on but Nell smelled the Bernardine stink right away, still so strong. "When's it going to be gone?" she said.

"What are you talking about?"

"The smell," she said. "From the flood."

Clay sniffed. "I don't smell anything." He glanced at her again. "Sure you're all right?"

Stop asking that. "Yeah, I'm fine."

The bars on Rideau Street went by—Boom-Boom, Lot 49, Screaming Meemy's, the Red Rooster. The wrecker from Yeller's Autobody was parked outside. Clay's eyes were on the road, straight ahead.

"You and Kirk talk about anything special out on the boat?" he said.

"He mentioned this expansion or whatever it is," she said. "And having an executive job for you."

"Duke told me."

"And?"

"It's something to think about."

"It is?"

"Why the surprise?"

"Kirk said it would mean retiring from the force."

"That's right."

"You say it so matter-of-factly."

Clay shrugged.

They passed Canal Street. Heavy equipment from DK Industries was in motion down at the end, where the water had first broken over the gates. There was still so much wreckage around, the area flattened except for mounds of mud; all that had stood before now reduced to scrap.

"I thought you were still passionate about it," Nell said.

"About what?"

"Police work."

Clay kept his eyes on the road.

"Aren't you?" Nell said.

"Things change."

"Things like the importance of your job?" Nell said. "How much you've done for the town?"

Clay's hands tightened on the wheel; beautiful hands, but for a moment or two blunt, flushed, almost unrecognizable. "They'd pay me two hundred grand a year," he said. "To start. Did you factor that in?"

Clay made $77,500; Nell almost $40,000, although pay had been suspended until the reopening. "We're not really about that, are we?" she said.

"No, we're better than everyone else."

"You know I didn't mean that."

"Then don't say it."

They drove through Lower Town. A few people turned to stare, that post-Bernardine faultfinding look in their eyes. Nell found herself stupidly hating what couldn't be hated, an act of nature, the storm that had brought so much trouble. And this conversation: stupid, too. She was about to leave it behind, delete it from the record, when Clay spoke.

"What else did you talk about?" he said.

"Who?"

"You and Kirk, on the boat."

"Nothing," she said, and felt ashamed, the lie coming so easily it arrived before the realization of what she was concealing: hypnotism, and how it might help her remember the face she saw on the Parish Street Pier.

"Nothing?"

"Nothing important. Chitchat." Adding a crummy little lie to the big one: somehow that felt worse.

Clay turned onto Blue Heron Road. After a few blocks it began to look like before, pre-Bernardine. The farther north they drove, the fewer people, the lighter their faces, the less hostile—and finally neutral—their expressions. The screens were hung at the tennis courts now, hiding the players from view, but a lob went up, the ball rising and then falling fast, like a symbol on a blue graph.

"What do you think of him?" Clay said.

"Who?"

"Kirk. Who else are we talking about?"

"I don't really know him," Nell said. "Why do you ask?"

"You've known him for, what? Eighteen years?"

"Not well," she said. "I always liked Duke better."

"Why?"

"Maybe because he's your friend. The way the two of you are together—it's special."

"Yeah?"

"You know that, Clay."

He nodded.

"Any particular reason you asked what I thought of Kirk?" she said.

"No."

"Was it because of this job opportunity?"

"Yeah," Clay said. "The job opportunity."

"But you wouldn't be working for Kirk, not while he's still mayor. And what if he becomes governor?"

"Where'd you hear that?"

"Vicki."

"Jesus."

"I like Vicki."

"She's not going to be around much longer."

"What do you mean?"

Clay turned on to their street, drove up the hill. "Duke met someone new."

"They're breaking up?"

"Appears so."

He parked in the driveway, between Nell's car and the Miata. A seagull, pure white, stood on the roof, poised with wings outstretched as though it had just landed, or was about to take off.

"Meaning Vicki doesn't know yet?" Nell said.

"That's right."

"But he took her to Little Parrot anyway?"

Clay didn't answer. There was something violent about this little tale of Vicki's last bit of Bahamian fun—not violent like the hurricane, or what had happened to Johnny—but violent nonetheless. For the first time in her life, Nell understood those women who hated men in a generalized way.

Inside the house:

"Norah?"

No response. Nell went up to Norah's bedroom, found the door open, everything neat, stuffed animals all in place, the monkeys dangling from the ceiling, swaying slightly in an air current. She left the bedroom, started down the stairs and at that moment heard a little bumping sound from the direction of her office. Nell went down the hall. The office door was closed. She opened it and saw Norah kneeling in front of the closet, boxes tipped over, papers strewn on the floor. Norah heard her and turned, but with no sign of haste or panic.

"What are you doing?" Nell said.

"Looking."

"Looking for what? You can't just go through my things."

"I don't care about your things," Norah said. "I'm looking for my father's things. Where are they?"

"I told you," Nell said. "We lost power. The pictures are ruined."

"But what about other stuff?"

"What other stuff?"

"His research, his papers," Norah said. "His clothes, for God's sake."

Nell hadn't thought about Johnny's things in years, had only a faint memory of his mother coming to box it all up. "Everything went back to his parents," she said.

Norah's eyes shifted, drawn by some inner thought. "There must be more," she said.

"I don't understand what you're doing."

Norah rose. "Someone killed him. Why don't you want to find out who?"

Nell didn't answer. It was true: she didn't want to know.

"Or do you know already?"

"What's happening to you? That's crazy."

"Comes with the territory," Norah said, stalking past her and hurrying out of the office. An invisible cloud of her breath lingered in the air for a moment; it had a syrupy, coffee smell. Nell remembered that the coffee place in the Blue Heron Plaza, not far from the tennis courts, had re-opened. She went down the hall, knocked on Norah's door.

"What do you mean 'comes with the territory'?"

"Nothing," said Norah, from the other side. "I mean nothing."

"You're keeping something from me. What is it?"

Silence.

"I can help."

More silence. Then: "I'm an adult. An adult who wants peace and quiet. Is that too much to ask?"

Nell returned to the office and repacked the boxes.

In the morning—Clay gone to work, Norah not yet up—Nell called the mayor's office, was put right through.

"Hey, there," said Kirk. "How're you doin'?"

"Fine." She saw herself in the mirror: cheekbones, never prominent enough, now too much so. Was she losing weight?

"Good to hear. Truth is I've been beating myself up pretty good about what happened out on the reef."

"No need to."

"If I wasn't in such lousy shape, nothing would have happened."

"Don't worry about it," Nell said.

"Feel just terrible," Kirk said. "Hope Clay's not too pissed at me."

"There's no problem," Nell said.

"Grateful for that, Nellie," said Kirk. "What can I do for you?"

"I'd like the name of that hypnotist you mentioned."

"Yeah?"

"If it's not too much trouble." Phone in hand, she walked into the bathroom, stepped on the scale; she'd lost ten pounds.

"No."

"No?"

"No trouble, I was starting to say. It's just that the guy's a little strange."

"In what way?"

"Kind of a quack."

"I thought he got rid of your tendonitis."

Kirk laughed. "Thing is, my tendonitis went away around the time I was seeing him—maybe a coincidence. What you're looking for, I don't know."

"It can't hurt to try," Nell said.

After a little pause, Kirk said, "Got a pen?"

The sign on the door—the office was in a strip mall in east Belle Ville—read LOUIS B. PASTORE, MSW, FAMILY AND OTHER THERAPY. Men in hard hats were working on the roof; what was left of the old one lay in heaps near a mound of mud at the back of the parking lot. Nell opened the door and went in.

She stood in a small reception room; no one waiting, no receptionist. Framed certificates hung on the wall; Louis B. Pastore—sometimes Lewis—had four or five degrees, all from institutions new to Nell.

"Hello?" she said.

"Come on in," a man called from behind a door in the back wall.

Nell entered another small room. A man with a big head and a thick gray ponytail sat at a desk.

"I have an appointment," Nell said. "Nell Jarreau."

"Of course, of course," the man said, rising and shaking her hand. He turned out to be short and skinny, his head way out of proportion. "Dr. Pastore," he said. "Have a seat in the comfy chair." He pointed to a La-Z-Boy.

Nell sat in the comfy chair, feet on the footrest; glad she'd worn jeans. Dr. Pastore—none of the certificates mentioned a doctorate—pulled up a stool, opened a notebook. "How long have you been smoking?" he said.

"I don't smoke," Nell said.

"No?" said Dr. Pastore. He leafed through the notebook. "Ah, here we go—long-ago assailant, nighttime, memory issues? That it?"

"Yes."

Dr. Pastore leaned forward, ponytail in motion behind him, almost like a separate being. Nell got a little queasy. "Ever been hypnotized?"

"No," Nell said. "I'm worried I might be one of those resistant types."

"Yeah?" Dr. Pastore looked interested, as though rising to a challenge. "Has anyone ever attempted to induce hypnosis on you?"

"No."

"Then the odds are this won't be too difficult." He looked less interested. "Comfortable?"

Nell wasn't, not at all, but she said, "Yes."

"I just want you to relax."

"Do I watch some kind of pendulum?"

Dr. Pastore smiled. "Just relax," he said. "Allow yourself to feel a certain heaviness—in your feet, your legs, your arms, your whole body. A heavy heaviness but nice. Nice and loose and heavy and reee-laxed. Your eyes are feeling heavy, too. It's okay to close them . . ." A little pause; Nell heard the turning of a notebook page, sound very clear but distant at the same time. ". . . Nell. It's okay to close those heavy, heavy eyelids of yours. That's good. Just reee-lax. Take soft, deep breaths. Feel the air inside you. The air is heavy, too."

Yes, heavy air. It spread through her body, relaxing every cell. And her eyelids, so heavy, too, as though she were asleep and dreaming.

"Hear me all right?" said Dr. Pastore.

She could hear him fine, distant but clear, somewhere outside the dream.

"Say yes if you do."

"Yes."

"Now let your mind drift back to the night of the incident. Is it a nice night?"

"Yes. Warm."

"A warm night. Anything else?"

"There's a full moon."

"Big and yellow?"

"More white than yellow. The little ghost brother."

"Little ghost brother?"

"That's what Johnny calls it."

"Is he with you?"

"We're holding hands."

"Where are you?"

"On the towpath. The pier is just ahead. I smell flowers."

"What do you see?"

"Nothing. I'm listening to Johnny."

"What's he saying?"

"It's hard to understand. The earth is dynamic. The bottom changes over time. There are some obvious conclusions, funnel effects, but no one seems in a hurry to . . ." Uh-oh.

"No one seems in a hurry to do what?"

"A man. There's a man on the pier. Something wrong with his face . . . like it's all misshapen . . ."

"Nell?"

"Yes?"

"You can still hear me?"

"Uh-huh."

"What's happening now?"

"He wants . . . no, it's a bandanna. Johnny's going to give him what he—oh, no. Oh, no. Oh, no."

"Nell? What is it? What's happening?"

"He . . . oh, God." She kicked out with all her might. Something fell to the floor. The bandanna slid down.

"Nell?"

"I see his face."

"Can you describe it?"

"Don't want to."

"You don't have to. Don't have to do anything you don't want."

"The eyes aren't blue."

"No? Do you recognize this man?"

Tears started flowing, wouldn't stop. The eyes were brown, soft and gentle.

"Nell? Nell? Do you recognize him? Who is he?"

Tears and more tears.

"Nell? Can you still hear me? I'm a little concerned. When I clap my hands you will awake and open your eyes."

"I'm awake."

"You are?"

Nell opened her eyes. For some reason, Dr. Pastore clapped anyway.

"You seem a little upset," he said, handing her a tissue. He picked up a book that lay open on the floor, as though dropped or thrown. "Visiting these memories can be . . . I don't want to say traumatic."

Nell dabbed at her eyes, stopped crying. She started to rise, her limbs still feeling heavy.

"No rush," said Dr. Pastore. "Just stay there as long as you like, no prob—"

Nell got to her feet.

"Are you all right?"

She nodded.

"In all the commo—" Dr. Pastore cut himself off, tried again. "Out of my concern, I forgot to say you would remember everything from the session upon awakening."

Nell remembered, way too much, way too clearly.

"Is there anything you'd like to discuss?" said Dr. Pastore, glancing at her, then moving behind the desk.

"Are these memories always true?" Nell said.

"You refer to memories induced through hypnosis by a properly trained professional?"

"Yes."

Dr. Pastore looked annoyed. "Why else would I be doing this?" he said. "Maybe if we got into the details of the memories I could be of some help, in a therapeutic sense."

Was this about therapy? Not now, Nell thought, and maybe never. The sound of footsteps came from above, workmen on the roof.

CHAPTER 21

The Yeller's Autobody wrecker was just pulling away from the house when Nell drove into the circle. She caught a glimpse of Norah squeezed against Joe Don in the front seat, and fought off the temptation to keep going, follow them down Sandhill Way.

The phone rang as she went inside.

"Hello?"

"Hi. Is Norah there?"

"Ines?"

"Yeah. Hi."

"Just missed her. You could try her cell."

"Is it working?"

"I think so. Why?"

"I've left a few messages, that's all," said Ines.

"And she hasn't gotten back to you?"

"No," Ines said. "Mrs. Jarreau?"

"You can call me Nell."

"Nell? How's she doing?"

Nell started to say something innocuous—all right, not bad—but stopped herself. "This is the second time you've asked me that," she said.

Ines was silent.

"Both times in a way I find a bit alarming."

"Sorry."

"Don't be sorry," Nell said. "But if there's something I should know, please tell me."

Silence.

"What is it, Ines?"

More silence.

"Ines?"

"Just . . . just tell her I called," Ines said. "Bye."

"Wait," said Nell.

But Ines hung up. Nell checked the caller ID menu, found Ines's number, called it right back. No answer.

Nell went into the office, turned on the computer and started reading up on hypnotism, specifically the accuracy of hypnotically recovered memories, something she should have done before her visit to Dr. Pastore. Or maybe not: because twenty or thirty minutes later, she was no further ahead. The answer to the hypnosis question was that no one knew. That left her with the image she'd seen in Dr. Pastore's office, a brown-eyed memory, persistent and unnerving.

Nell rose. She felt disoriented, as though in some strange place instead of her own home. She went into the laundry room, took her bathing suit from the dryer and walked out to the pool.

Nell swam. Lap by lap, her body took over. Her mind shut down, almost unaware of how well she was swimming, so smooth and easy, as if the water had been shot full of air and lost its resistance. The disoriented feeling ebbed away. She swam herself into a state of peace.

It didn't last. When the effortless period ended and she climbed out of the pool, she found Clay seated at the outdoor table a few yards away, very still, watching.

"Hi," she said, reaching for a towel. "How long have you been here?" She checked her watch: 12:30. He almost never came home in the middle of the day.

"Where were you?" he said.

She paused, the towel against her chest. "When?" she said.

"You didn't answer my calls."

She gestured toward the pool. "I've been swimming."

"For three hours?"

"No."

"Then where were you?"

"Clay, what is this? You're interrogating me."

He didn't say anything, just gazed at her; brown eyes, yes, but not at their softest: the professional look was back.

"I was at the museum, if you must know," Nell said. A lie that burst out on its own, and probably a stupid one: Hadn't he once told her that good interrogators often knew the true answers to the questions they asked? Was it possible Dr. Pastore was some kind of informant? She rejected the thought; that way lay paranoia.

"You were at the museum," he said.

"Yes," said Nell, now locked into the lie.

"Okay, Nell." He turned and walked into the house. A few moments later she heard his car starting up out front.

Nell sat at her desk. Was there any possible connection between Clay and Johnny? Johnny had never been in trouble with the law. A safe driver, uninterested in drugs, and hardly drank at all: he found excitement in other things. So: no connection, and therefore how to explain her hypnotically induced memory? Perhaps she'd entered paranoid territory before her visit to Dr. Pastore, drifting in deep and unaware, and paranoia had sketched out a memory of its own.

The phone rang. It jolted her, as though electricity had jumped right out of the wire. Nell let it ring. The answering machine took the call.

"Nell? Lee Ann here. Please give me a—"

Nell picked up. "Hello?"

"Screening your calls?" said Lee Ann.

"Then why would I be talking to you?"

"Whoa," Lee Ann said. "You don't sound like your usual self."

How could I? Nell managed to keep that thought to herself. "What's up?" she said.

"A few things," said Lee Ann. "First, Sheriff Lanier cut Kiki Amayo loose."

"Who's that?"

"The drug dealer he arrested in the Nappy Ferris murder. He's a gangbanger, all right, but he alibied out."

"What does this mean?" Nappy, in his last moments, stirred in her mind, toppling over outside the cabin up in Stonewall County, the sound of his bourbon gurgling away.

"It means the investigation's wide open, according to the sheriff. Here's a quote from him." Nell heard Lee Ann flipping pages. "Asked about a possible connection between the Ferris murder and the DuPree case, Sheriff Lanier said, 'Everything's on the table.'"

The handset was damp with Nell's sweat.

"Nell? Still there?"

"Yes."

"Any comment?"

"For the paper?"

"Preferably."

"No."

"What about off the record?"

"No."

"What if I told you that Nappy Ferris had a long history of dealing marijuana himself, mostly right out of his store?"

Nell remembered Clay in the clearing: *Ferris had two drug priors—one for possession, one for dealing, marijuana both times.* "Didn't we know that already?" she said.

"In a way," Lee Ann said. "I looked into those priors. They're both over twenty years old."

"So?"

"So my sources tell me he kept dealing out of the store all those years, right up until Bernardine."

"I don't understand," Nell said. "You're saying he was killed because of drugs after all?"

"Not really," said Lee Ann. "Doesn't mean that's not

what happened, of course. But what I find interesting is how Nappy kept his nose clean, at least in terms of the law."

"Meaning?"

"This sideline of his. I'm not suggesting he was a big-time dealer. But it wasn't a secret, not in Lower Town."

"How do you know?"

"Fifteen years with the paper, Nell. What kind of a reporter would I be if I hadn't cultivated Lower Town sources in all that time?"

"I don't know," Nell said; kind of a stupid answer, especially since it was obvious that Lee Ann was a good reporter, and very clever; maybe clever enough to tape phone conversations. She felt Lee Ann was homing in on something, irresistible.

"A lousy one is the answer," Lee Ann said. "But what keeps snagging in my mind is this issue of how a borderline or maybe full-fledged alcoholic like Nappy Ferris managed to stay out of trouble while running an illegal second career."

"Maybe it caught up with him in the end."

"Maybe," said Lee Ann. "Any guesses on who pulled the trigger?"

"Of course not," Nell said. "I don't know anyone in that world."

"What world?"

"The drug world."

Pause. "No offense," Lee Ann said, "but I'm finding you a little obtuse right now."

"My apologies," Nell said. The mouthpiece reflected her voice back at her, hard and cold.

"None necessary," said Lee Ann. Another pause. "Everybody likes you."

"You told me that already," Nell said. "The first time I believed you."

Lee Ann laughed. "There's something I want to run by you. Any chance at all you'd be willing to meet with Alvin DuPree?"

"Why would I want to do that?" Same hard, cold tone, but Nell was shaking.

"I can't speak for you, even though I think I know you a little bit," Lee Ann said. "But it wouldn't surprise me if the answer's yes."

"It's no," Nell said.

"Don't decide now," said Lee Ann. "Sleep on it. I'd be there the whole time, if it's the one-on-one aspect that's worrying you. He's still at the Ambassador Suites—I can swing by and get you anytime you say."

"No."

"No you don't want me to be there or no to the whole thing?"

"The whole thing," Nell said.

A tall bookcase stood in the family room. It had two big drawers at the bottom, both filled with letters, game programs, award certificates, report cards, souvenirs. Nell pawed through all that until she found what she was looking for: an old clipping from the *Guardian,* the caption headed *Young Sharpshooters.* She took the clipping to the window, examined it under bright light.

The picture showed Clay and Duke, both in profile, aiming rifles at an unseen target. The caption read: *Clay Jarreau and his friend Duke Bastien, both thirteen, shown competing in the Southern State Riflery Championships. Clay finished second. The winner, not shown, was Duke's eleven-year-old brother, Kirk Bastien. Good job, boys!* Did it mean anything? Probably not: What had Sheriff Lanier said? *Just pointing out the level of shooting ability around these parts—kind of like at the Olympics.*

And what was she allowing herself to think? Clay couldn't shoot anyone, not the way Nappy Ferris had been shot. He actually had killed a man once, but in the line of duty—he'd stepped into a shoot-out already in progress, saving the life of a convenience-store clerk and earning a commendation for heroism. *So stop this right away.*

Nell told herself to stop but at the same time she went into their bedroom, opened the closet and checked his guns, locked in the rack: a Smith & Wesson revolver and a rifle. Nell found the caliber, stamped on the stock, the number she didn't want to see: .30–06. She sniffed at the muzzle, smelled nothing. How long would gunpowder smell linger? She didn't know. But what about all this dust on the barrel? Didn't it prove that the rifle hadn't been touched in months, maybe years?

Nell wandered around the house, agitated again, as agitated as she'd been before the swim, or more. That oppressive feeling came down on her, as though she were in some alien place. Another swim? A crazy thought, but she came close to getting back in her bathing suit. Instead she got in her car, a minivan she'd had for years, and went for a long drive, headed nowhere particular. She ended up downtown, in the parking lot of the Ambassador Suites.

"Mr. DuPree?"

"Yeah?"

"This is"— somebody or other, name not quite catching in Pirate's head—"at Southern State Bank and Trust. Your account has been credited with a deposit of four hundred thirty-two thousand seventy-one dollars and sixty-three cents."

"Oh."

"Minus a fifteen-dollar fee for wire transaction."

"What's that?"

The woman explained. Pirate stopped listening.

"Anything else I can do for you today?" she said.

"What's it like out?" said Pirate.

"I'm sorry?"

"You know, the weather."

"I think it's nice."

Pirate hung up. He opened the curtains. Nice? Way too bright to be nice; for some reason he felt the brightness only in his non-eye. He opened a pack of Twizzlers and watched a minivan drive into the parking lot, down below.

The phone rang a minute or two later.

"Someone to see you, sir."

"Norah and Joe Don?" said Pirate. "Send 'em up."

"Um, no, sir, it's just the one person."

"Who?"

"One moment." *Muffle muffle.* "She says her name is Nell."

"Don't know any—" Hey! But he did! "Yeah, send her on up."

Muffle muffle. "Actually, sir, the lady says could you come down."

"Nope."

More muffle. "She's on her way."

Pirate hung up, looked around. Should he tidy up? Not much to tidy: that was the cool thing about maid service. He got one of those Kahlúa bottles from the minibar, took a sip or two, thought for the first time in a while of the tiny weapon—maybe reminded by the tininess of the Kahlúa bottle. Funny, how the mind worked. Pirate went into the bedroom, raised the mattress. Yes, the tiny weapon, safe and sound. The tiny weapon wanted him to pick it up, but who was master? A very rich master! He let go of the mattress— *thump*—and moved to the desk, where his Bible lay. As he opened it to read that last part—Job's final reward—he caught a glimpse of himself in the mirror, saw he wasn't wearing the patch. Was that any way to receive a lady? Pirate was going back and forth on that question, fingering the gold tassel, when he heard a knock on the door. Just an ordinary knock, but it sounded in his head like a starter's pistol.

Starter's pistol—like for the beginning of a race. He remembered that from his sophomore—and last—year of high school, when he and his buddies, now forgotten, had smoked weed under the stands by the cinder track. Funny, how the mind worked. He reached for the patch.

CHAPTER 22

Pirate opened the door. Yes, her: the tanned, in-shape one, older than Susannah but just as pretty in a softer way, and close up like this—she wore a skirt that came to the knees and a short-sleeved shirt buttoned up high—no doubt about her being strong-looking, for a woman.

"Hi, there," said Pirate.

"Hello, Mr. DuPree," she said. Her gaze went to his patch, then quickly away. Pirate got a kick out of that. "Thanks for agreeing to . . . thanks for seeing me." She seemed nervous. Pirate got a kick out of that, too.

"Seeing is believing," he said. A joke: one of his very best, and so quick.

She blinked. Her mouth—nice and soft—opened slightly, but she couldn't come up with anything to say.

"Nell, right?"

"Yes."

"Come on in, Nell," Pirate said, stepping aside and making a broad gesture with his hand. "It's a suite."

She entered, glanced around. Bedroom to the left, sitting room to the right. She turned right.

"Take a seat," Pirate said, indicating the sofa.

"I won't stay," she said.

"Take a seat anyway," said Pirate.

"Thank you."

She seemed polite, a nice and polite lady who'd fingered

him for a crime he didn't do. Only a test: yes! This visit, this being so close to her, was only a test of how at peace he really was. At that moment, Pirate was sure of something, had never been so sure of anything in all his life: he was going to pass with flying colors.

"Care for a drink?" he said.

"No, thanks," she said. "I only came to—"

Pirate interrupted, talked over her—not in a rude way, but didn't he have a right to—what was the expression? Set the tone? Yeah. He had a right to set the tone. "There's Coke, OJ, Sprite and Kahlúa," he said, opening the minibar, "plus liquor, beer and wine. Personally, I'm having Kahlúa."

"Nothing for me, thanks," she said, sitting at one end of the sofa.

"Too bad," said Pirate. "I was going to propose a toast." A toast: what a great idea, and coming to him out of the blue. His mind was in overdrive, cranking out shit like it hadn't in . . . in years, twenty of them to be precise. It was starting to feel like the old days. He glanced over at the Bible, lying on the coffee table, and overcame a sudden urge to fondle the gold tassel.

"In that case," she said, looking embarrassed.

"I'll pour two," said Pirate.

"Not much for me."

"Just a dainty splash."

He handed her a glass. Their fingers touched. Her skin—the skin of the finger that had fingered him—felt hot. Was there a message in that? Pirate, not knowing, filed the fact away for some future use. And then came the perfect toast.

"Peace," he said, towering over her. They clinked glasses. She took a sip, her eyes shifting for a moment, as though she'd had some thought, or maybe didn't like the taste. Pirate sat in a chair angled toward her, four or five feet away.

She put down her glass, faced him. "I realize there's nothing I can say to make up for what you've been through," she said.

"Say or do," said Pirate.

She flinched. That was nice. "You're right," she said. "Nothing I could say or do. But for my own sake, then, I want you to know how sorry I am and that I never meant to do you any harm."

Pirate took a slug of Kahlúa, settled things down inside. "Sorry I get," he said. "Run that no-harm part by me one more time."

She nodded. A woman from another world, a finer one: Pirate could see that. And guess what. Norah had the same quality, Norah the daughter. This was getting interesting. What did Momma know? Probably nothing; in fact, unless Nell said something about Norah in the next minute or two, a sure thing. That made Norah one of those eight-hundred-pound gorillas in the room. Pirate tried to stop himself from rubbing his hands together, and almost did.

"I meant harm for the real killer, of course," Nell was saying. "But I made my identification in good faith."

"Faith?" Wasn't he the expert in that area? Also, except for that fineness, he couldn't see much resemblance between mother and daughter. Were they trying to pull something? Pirate was ready for that, ready for anything. He smiled a friendly, misleading smile.

"Meaning," she said, "I really thought the killer looked like you. I know now I made a terrible mistake."

"Looked like me how?" said Pirate.

"Do those details matter now?" Nell said. "I've already admitted I was wrong."

"Looked like me how?"

She flinched again, not as much this time, less fun for him. He began to decide he didn't like her. Hey! How funny was that? Because of course he hated her guts. Correction: would have hated her guts, if he hadn't come to peace with life.

"It was the shape of the face," Nell said. "And mostly the eyes."

"The eyes?" He turned his head so just the patch was visible from where she sat.

Her voice fell, real quiet now. "They were pale blue," she said. "Like yours."

"Like mine?" Pirate said. He raised the patch, gave her a real good look.

Silence.

And then came a voice, an angry, heavenly voice that spoke through him. "My power lives in this secret place." The voice of God, no question. Pirate felt like a giant.

He lowered the patch, turned so he could see her. She was crying—silent crying, but with tears rolling right down her face in two silvery tracks. He watched. For a few moments he felt pretty good, but then it wore off. He rose, got the Kahlúa bottle, topped her up, offered the glass.

"Enough of that," he said. "Drink up."

She took the drink, this time knocking back a real grown-up snoutful. What else could he get her to do? But that was a nasty thought, not him at all. He clinked her glass again, again said, "Peace."

She nodded, found some tissue in her pocket, wiped her face. "I'm sorry," she said, squaring her shoulders, pulling herself together. "This is unforgivable."

Sending an innocent man up to Central State for twenty years? Is that what she meant by unforgivable? Or something else? All at once Pirate was tempted by three magic words: *I forgive you.* Wow. The power of words; maybe they were wasted most of the time, but now this, a chance to wield them like . . . like God. The catbird seat! Pirate came close to saying the magic words, if for no other reason than to feel like God. Then, at the last second, he remembered from Job what God was really like, not the kind of guy for making nice right from the get-go, more the kind of guy for drawing things out. For example, if God knew about the eight-hundred-pound gorilla in the room, would He be spilling the beans, tidying up everybody's lives? No way. So Pirate kept the magic words to himself, just sat back and watched her get herself all groomed and composed, the way she'd been before this visit. She came pretty close, but still looked a little different. Would it be cool if she never got all the way back? This—thinking like God—was giving him a nice rush. He refilled his glass.

"Funny about the hurricane," he said.

She sat with her hands in her lap, folded around the tissue. "What do you mean?"

"You know." Another God-like line: he was getting good.

"The way it did so much damage but also helped you?" she said.

"Couldn't have put it better myself." Although actually he could have: *The great rain of his strength.*

"I've been thinking a lot about that," she said.

"Yeah?" Pirate was surprised.

She met his gaze. For a moment, he was sure that the waterworks were starting up again, but they did not. "The way something good managed to come out of the storm," she said.

"Something good?" he said. "Me getting out?"

She nodded, and as she did, seemed to notice his feet. Pirate realized he was still in bare feet; he had really big ones. And he'd picked up a case of nail fungus, thick and yellow, like all the lifers. She squared her shoulders again.

"Yes, you getting out. That was good. You're innocent."

Was there just a trace of question mark at the end of that sentence? If so, he let it hang there. Did he need to prove anything to anybody? Four hundred and thirty-two grand did all the talking necessary.

She rose, walked over to the window, looked out. It was nice watching her move. "What I'm trying to do now," she said, "is figure out how it happened."

Pirate knew the answer to that, had it on good authority, straight from the mouth of that potbellied cop: frame job. But more fun to let her work it out for herself. Unless . . . unless she already knew, was in fact in on the frame job, a key player, and all this chitchat was part of some game.

Pirate thought of the tiny weapon. "And?" he said. "What you got figured out so far?"

"Not much." She turned to him. "Were all of these people strangers to you before the murder?"

"What people?"

"The ones involved—Bobby Rice, Johnny Blanton, my husband."

"Which one doesn't belong?"

"I don't know what you mean."

"Murder victim's on your list," Pirate said. "Asking me if I knew him makes me wonder where you're going with that."

"I'm just trying to see how the investigation went wrong."

"Like maybe they thought I had some grudge?" Pirate said. "A motive?"

"Exactly."

Pirate took another drink. "Blind alley," he said. "Complete strangers, all three of them. Next question?"

"But you had a—you'd had legal problems before," she said.

"So?"

"Maybe those legal problems brought you into contact with my . . . with the detectives."

"Nope," he said. "How about you?"

"Me?"

"Yeah you. Any chance of you being acquainted with a detective or two, back in the day?"

"What are you saying?"

"Motive works both ways." He was cookin', simply on fire. In case she'd missed anything, he hammered it home. "What goes around comes around."

"Are you suggesting it wasn't a mistake?" she said, her voice rising in a way that grated on him. "That I did it deliberately?"

"In cahoots," said Pirate. In the beginning was the word, right? So God always had the right ones at hand.

"But I just told you," she said, her eyes filling up again in a gratifying way. "There was nothing deliberate. I made a mistake, the worst mistake of my life. You've got to understand that."

Oh? He was on the receiving end of some order? Weren't twenty years of that enough? When was it his turn to dish it out? All at once the expression on her face changed and she stepped back, as though frightened. Had some look shown on *his* face? He gave her a smile, a real big one, and said, "Mind excusin' me for a second?"

Pirate went through his bedroom, into the bathroom, splashed cold water on his face; a face, as he saw in the mirror, not particularly scary, more like a kindly buccaneer. So her reaction pissed him off even more. And at that moment, pissed off even more, he remembered one of the most important bits of God's wisdom in the whole Bible, maybe the king of them all: *An eye for an eye.*

How perfect was that? His heart started pounding. He shook with the force of the idea, his image blurring in the mirror. Pirate lowered his head, drank from the tap, calmed himself. Then he returned to the sitting room, pausing by his bed for just a moment to retrieve the tiny weapon from under the mattress and drop it in his pocket.

She was sitting on the sofa again, hands folded, composed—*mine enemy*. God had delivered her into his hands.

"Hey," he said, "how's it goin'?"

She blinked.

"Hungry?" he said. "I've got Twizzlers."

"No thanks."

"Jujubes?"

"I'm really not hungry." She rose, approached him, stopped within arm's reach. "I've realized something today," she said.

"Oh?"

"Up until coming here, I didn't want to find out who the killer was," she said, "wanted to leave it all behind. Now I know we'll never have peace that way."

"Who's we?" said Pirate. "I'm at peace."

"You are?" she said, gazing up at him.

"Hundred percent," said Pirate, focusing on her right eye, a light brown eye with tiny gold flecks, almost like a gem. He felt some shaking coming on, went to the window. Down below, the Indian woman with the tits was waiting at the bus stop again. All kinds of thoughts swirled through his head, fighting for attention. If she couldn't pick up his heartbeat now, there was something wrong with her hearing.

But maybe there was something wrong with his, because he didn't hear her approaching from behind until it was too late. She laid a soft hand on his shoulder, just a touch, light and gone. Pirate jumped, spun around, reaching into his pocket. How had that happened? His hearing, since that long-ago run-in with Esteban Malvi, had been amazing, practically superhuman. Was he losing his edge, here on the outside?

"Sorry," she said, backing away. "I didn't mean to startle you. But if you're really at peace, I'm grateful, that's all."

"You doubt my word?" he said, getting a grip on the tiny weapon.

"No, no, not at all," she said. "It would just be so . . . so rare for anyone to feel like that."

Rare? Interesting.

"That's all I have to say," she said. "I won't take any more of your time."

"Getting on back to hubby and kids?" he said, but not with total concentration, his mind still stuck on the rarity idea.

"I don't have any kids," she said.

"Say what?"

She said it again.

Wow. Things were not what they seemed. Of course she had a kid, his new pal, Norah. On one hand, there was justice, an eye for an eye. On the other hand was mystery. Did he care about getting to the bottom of things, about the truth? Kind of. Besides, justice had to be meted out in the right way, a way that let him hold on to freedom and the four three two. And then there was the example from above: drag things out, especially ordeals.

"But you've got a husband."

"You know that."

"I surely do." And then came yet one more great idea, out of the blue. "I'd like you to be at peace, too," he said, trying to imitate that reverend's wimpy voice, Proctor, or whatever the hell his name was.

It worked. He could see it on her face: she was moved by his goodness, his turning the other cheek, or maybe not quite that, but something Jesus-like.

"And I'm with you on one thing," he said, setting it up so well: "You won't be at peace until you get to the bottom of things."

She was watching, concentrating so hard he could almost feel her mind.

"So maybe there's something you should know." He went to the window, glanced out, just to get the timing right. The Indian woman was gone.

"What should I know?"

She couldn't hold back; he was getting good at the dragging-it-out thing. Pirate turned to her. "First, I better make sure of the facts," he said. "Your husband was the white detective?"

"Yes."

"Okay," he said, then took a deep breath, like a guy struggling with something. "Only saw him the one time, down in the cell. Just the two of us. He said, 'Last chance to confess.' 'Why'd I want to do that?' I said. He said, 'Because this witness is going to sink you, my man.' 'Course I didn't confess, but on the way out he said one last thing."

"What was that?"

"'And when you're locked up I hope she'll be grateful. She's one hot babe.'"

Nell went white. It wasn't just an expression. The power of words: and not just words but all this speechifying, out of nowhere, so real-sounding. Losing his edge? No way. He was smokin'.

From his side window, Pirate watched her walking across the parking lot. Her tits didn't stick out like the Indian woman's, but they weren't bad. He thought of another use for the tiny weapon, and got a little mixed up.

CHAPTER 23

W as it possible?

Nell crossed the parking lot at the Ambassador Suites. She felt sick—hot and nauseated, as though coming down with something, a one-two punch. Punch number one: the brown-eyed vision at Dr. Pastore's office, eyes of the murderer. Punch number two: *I hope she'll be grateful.* Only hearsay, that long-ago wish, she reminded and reminded herself, and maybe not even hearsay, maybe simply an outright lie. But why would DuPree invent something like that? Was he even capable of it, clever enough? DuPree didn't seem especially clever, was in fact a little plodding, moving from one cliché to another, if that wasn't too harsh. Did that mean she should trust him? No. Despite her guilt—like a clamp around her heart—despite his suffering, Nell still recognized that there was something scary about him. The way he'd raised his eye patch—that was scary, and so were his feet. Where was the fairness in that? What could he do about his feet or his missing eye? But just as the image of those huge feet with the diseased nails rose in her mind, she stepped between the Ambassador Suites and its garage, and a hot breeze caught her full face, the first hot breeze of the year, and heavy with Bernardine stink. It combined with the already curdling Kahlúa inside her, and the next moment Nell was bent double, vomiting on the pavement. Her insides emptied out, and there was nothing she could do about it.

Nell straightened, hurried to her car, flung open the door. Breathless, out of air: she could have been back on the reef at Little Parrot Cay, trapped this time not under the collapsed coral shelf, but under a rubble of possibilities. Was it possible that Clay had killed Johnny? And more, was it possible that she herself was the motive? Had she ever seen Clay before the night of the murder? Had he seen her? Was her whole marriage a delusion? Nell stood in the parking lot, paralyzed. But how crazy, this motive, she told herself. She was no great beauty, no great anything, couldn't be the object of an obsession with such destructive power, the power to sink a knife through flesh and bone. But much more important, she knew her own husb—

"Mrs. Jarreau?"

Nell swung around, saw a skinny uniformed cop coming toward her, a cup of coffee in his hand; his face was young, familiar. "Timmy?" she said.

"Yes, ma'am." He looked worried, a single horizontal line appearing on his smooth forehead. "Everything all right?"

Oh, God—had he witnessed her little episode? "Yes," she said. "I'm fine."

"Just on my break," he said, gesturing toward his cruiser, a few cars away. He rocked back and forth on the balls of his feet, awkward. "We get breaks," he said. "It's a real good job, ma'am." More rocking back and forth. "That little Miata get fixed up okay?"

"Yes, thanks."

"And, um, your daughter?"

"She's fine. Thanks for all your help."

"Oh, I didn't do nothin', only . . ." Timmy looked down. "Just glad no charges—just glad it all ended good."

Nell got in her car. Timmy closed the door for her, tapped the roof. She drove home.

* * *

The phone was ringing as she walked in. Things were speeding up, and downtime, time she badly needed for thinking, for sorting things out, was shrinking, the events of her life bumping up against one another. Johnny had once talked about that, maybe in the context of Einstein. *Could use you now, Johnny.* She picked up the phone.

"Hi," said Lee Ann. "Quick question. How—"

Nell interrupted. "I'm not answering any more questions."

"Why not?" And then quickly: "Has something happened?"

"Lee Ann, you missed the point. I don't have to answer your questions."

A moment of silence, and then Lee Ann said, "This one isn't even about you."

Despite everything, Nell almost laughed; Lee Ann was irresistible. "Go on," she said.

"How well do you know Velma Rice?"

"How is that not about me?" Nell said. "And her name's not Velma."

Nell heard the rustle of paper, Lee Ann searching through her notes. "Bobby's widow's not Velma?" she said.

"Veronica," said Nell.

"Christ," said Lee Ann, "my editor's such a moron. Why is he incapable of the simplest—" She cut herself off. "The problem is Veronica Rice doesn't seem to be returning my calls."

"So?"

"So I was hoping maybe a word from you might encourage her."

"I haven't seen Veronica since Bobby's funeral," Nell said. "And I never really knew her that well."

"How's that possible?" said Lee Ann. "He and Clay were partners."

True, but the men had grown apart after Clay started getting promoted. Was any of that Lee Ann's business? "I'm just telling you I didn't know her well," Nell said. "Believe what you want."

"Sorry," Lee Ann said. "Didn't mean to upset you."

"You didn't upset me." Silence. And in the silence, Nell thought of the obvious question. "Why do you want to talk to her in the first place?"

"The tape was found in Bobby's locker," Lee Ann said. "How did it get there? Did he ever speak to Veronica about it? What does she think happened? And a thousand other questions I'm sure you could come up with on your—hang on a sec; got to take this call."

Nell clicked off. She heard a sound somewhere above, as though a small animal was running across the roof.

"Norah?"

Nell went upstairs, looked in Norah's room. No Norah. The stuffed monkeys swung gently on their trapeze.

Downstairs, Nell found Ines's number on her phone and dialed it.

"Hey, this is Ines. Leave a message, I'll get back." The recording had captured what sounded like a party going on in the background. Nell even thought she heard Norah's laugh. She was dialing the number again, just to be sure, when the front door burst open.

Clay strode in, saw her; he stopped, almost swaying forward from the force of his momentum.

"Clay," she said. "What's wrong?"

"Nothing," he said. She could see the vein throbbing in the side of his neck, like an agitated blue worm. "Why would anything be wrong?"

Nell stood there in the front hall, everything around her so familiar, except the expression on Clay's face, and the tone of his voice.

"Answer me," he said. "Why the hell would anything be wrong?"

"Something is, clearly," she said. "Tell me."

"Things are peachy," he said; this sort of heavy sarcasm didn't suit him it all, as though a crude ventriloquist had taken over his speech. "I'm having a fine, fine day. How about you?"

"Clay. What is it?"

"I asked you a question," he said, "one of those married-couple basic questions." He smiled, a smile that had a friendly shape but nothing else: "How's your day going?"

"I don't know," she said. "Not well, I guess, seeing you like this."

"My apologies," Clay said. "Anything else happen, besides me pissing you off?"

Nell tasted a bitter, coffee taste in her mouth. "Nothing much."

The smile stayed on his face. "Things'll be better when the museum opens, give you something to do."

"Yes," she said, a new little disturbance—did he see her now as some kind of bored housewife?—trailing in the wake of all the big ones.

"So you've just been hanging around the house all day?"

"Pretty much."

"Pretty much," he said. "Pretty much, would you say, or totally?"

"I don't understand what you're getting at." But she understood perfectly, and also felt what was coming, like a storm on the way.

"I'll try to be more clear," he said. "Remember Timmy? The rookie? Looks about ten years old?"

"Of course."

"Of course, huh? So I'm making myself clear at last. What do you think of him?"

"You're asking what I think of Timmy?"

"Yeah. The kid who helped out with Norah, kept her name off the sheet for you—what's your take on him?"

"For me? That was just for me, keeping her name off the sheet?"

"Now you're going to start lying to yourself?" he said. "Who else was it for? Think it did *her* any good?"

He was right—the cover-up of Norah's accident was her

doing, and maybe letting Norah suffer the consequences would have been better. But *lying to yourself:* that infuriated her, and she pushed on. "You want to talk about lying?" she said. She'd never spoken to him like this in their whole marriage—nor he to her—yet now this crude dialogue was flowing on both sides with an ease any outsider might have thought habitual. Nell felt self-disgust, but couldn't stop; something horrible was in the air.

"Yeah, let's," said Clay. And she knew that he couldn't stop either. "Let's talk about lying. Where were you today?"

"How can you speak to me this way?" she said. "Like you're interrogating some criminal?"

"It's easy. You're acting like one."

"I'm acting like one?" Her voice rose, carrying her away. "Why don't you try explaining—"

The phone rang. They both turned to it. Three rings, and on the fourth the answering machine picked up. Lee Ann spoke, her voice loud and clear in the front hall. "Nell," she said. "Still there? Had to take that call. And guess who it was? The man of the hour. Changed your mind about meeting him, it seems—he mentioned your visit to the Ambassador Suites. I wish you'd told me. Going to pick up now? There's more and more to talk about all the time . . . No?" *Click.*

Nell turned to Clay. All at once he didn't look angry; colder now, more impassive, almost withdrawn. "What are you doing?" he said. "Or do you even know?"

"I apologized to him," she said. "It was the right thing to do."

"Then why hide it from me?"

"Because I didn't want this—what's happening now."

"That's not good enough."

"No?" Her voice began to shake. "Then how's this, since you're so good at seeing through me? You manipulated my statement, got me to accuse an innocent man and send him away for life. And I want to know why. Is that good enough?"

The shakiness jumped the space between them, infected his body. He came toward her, his right hand rising slowly, and shaking most of all. "Don't you ever say that again."

"That you manipulated me?" she said. "Or that I want to know why?"

He didn't come any closer. His gaze went to his hand. He lowered it; the effort seemed to take a lot of strength. "Don't you do it," he said, his voice growing softer. "This has to stop."

"Stop? I'll never stop wanting to know why," Nell said. Then a question burst out of her, uncontainable at that moment, the biggest question of all. "Where were you when Johnny got killed?"

Clay moved, so fast Nell didn't have a chance to dodge him or protect herself in any way. All she saw was his fist— somehow strange and alien, like a new weapon designed by engineers—flying toward her face. But it halted, quivering in midair, inches away; and then dropped like a deadweight to Clay's side.

He backed away, actually stumbling—she'd never seen him stumble before, his movements always so smooth and athletic—but now he stumbled and almost fell, his face white and deformed by shock and disgust, disgust for them both, and other forces Nell couldn't identify. "We'd better not be together right now," he said, one hand on the wall, holding himself up. "I'll be at Duke's. If you need me."

He didn't slam the door, didn't even close it, just walked out and went away. Nell closed the door and sagged against it.

CHAPTER 24

This was nice, to play a little music in Joe Don's barn, way at the back of his old man's spread, to relax, to smoke some weed. Nothing wrong with smoking weed. Weed was natural, grew right out of God's own ground, had no other use, meaning smoking it was okay with Him. And the nicest part? To do all this with a young, female beauty close by. Norah—he could see her now, behind a tiny cloud of pot smoke, gauzy like one of those old black-and-white movie actresses—was a beauty, no doubt about it. More than that. There were other beauties around: Pirate knew that very well, had checked out the porn on his TV at the Ambassador Suites. Norah wasn't like that. She had this innocent thing about her. Hey! And he was innocent, too. They had something in common. He reached over to pass her the joint, but Joe Don, in mid-riff, intercepted it with his fretting hand.

"Good dope, huh?" said Joe Don, somehow continuing a *thudda-thudda-chunk-chunk* run too quick for Pirate to follow with his eye, a run that led to the chorus of this song Joe Don was working on:

> *Saw your face*
> *Down the hall*
> *Nothin' else*
> *Matters at all.*

Joe Don had a good voice, a bit like Marty Robbins', but deeper. Norah sang along, not doing a second part, just trying to hit the notes, which she mostly missed, but it didn't matter, her voice so whispery, almost not there at all. Joe Don played a little tag, came to a stop.

"And I used to hate country music," Norah said.

Joe Don started laughing. Pirate laughed, too. Joe Don leaned over and kissed Norah's cheek. Pirate stopped laughing.

"Maybe got a title for it," said Joe Don.

"Let me guess," Norah said. "'She Matters.'"

"Wow," said Joe Don. "Like that one, Alvin?"

"Cool," Pirate said.

"Better'n what I got," said Joe Don. "Almost."

"Almost?" Norah said, giving him a poke in the ribs. She and Joe Don sat on an old couch, dusty and threadbare. Pirate was on a worn footstool with cigarette burns through the leather. "What's yours?" she said.

"'Norah's Song,'" said Joe Don.

Norah gave him a look. He gave her a look back. For a moment, Pirate felt like a fifth wheel, a mixed-up feeling that threatened to swallow up all this fun. His fingers itched for the gold tassel, but his Bible was back in his room at the Ambassador Suites. He reached instead for the joint, burning unnoticed now in Joe Don's hand—had he overheard her saying something about the perfect shape of Joe Don's hands?—and took a deep drag. Ah, freedom, he thought to himself, but for some reason didn't feel free. "Ah, freedom." Too late, he realized he'd spoken aloud.

They both turned to him and smiled. "Must feel good, huh?" Joe Don said.

"Must," said Pirate.

They laughed, like he'd made a funny joke. Pirate joined in. They laughed and laughed, got a bit delirious, although maybe not Joe Don, who went and picked up the phone.

"Wreck on the interstate," he said, hanging up. "Back soon."

Pirate rose. "Maybe, uh, drop me off at the hotel."

"Hang here," said Joe Don. "Won't be long."

"Yeah?"

"Why not?" Joe Don glanced at Norah.

"Sure," said Norah.

"Okeydoke," Pirate said, sitting back down. "How about if I fool around some on the Rickenbacker while you're gone?"

Joe Don shook his head, like he really wanted to give the go-ahead but couldn't because of some iron rule. "Just this superstition I got, me and the instrument, one-on-one relationship, you know? But there's the Telecaster—no problem you using that."

"Cool," said Pirate.

"Turn it up to eleven," Joe Don said.

Norah laughed, but whatever the joke was Pirate didn't get it. Getting a little tired of not getting things? Oh, yeah—especially of not getting things he would have known if he'd spent the past twenty years on the outside. But payback was on the way, had already begun, and he was at peace.

"Turn it up to eleven," he repeated, adding a chuckle, if *chuckle* was the word for a quiet laugh that died abruptly away.

"Don't you love that movie?" Norah said.

Pirate had never heard of a movie called *Turn It Up to Eleven*. "One of my favorites," he said.

"Adios," said Joe Don, resting the Rick on its stand.

"What other movies do you like?" said Norah, a few moments later.

Movies. That was a tough one. Four o'clock Wednesday was movie time in the C-block lounge, but Pirate's mind had tended to wander during the showings and he seldom stayed till the end; except for *The Passion of the Christ*—that one stuck. "Lots of them," he said, "but I can never remember the names."

Norah took a hit off the joint. "I used to like movies about history," she said. Then came a long silence. Pirate started to get the squinting feeling in his non-eye, like one of those behind-the-scenes visions was on the way. Beyond the gauzy smoke, Norah's eyes looked damp. "*Shakespeare in Love*," she said. "*Master and Commander. The Last of the Mohicans.*"

Those had to be movies. "Yeah?" he said. "And then what happened?"

"What happened after *The Last of the Mohicans*?" she said. "There were no more Mohicans."

Norah started laughing, did the delirious thing again. Pirate tried to join in, but he didn't think it was funny, and besides, he'd asked a serious question, so this was pissing him off. After a while, the room got quiet. The behind-the-scenes vision came, and for a moment, he saw through the gauze, through the skin, down to the face of a girl about ten or eleven years old. Just a glimpse; and then that squinting pressure let up and normality returned.

"Hungry?" said Norah. "There's some salsa and chips."

Pirate wasn't hungry, but an idea came to him and he said, "Salsa and chips—sounds good."

She got up and went into the kitchen. Pirate was on his feet the next second, and a second after that he had the Rick in his hands. The chords to "You Win Again" went E, B7, E, A. He didn't plug in, just played them off-amp, real quiet, but they sounded so good on the Rick. Pirate knew he could always fork over the $995 for the Rickenbacker in the pawn-shop window—a hundredfold!—play "You Win Again" on any Rickenbacker in the world, pile Rickenbackers to the sky. He heard Norah coming and put the guitar back in the stand. The problem was Pirate wanted this one, Joe Don's.

She spoke behind him. "He's funny about the guitar."

"I didn't touch it," Pirate said, not turning.

Pause. Then she said, "I know. It's just one of those musician things."

Now he turned, gave her a nice smile. "No problemo," he said.

They scarfed up all the chips and salsa, maybe in a minute or two. *Your mom wouldn't even eat a Twizzler with me.* Pirate came close to saying that—Norah was so much easier to be with than her mother—but decided against it for no real reason, just instinct.

"Good salsa," he said. "And chips."

She nodded. Her eyes had an inward look.

"History movies," he said.

"What about them?"

"How come they're your favorites?"

"I said they used to be. Because history was always my favorite subject. I loved imagining the past."

"Like *The Passion of the Christ*?"

"Didn't see that one," Norah said. "Too gory for me."

How did she know if she hadn't seen it? Plus Pirate hadn't found it particularly gory. But he just said, "Yeah, too gory."

"I don't like the sight of blood," she said.

"No?" said Pirate. He remembered blood spurting from the neck of some dude who'd pissed off the Ocho Cincos: like a tiny red fountain, actually a pretty sight if you could have taken a picture of just that part. Hey! An interesting observation. Was it worth passing on? Why not? "I was just—" he began, but she interrupted.

"I know what you're going to say," she said.

"Yeah?" How was that possible? She'd never done time, never been involved with anything violent.

"You're going to say how come I used to like history but don't anymore."

The furthest thing from his mind: How would he have known something like that? "So?" he said. "How come?"

"Because," she said, "the past turns out to be horrible. Twisted and horrible."

"Tell me something I don't know."

"Exactly! That's it exactly, so messed up. The innocent goes to jail, the guilty goes free and my father . . ." Her face got all out of shape—actually looked ugly, which he wouldn't have thought possible—like the waterworks were about to open up, but it didn't and her face smoothed back out. "What happens to him?"

"He got killed?" Pirate knew that for a fact, the big fact that started this real bad ball rolling, but he said it like a question—her line of talk was getting a little strange, confusing him.

"Yeah," she said. "It's like a fucked-up triangle."

That one went over his head. He reached into the chips bowl, foraged for the last crumbs.

"Have you ever seen his grave?" she said.

How would that have happened? "Nope," he said.

"Would you like to?"

Not really. What Pirate wanted to do was try out the Rickenbacker with the amp on and no one hassling him. He was about to say, *Rain check,* but then thought—maybe some fresh air might be good. And piggybacking on that: "Can I drive?"

"Sure," said Norah. "Why not?" The ten-year-old's answer, no boring complications about license, insurance, vision: Pirate was feeling ahead of the game; that was new.

It's like riding a bicycle," Pirate said, top down, wind in what was left of his hair, needle touching seventy. And he could see just fine, except for the lane where his nose got in the way. "You know what I mean? The way you never forget."

"Yeah," said Norah. "Um, this is a forty zone."

A forty zone? For a moment he didn't understand what she meant. Then he got it and reached for the shift to gear down, only it was an automatic, which he already knew but remembered too late. There was a high-pitched revving shriek as he shifted into N, his left foot pressing down through clutch-less space. He banged the stick right back into D, braked smoothly, drove the rest of the way without incident, but the fun—feeling young, rag top, open road—was gone. Not his fault: he blamed Norah. She'd gone grown-up on him; he preferred the ten-year-old version.

Johnny Blanton was buried in a cemetery on high ground on the north side of Belle Ville, near the county line. He had a white stone marker with his name and dates, not as big as the stone markers on either side.

"We should have brought flowers," Norah said.

Pirate glanced around, saw a bouquet of flowers lying on a nearby grave. He went and got them, handed them to Norah.

"Thanks," she said. She smelled the flowers—Pirate liked the way her nostrils flared—and leaned them against the stone. "Half of my DNA is his," she said.

"Yeah?"

"You'd think if half of someone's DNA was in you, you'd know them, just automatically. But I don't know him."

Pirate gazed up at the sky. Clear blue. The air was warm, the breeze soft; he heard birds chirping somewhere far away. This was nice.

"I've tried to get to know him from his writing," Norah was saying. Or something like that. She was talking too much. Why couldn't she just enjoy the day? And now she was watching him, maybe waiting for some reply.

"He was a writer?" Pirate said.

She shook her head. "A scientist. You didn't know that?"

Huh? Why should he know that? Why should he know anything about this guy? He, Pirate, was the victim. "Nope," he said.

"A brilliant scientist," Norah said. "He would have been famous. But all his writing is so technical—I really can't get a sense of him at all."

"What about old pictures?" Pirate said; he didn't want to encourage this discussion but it was an obvious idea.

"That turned out to be a problem."

"Oh? Too bad." He was ready to get back behind the wheel, but Norah didn't seem to be in any hurry. She stood there, lost in thought. More to break the spell than anything else, Pirate tossed out another idea. "How about asking your mom about him?"

"I used to," Norah said. "Now that's a problem, too."

Christ. "How come?"

Norah turned to him. "It's this whole *Hamlet* thing."

Hamlet thing. That meant Shakespeare. Pirate had never read Shakespeare, but she'd been talking about him, back at Joe Don's barn, something about . . . movies, that was it.

"You're talking about the movie?"

"No," she said, "just the plot."

Pirate didn't know the plot of *Hamlet,* kept his mouth shut.

"Specifically, the central problem Hamlet has," Norah said.

"The central one, huh?"

She nodded. "Whether to believe the ghost or not."

"There's a ghost in it?" *Hamlet* was starting to sound not bad.

She glanced at him. He read her look, easy to read, right out in the open: she was getting hit by the fact that he knew squat about *Hamlet,* and seeing him different. Pirate felt the presence of the tiny weapon, even though it was back at the Ambassador Suites, under the mattress.

She smiled, a soft, friendly smile, but not enough for him to forgive her. "The ghost of Hamlet's father says he was killed by the uncle, who takes the wife and the crown. Hamlet doesn't know whether to believe the ghost. He keeps agonizing and agonizing."

"And did he do it, the uncle?"

"Yes."

"How?"

She closed her eyes, thought. "I don't remember."

How was that possible? "Stabbed him, maybe?" Pirate said.

"I don't think so." Her eyes opened. They were red, maybe from the weed, maybe from being upset; it was her father's grave, after all, and she was the emotional type. "There is a sword fight, at the end," she said. "By that time Hamlet knows his uncle is guilty, but it's too late."

The story was getting hard to follow. "Why are we talking about this, again?" he said.

"Because of you," she said.

"Me?"

"The fact that you didn't do it means someone else did."

That again. The mother had made the same point, or close to it. She'd also denied having this daughter, having kids at all. Why? Any danger for her in him knowing? Not that Pirate could see. "Yeah," he said. "Someone else did it. Party or parties unknown."

"That's what brings up the *Hamlet* problem."

"How?"

"My grandfather put the idea in my head, all about the killer ending up with the widow."

"You've got a grandfather?"

"Two. I'm talking about my dad's dad. He lives in New Orleans, but I never saw him, growing up."

"No?"

"Until last semester. And you know what he told me—and this was before the tape and everything? He said he didn't think the right man was in jail."

"Sounds like a cool guy," Pirate said.

"But that wasn't the most horrible part."

"No?"

"The most horrible part was who he thought did it."

Was that the most horrible part? Far from it, but now Pirate was curious. "And who's that?"

Tears came, silent ones, just like her mom's. "He always treated me so well, brought me up as his own daughter. I can't believe he'd do something so awful. And why? There's no reason." Norah's face twisted up in that ugly way.

Pirate realized who she was talking about. Everything clicked into place. He already had a perfect story for this moment, had used it once already to great effect.

"There was this thing that happened down in the cell," he said. "Way back when. Just the two of us, detective and me. He said, 'Last chance to confess.'"

And Pirate told his little tale; he had it down pat. The response? Socko, one more time. Tears rolled down, silent, in two silvery tracks. It must have been in her DNA.

CHAPTER 25

N ell?"
      "Yes?" A woman, black and educated, but Nell didn't recognize the voice.

"Veronica Rice."

"Yes. Hi, Veronica."

"I'd like to talk to you for a few minutes."

"Sure," said Nell. "Go ahead."

"If it wouldn't be too much trouble and all, I was hoping we could make it in person."

"All right. You know where I live?"

"I do, and thanks," said Veronica. Pause; and after it, she sounded a little uncomfortable. "But is there any chance you could come here? I'll have some time at practice."

"I thought you'd retired," Nell said, realizing Veronica didn't want to come to the house and wondering why. Some racial thing? Not possible.

"I unretired," said Veronica. "There's been some delay with Bobby's pension."

Veronica Rice taught history at East Middle School, and also coached softball. Nell found her sitting in the bottom row of the bleachers, watching the girls warm up, clipboard in hand. Veronica patted the bench beside her. Nell sat down.

"Thanks for riding over," Veronica said.

"Not at all."

"You're looking well."

That was a lie: Nell had checked herself in the mirror before leaving. "You, too," she said. Also a bit of a lie: Veronica had lost some weight, but she was one of those powerfully built women who actually looked worse when that happened, no longer quite themselves; and her broad face was ashy, as though she hadn't been sleeping.

"I'm sorry to hear about Bobby's pension," Nell said.

Veronica shook her head, a small, hopeless movement. "The medal came prompt enough," she said.

"What's the holdup, if you don't mind me asking?" Nell said. Was that why Veronica wanted this meeting, to speed up the pension?

Veronica turned to her, gave her a close look. "Don't mind at all," she said. "Always considered you a friend."

"I'm glad."

Veronica glanced out at the field. "Follow through, Aliyah," she yelled. "And turn your body, child." She lowered her voice. "It's some paperwork problem," she said. "Records got destroyed in the . . ." Veronica bit her lip. ". . . in the flood. All the vacation days, sick days, overtime cards—gone. But everybody knows Bobby was with the department for twenty-seven years, common knowledge. The storm took away some people's good sense."

"That's not all it did."

Veronica gazed at her. For a moment, Nell thought she was angry. But Veronica's face was hard to read, at least for Nell, because she smiled and said, "Amen." The smile faded. "Never gave you proper thanks for coming to the funeral."

"Of course I—we came." Bobby's church, Fourth Street Baptist in Lower Town, had still been half underwater at the time of the funeral, which ended up at a small chapel in Stonewall County, the walls lined with blown-up photos of Bobby, including that last one—balanced on a rooftop, passing a baby to a man in a dinghy—taken seconds before something gave way beneath him. It took divers more than a day to find his body in all the rubble.

"Now there's this reporter wants to talk to me," Veronica said. "Ms. Bonner. Claims she's a friend of yours."

"That's true," Nell said. "But she's a reporter first."

"Uh-huh," Veronica said. And then, louder: "Butt down, girl, butt down on grounders." She shook her head, turned to Nell. "No excuse for a grounder going through your legs, not never. Ms. Bonner wants to talk to me about the tape."

"I thought so."

"What did you tell her about it?"

"The tape?" Nell said. "I don't know anything about the tape."

"Your husband never made mention of it?"

"No. Did yours?"

Veronica's eyes were expressionless but she nodded, very slightly. "Talking to Ms. Bonner don't feel right," she said. "Bobby never trusted the press." There was a long silence. Nell forced herself to be still, keep her mouth shut, but her heart was beating faster and faster. "On the other hand, the tape turning up in Bobby's locker, how it might look, that don't feel right neither."

More silence. When Nell couldn't endure it another moment, she said, "Can you explain that last part?"

"Not much to explain," Veronica said. "Why would I go and feel right? No one likes when folks pass tales."

"What kind of tales?"

"You must have heard—tales about evidence that gets hidden, frame-ups, what all. Not saying that Bobby was a perfect man—ain't no man nor woman perfect on this earth—but he was straight up in his job, by the book."

"So is Clay." That just popped out, almost like a reflex from some dead creature poked in a biology lab.

"Uh-huh," said Veronica.

That *uh-huh:* two little syllables but they contained a powerful inertial force. Nell realized what should have been obvious from the start: their interests were not the same. "I think you know more than you're telling me, Veronica."

"Likewise," said Veronica. Maybe Veronica did consider her a friend, but at this point there was no sign of it in her eyes.

"I don't really know anything," Nell said. "I'm just trying to figure it all out."

"And let the chips fall wherever they may?" Veronica said.

Nell wasn't sure about that. She said nothing.

Veronica called out, "Three laps, team. Then we'll take BP." Groans rose from the field, but the girls started running, feet thudding softly on the turf. "Think Ms. Bonner has a theory 'bout all this?" Veronica said.

"I don't know," Nell said. "She's still gathering facts. With someone like Lee Ann, I think theories come later."

"Makes sense."

"Glad to hear you say that," said Nell. "Because that's what I'm doing, too, if there's anything you can tell me."

"Such as what?"

"Such as maybe Bobby said something to you about the tape."

Veronica gazed past her, expression unreadable.

"A long time ago," Nell added. "Just a hint, a suggestion. You might not have even understood it at the time. Maybe it's starting to make sense only now."

"And if we're discussing maybes," Veronica said, "maybe someone said something to you, too." Her eyes were on Nell now, and readable again; readable and unsettling.

"No," Nell said.

"No, just like that, no?" Veronica said. "Couldn't have been a suggestion in *your* case, a hint *you're* only understanding now?"

"There wasn't," Nell said. "I'd tell you."

"Yeah?" said Veronica. "Why?"

"Why? Because you'd deserve to know."

Veronica shook her head; the gesture had an ancient finality, as though it dated from the dawn of humanity. "What

a world that would be," she said. "But I was born in Belle
Ville. Family's all from around here, going way back. So I
understand how things work."

"What do you mean?" Nell said.

"Power structure," Veronica said. She rose, stepped onto
the field. "Can't help," she said. "Sorry, because I always
liked you, still do. But this is what I was fearing."

"What?" said Nell. "What were you fearing? What do you
think happened?"

But Veronica was no longer talking to her. She clapped
her hands. "Everybody in." She picked up a bat.

The Miata was parked in the driveway when Nell got home.
She found Norah in the kitchen, eating ice cream from the
carton. Nice to see her eating, so nice that Nell smothered
the urge to bring her a bowl from the cupboard: Norah
still looked much too thin. For a moment, in the quiet of
her kitchen, Nell thought, despite everything, that a happy
ending was possible.

"What kind is that?" Nell said.

"Good question," Norah said, turning the carton in her
hand, reading the label. "Macchiato Crunch. Want some?"

Nell had no appetite at all, but she said, "Sure," and fetched
a spoon. She sat beside Norah, dipped into the carton. A
stillness descended, as though time was making a brief stop,
lingering over a mother-and-daughter moment. "Mmm,"
Nell said. "Good."

"I like the crunch part," Norah said.

"Me, too."

"Crunch crunch," said Norah.

Nell gave her a quick glance, saw nothing abnormal.
"Been into town?" she said.

"Affirmative."

"How was it?"

"No complaints."

"Do anything interesting?"

"Just hung out."

"With?"

"Joe Don."

"How's he doing?"

"Good."

"Tell me a bit about him," Nell said. "What's he like?"

"Nice," Norah said. She tapped her spoon against her teeth, seemed lost in thought. "Real nice."

Nell smiled. "Go on."

Norah's eyes shifted toward her, then away. The sense of stillness disappeared, and tension rose in Norah's body, communicating itself to Nell. "Tell me something, Mom. Did you love my father?"

"Of course."

"More than your present husband?"

"My present husband?" Now the happy-ending feeling vanished, too. "Why do you call him—"

"Less?" said Norah. "The same?"

"I don't—"

"Come on, Mom—did you love him more, less or the same? It's easy—multiple choice." Norah's voice rose, high and thin, toward hysteria; and now Nell noticed how red her eyes were, like she'd been crying. She reached out, touched Norah's shoulder. Norah flinched away from her hand, jumped up.

"Norah, please. What's happening to you? What's going on?"

"You really don't know? Read *Hamlet*." Norah ran from the kitchen, banging the door closed.

Read *Hamlet*? What was she talking about? Nell went upstairs, knocked on Norah's door.

"Don't come in."

"I loved your father," Nell called through the door. "Of course I loved him. But comparing them—why is that so important to you?"

No response. This was unbearable. Nell turned the knob, pushed the door open. Norah was standing by the chest of drawers, throwing clothes in a suitcase.

"What are you doing?" Nell said.

"More, less, the same?" said Norah, not looking at her, camisole top, jeans, her cute little hat from Urban Outfitters, all missing the suitcase and spilling across the floor. "More, less, the same? More, less, the same?"

"Why do you want to know?" Nell said. "What difference does it make?"

Norah faced her. She was shaking. "How can you ask that? Are you stupid?"

Now Nell was shaking, too. "Out with it," she said. "Whatever's on your mind, out with it. This can't go on another moment."

"What's on my mind?" Norah said. "Who killed my father—that's what's on my mind. What's on yours?"

"The same thing," Nell said. "Of course, the same thing."

"And?" Norah said. "Any ideas?"

"I—" Nell's throat closed up; her body refused to let her name names.

"You're despicable," Norah said. She spun away, zipped up the suitcase, a silk sleeve hanging out, and strode toward the door.

"What are you doing?" Nell said. She stepped in front of Norah. Norah kept moving, bumped right into her.

"Now comes a mother-daughter fistfight?" Norah said.

Even the idea should have been unimaginable. Nell stepped aside. Norah passed by without further contact.

"Where are you going?" Nell called after her.

Already on the stairs, Norah said, "I'm not spending another night in this house."

A minute later, Nell heard the Miata starting up. What could she do? Norah was nineteen, an adult. Her family was walking out on her, one at a time. Nell was left alone in her daughter's room—alone and shaking—with the stuffed animals on the shelves, and the monkeys, swaying very slightly on the trapeze.

Plus all of Norah's high school books. It took her just a few moments to find *Hamlet*. She leafed through the pages, and soon came to:

> *Seems, madam! Nay, it is; I know not "seems."*
> *'Tis not alone my inky cloak, good mother.*

In the margin, Norah had written in red—tidy penmanship, the letters fat and somehow cheerful-looking: *What's up with Hamlet's mom?*

And below that, in some other student's spikier hand: *She's a whore.*

CHAPTER 26

N ight: a warm night with soft sounds in the air. Pirate, with his excellent hearing, didn't miss any of them—a woman's laugh, ice cubes in a glass, a passing plane, the kind that flew very high, on the way to Paris or Rio or some other place Pirate had never seen and had no desire to. He pressed record on Lee Ann's digital recorder, said, "Twice as much as before," and "she asses," and listened to the sound of his voice. Then he tried gazing down at the bus stop, hoping the Indian woman would show up, wearing something skimpy. She did not. No buses came. He got restless and went for a walk, ending up at the Red Rooster.

"Kahlúa," he said. "Rocks."

"Coming right up," said the waitress, a waitress he didn't know, not pretty, no tits, barely registering on his consciousness. Despite his wealth—he was rich!—and freedom, he wasn't in the best mood, which didn't make sense. He found himself thinking of what he'd be doing at this hour up at Central State: lying on his bunk, most likely, fingering the gold tassel, at peace. Pirate glanced at the empty stage. Music was what he needed.

"When's the band start?" he said to the waitress when she brought his drink.

"No band tonight," she said. "It's Tuesday."

"How come?"

"No band on Tuesdays."

His mood got a little worse. "Make it a double," he said.

She glanced at his glass, looked confused; no reason for that, and it pissed him off more. "Turn this one into a double?" she said. "I don't think we can do that."

"What can you do?"

"I could bring you another one," the waitress said.

"A double?"

"If that's what you want."

"I want," Pirate said.

He drank the single and the double. He stopped feeling pissed off, but the restlessness remained. Pirate went into the bathroom, splashed cold water on his face. There he was in the mirror: with the patch and now the earring, really looking like a pirate. He cheered up, paid his bill, leaving a big tip, and walked out of the Red Rooster, into the night.

Pirate headed nowhere particular, just wandered, a special kind of wandering that led him in the direction of Joe Don's place. Too far to walk, of course, unless you had time, and he had lots. So what if he got there in the middle of the night? He wouldn't disturb anyone. The barn where Joe Don lived had a window at the back. He could just peek in. Would Norah be there? A possibility. Maybe they'd be sleeping. He could watch over them, like a guardian angel. Pirate liked that idea a lot. He was starting to pick up the pace when a car pulled over to the sidewalk and crept along beside him.

Not a car, but a pickup; it came up on his good side, so Pirate didn't have to turn his head to see the passenger window sliding down. He heard a man's voice: "Get in."

The voice: slightly familiar but Pirate couldn't place it. And the tiny weapon? Under the mattress. At that moment, he and the pickup entered the cone of light under a streetlamp. Pirate, still walking, not slowing down, peered through the open window and got a good look at the driver. Slightly familiar, all right: former detective, now chief of the Belle Ville police, dressed like any normal guy in jeans and T-shirt.

"Don't think so," Pirate said, and he kept moving.

"Thinking's not your strong suit," the chief said.

A coplike thing to say. Pirate had never liked cops, not even before the whole—uh-oh. Something gleamed inside the pickup. Pirate spotted an automatic, held loosely in the chief's left hand, half resting on his leg and pointed in Pirate's general direction. Would anyone really think he could shoot a man down out in the open like this and get away with it? Yeah, this guy, this particular cop. Didn't Pirate pretty much know that for a fact? He didn't take another step. The car stopped. He got in. The window slid up. The door locks clicked shut. The pickup rolled forward, gained speed, turned a corner and entered a dark street, with nothing but rubble piles from the hurricane on both sides.

"We need to talk," the chief said.

"What about?"

"Your plans."

"Got none," Pirate said. "Be at peace, that's all."

"Save that line for someone else." Did the automatic twitch in the chief's hand? Pirate thought so. He kept his mouth shut. The chief drove to the end of the street, circled an earthmover with tires as tall as a man and stopped at the edge of some water—black and still, maybe the canal. Pirate glanced around—canal on one side, earthmover on the other: invisible. The chief lowered the windows, switched off the engine. It got quiet. Pirate heard tiny lapping sounds from the canal. How deep was the water? Pirate couldn't swim.

The chief shifted a little, facing him. "Your plans," he said.

"Nothing special," Pirate said. "Relax. Do some writing."

A muscle moved in the chief's face, casting a shadow on his skin. "What kind of writing?"

Maybe not a good idea, bringing up the writing. But what if the chief already knew about this project with Lee Ann? Some inmates up at Central State bought into that old idea that cops never asked a question they didn't know the answer to; not Pirate. On the other hand, there was such a thing as getting too cute. Pirate went back and forth in his mind. And then: "Songwriting," he said. Came to him out of the blue, so sweet.

"Done much songwriting?"

"Workin' on one now, matter of fact," said Pirate. "'Saw your face down the hall, nothin' else matters at all.' That one's called—" Whoa, boy: "Norah's Song." "Doesn't have a name yet."

"So your plan is to make it in the music business?" the chief said.

"Yeah," said Pirate; that hadn't been his plan, exactly, but why not?

"Not much of a music industry here in Belle Ville," the chief said.

"Nope."

"Leading to the obvious question."

"What's that?"

"Where are you going to go? Nashville? L.A.?"

Pirate shrugged. "I kind of like it here."

The chief's hand tightened on the gun. Pirate smelled an oily smell, rising off the canal. He could end up down on the bottom, and no one would ever know.

"Again, the thinking problem," the chief said.

"No?" said Pirate. "I don't like it here?" And at that moment, the moment of the thinking-problem accusation, Pirate remembered Lee Ann's digital recorder, the one for recording anything that fleshed out the story. He felt its little presence in the right-hand front pocket of his pants. Sticking his hand in the pocket: out of the question, of course, but how about just casually sliding a finger over the material like so, maybe feeling that tiny record button? Yes. He pressed down.

"This isn't the best place for you," the chief said.

"How come?"

The chief gazed at him, his eyes just two pockets of shadow. "Belle Ville's not your lucky town," he said. "That should be clear by now."

"I'm at peace with it," Pirate said, remembering, too late,

about saving that line for someone else. Then, at the same instant as that memory coming too late, the automatic was in his ear, the muzzle pushing up inside, hurting him.

The chief spoke, his voice soft, asked a question as though really interested in the answer. "What did I tell you?"

"Save that line for someone else."

The chief nodded. "I've known a lot of ex-cons," he said. "Comes with the territory. You've got a big advantage over just about all of them. Know what that is?"

"I was innocent?"

The gun pressed in his ear, harder. Wrong answer —even though it seemed so right. Pirate couldn't think of another; probably safer not to try any wild guesses.

"You tell me," he said. "What's my advantage?"

"Did you grow up rich?" the chief said.

"No."

"Any reason to think you'd have been rich by now?"

There was: What if he'd actually hit the big time in Nashville or L.A.? But Pirate felt the rhythm of the conversation and fell in step. "No," he said.

"So how come you're so casual about four hundred grand?" the chief said.

"That's the answer," said Pirate. "I got money and they don't."

"Now you're talking," the chief said. A common expression: Pirate had heard it many times before, but always with the word *now* sounding the most important; the chief's way, *talking* came first. "Much better," he said, the gun pressure easing a bit, but still making him sick in the stomach, like an alien in his body. "Let's try the writing question again."

"The writing question?"

"What are these writing plans of yours?"

Pirate was about to run through the songwriting thing again, when he heard a click. This click sounded just like the cocking of a gun, but the chief hadn't done that. Instead he'd made the sound in his mouth, a crisp, metallic click. How come that was scarier?

"My story," Pirate said. "I was planning on writing a book about my story."

"Which is?"

"You know," said Pirate. Who'd know better? "What happened to me."

The gun slid out of his ear. An animal squealed somewhere on the far side of the canal. "Written any books?" the chief said.

Pirate shook his head. A simple movement but he was free to do it, no gun in his ear. Had to be a good sign, a sign that he was going to live.

"Then how are you going to go about it?" the chief said.

"Still working on that."

"Some people in your position might get a professional writer involved."

"Yeah?"

"A reporter, for example," the chief said. "Especially one who'd already been following the case."

"Hadn't thought of that," Pirate said.

"Any names come to mind?"

Did the chief already know about Lee Ann? Was his knowing necessarily a bad thing? Pirate couldn't figure out the answers to those questions. But sharing information with a cop? How could that ever be right? "Nope," Pirate said. "I'll handle it myself."

"Starting how?"

Pirate shifted in his seat. He wanted out, now. The gun was back on the chief's leg, loosely held. "Interviews, I guess," Pirate said.

"You're going to conduct some interviews?"

"Yeah."

"With who?"

"Not sure," Pirate said. "Maybe I'll make a list."

"Maybe," said the chief. The animal on the far side of the canal squealed again, a frightened sound abruptly cut off. Pirate's fingers itched for the gold tassel. He took a deep breath to calm himself. The night reeked.

"If we're all done here—" Pirate began.

"Shh," said the chief, his voice quiet, like he was shushing a baby. A long silence went by. Then something made a splash in the water. "Who'd be on this interview list?" the chief said.

"Don't know."

"How about me—would I be on it?"

"Wouldn't want to inconvenience you," Pirate said.

"No inconvenience," said the chief. "Want to interview me? How's right now?"

"I'm not, um, prepared," Pirate said.

"Don't be shy," the chief said. "What's the worst that can happen?"

Bullet in the head, oily water, going down. "Thanks for the offer," Pirate said. "How about a rain check?"

"Your call," said the chief. "But I'm pretty sure you've got to be more aggressive to make it in the writing game."

"I'll try," Pirate said.

The chief laughed. "This is a funny situation."

"Yeah?" Pirate's shirt was damp now, stuck to the seat back.

"Here I am telling you how to write your own book," the chief said. "When all along I'm perfectly aware that you're off to a flying start."

"I am?"

"Sure," said the chief. "Take your interview—that's what it was, I get it now—your interview with my wife."

"Interview with your wife?" said Pirate. "I don't know what you're—"

Pirate got surprised by the chief's quickness for the second time. Things came in the wrong order: first the pain across the left side of his face; then the blow itself from the heavy barrel, the sighting mechanism slicing through his skin; and finally the whoosh of air as the chief whipped the gun at him.

"Careful, now," the chief said.

Pirate's head filled with sound, like waves crashing on a

beach. He touched his face, felt blood and sweat, all sticky together.

"The interview," the chief said.

The tiny weapon: Would he leave it behind again? Never. But just the thought of it gave him strength. "You can call it an interview," he said. "But she came to me."

"And?"

Pirate shrugged. His head began to clear. "She was sorry about what happened. I told her not to worry about it."

The chief gazed at him, just those two black pits, same color as the canal. "How did you put that? The exact words."

"Just like I said—don't worry about it. I forgive you."

"You forgave her?"

"Why not? It was . . ." What was the phrase she'd used? "It was in good faith."

"What was?"

"The ID," Pirate said. "Naturally she's upset about it, kind of wanting to know how it happened and all."

"And what did you have to say about that?"

"Not much," Pirate said. "I told her mistakes happen."

"That's it? Mistakes happen?"

"Yup."

"What about the tape?"

"Truth is I don't know much about that. My lawyers are the experts."

"So you didn't pass on any theories to my wife?"

"Not a one. Asides from mistakes happen." Then came a long silence, except for the tiny sound, audible only to someone with Pirate's acute sense of hearing, of blood dripping off his face and onto his shirt. "What I'm trying to tell you, Chief, is I just want to move on."

More silence. The chief holstered the gun. "Sounds like the right move," he said. "Two things to remember, Mr. DuPree. One—Belle Ville's not the place for you. Two—the book's not going to help you with moving on. Message clear?"

"Yup."

The chief turned the key. "Get out," he said.

Pirate got out. The pickup turned, drove around the earth-mover. Not quite around: the brake lights came on, and the pickup backed up, stopping beside Pirate.

The chief spoke out the driver's-side window. "And there's a third thing, so obvious it's hardly worth saying."

"What's that?"

"If you see my wife again, talk to her, make contact in any way, I'll kill you."

It took thirty minutes or so for Pirate to walk back to the Ambassador Suites. In his room, he listened to the digital recording device. The sound was first-rate, radio-station quality. He called Lee Ann.

"Sorry to wake you," he said. "I've been doing some research on the book."

CHAPTER 27

Alone in her house all night: Nell hardly slept. And this house she'd always loved didn't even seem like hers anymore. She went downstairs, looked out at the lap pool. A huge bullfrog sat at one end, the biggest she'd ever seen. His thick throat pulsed. For some reason the sight of the frog made her ill. She threw up in the kitchen sink.

Nell called Yeller's Autobody, got a number for Joe Don, dialed it. Joe Don answered on the third ring, sounding sleepy.

"Nell Jarreau," Nell said. "Is Norah there?"

"Yes, ma'am," said Joe Don. "Hang on." Then came muffled voices, Joe Don's and Norah's, before Joe Don returned to the line. "Um, ma'am? She's in the shower right now?" He was a bad liar.

"Okay," Nell said. She waited for what should have followed: *Can she call you back?* But it did not. "Tell her I'll call later," Nell said.

"Yeah, sure," said Joe Don. "Good idea."

This, her family falling apart, was intolerable. Nell got in her car, drove out to Lake Versailles. The Bastiens' compound, walled and gated, stood at the eastern end of the lake. The walls were high, overgrown with flowering vines; the gates were closed but swung open just as Nell arrived. Kirk was on his way out, at the wheel of a big SUV. He saw Nell, smiled, waved at the gateman to let her through. She followed the long gravel driveway to the end and parked beside Duke's Porsche; no sign of Clay's pickup.

There were two main houses on the compound—antebellum restorations, identical except that Kirk's had more columns and an observation tower—several guesthouses, acres of lawn, the green so saturated it didn't look real, and five or six boats down at the dock, lying still in the calm water. She walked up to Duke's house, and was raising her hand to knock when her cell phone rang: Lee Ann.

. "Hi," Lee Ann said. "Got a moment?"

"Not really."

"Maybe we can talk later. I just wanted to thank you for your help with Veronica Rice."

"I don't understand."

"Whatever you told her did the trick," Lee Ann said. "We had a very productive talk."

"You did?" Nell said.

"Why the surprise?"

Because Nell didn't think she'd done the trick at all; Veronica's face had closed up and she'd started talking about the power structure. Nell was wondering whether to bother going into all that, when the door opened and Duke looked out.

"Maybe we can talk later," Nell said.

"How about lunch?" Lee Ann said. "Foodie and Company, twelve-thirty?"

"Fine."

"I've been making progress," Lee Ann said. "Lots."

"What kind of progress?"

"Tell you at lunch."

Nell clicked off.

Duke was wearing a dark-blue silk robe decorated with

crescent moons. He ran his hand through his hair and said, "Nell?"

"I'm looking for Clay," she said.

"He's gone to work."

Nell's gaze rose up the facade of the house. Pickup gone, and it was past the usual time for Clay to have left for work, so why should she doubt Duke's word? Because: her family was falling apart.

"But you're welcome to come in," Duke said. "In fact, please do." He opened the door wide. Nell went in. "Coffee?" Duke said. "Breakfast?"

"Coffee, thanks."

They went into the kitchen. A uniformed maid was at the stove.

"Tina," Duke said. "Coffee for two in the breakfast room, please. And maybe some of those beignets."

"Right away," said Tina.

"And a little fruit."

"Yes, sir."

Nell gave Tina a smile, but Tina didn't seem to catch it. The idea of servants just didn't sit well with Nell, even though some people she knew had them; she saw the fruit bowl on the counter, had to stop herself from carrying it into the breakfast room herself.

Duke's breakfast room was at the end of a short corridor off the kitchen. On the way, Nell said, "How's—" Deleting Vicki at the last instant, substituting "everything?"

"No complaints," Duke said.

They sat at the table, a pink marble table with a vase of orchids in the center, maybe two or three dozen.

"These are lovely."

Duke pointed out the picture window with his chin. Two young women were on the tennis court, hitting the ball hard. "Mindy likes orchids," he said.

"Which one's Mindy?"

Duke laughed. "The pretty one, of course."

Nell tried to decide which was the pretty one. They both looked pretty—blond, tall, great bodies.

Duke helped her out. "Mindy's in blue. The other one's the pro—played for LSU a few years back."

Making her—what? Twenty-six or -seven? "How old is Mindy?" Nell said.

Duke laughed again, but said nothing. Tina arrived with coffee, beignets, fruit, yogurt.

"Milk and sugar, ma'am?"

"Black's fine."

Duke had milk and sugar, lots of both. He stirred the cup, eyes on the tennis court. After Tina left the room, he said, "Not too many good marriages in this part of the world these days. That's what's so tough about all this—not just knowing both of you so well, but how your marriage was kind of an example to the rest of us."

Her marriage was not something Nell wanted to discuss with Duke—or anyone, except for Clay. She sipped her coffee, gazed at Duke over the rim of the cup.

"He's real upset, Nell," Duke said. "I've never seen him like this. Tell me what I can do."

"What you can do, Duke? What does it have to do with you?"

Duke's eyes shifted to her, then away. "That's a little hurtful, you saying that."

"I'm sorry," Nell said. "But why?" Out on the court, the pro hit a ball that ticked the net cord and popped up over Mindy's waiting racquet for a winner. Both women started laughing, as though it was the most hilarious sight ever. Nell wondered whether she'd be carefree like that again; maybe not quite like that, but at least carefree for her.

"For one thing," Duke said, "I always thought you and I had a good relationship." He smiled. "In fact, you're the only woman—the only attractive woman—I can have a normal conversation with. Because you're out of bounds, if you see what I mean." He tightened the knot on the belt of his robe.

"God," Nell said. "It must wear you down."

"The hormone flow, or whatever it is?" Duke said. "Not yet. Is wearing down inevitable?" He picked a strawberry from the bowl, bit off the pointy tip, looked thoughtful. "Clay's not like me that way. But you don't need me to tell you that."

"Tell me what?"

"That he's a one-woman man." Duke ate the rest of the strawberry. "Even back in high school—he dated and everything, girls all over him, football hero, but he always had someone special in mind. And that turned out to be you. Which is why this, what's happening now, is so disturbing. I want to do something, Nell. How can I help?"

"Thanks," Nell said. "It's very kind. But there's nothing you can do."

"I'm a little surprised," Duke said.

"Why?"

"I didn't think you'd give up so easily."

That annoyed her. "Who said anything about giving up? Why do you think I'm here? I want to talk to him."

Duke showed no reaction to the change in her tone, maybe hadn't noticed. "Point taken," he said, reaching for another strawberry. "I'm surprised you're not using every available resource, is what I should have said."

"What resource are you talking about?"

"Me," Duke said. "Clay and I are like brothers."

"Wouldn't that only make it harder for you?" Nell said. "Besides, you have a real brother."

Now Duke's face did show a reaction, creases appearing in his forehead, still peeling slightly from the Bahamian sun. "What's that supposed to mean?"

Nell actually wasn't sure; the remark had almost made itself. "I was referring to Kirk, that's all."

"What about him?"

"Nothing. He's your brother. Your real brother." *So you don't need my husband for a brother? Is that what she was trying to tell him?*

Duke gave her a long look. "The primary relationship is husband and wife—I get that," he said; Duke was smart, almost in her head. Down on the tennis court, Tina was bringing Mindy and her pro cold drinks on a silver tray. Mindy looked up, saw Duke watching, gave him a girlish little wave, identical to Vicki's as far as Nell remembered. "I've got a proposition," Duke said, waving back. "For you and Clay both."

"What is it?"

Duke turned to her. At that moment a cloud passed over the sun, and Duke's face changed, suddenly careworn; she saw how he would look in thirty years. "It's all predicated on him taking this new job," he said. "I thought I had him all persuaded, but he says you're against it."

"I wasn't really against it for me," Nell said. "I was against it for him."

"What does that mean?"

"The department has been his whole life. I didn't think he was ready to quit."

"First of all," Duke said, "he's already given plenty, more than anyone could ask. Second, you're using the past tense—does that mean you've changed your mind since the two of you discussed it?"

Yes: he was very smart, probably smarter than Clay, or than her, for that matter. How had she not seen this side of him? She began to understand the success of DK Industries. But what to tell him? Certainly not the truth: that she suspected Clay—knew beyond almost all doubt—that he'd sent an innocent man to jail for life on a charge he knew to be false; and that she feared far far worse than that. Duke's head was tilted to the side, maybe looking at her from a new angle in both senses; he was waiting for an answer.

"This case," she said. "It's just . . ." And all at once Nell was close to tears. She rose, went to the window, her back to him. Crying in front of Duke: not that. The pro ripped a backhand down the line for a clean winner. Mindy applauded tennis-style, clapping with one hand and the strings of her racquet, silent. Nell got a grip, turned, faced Duke dry-eyed. The sun had come out; the old-man preview faded, and Duke looked his normal self.

"You don't have to say anything about the case," he said. "It's horrible. I've never seen him like this, so distraught. And the worst part is this rift it's opened up between the two of you. I just don't understand." Duke seemed a little distraught himself, his pale blue eyes full of emotion.

"What do you suggest?" Nell said.

"That's my cue," said Duke. "Stay right there." He hurried from the room.

Nell poured herself another cup of coffee, regretted it after just one sip, a sip that pushed her over some edge, piling coffee jitters on top of all her other instabilities. She walked over to the side wall, cream-colored, with several photos, all of Little Parrot Cay, on display. One, probably the most recent because of Vicki's presence—she was in the background looking happy and drunk—showed Duke and some Bahamians admiring a marlin hanging upside down from a scale. Nell's gaze wandered over the others, searching for Clay without success. They were almost all fishing photos, except for one in the bottom row, somewhat yellowed with age, in which a younger and much trimmer Kirk, a dive mask pushed up on his forehead, raised a plaque: *Eleuthera Free Dive Champion, Kirk Bastien: 115 feet.* Nell heard Duke coming and returned to the table.

"Feast your eyes on this," he said, handing her a brochure.

It was all about a villa on Lake Como. She leafed through. *Villa Serena.* "Beautiful," she said.

"I guess," said Duke. "The crazy thing is we kind of own it. Fell into our hands, too complicated to explain—I'm not sure I understand it myself. We're putting the place on the market, of course, but not till next year, something about euro accounts. But the point is, there's no one in it right now, just standing empty. And, well—how does Italy sound?"

How did Italy sound? Nell hadn't traveled much outside

the United States, had never been to Italy, and there was nowhere she'd always wanted to see more. "What are you saying?"

"I was thinking you and Clay might like to go there, house-sit for a month or two, long as you like."

"How could we do that? Clay could never get away from work for that long, and the museum'll be reopening soon."

"You're forgetting about Clay's new job," Duke said.

"If he takes it."

"I think that's going to pretty much depend on you. One more thing to factor in—for some time now we've been wanting to make a move or two in the art game."

"The art game?"

"Sorry," he said. "That just proves how bad we need you."

"To do what?"

"Manage this collection for us, buy and sell, be the brains."

"What collection?"

"We've got these new consultants," Duke said. "They're pushing art collection on us."

"You're offering me a job?"

"In my clumsy way, yeah," said Duke. "You'd have a pool of two or three mil at the outset."

"The outset of what?"

"Buying art. But if you needed more—some Picasso pops up, that kind of thing—we'd try to be accommodating. Salary would be industry standard or better—ballpark a hundred grand or so, I'm told—and you could start when you came back from Italy."

A dream she'd never even dared to dream, come true. It was all so sudden, like a rocket out of all their problems—hers and Clay's—a miraculous escape. Duke was watching her, mouth in smiling form, eyes sharp. "It's all so sudden," Nell said.

"True of most good things, in my experience," said Duke.

Nell had a strange thought: if Bernardine had been worse,

bad enough to wipe Belle Ville completely off the map with-out a trace, as though it had never existed, then accepting this offer would have been possible. But Bernardine hadn't been bad enough. The past remained, and with the past came questions, big ones, undermining her whole life.

"Thank you, Duke," she said. "But no."

His mouth changed shape, conformed with his eyes. "No? Just like that?"

"I'm sorry. It's such a generous offer, but I can't." More than generous: perfect, as though designed with her and only her in mind.

"Mind explaining?" Duke said. "Don't mean to be rude— just that I thought I knew you a bit."

"It's personal," Nell said.

"Meaning between you and Clay?"

She nodded.

"And I respect that personal relationship," Duke said. "I hope you know that. But—maybe just like you—there's no one I'm closer to than Clay. I need to help."

"There's nothing you can do," Nell said. "Unless . . ."

"Unless what?"

Nell gazed at Duke. She'd always liked him; a reprobate, maybe, to use an old-fashioned word, but he also had a lot of old-fashioned virtues, loyalty most of all. Clay was that way, too—wasn't he? She made a quick decision.

"What do you think happened?" she said.

"Mistakes were made," said Duke.

Nell knew that. The next word got stuck in her throat, almost didn't get out: "Deliberately?"

"A deliberate mistake? Deliberate on the part of who?"

"I'm asking you," Nell said.

"I don't see why it has to be deliberate," Duke said. "In-nocent people end up in jail sometimes."

"We're way past that," Nell said. "Don't you see? The tape changes everything. There was a cover-up."

Duke gazed at her, then looked down at his coffee, began stirring it. The room was silent, except for the clink of his spoon and the faint thud of tennis balls. Nell thought the conversation was over. Then, eyes still on the swirling coffee, Duke said, "A cover-up engineered by Bobby Rice?"

Nell hadn't been suggesting that, but her mind responded to the theory at once, reordering facts and suspicions around it. "Is that what happened, Duke? Did Clay tell you?"

He looked up, met her gaze. "Clay and I haven't discussed it."

"He's protecting Bobby's memory? Is that what's going on?"

"You'll have to move on from this, Nell. I hope to God you realize that soon."

Her mind was racing, adding, deleting, reshaping. Johnny's murderer was white, not black, ruling Bobby out. Therefore, if Bobby was behind the manipulated ID and the cover-up of the tape, he'd been doing it for someone else. And that someone else? The murderer? Nell couldn't come up with any other possibility. The murderer: Clay himself? Something deep inside her fought against believing that, and always would; could deep-inside things be wrong? But if not Clay, then the murderer was . . . close, somehow, close to Bobby or Clay or both. She began to feel the weight Clay was under; and maybe had been under all along.

"Does Clay know who the murderer was?" she said. "Has he known the whole time?"

"I told you—we haven't discussed it," Duke said.

Nell didn't believe him. And more than that: "You know, too," she said.

"Know what?" said Duke.

"Who the murderer was."

Duke's face turned bright red, a redness that began as spots on his cheeks and spread to the tips of his ears. "You're not making sense," he said.

"Tell me," she said.

"You've got to stop," he said. "So much depends on it."

So much depended on her stopping? "Like what?" she said.

Duke paused, looked like he was arranging words in his mind. At that moment, a door opened and Mindy came in, racquet dangling over her shoulder, hair damp with sweat, skin glowing.

"Hi, baby," she said, "when are we—oh, sorry."

Duke made proper introductions.

Nell went to her car. Kirk was back, parking his SUV. He got out, didn't appear to see her, walked toward his house, fast, but with a limp. He entered by a side door, pulling a cell phone from his pocket.

Nell got to Foodie and Company at 12:25. Lee Ann wasn't there. She took a table at the indoor garden at the back, drank iced tea and waited. At 12:45 she tried Lee Ann's cell. No answer. At one she tried again, this time leaving a message.

"Missed you at lunch. I'd be interested to hear what—just give me a call."

CHAPTER 28

Nell left Foodie and Company and drove home. As she entered the Heights she thought she heard her phone ringing. Lee Ann? She dug the phone out of her purse, swerved over the centerline, heard angry honking. But the phone wasn't ringing, and a quick scroll-through showed she hadn't missed a call: now she was hearing things.

Nell turned onto Sandhill Way. No Miata in the driveway, but a sedan with a Vandy bumper sticker sat in front of the house. Nell steered around it—four girls inside, none of them Norah—and parked in the driveway. One of the girls—tiny, dark, lovely—got out of the sedan and approached her.

"Mrs. Jarreau?" she said.

"Ines?" said Nell.

"Yes," said the girl, a little surprised. "We were just passing through, on break. Is Norah around?"

"Not at the moment," Nell said, "but I might be able to . . ." She tried Joe Don's number on her cell phone. It rang three times and then she was in voice mail. "Norah? Ines has just stopped by. Um." She clicked off. Ines was watching her; Ines's eyes were huge and expressive. "Why don't you come inside?" Nell said. "All of you. A snack, maybe? Iced tea?"

"Thanks, Mrs. Jarreau, but—"

"Nell. Please."

"It's really nice of you but we're trying to get to Miami tonight."

"Tonight?" Nell glanced at the car. One girl was gazing at the house; one was twirling her hair; one had her eyes closed.

"Let's say while it's still dark," Ines said. "I just wanted to know how Norah's doing."

"You haven't talked to her yet?"

"She's not . . . she doesn't seem to be calling me back."

"And you're worried about her."

"Well. I wouldn't say worried, exactly." Ines shot a quick look at the car, probably trying to think of a nice way to say good-bye, get back to the road trip, and fun.

"I am," Nell said. "I'm worried. And I believe you are, too, and not only that, but you have information that might help."

Ines shook her head.

"I don't know what went wrong at school," Nell said. "But now there's a problem here at home and I'm afraid it's all going to be . . ." She choked up, hated herself for doing that, pressed on. " . . . too much for her."

"A problem here?" Ines said.

Going into the problem at home with this girl she didn't know went against Nell's nature, but was there a choice? "I have no idea what you know about Norah's real father," she said. "That he was killed and how the wrong—how it looks like the wrong man went to jail."

Ines was silent for a moment. Her big, dark eyes got bigger and darker. "Oh, God," she said. "It's my fault."

"What is?"

"Norah," Ines said. "How she got so . . ." She searched for a word, couldn't find it.

"I don't understand," Nell said.

Ines's eyes shifted to the car again. All the girls were watching now. Ines took a deep breath. "I'm a geology major," she said. "I found—no, I should go back before that." She took another deep breath. "Last year. Late one night, just talking, you know? And Norah happened to mention about her real father. Getting killed and all, like you say. She wasn't upset or anything. I think we'd been talking about divorce—my parents are divorced, that's how it started. Plus she told me about him being a geologist—because of my major?"

"I understand."

"So then this fall—last semester—I was doing research on the New Madrid Fault Line and I found this paper he'd written about it. Dr. Blanton, I mean. It wasn't online—an actual paper, in the library. Anyway, I showed it to Norah, kind of explained it to her. After that, she started getting pretty intense about it."

"About geology?"

"More about tracking down her dad's papers," Ines said. "I found maybe three of four, all technical and dry, no personality in them. They're scientific papers. But in one of them he thanks his father—for helping him with his first rock collection, I think it was. And that's when she got the idea."

"What idea?"

"To look him up, maybe get to know him a little."

"You're talking about looking up my—Johnny's father?"

"Uh-huh. Norah's grandfather. She drove down to New Orleans, spent a day or so." Ines bit her lip. "When she came back she just wasn't the same."

"How?"

A sound came from the car, maybe a fingernail tapping on the windshield. Ines turned. One of the girls mouthed something to her.

"How?" Nell said, a little louder. She almost added *Lives may be at stake,* a completely unwarranted and over-the-top notion that came out of nowhere.

Ines sighed. "Not cheerful anymore. Staying in her room. Falling behind. You know."

"And what did she tell you?"

"Nothing. She wouldn't talk about it. Then she started hanging with another crowd, ended up kind of living off-campus."

"With who?"

"Guys from this other crowd."

"Students?"

"One of them," Ines said. "I think."

"How old were these people?"

Ines shrugged, wouldn't meet her eye. "The next thing I knew she'd gone home. That's all I know." Ines looked miserable.

Nell put her hand on Ines's shoulder. "Thank you," she said.

"Please don't tell her I told you all this."

"I can't promise that," Nell said. "But now I can help her. That makes you a real friend."

Ines wasn't buying it. She said good-bye, and thirty seconds after that, the girls' car was squealing around the corner at the bottom of the hill and vanishing from sight.

Nell called Norah. Voice mail. Joe Don. Same thing. She drove over to Joe Don's barn. No answer to her knock, and the Miata wasn't there. She went to Yeller's Autobody. Joe Don's day off, said the woman at the desk. Prob'ly gone fishin', said someone else. Nell got back in her car and headed for New Orleans.

I'm sure they *like you,* Johnny had said about his parents. *They just take some time to get to know.* But there hadn't been time, and she'd never had the chance to see whether Johnny was right: that the faint disapproval she'd felt coming from them was just her imagination misleading her, misinterpreting the normal feelings of two adoring parents for an only child. There'd been almost no contact after Johnny's funeral—one brief and strained visit to New Orleans with baby Norah, a note to Mr. Blanton after Mrs. Blanton died, a formal reply, not much else. And then, after her session with Professor Urbana, she'd caught that glimpse of him in his garden, an old man now.

Nell got off the freeway, drove down Carrollton, turned onto St. Charles and parked in front of the Blanton mansion. She walked up to the wrought-iron fence, found the gate locked, pressed the buzzer. No response. She was about to press it again when Mr. Blanton backed out from behind a rosebush, shears in hand. He wore a straw hat, seersucker pants, a white shirt, suspenders; was muttering under his breath; didn't see her.

His name was Paul, but even when he'd been her prospective father-in-law, she hadn't felt comfortable calling him by it, and now it was impossible. "Mr. Blanton?"

He turned. He'd never looked much like Johnny, and now the resemblance was even less, his cheeks thinned out, his nose beakier, the downward grooves in his face dug deeper. "Yes?" he said, squinting at her.

"It's me, Nell."

He went still for a moment, sunlight gleaming on the shears. "What do you want?" he said.

"To talk to you."

"I'm busy."

"It won't take long," Nell said. "And it's important."

"To whom?"

His tone ruled out almost every possibility. Nell tried the only one with any chance at all. "Your granddaughter."

"How is it important to her?" he said.

"Norah's in a bad way," Nell said. "She needs help."

"Whose fault is that?"

"If there's fault, we can deal with that later. She needs help now."

"There's nothing I can do."

"How do you know until you've heard what I have to say?" Nell said.

He came forward; he was shaking, and his voice shook, too. "You've got nerve. Shutting me out of her life all these years and now you come crawling."

"You shut yourself out."

His voice rose. He stood within a foot or two of her, facing her through the bars. His breath was awful; decayed and alcoholic. "Why would I do a damn-fool thing like that?"

"Because you never liked me." How obvious that suddenly seemed, how stupid her long-ago rationalizations, how uneasy—in retrospect—Johnny had been about her and his parents. "You could have gotten in touch anytime."

"That's right," Mr. Blanton said. "We never liked you. He was a prince, that boy. Why you? Why on earth? He could have won the Nobel Prize." Spittle was flying now; she felt it on her face. "And now sins come home to roost, as I told her."

"You told Norah that?"

He jabbed his finger through the bars. "The murder was a setup. Don't know about the exact mechanics, don't care, but it didn't take me long to sniff out the basic truth, what with how quick you were to jump into that cop's bed. Much more your level, of course, made perfect sense."

Nell backed away. "You told her that, too?"

"And the reporter. I'll tell the world. I'm sick of the stink, sick to death."

"What reporter?"

"Goddamn thief from that rag of yours."

Was he insane? She felt herself hardening inside, tried to hurt him with her gaze. "What the hell are you talking about?"

"Sweet-talking whore, she was. I let her look through Johnny's papers, the pathetic little I have, thanks to you—where's his computer? You squirreled that away, didn't you?"

"I didn't squirrel anything away." His computer? Nell tried to remember. Hadn't they shared one, an old IBM desktop?

"Liar. You're a liar just like her. She sent me out of the room on some pretext, and after she left, his address book was missing."

His address book? Nell tried to control her anger—fury, even, at this old man for the trouble he'd stirred up. "Why would she want that?"

"Because she couldn't have it—why does anyone want anything? I told her the rules—no taking, no copying—but we all know what happens to rules nowadays."

Johnny's address book: Nell remembered it, leather-bound

with *University of Texas* in gold. "Johnny's papers, whatever else you have—I want to see them."

"Never."

"It's important," Nell said. "Norah's at risk. She's your flesh and blood."

"Polluted by you." He raised the shears, brandished them. A passing car slowed to a crawl.

Nell got back on the freeway, doing ninety. She called Lee Ann, got a message that her voice mail was full. She called the *Guardian* and was told Lee Ann was on assignment. She tried Norah, Joe Don and finally her own home phone, where her own recorded voice invited her to leave a message.

Pirate sat in his room, waiting. He had the digital recorder out on the desk, all set for Lee Ann's arrival. Last night, when he'd woken her, she'd said she'd be over in the morning. Morning came and went. Maybe she'd said early afternoon. That came and went, too. He called her, got sent to that voice-mail thing. "Hey. Was it morning or afternoon?" A few minutes later, he realized he might not have waited for the beep—Pirate hadn't done much phoning at Central State, was still getting used to all the changes. He called again. "Customer mailbox is full." So therefore? "Still here," he said, just in case there was a tiny bit of room for a two-word message.

After a few more hours, Pirate was restless and hungry, and a little pissed off at Lee Ann. He played back what was on the digital recorder. Real nice. Lee Ann was going to like it, like it fine. She'd sounded excited in the night. So where was she? Then he got to thinking maybe she hadn't been alone. That disturbed him for some reason, even though she wasn't particularly good-looking. After a while, he figured out the reason: they were partners; he didn't want anyone messing up the partnership. Not an unknown anyone.

Pirate got more and more restless. He tried reading the Bible, but the words got blurry, like on the little Kahlúa bottles. He opened the phone book, leafed through the Bs. Would a reporter be listed? Pirate had no idea, but there she was: Bonner, L.A., 207 Beauregard Street. Pirate knew Beauregard Street, on the edge of Lower Town, not far away. He slipped the recorder in his pocket, started out; remembering at the last second the promise he'd made to himself, the promise not to leave his room—his suite—without the tiny weapon. Pirate went into the bedroom, raised the mattress, kept his promise.

CHAPTER 29

B eauregard Street had changed, or else Pirate was remembering wrong. What he remembered were crumbling old warehouses, bums on the street, flies buzzing around, the slow, fat kind of flies, easy to kill. What he saw were warehouses all sandblasted like they were built yesterday, windows shiny, trim freshly painted, no bums, no flies, prosperity on the way. Across the street from 207, workers were hoisting a sign: CAFÉ HURRICANO. And in a lower window of 207 itself, Pirate read: BEAURE-GARD LOFTS—LUXURY CONDO AND APARTMENT LIVING— CONTACT BASTIEN RESIDENTIAL REALTY.

Pirate walked up to the door at 207, a cool-looking door, blue and silver—he could afford to live here!—and tried the handle. Locked. He checked for buzzers and found none. "Hey, Lee Ann." He raised his fist to bang on the door, but at that moment heard footsteps descending stairs inside— heavy footsteps, not Lee Ann's. He backed away, into the street, just letting his instincts take over. His instincts were good: he realized that now, maybe a little late in life. The door opened and a man came out, wearing white overalls and carrying paint cans. He left one of them against the door to keep it from closing and went to a van parked a few spaces away. Pirate walked into 207.

A small foyer: Pirate glanced around, took in a Wet Paint sign, an inner door, this one propped open with a paint roller, leading to stairs, and four buzzers on the wall. The spaces beside the first three were blank; number four read: *Bonner.* No point pressing the buzzer, not with the door already open. Pirate went on up. He felt good. Why not? He had his instincts, and then there was this partnership: his very first partnership, solid and real. There was a signed contract! And what he had on the digital recorder, his contribution—it meant he was holding up his end, no question. Why couldn't *Only a Test* turn into one of those books that hit it big, maybe became a movie? Pirate tried to think of the right movie star to play himself, but he didn't know much about movie stars. Maybe Lee Ann would. That was what partners were for, to pick up the slack. But how about the Scottish guy with the blue face, who'd fought the English? Maybe him.

The stairs were covered with a paint-spattered drop cloth. Pirate climbed to the first landing. The door to number two was closed; door number one hung open, revealing a glimpse of stepladders, light fixtures lying on the floor, a sawhorse. He kept going. On the second landing, both doors were closed. Pirate knocked on number four.

No answer.

"Lee Ann? You there?"

Nothing. He knocked again, harder. "Lee Ann?" Maybe she wasn't home. Either that, or she was avoiding him. That possibility pissed him off. He knocked one last time, hardest of all, more like pounding. "Hey! Lee Ann!" He listened for some sound inside, a quiet footstep, a door softly closing, and heard nothing. "Okay. Guess you're not home." Pirate took a few loud steps toward the stairs, a few silent ones back. He put his ear to the door. A few seconds passed. Then—oh, yes, his hearing, superhuman—he heard a faint moan, very soft, very light.

Bad news. Lee Ann was home, all right, avoiding him and not alone. Home with some loverboy. She wasn't beautiful, nothing like Norah, with that soft soft skin, but they were partners. They had a signed contract. He was getting sick of this. Who did she think she was dealing with? He was a man of means, not some pushover. Pirate leaned back, lowered his shoulder, lunged at the door. A brand-new, well-made door: it barely splintered on the first try, but the third took him inside Lee Ann's apartment or condo or whatever it was, bursting his way through and feeling strong and angry.

Pirate looked around. Lee Ann's place was some kind of open design, with high ceilings, walls that were part wood and part concrete, hardwood floors, dark stone countertops. Without taking another step, he could see just about every-thing: kitchen, office, living room, all unoccupied. He went down a little hall, past a washer and dryer, into an empty bathroom. That left the bedroom, which had to be through the closed door on the far side of the open bar.

Pirate went to the bedroom door, put his ear to this one, too. This time he heard nothing. He tried the knob. It turned; but before going in, he knocked. He had manners.

Pirate entered Lee Ann's bedroom. It was a big room with paintings on the walls, a soft rug, a king-size bed. The bed was unmade, no one in it. There was a second bath-room off the bedroom. He poked his head in: a big bath-room with lots of mirrors, a huge bathtub, a stall shower. Pirate went in, opened the shower door: lots of soaps and shampoos, but no Lee Ann. He returned to the bedroom, knelt, peered under the bed: nothing, not even dustballs. She wasn't home.

And therefore? Therefore there'd been no moan, no lover-boy, no attempt to avoid him. He'd misjudged her, doubted the partnership for no reason. Pirate didn't feel good about that. All she wanted was to tell his story. She'd always been straight up with him. He owed her for that, although what, exactly, he didn't know.

He sat down at the kitchen table. On the table lay a fruit bowl with some nice peaches in it, a half-full mug of coffee and an address book with *University of Texas* in gold on the front. Was his name in it? Pirate leafed through, found day-by-day appointment pages in the front and names and addresses in the back; lots of names, but not his. He laid the address book aside, stuck his finger in the coffee: cold. He realized he was thirsty and drank it all down.

Pirate went to the desk, found a sheet of paper, wrote a note. *Hey. Heres the recording thing. Digital. Check out this inturvue with the cheif!! Sory about your door. Mistake. I'll pay. A. DuPree.* He took the recorder from his pocket and laid it on the note. Then he peeled $320 off the roll he'd started carrying in his pocket—an amount that came to him out of the blue—and set it on the note, beside the recorder. He circled *I'll pay* and drew an arrow from there to the money.

Now what? Kahlúa sounded good. Did Lee Ann have any? Pirate went to the bar, opened the cupboard: two bottles of white wine, a bottle of vodka. Vodka and wine—booze, no question about it. Was it true what they said about vodka, that it had no smell? Pirate couldn't remember. He twisted off the cap—not to drink, only for a smell test—and had his nose to the opening, taking a deep, scientific sniff, when he heard a moan.

Pirate froze. *Froze* was the word, all right: he felt a strange iciness on the back of his neck, something brand-new. A moan, without a doubt, but how could that be? He was alone inside Lee Ann's place.

"Lee Ann?" he said, but very softly, too soft for anyone to hear.

Pirate put down the vodka bottle, moved toward the bedroom, all movements slow and silent. He looked in the bedroom, saw nothing he hadn't seen the first time. Was it possible she lay under the rumpled covers on the unmade bed? No; but he pulled them back anyway, revealing a red plastic hair clip, nothing more. He picked up the hair clip, sniffed it, too, smelled something nice. At that moment, he got the squinting feeling in his non-eye, as though it was getting ready to see through the surface of something. Why wouldn't it? That was where God kept his secret power.

But what surface was he supposed to see through, what insight was waiting to be discovered? Pirate glanced around the room and noticed what he'd missed before, a tiny glint on the dark rug. He went over, bent down, and picked up a pair of glasses: those strange glasses Lee Ann had, the glasses that made her look so smart and at the same time uglier than in real life. They were twisted out of shape, maybe like she'd stepped on them. Pirate could picture that happening. Lee Ann probably couldn't see well without the glasses, so after she dropped them it would be easy to—

Another moan.

Unmistakable. A woman's moan, and it came from the closet—at least, Pirate had assumed it was a closet, with one of those wood-slatted doors, so air could get in. Was she in there with loverboy, after all? Should have checked it the first time. Pirate went over and checked it now, flinging the door open.

This was a closet? It was like another room, extending way back, lined with lots of clothes hanging on both sides. The only light came from a ceiling window. It fell on rows and rows of gleaming shoes, a distracting sight that kept Pirate from noticing what lay at the rear of the closet.

Lee Ann, on her back. She had her skirt hiked way up and her legs spread, but there was no loverboy. Great legs, it turned out, and she wore a tiny black thong, also a surprise. A surprise and another distraction. Pirate didn't notice what had happened to her face until he'd taken another step or two.

"Oh."

Bad things. Her face was not the same, looked like one of those modern artists had got hold of it, all bashed in here and bulging there. Her spiky hair was bloody and her eyes were closed, one of them closed like a normal eye, but the other eye, the left, was ruined, a puffball leaking a jellylike glob between the lashes. Pirate got the squinting feeling in his non-eye. An insight was coming after all. His partner: someone had killed her, bashed in her head. But Pirate was expecting more of an insight than that. He was still waiting for its arrival when she moaned.

Pirate jumped back. "Lee Ann?" He forced himself to go closer, bend over her. "Lee Ann?"

Nothing.

He bent a little more, reached down to take her wrist, feel for a pulse, and at that moment noticed a gun on the floor, a foot or so from her hand: a little revolver with a grip that looked like pink pearl. Had she been shot, too? He didn't see any bullet-wound signs. Maybe if he rolled her over and— but Pirate didn't want to do that. In fact, all he wanted was to get the hell—

Lee Ann's good eye opened. It shifted, found him. Her lips moved, very slightly. She said something, all gurgly. He didn't catch it.

"What happened?" he said. "Who did this to you?"

She spoke again, just one word. It sounded like "bastard." Blood trickled from between her lips.

"Goddamn right," he said. "We'll get the bastard." And he meant it: whoever had done this was going to pay.

Was she trying to shake her head? Pirate couldn't tell. And her eye might have been trying to communicate something as well, but he didn't know what. Maybe he should touch her shoulder, make some reassuring move. He was wondering about that when she said, "Book."

Very clear. Book, not bastards. But just to be sure, he said: "Book?"

Lee Ann moaned again, very softly, mostly from the pain or agony or whatever it was, but maybe a little bit too from frustration, at him, for being slow on the uptake. That pissed him off, but just as he was about to say something, he got it: "The address book?"

The expression in her eye changed, told him *yes*. They really were partners.

Pirate rose, hurried to the kitchen: fruit bowl with peaches; coffee mug now empty; address book with *University of Texas* on the cover. "Got it," he called, and hurried back through the bedroom and into the closet. "What am I supposed to do with the thing?"

No answer.

He went a little closer. Her eye was very clear in the light from the ceiling window. There was no life in it now, none at all. Pirate stuck the address book in his pocket, knelt and felt Lee Ann's wrist. No pulse; and the skin itself was different, more like an imitation of skin meant to fool the eye but not the touch. Pirate, real gentle—although he was reminded of doing something similar, less gentle, to Esteban Malvi— closed Lee Ann's eye. Then he tugged at the material of her skirt, trying to cover her legs, make what was left of her more modest. Tugging the skirt down involved moving her legs closer together. Pirate was still busy with all that, at the same time trying to find some proper words to say, maybe from Job, when he heard a footstep, soft on the bedroom rug, behind him.

He whirled around, reaching without thought for the pink-handled gun. There, not ten feet away, stood the in-shape, tan one, his enemy: Nell Jarreau. She looked past him, at Lee Ann, took in everything. Her hands rose, as though to cover her mouth or face, some womanly gesture, but she stopped them—he saw the effort it took.

"She's dead," he told her. But it must have been obvious: he began noticing blood he'd missed before, blood all over the closet.

Nell's face went pale, practically white. But her eyes, nostrils, mouth, were dark, like black holes. Something about that black-and-white look scared him. She said, "You are a murderer after all."

"Me?" Was it possible she thought that he was the—? Oh, God. "We were partners." His voice rose. "Some bastard did it." Nell's face didn't change. It took a few moments for Pirate to feel the truth sinking in. *This was happening again?* Not even to Job. The happening-again thing sank in, sank in deep, and when it did, when it pierced all the way down to the core—she was going to frame him for the second time!—Pirate boiled over like some steaming gusher.

"Frame me again? You want murder?" He sprang, lashing

at her face with the barrel of Lee Ann's pink-handled gun. Somehow he missed—she turned out to be quick, twisting away; but not quick enough to avoid the barrel completely. It caught her on the shoulder, good and hard, and she cried out, and the sound was right. An eye for an eye: the truth of that was confirmed forever in his heart. The only problem, which he missed at first, was that the force of the blow, so strong, knocked the gun from his hand. He heard it fall, bounce off the rug onto the hardwood floor, and then it was on his blind side and so was she; just for an instant, but as he turned, bringing everything in view again, he saw her rolling on the floor, into the corner. Pirate lunged. Too late: she sat up, pointed the gun right at his chest, like she knew how to use it, no surprise for a cop's wife. He took another step, bent forward, hands extended like claws.

"Don't," she said. Just one word, but something about the way she said it—scared yes, hysterical no—plus the black holes of her eyes, and the hardness he knew to be in her from what she'd done to him already, convinced him that she was not one of those women who could never shoot someone. He raised his hands. But shooting someone with his hands up as he backed out of a room? A different matter. That took a little more than she had going for her, in Pirate's judgment. He started backing out of the room, hands up. The barrel swung, following him: a bad moment. Then he was out of the line of fire.

And gone.

CHAPTER 30

N ell got off the floor. Pain shot up and down her left arm, from the shoulder to the wrist. But she could raise the arm, lower it, move it side to side. No damage; not worth another thought. So why this shaking?

Nell went in the closet, knelt beside Lee Ann. She took Lee Ann's wrist—cold skin, as though Lee Ann had spent a subzero day outdoors—and felt for a pulse. Nothing; but maybe she was doing it wrong. Nell put her ear to Lee Ann's chest. Silence. She'd seen a murder victim—and been this close—once before. Maybe that experience down at the Parish Street Pier, the worst of her life, steeled her, kept her from crying. Or maybe it was the realization that the two murders were connected, a realization that got her mind working at once; no time for self-indulgence. Two connected murders, yes: but how?

Nell became aware of Lee Ann's gun, still in her hand. She had never fired a gun in her life, although Clay had invited her out on the police academy range several times. Could she have fired it at DuPree? Yes, if he'd taken one more step.

Nell went into Lee Ann's bedroom, found her purse on the floor, took out her cell phone, tried Clay's number at One Marigot. Nothing appeared on the cell-phone screen; no lights shone on the keypad. The phone was broken.

Raising the gun to waist level, Nell left the bedroom,

walked down the little hall, looked around: fruit bowl; reproduction of *Guernica* hanging on the wall; splintered front door. He was gone. She went to the window. The painter who'd let her in downstairs had been on his way out; she saw no sign of his van.

Nell moved into Lee Ann's office alcove, picked up the desk phone, tried Clay's number again.

"Jarreau," he said, answering on the first ring.

"Clay?" Her tone betrayed her, wobbling a bit.

"Yes?" he said; his tone was reserved, emotionless.

Nell tried to make hers that way, too. "You'd better come here."

"Where?"

"He . . . he beat her to death."

"What are you talking about?"

She started to tell her story, a badly organized jumble she was only halfway through when he interrupted.

His tone changed. "Lock yourself in the bathroom. I'm on my way."

"There's no—"

Click.

Locking herself in the bathroom? That sounded scarier than not. Nell decided to stay where she was, by the phone. A second or two later, her gaze fell on a small digital recorder, about three inches by two; some money; a handwritten note.

Hey. Heres the recording thing. Digital. Check out this inturvue with the cheif!!

Nell picked up the recorder, her hand unsteady. She pressed play.

Clay spoke: "Shh," he said. From the tiny speaker, came a faint splash. Right there and then in Lee Ann's air-conditioned apartment, Nell's nostrils filled with the Bernardine stink. "Who'd be on this interview list?" Clay said.

DuPree spoke. Nell jumped at the sound of his voice. "Don't know," he said.

Clay: "How about me—would I be on it?"

DuPree: "Wouldn't want to inconvenience you."

Clay: "No inconvenience. Want to interview me? How's right now?"

DuPree: "I'm not, um, prepared."

Clay: "Don't be shy. What's the worst that can happen?"

DuPree: "Thanks for the offer. How about a rain check?"

Clay: "Your call. But I'm pretty sure you've got to be more aggressive to make it in the writing game."

DuPree: "I'll try."

Clay laughed, a laugh so unlike him it terrified her. "This is a funny situation."

DuPree: "Yeah?"

Clay: "Here I am telling you how to write your own book. When all along I'm perfectly aware that you're off to a flying start."

DuPree: "I am?"

Clay: "Sure. Take your interview—that's what it was, I get it now—your interview with my wife."

DuPree: "Interview with your wife? I don't know what you're—" Then came a thud, followed by a cry of pain. A heavy thud: Nell knew for certain Clay had his gun out, had struck DuPree as DuPree had struck her. And she, too, had a gun in her hand. The civilized world was speeding away.

Clay: "Careful, now. The interview."

DuPree: "You can call it an interview." Now his voice was pinched by pain. "But she came to me."

Clay: "And?"

DuPree: "She was sorry about what happened. I told her not to worry about it."

Clay: "How did you put that? The exact words."

DuPree: "Just like I said—don't worry about it. I forgive you."

Clay: "You forgave her?"

DuPree: "Why not? It was . . . it was in good faith."

Clay: "What was?"

DuPree: "The ID. Naturally she's upset about it, kind of wanting to know how it happened and all."

Clay: "And what did you have to say about that?"

DuPree: "Not much. I told her mistakes happen."

Clay: "That's it? Mistakes happen?"

DuPree: "Yup."

Clay: "What about the tape?"

DuPree: "Truth is I don't know much about that. My lawyers are the experts."

Clay: "So you didn't pass on any theories to my wife?"

DuPree: "Not a one. Aside from mistakes happen. What I'm trying to tell you, Chief, is I just want to move on."

Nell heard another faint sound, maybe the fastening of a metal snap, the kind on a holster. Then Clay said, "Sounds like the right move. Two things to remember, Mr. DuPree. One—Belle Ville's not the place for you. Two—the book's not going to help you with moving on. Message clear?"

DuPree: "Yup."

A key turned; an engine fired. Clay said: "Get out."

Then, after a long pause: "And there's a third thing, so obvious it's hardly worth saying."

DuPree: "What's that?"

Clay: "If you see my wife again, talk to her, make contact in any way, I'll kill you."

And then silence. Nell didn't understand. When had this happened? She needed some sort of timeline, maybe going back twenty years; it snarled in her mind before she could even begin. But way more important, Clay's brutality knocked her completely off balance—she finally knew from hearing him on this recording that he was capable of murder. There was more: DuPree's lies—they threw her, too. DuPree hadn't forgiven her at all, so why would he tell Clay that he had? And what had he said about theories: that he hadn't passed on any to her? What about that scene of Clay and him down in the cells? *And when you're locked up I hope she'll be grateful. She's one hot babe.*

Nell didn't understand. She was missing so much. Was it possible she'd misheard the recording, or misinterpreted what she had heard? She hit the back button, then play.

"Two—the book's not going to help you with moving on. Message clear?" Was DuPree's motive somewhere in there? Had there been a disagreement between him and Lee Ann, something that had set him off, caused him to—

Nell heard someone coming up the stairs, very fast. She pressed *off*, tucked the recorder and note in her pocket, and turned, raising the gun. A man—not DuPree—ran through the open doorway, splintered door remains cracking under his feet. Clay? Yes, Clay: for a moment, she hadn't even recognized him. Two men in full SWAT-team outfits charged in after him. They saw Nell, halted, snapped their rifles up, took aim. The *Guernica* reproduction fell off the wall with a crash.

"Don't shoot," Clay said, waving the men back. And to Nell: "Drop that fucking gun."

She dropped it.

Clay came closer. "Who's here?"

"No one. Me."

"I heard you talking."

"I wasn't."

He faced her, probably looking expressionless to everyone else, but grim to her. "I told you to lock yourself in the bathroom."

Nell said nothing, just tried to stop shaking. She could hear the SWAT men breathing behind their face shields; their chests heaved.

"Search the place," Clay said, his eyes staying on Nell.

"There's no one here," Nell said. "Except Lee Ann. She's . . . she's in the closet." Clay watched her face; his expression didn't change.

The SWAT men hurried into the bedroom, rifles raised. Clay bent down, picked up the pink-handled gun. "This yours?"

"Of course not—you know that," Nell said. "It's Lee Ann's."

"Who got shot?" Clay said.

"Nobody," Nell said. "He . . . he beat her. I told you."

"Then what's that?" said Clay. He pointed to a shell casing on the floor, bright and clear on the gleaming hardwood outside Lee Ann's bedroom; how had she missed it? Clay moved closer to the shell casing, then spotted something else. Nell followed his gaze; and she spotted it, too: a drop on the floor, oblong, dark-colored—possibly a deep shade of red. And there were others, some bigger, some smaller, marking a trail to the front door. Clay had already taken that in. He moved into the bedroom. Sirens sounded, coming from all directions. Nell walked over to one of those deep red drops and touched it with the tip of her finger: not wet, or even sticky, but completely dry.

Crime-scene investigators came; and soon the M.E. They took photographs, took measurements, took Lee Ann away. The SWAT team searched the whole building. Clay ordered the duty captain sent over from One Marigot. For a minute or two, Clay and Nell were alone in Lee Ann's apartment. He gave her a look, intimate and strange at the same time. Nell knew she was looking at him in the same way.

"What happened to your arm?" he said.

"I'm fine."

Clay opened Lee Ann's freezer, approached her with an ice pack. He moved as though to lay it on her shoulder, but stopped himself and handed it to her instead.

"Thank you," she said.

He nodded. Nell felt the weight of the recorder in her pocket. Like so many electronic devices, it seemed to have a primitive intelligence, but this recorder had developed some sort of will, too: she felt its desire to come out in the open, get handed over to her husband.

Deputy Chief Darryll Pines walked in, a little breathless from climbing the stairs.

"What are you doing here?" Clay said.

Darryll looked surprised. "Didn't you ask for the duty captain?" he said. "I was on, noon to eight."

A vein pulsed in Clay's neck. "I want you to take Nell's statement," he said.

"Whatever you say."

"And I'd like to listen in, if that's all right with you," Clay said.

Darryll shrugged. "You can run the whole show, if you want."

"I told you what I want."

"Yes, sir."

They sat in Lee Ann's living room, Nell on the sofa, Darryll in an easy chair, Clay on a stool he brought over from the bar. Darryll took out a notebook, rested it on his belly.

"So, uh, ma'am," he said, "what was it brought you over here in the first place?"

"Lee Ann and I were supposed to meet for lunch," Nell said. "She didn't show up and I couldn't reach her. I got worried."

"This lunch date, what time was that?"

"Twelve-thirty, at Foodie and Company."

"And you got here?"

"Around five."

"What happened then?"

Nell told her story: the painter letting her in the building, finding Lee Ann's door broken down, her first sight of DuPree, hunched over Lee Ann's body, fumbling with her skirt.

"Rape kit," Darryll muttered to himself. He made a note, the pen tiny in his thick fingers. "And then?"

"He saw me and said, 'She's dead.'"

"Did you say anything to him?"

"I accused him of murder."

"Yeah? What was his reaction?"

"He said something about not letting me frame him again. Then he attacked me."

"What did he mean by that—not letting you frame him?"

Nell felt Clay's eyes on her. "I think he was referring to my eyewitness testimony in the Blanton case."

"Oh, right," said Darryll. "Stupid of me." He made another note; it seemed to take a long time. "The attack—now, how did that go?"

Nell described the attack, not well. When she came to the part about the gun falling loose from the force of the blow, she glanced at Clay. He was watching her, no strangeness now in his expression, instead the husbandly expression of a man who cared. But he caught her glance and everything changed.

"So once you got the gun, he booked?" Darryll said.

"Yes."

"Any idea where he—"

Clay's cell phone rang. He answered, listened for thirty seconds or so, clicked off. "There are no bullet wounds on the body," he said. "But the gun was fired." He turned to Nell. "Was DuPree bleeding?"

"Not that I saw."

"Any sign he'd been hit? Was he limping, for example?"

"No," Nell said.

"Think she shot him?" Darryll said.

"We've got a shell casing but no bullet hole," Clay said. "And a bloody trail leading out the door."

Darryll nodded. "He come at her," he said. "She put a bullet in him, but not in the right place, not enough to stop him. He did what he did, with a hammer or whatever, took it with him."

"Something like that," said Clay.

"I didn't see a hammer," Nell said.

"Or could have had a tire iron down his pant leg," Darryll said. "So now we go get 'im? Unless there's more you want me to go over here, Chief."

"Is there more, Nell?" Clay said. They exchanged a look. There was more, lots more, and she saw him registering that on her face.

But she couldn't trust him. "No," she said.

"Then we go get him," Clay said.

"Thought of one more thing," Darryll said.

"What's that?" said Clay, looking impatient.

"Maybe not important, but I should of asked if there was anything special about the lunch."

"I don't understand," Nell said.

"Reason for meeting, kinda thing," said Darryll.

"We're friends," said Nell.

"Gotcha." Darryll made one last note, missing the angry glance Clay shot him. Then he rose, a little unsteady, and started for the doorway, favoring his left leg. "Goddamn arthritis," he said.

Nell hung the *Guernica* reproduction back on the wall. She couldn't get it to line up straight.

CHAPTER 31

Timmy drove Nell home. His uniform was crisply ironed and he smelled of aftershave; lots of it, but not enough to smother completely the Bernardine smell. For the first time, Nell realized she might end up living somewhere else, maybe far away.

She went into the house and immediately got a strange feeling, the feeling of revisiting a place lived in long ago. But this was her house, the house she loved, and lived in now, so what was going on? She called Norah, got no answer. "Norah, I need to talk to you. It's urgent. Call as soon as you get this. Please."

Hanging up, she noticed the cruiser, still parked in the driveway, windows open, Timmy behind the wheel, eating an apple. She went outside.

"Timmy?"

He glanced at her quickly, dropped the apple out of sight, as though caught doing something bad. "Ma'am?"

"Is there anything I can help you with?"

"No, ma'am."

"Are you having car trouble?"

"Don't think so, ma'am."

Nell remembered how Timmy had told Clay about her visit to the Ambassador Suites, and her voice hardened, despite Timmy's fresh face and good manners. "Then what are you still doing here?"

He turned bright red. "Very sorry," he said. "Orders."
"Orders?"
"The chief wants me to remain on location," Timmy said.
"For protection, what with the killer on the loose, and all."
"I don't think it's necessary," Nell said.
"Very, very sorry," said Timmy. "Orders."
"But it's my house. This is my driveway."
"Yes, ma'am," said Timmy.

He looked miserable, but something in her didn't want to
relent, even prodded her to push harder, kick the car, key
the shiny paintwork, make the kind of irrational statement
that she had never even been tempted by in her life so far.
Instead she turned on her heel and strode back into the
house. She heard Timmy's sigh of relief, but she was in the
front hall by that time, door closed, so it must have been
her imagination.

Nell went up to her office, sat down. She took out the
digital recorder, listened once more. Easy to understand
why DuPree had said nothing to Clay about the scene in
the cells, but if Clay had been asking about that night, if
events had really happened the way DuPree had told her
and both men knew it, then why would Clay have called it
a theory? It would have been a fact, a cold-blooded setup
that explained almost everything. And why had DuPree
told Clay that he'd forgiven her, that it had been a mistake? If the scene in the cells had happened, then the whole
mistaken identity story would have been nonsense to both
men. And therefore?

On a sheet of paper, Nell drew little boxes. Someone killed
Johnny, and that someone was not Alvin DuPree. DuPree
gets out of jail, soon kills Lee Ann. And someone shot
Nappy Ferris—according to Sheriff Lanier, that case was
now wide open. One known, two unknowns; at least to her.
But in Johnny's case, Nell was almost sure two people knew:
Clay and Duke. She remembered Duke's blush—brighter
than Timmy's, although not much freshness remained on
Duke's face—when she'd suggested he knew the identity of

Johnny's murderer. And Clay was Duke's best friend; they were like brothers, went way back.

Her pen trailed off the paper. She just wasn't smart enough to figure this out; it required a brain like Johnny's. That was the kind of cheap irony that had never appealed to her in art or in life. "Think." She said it aloud. What had she left out? Bobby, of course. She drew another box, wrote his name inside.

Bobby. Had the tape been in his locker all those years? Once, at the police picnic, she and Bobby had worked the grill together. He'd told her a funny joke, made her laugh. What did the duck say to the horse? Answer: Why the long face? Had he been thinking at the same time: *Laugh, honey, but you don't understand the most important event of your whole life*? And, so much worse, but undeniable no matter what the play-out: Clay had known that, too, known the depth of her delusion.

Who else? Her world was divided, had been divided for a long time, between those who knew more about her than she did, and all the others. Who else was in that first group? Veronica? At that moment, Nell remembered Lee Ann's last call: *I just want to thank you for your help with Veronica Rice.* And then: *Whatever you told her did the trick. We had a very productive talk.*

What help? Nell hadn't understood then, didn't understand now. She called Veronica, got no answer.

"Veronica? Nell. Lee Ann tells me you spoke. I really need to talk to you about that. It's . . . it's an emergency, Veronica." Too dramatic? Maybe, but also too late to take it back.

Two or three minutes passed, Nell staring at the boxes on her sheet of paper. She rose, looked out the window, saw the cruiser in her driveway, Timmy's arm out the window. That reminded her of Joe Don. She tried Norah again, without success. What had Johnny told her about the universe, that everything was speeding away from everything else? She felt it happening now; a lot of those big, abstract things he'd liked to talk about turned out to apply in the tiny universe of the human heart. What would he say to that idea? Nell would have given a lot to know. He'd left so little behind. She tried to picture his face and could not.

Almost without knowing what she was doing, Nell opened the closet, unstacked boxes until she came to the one lettered UNC. She pulled it out, looked inside, found what she had before: her old art notebooks, research for her unwritten thesis, introductory geology textbook, souvenirs that didn't bring back any important memories and the photo album full of pictures of Johnny, all ruined by Bernardine. She flipped through, saw his blurred smile here, what might have been his torso, so lean and strong from the pool, there. This was stupid: she knew what she was doing, all right—running for help to a dead man. Nell began repacking everything, and as she did, her gaze fell on an old computer sitting at the back of the closet.

Her old computer, dating to her undergraduate days: an IBM desktop that now looked not much different from something invented by Edison. But not just her computer: in that last summer in Belle Ville, she'd been sharing it with Johnny. *Where's his computer? You squirreled that away, didn't you?*

Nell dragged the computer out of the closet, keyboard and mouse trailing behind, swept away cobwebs, blew off dust. An old Post-it note that had hung on the side of the computer all those years drifted to the floor. She recognized her own handwriting, somewhat different, the letters fuller than now, everything more spacious: *wine and cheese Tues. 7:30*—invitation to a party now completely forgotten.

Nell plugged in the computer, hit a key. Nothing happened. She tried several other keys, the mouse, a button, another button. Nothing. "Come on," she said, and gave the thing a little tap, followed by a harder one. The computer beeped and the screen flickered to life. She saw some icons, scanned them, their labels mostly meaningless now—lease 1.doc, cat copy courbet, Q&A 3.doc, jbletters.doc.

jbletters.doc? Nell clicked on that. A letter appeared.

> *Dear Mr. Bastien,*
> *I am very disappointed by your*

The computer beeped and the screen went dark. Nell tried her routine again, hitting keys, the mouse, different buttons, slapping the box itself, not hard, then harder. No response. She unplugged, replugged, went through the routine once more. Nothing. She yelled at the thing, fought off the urge to throw it through the window.

Nell rose, went to the window, looked down. Timmy was standing in front of the cruiser now, buffing the headlights with a cloth. Nell opened the window. "Timmy?"

His head snapped up. "Ma'am?" His hand went to his belt. "Everything all right?"

"How are you with computers?"

"Computers?"

"Are you good with them?"

"Honestly? Couldn't say real good, no. Not yet, anyhow."

"Not yet?"

"I'm taking level-three computer tech at night school," Timmy said. "BVCC. But I don't graduate till November."

"Mind coming in for a minute?" Nell said.

"In the house?"

"I need some computer help."

Timmy thought that over. "Is the door locked?"

"No. Just come in."

"It should be, ma'am."

"Well," said Nell. "It isn't."

"Wow," said Timmy. "What's this?"

"A computer," Nell said.

Timmy knelt in front of it. The desk phone rang. Nell picked it up.

"Hello?"

"Veronica Rice calling. I got your message."

Nell glanced at Timmy. He was examining the back of the computer. She stepped into the hall, the cord dragging behind her. "Thanks for calling me back," she said.

"You said it was an emergency."

"Lee Ann Bonner is dead. Alvin DuPree killed her."

Pause. "I'm sorry to hear that."

"He's on the run."

A longer pause. "Is that a warning?"

"Warning?"

"Are you saying he's coming here?" Veronica said.

"No," Nell said. "Why would he do that?"

Silence.

"I need to talk to you, Veronica. Can you—" She was about to ask Veronica to come over, but with the cruiser in the driveway, and Timmy? "Can we meet somewhere? Now?"

Silence. Just when Nell had decided that no answer was coming, that she had only a second or two to find the magic words, Veronica said, "And let the chips fall wherever they may?"

Nell felt a moment of dread; it turned out to be a real physical feeling, located inside her, on the border between chest and stomach. But there were things she had to know, that she couldn't live without knowing, leaving only one answer. "Yes."

"Because that's where the problems always start," Veronica said.

"You mean racial problems? This has nothing to do with that."

Veronica made a little sound, part laugh, part snort. "You know where I live?" she said.

"Timmy?" Nell said. He'd opened up the back of the computer, was gazing inside. "Timmy?"

He looked up quickly, as though startled. "Ma'am?"

"I'm going to lie down for a while."

"Okay," said Timmy. "Have a nice rest."

Nell walked along the hall, opened and closed her bedroom door—louder than necessary—then continued down the stairs and into the garage from the kitchen exit. She got in her car, hit the garage remote, backed out, hit the remote again. Turning onto the street, she glanced up at the office window, didn't see Timmy. She drove away.

Nell knew where Veronica lived—in the nice part of the East Side, several blocks north of the high-water mark, just above Penniman Street. She parked in front of Veronica's house, white with violet trim, and pressed a button by the door. Chimes sounded inside; a long time since she'd heard door chimes. She also heard a dog barking ferociously in the house next door. Glancing over, she saw an old man in a round African hat sitting on the porch, a puppy on his lap. The puppy's eyes were on Nell; the old man stared straight ahead.

Veronica's door opened. She wore a dress that matched the trim of the house, and seemed to have gone to some trouble with her appearance; Nell hoped it was because she was on her way to somewhere nice after this visit. "Come in," she said.

Nell went in, her first time inside Veronica's house. Spotless, comfortable, a little dark; a signed photograph of Martin Luther King stood on a table in the front hall. Veronica led her past it, into a small sitting room with brown furniture and a cream-colored wall-to-wall carpet. Black-and-white photographs hung on the wall, all of them scenes of Belle Ville before the flood.

"I love the photos," Nell said.

"Bobby took them."

"He did?"

"It was his hobby," Veronica said.

How had she not known that? The pictures were really

good; the one of the Fourth Street Baptist Church, now destroyed, with a thoughtful-looking girl in a party dress going up the stairs, was as good as anything in the museum's collection.

"Something to drink?" Veronica said. "Coke? Iced tea?"

"I'm all right, thanks," Nell said.

Veronica nodded. Maybe accepting a drink would have been the way to go; Nell felt off balance, as though in another country, which was crazy: this was her town and she'd been around black people all her life, considered a few of the black women at the museum her friends. They sat on easy chairs angled toward each other.

"Ms. Bonner is dead?" Veronica said.

"Yes."

"I turned on the news. They didn't say anything."

"I'm sure they'll have the story soon," Nell said. "Maybe the delay has something to do with the search for DuPree."

Eyes focused on some point beyond Nell, Veronica said, "He's the real killer this time?"

"I practically saw it happen." Nell described the scene in Lee Ann's condo; and as she did, Veronica's gaze shifted slightly and met hers.

When Nell came to the end, Veronica said, "I'm glad you weren't harmed."

"Thank you," Nell said. "I was supposed to meet Lee Ann for lunch. I think she was going to tell me whatever it was you told her."

"Why is that, if you don't mind me asking?" Veronica said.

"Why do I think she planned to tell me?"

Veronica nodded, a slow movement, almost grave; and there was a deep gravity about this woman: to shift her against her will off some position she'd taken would be almost impossible.

"Because," Nell said, "I could hear it in her voice." Veronica's face remained impassive. "And she seemed to think the little visit you and I had at the school played a role in your decision to talk to her. She said it was productive. Meaning she was grateful to me."

Another slow nod.

"So whatever you told her about the tape, I'd like to hear, too," Nell said.

"The tape?"

"How it got in Bobby's locker," Nell said. "The whole story, I guess, from where you sit."

"From where I sit." The way Veronica said that seemed to imply some huge distance between them. "Truth is I didn't speak a word about the tape, except for I had nothing to say on that subject."

"Then what did you tell her?"

"That Bobby's death was an accident."

"Of course it was," Nell said. "He died saving the baby—everyone knows that."

"There's everyone," Veronica said, "and then there's the power structure. To satisfy my mind, I hired a private detective out of Houston."

Nell was bewildered. "To do what?"

"To make sure Bobby really died—" She went silent, her eyes moistening; then her face changed—Nell caught a look of self-disgust—her eyes dried up and she continued: "To make sure Bobby really died the way they said."

"But the picture was in the *Guardian*."

Veronica gestured at the photos on the wall. "Anything can be done with pictures—Bobby taught me that."

All at once the room felt airless; the edges of everything went yellow. Nell tried to grasp the implications of what she'd just heard. "Lee Ann believed Bobby might have been murdered?" she said.

"She's—she was a smart lady," Veronica said.

"But—" Nell stopped herself. Had she read some poll result seeming to show that blacks had a more conspiratorial worldview than whites? Nell wasn't sure, but the thought came to her: *You need to be blacker now.* "What did the detective find?" she said.

"No foul play," said Veronica. "He satisfied my mind."

"I'd like something to drink now," Nell said. "Water, if it's no trouble."

"No trouble," Veronica said. She rose, quite easily for such a big woman, and left the room. Nell got up, too, breathed deeply; the yellow edging faded away. She took a closer look at the girl in the party dress and noticed something she hadn't before—a man's face in one of the church windows. For some reason, the sight chilled her.

She went into the hall, followed sounds of running water to the kitchen. Veronica stood at the sink, filling a pitcher. "The fact that you believed Bobby might have been murdered means you know someone who had a motive, doesn't it?" Nell said.

Veronica lost her grip on the pitcher: startled by Nell's sudden appearance? . . . or by what she'd said? The pitcher fell and smashed in the sink. Veronica didn't move. The water ran.

"Who?" Nell said. "Who had a motive?"

Veronica was silent.

"I have to know, Veronica. It's about the tape, isn't it?"

Veronica went still. Somehow she'd cut the palm of her hand. Not badly: she didn't seem to notice the thin red trickle. "Why should I say anything?" she said.

"Because it's all going to come out now," Nell said.

"It never does," said Veronica. Now she became aware of the cut. She frowned at it, held her palm under the water for a moment, then shut off the tap. The bleeding stopped. It was very quiet in the kitchen.

A conspiratorial kind of quiet. "You can tell yourself that's the reason," Nell said. "But what if the truth is you're covering up something Bobby did, something bad?"

Veronica turned on her, so fast Nell took a step back, afraid that Veronica was about to attack her. "Bobby did nothing bad," she said, her voice shaking. "Nothin'."

"Then who did?" Nell said.

Veronica's head tilted back a little. Nell knew the answer right then.

"My husband?" she said.

Veronica nodded, a tiny motion, almost imperceptible.

"What happened?" Nell said.

"Chips fall wherever they may?" Veronica said.

"They're falling right now," said Nell. What could be more obvious? Chips falling and falling, a blizzard.

"It was like insurance," Veronica said. "We take insurance wherever we can find it in this life."

Who did? Black people, or everybody in general? Nell didn't risk the question.

Veronica gazed down at her hand; Nell saw she still wore her wedding ring. "One night," she said. "After work on the late shift. Bobby's sitting in his car, the old blue Chevy, in that lot between One Marigot and where that ribs place was back then. Pouring rain, the ribs place is closed, everything dark. Out the back of One Marigot comes Clay Jarreau." Veronica looked up, her eyes meeting Nell's. "Clay glances around real quick, doesn't see Bobby, doesn't see anyone, on account of the parking lot's deserted, late at night, the rain. He goes over to the Dumpster by the ribs place, tosses something in, closes down the lid. Then he gets in his car and drives away. Seems strange to Bobby. Bobby's a curious man, a detective, right?" Veronica turned and began picking up the broken glass, dropping it in a trash pail in the cupboard under the sink.

"It was the tape?"

"Bobby brought it home," Veronica said. "Showed it to me. I told him one thing—it's not staying in this house."

"Why did he keep it secret? Out of loyalty to Clay?"

Veronica gave her a strange look, a look that said *no* and more besides. "Bobby liked his job," she said. "Liked the life we were having."

"But an innocent man went to jail," Nell said.

Veronica made that sound again, half laugh, half snort.

"I don't understand," said Nell.

Veronica shrugged. "What did all the folks involved have in common?" she said. "Except Bobby."

All white. That was easy, maybe too easy. "Why did Bobby keep the tape?"

"I told you—insurance."

"Was he planning to use it on Clay someday?"

Veronica's back stiffened.

"Did he know who the real killer was?" Nell said.

No answer.

"Was it Clay?" Nell said.

Veronica spoke quietly. "Bobby was never sure." She dropped the last piece of broken glass into the trash.

Nell drove home, saw the cruiser still outside, no one in it. She parked in the garage, went upstairs, entered the office. Timmy had the old computer on the desk now, was playing some primitive-looking video game on it. He turned.

"Have a nice rest?" he said.

"You got it working?" Nell said.

"Oh, yeah," said Timmy. "Sixty-four kilobyte CPU! Hard to believe." He rose. "I'll be heading back outside."

"Thanks, Timmy."

"Hey."

Timmy left. Nell sat at the old computer. A few seconds later, she'd opened jbletters.doc.

Mr. Kirk Bastien
Vice President, Operations
DK Industries

Dear Mr. Bastien:
I am very disappointed by your response in the
matter of the pending ship canal construction plans.
As I indicated in my earlier letters and phone calls,
my computer modeling (see attachment to my letter
of July 2) demonstrates that the Canal Street flood-
gates, as designed, are insufficient to withstand a
direct hit from a category 4 hurricane and above, or
even a category 3 on a rising tide. The position you
seem to have taken—that all the various permitting
agencies have given their approval—does not change

*this fact. Furthermore, their approvals do not appear
to take into account recent surveys, which, although
still partial, indicate a worrisome "funnel effect"
under certain conditions. I would add also that the
computer modeling techniques employed by your
engineers are flawed and out-of-date. Your failure to
take these findings seriously leaves me no alternative
but to begin contacting all relevant agencies—and
possibly the press—myself. Let me add that I was
taught by two scientists presently employed by the
Army Corps of Engineers.*

> *Sincerely,*
> *Johnny Blanton*

Nell checked the date on the letter, July 21, twenty years
ago: two days before Johnny's death.

CHAPTER 32

Pirate poked his head around a corner, got a partial view of the Ambassador Suites: three cruisers parked outside. No go. That was bad. Why? Because his Bible was in there, in his rightful suite, and his fingers itched for the gold tassel.

A door on one of the cruisers started to open. Pirate ducked back into the alley, real quick, like an animal. Why not? That was how they were treating him. Something was very wrong. Wasn't he supposed to end up with twice what he had before? And what about his book, *Only a Test*? What was going to happen to that, now that they'd killed his partner? Someone beat her head in, and the worst part? That same bitch, Nell Jarreau, was going to finger him for it, do him bad for the second time. No second time in Job, oh, no: and that was the word of God. Therefore ungodliness was doing the talking for the moment, and all rules were suspended. Pirate hunkered down behind a pile of wreckage from the flood and waited for nightfall, his fingers itching for the gold tassel.

Pirate slept. And in his sleep he dreamed, not a nightmare or even one of those anxious dreams, but instead something wonderful. In this dream he had both eyes and a Rickenbacker, and he could play. He ripped through dazzling solos on "Devil Woman," "You Don't Know Me," "He Stopped Loving Her Today." Norah gazed up adoringly.

* * *

Pirate woke. Late-evening sky, full of wild colors: it reminded him of the cover of a gospel album an old neighbor biddy had had when he was a kid. That sky—the sky on the album, the sky above this crappy town—was what heaven looked like. For a few moments, he just lay there in the flood wreckage in a peaceful, quiet mood, watching heaven grow dark. Then various memories started trickling back, and the situation he was in took its hard shape in his mind. Lots of different—what was the word? factors?—but one sure thing: he wasn't going back to prison. That was out, stone-cold out.

He sat up, felt something in his pocket. What was this? The address book, leather cracked with age, *University of Texas* in gold on the front. He realized that Lee Ann had left it to him, her very last act before dying. So it must be important, right? Pirate remembered her face at the end: reduced to one eye, just like him. They were partners, all right. Someone— *bastard,* she'd said—had to pay. But bastard: What kind of a clue was that? Bastard meant just about everyone. He'd never killed anyone in his life, but, oh boy.

Pirate moved toward the street, got close to the cone of a streetlight, stopped short of stepping into it. He saw a single cruiser parked outside his hotel. That was the way they thought: he wasn't coming back. What else were they thinking? Pirate didn't know. He opened the address book, his inheritance from Lee Ann. This time he didn't leaf through, but examined the thing with care, starting at the first page. And right away he learned something: this was Johnny Blanton's address book. Pirate knew that because at the top of the first page it said: *My Address Book;* and in the space underneath was written *Johnny Blanton.* Below that he saw a crossed-out address in Chapel Hill, North Carolina, and under that a West Side address in Belle Ville and in parentheses: *Nellie's folks.*

He had Johnny Blanton's address book. It had to be important. But to who? And then he remembered something Norah had said: *I've tried to get to know him from his writing.* Here in this book—beat-up, the writing faded, like in a real historic document—had to be his friends, business associates, whatever: a handy little guide to Johnny Blanton's life.

Pirate heard a distant siren. He walked down the alley, away from the Ambassador Suites. The first crossing street was Peach, run-down in the old days, run-down now, not well lit. He spotted a convenience store partway down the block, one of those convenience stores with a couple gas pumps and a pay phone outside.

Pirate, staying in the shadows, made his way to the pay phone. A light pole stood over the pay phone, but it wasn't working. Pirate had Joe Don's number on a scrap of paper in his pocket. He dialed it. The phone rang a few times, then went to the message machine. "Um," said Pirate. "It's, like, me. I've got, uh—"

At that moment, he heard a funny little sound, like a reverse click, and Norah spoke. "Hi," she said.

"Hi." Too late, Pirate thought: *What if she knows about Lee Ann?*

"Sorry about that," Norah said.

"About what?"

"Screening," she said. "We've kind of been screening our calls a bit." She laughed, a high little laugh, close to a giggle. Was she stoned? "What's new with you?" she said.

A question like that had to mean Norah wasn't in the know. Pirate could picture the scene: Norah and Joe Don rolling around in that fixed-up barn of his, then maybe taking a little spin in the Miata to cool off, followed by back to the barn and more rolling around. He could picture it vividly, although nothing like that had ever happened to him. Was it too late?

"Not much," he said. "One little thing you might be interested in."

"Yeah? What's that?"

"I think I can help you some with that . . . quest of yours."

She laughed again; yes, stoned for sure. "I have a quest?"

Now she was starting to piss him off. Did he have time for this? Night had fallen and the moon hung in the sky, a sliver-type moon with pointy ends, like devil ears. "Thought you did," Pirate said. "Like you told me the other night—finding traces of your father."

Her voice changed, got more serious. "Yes," she said. "You're right. You can help me?"

"It just so happens," Pirate said. A cruiser pulled around the corner, drove down the street, not fast. Just as it neared the convenience store, two big black guys appeared on the far sidewalk, and the cop turned his head to look at them.

"Still there?" Norah said.

He lowered his voice. "Just so happens I managed to lay my hands on his old address book."

"My father's address book?"

"From back then," Pirate said; although what sense did that make? When else would it be from? But Norah didn't seem to notice—he heard her suck in her breath just the tiniest bit, kind of in surprise, a sound ninety-nine out of a hundred would have missed, but not him, not with his hearing. "Has all his friends in there," he added. "Business associates. Whatnot. Care to see it?"

"Oh, yes," she said. "When would be—"

"How about if you swing by, pick me up right now?"

"Sure that's all right?"

"Huh?"

"Convenient for you," Norah said.

"Yeah, it's convenient," said Pirate. *I'm at a convenience store, for Christ's sake.* "I'm out for a walk right now. How about meeting me on Peach Street?" He named the next corner.

"Peach Street?" said Norah. "That's not a very nice area."

"Shaking in my boots," said Pirate.

She made that giggling noise again. He felt pretty good.

Pirate heard thunder, very far away, maybe someplace in Texas; that was the kind of hearing he had. A few seconds after that, he felt a raindrop, then another. He looked up: the devil moon was gone.

Headlights shone a few blocks down Peach Street, low and close together, small-car-type headlights. As they came closer, Pirate stepped out of the shadows. The car—yes, the Miata, top up, wipers on—pulled over. Pirate opened the passenger-side door, got in; only then noticing that Joe Don, not Norah, was behind the wheel.

"Hey," said Joe Don.

"Where's Norah?"

"Back at the place. She's a little tired."

"Yeah? You two been busy?" That just popped out; Pirate regretted it right away, at least a little bit. On the other hand, why did he have to pussyfoot? Where did that get you?

Joe Don's eyes shifted toward him. "Not too much," he said. "Been traveling some—we spent a day in Baton Rouge."

"What's up there?" Pirate said.

Joe Don turned a corner, headed north. A cruiser sped by in the opposite direction. Headlight beams shone for a moment on Joe Don's face, with its prominent cheekbones and perfect skin; all very clear to Pirate—Joe Don was on his good side. "Fact is," he said, "I got a bit lucky."

"How so?" said Pirate.

"Dude from Swampland Records heard me down at the Rooster," Joe Don said. "They signed me to a contract."

Pirate wasn't following. "To do what?"

Joe Don laughed; maybe a happy, innocent laugh, but Pirate didn't like it at all. "To make a record," he said.

"You got a record deal?"

It was raining harder now, drops splashing up off the hood. "Not with EMI or anything like that," Joe Don said. "Swampland's just a little indie label, but they got big plans."

Pirate sat, silent and still, watching the wipers. His dream came back, the dream with him up onstage, reeling off solos, rippin' and rockin', on fire. "I had this dream," he began, then stopped himself.

"Yeah? What happened?"

"Guitar dream. I was playing out of my fuckin' mind."

"Never had a dream like that," Joe Don said, slowing down for a red light. "And one little thing, Pirate. I heard you were playing the Rick."

"How'd you hear that?"

"Doesn't matter," said Joe Don. "Maybe it sounds goofy to you, but I've got a thing about the Rick. A superstition, like." There was a silence. "We square on that?"

"Sure thing," Pirate said.

Joe Don stopped at the light. He looked like he was getting ready to say something nice and friendly, back to being pals. Pirate pivoted his upper body around, toward the door, just loading up, then swung back the other way, elbow leading, with all his strength. And that was a lot. His elbow caught Joe Don square on that beautiful cheekbone, and made a satisfying crunch. "Square enough?" Pirate said, but probably not; there was barely time to think the thought let alone say it before his right fist, continuing the same movement, landed on the same cheekbone, exact same spot. A real crusher. And once more. Why not? Pirate felt tremendous—what was the word? something from a Bob Dylan song?—release. But that last blow had been selfish, unnecessary, because it was clear Joe Don was no tough guy, no fighter. In fact, Joe Don wasn't doing much of anything. Pirate leaned across his motionless body, opened the driver's-side door, pushed him out. Joe Don's head made a coconut sound on the pavement. Somehow Pirate got himself across to the driver's seat, slid it back to the right position for a big guy like him, and was all set to go when the light turned green. He thought of looking back in the rearview mirror but decided against it.

* * *

Pirate knocked on the side door of Joe Don's barn. Norah opened up. "Oh, it's raining," she said. Then she looked past him. "Where's Joe Don?"

Pirate was all set. "Ran into a guy. They're having coffee."

Norah frowned. She was beautiful, no doubt about it. Pirate felt this strange urge, an urge he'd never felt for another human being, to explore all her emotions. "What kind of guy?"

He was set for that, too. "From Swampland," he said. "Wanted to go over some charts. Something like that."

She looked past him again. Meanwhile, Pirate was getting wet. "Why didn't they come here?" she said.

He shrugged. "The music business," he said. "But, hey— don't you want to see the address book?"

"Sorry. Come in."

Pirate went in. A book lay open on the couch, cover side up: *Last Train to Memphis;* there was a picture of Elvis Presley on the cover. Pirate's gaze went right from that to the Rick, almost glowing in its stand.

"Did he say if he wanted me to come get him?" Norah said.

"Who?" said Pirate.

Norah blinked. "Joe Don."

"Nah."

"But it's raining."

"He'll call. Or maybe the Swampland guy will give him a ride."

"Was it Big Ed?"

"Who?"

"The Swampland guy."

"Didn't catch his name."

"A big guy with a droopy mustache?"

"Yeah, him. Big Ed."

Norah nodded, but then seemed to have another thought. It made her frown again. Of the frowning emotions, Pirate had already had enough. "I thought Big Ed was flying to L.A. today," she said.

"The music business," Pirate said. Norah had prominent

cheekbones, too, but much more delicate than Joe Don's. Pirate took the address book from his pocket before she had a chance to go down some line of questions she'd regret. "Here," he said.

Norah's mood changed completely. She gazed at the thing like it had magic powers. "Oh my God," she said.

"Take it."

She took it, real careful, reverentlike. Pirate's fingers understood: they got the itchy feeling.

Norah sat on a stool, paging through the address book, very quiet. Pirate stood by a window, watching the rain, trying to figure things out. He needed the Miata. That was clear. The only question was whether he was leaving alone.

After a while, he heard her crying. He turned. "What's wrong?"

Tears were streaming down her face. "All his appointments and everything are here," she said. "Of his last days and beyond."

Well, of course; he hadn't known he was going to die. "That's so sad," Pirate said. He went closer, looked over her shoulder.

"See," she said, pointing to a page with horizontal lines, all blocked out in chunks of time. Pirate had never had a book like this. He read: *call Prof. Myers re cone theory; dentist, 1:30; Sallie Mae re questions; lunch with Nellie.*

"What's cone theory?" Pirate said.

"I don't know," said Norah. "He was brilliant." She turned the page, spoke again, very softly. "This is the day he died."

Pool 7–8, intervals; revise cat. 3 model; call Kirk Bastien—last chance; dinner w/Nellie. She turned the page. "And here's the next day."

Bastien? "Wait," said Pirate. "Turn back."

"Turn back?"

Pirate seized the book, turned the page himself, pointed. "How do you say that?"

"Originally it must have been French, like Bastienne. But they say Bastin."

"Bastin? They say Bastin?"

Was he shouting? She looked a little scared. "Yes," she said. "Bastin. They're friends of my par—of my mother and stepfather. More my stepfather's, really. He and the other brother—"

"Bastin? Like that? You say it like Bastin?"

"Kind of. But why—"

"Are there lots of them in town—Bastiens?"

"Just the two, as far as I know. Kirk's the mayor."

Pirate had a faint memory: *You're on a bit of a roll, Mr. DuPree.* But before it could sharpen—something about that fancy Italian restaurant?—it got pushed aside by bigger thoughts.

Bastard. That wasn't what Lee Ann had said, dying on the floor of her closet, blood trickling between her lips. It was what he'd heard, not knowing this strange name. But she'd said Bastin, Pirate was sure of that. Lee Ann had been trying to tell him the name of her killer. A dying person naming her killer: that was practically a message from God. Would he ever have a better partner? He owed her, big-time. And then it hit him, a revelation like an earthquake, strong enough to make him shake. There was a big difference between these two false accusations in his life. The first time, with Johnny Blanton, he hadn't known the identity of the real killer, in fact, still did not. But this time, now, with Lee Ann, he knew. A lifeline! Bastien was the killer: he had the victim's dying word.

"Where is he?"

"Who?"

"Bastien."

"I don't know."

"Does he live around here?"

"They've got a big place up at the lake."

"Show me."

"Show you?"

"Now."

"But why? Why is it so important?" She reached for the address book, read out loud, "'call Kirk Bastien—last chance.'" She looked up, a thought dawning in her eyes. "Does it have something to do with my father's death?"

"Yeah," Pirate said, just to get her cooperation. He grabbed the Rick on the way out.

"What are you doing?" Norah said.

"Joe Don wanted me to bring it."

"Bring it where?"

"Didn't say. He'll call." Pirate almost said *the music business* one more time, decided not to bother.

"Okay," Norah said. "I've got my cell."

"Let's rock and roll," said Pirate.

CHAPTER 33

N ell gazed out the window. Rain pounded down on the cruiser, Timmy invisible inside, sitting in the dark. She'd called Clay three times, been told he was on the case, wanted her to stay right there, would be in touch soon. But everything was speeding away from everything, as Johnny had taught her. Her mind was speeding most of all. It left a trail of disturbing images: Kirk, mask pushed up on his forehead, holding his free-diving trophy; Clay and Duke, both thirteen, at the riflery championships: *the winner, not shown, was Duke's eleven-year-old brother, Kirk Bastien;* and just yesterday, Kirk getting out of his SUV up at Lake Versailles, and limping up to his house. She could hardly breathe. The sensation of being trapped under the reef off Little Parrot Cay came back to her, real enough that she opened the window wide, let in the wind and rain. The rain was so loud she almost didn't hear the phone.

Nell ran to the desk, grabbed it. "Clay?"

But not Clay: some man's voice she didn't recognize: "Norah?" he said. "That you?"

"No. This is her mother."

"Mrs. Jarreau? Yeller here. You seen her anywheres, Norah, that is?"

"No. I've been calling and calling. Is something wrong?" She knew the answer to that already, from the sound of his voice.

"Yes, ma'am, you could say that. Joe Don's in a bad way."

"What happened?"

"They found him laying in the middle of the street. Princess Street. All messed up, like some boys put the boots to him pretty good."

"Is he going to be all right?"

"Doc's goin' to be operating anytime now. Got him down at Mercy, where I am at this moment, Mrs. Jarreau."

"Operating?"

"Bleeding on the brain, doc says. They got to go in, plug it all up. But why I called, there's this report of maybe that l'il Miata gettin' seen nearby."

"Oh, God."

"I sent someone up to that old barn of Joe Don's—she weren't there, the car neither."

"I don't know where she is. Are the police involved?"

"They's what found him. Thing is, ma'am, they got some eyewitness says a man was at the wheel of the car, an' he was by hisself. Not Norah in her own ride, what I'm saying. Any idea who that man could be?"

"No. None."

There was a little pause. Nell could hear some machine beeping in the background, and a voice on a speaker. "Sure about that?" Yeller said.

"Yes," Nell said. "What are you saying?"

"Joe Don said he was harmless, and all, and 'course with him bein' innocent in the end, there shouldn't be a problem, but still I—"

"Mr. Yeller? Who are you talking about?"

"Alvin DuPree," Yeller said. "Turns out he's a music lover. Been hangin' out at the Red Rooster, maybe even paid a visit or two to the barn."

"Are you telling me DuPree has met my daughter?"

"Oh, yes, ma'am. Pretty sure of that."

* * *

Nell ran out into the rain, slanting down now in icy sheets, and tried the cruiser's passenger-side door. Locked. She banged on it. The inside of the car was all fogged up, but she could see Timmy flinch. The window slid down.

"Ma'am?" he said.

"Let me in."

"But—"

"Don't argue. Norah's in trouble." The lock popped up. Nell got in.

"What kind of trouble?" Timmy said.

"I don't know," Nell said. "And she's not the only one."

"Not the only one in trouble?" Timmy said.

"Drive," said Nell.

"Where?" But he turned the key, hand not quite steady, as though her inner state had invaded his.

Where? Only one idea came to mind, not very promising. "The Red Rooster," she said.

"That dive over on Rideau?" said Timmy. "Doubt someone like her—"

"Drive."

Timmy slid the car in gear, turned onto Sandhill Way. Water was sluicing down both sides of the road in thick, writhing streams. Timmy radioed in, gave his number. "Proceeding east on Crosstown, destination Red Rooster club on Rideau. Have Mrs. Jarreau."

"I want to speak to Clay," Nell said.

"Wants to speak to the chief," Timmy said. "Soon as possible. Over."

They came to the upper end of Rideau, turned south. A half mile or so down there was water in the street, three or four inches. And a few blocks later? Flood conditions, with abandoned cars, all buildings dark, wreckage from Bernardine floating in from the back alleys, like a recurring nightmare.

"Jesus," said Timmy, stopping the car. Voices crackled on the radio, one of them Clay's.

"There he is," Nell said.

Timmy called in, gave his number. "Got Mrs. Jarreau here. Any way you can patch the chief in for her?"

"On his way to a reported disturbance," the dispatcher said. "Trying for you now."

Nell heard static, and then nothing. "Ask her where the disturbance is," she said.

"They'd call me if—" A hanging traffic light came loose on the next corner, fell with a big splash. Timmy radioed in, asked the question.

"Lake Versailles," said the dispatcher, adding the street address. But Nell already knew.

"Timmy?" she said. "You won't do much good here."

He nodded and backed the car.

"It's really raining," Norah said.

"Yeah," said Pirate, behind the wheel. She'd told him she didn't like driving in the rain, so he'd done the gentlemanly thing. But he found, after so many years off the road, that he didn't like it either. He had the wipers cranked to the max, a rhythm that bothered him, something going way too fast, deep in his brain, but there was no choice if he wanted to see. And he wasn't seeing too great, some new night thing with the one eye, another pisser. Plus in between giving him directions, Norah kept making calls on her cell phone and getting no answer. Why did that piss him off even more? He got a funny sensation in his right elbow, like it wanted action, maybe do like the left one could do.

"Who're you calling?" he said.

"Joe Don," she said. "It's not like him not to answer."

"Maybe him and Big Ernie are talking business."

"Big Ernie?"

What the hell? "With the droopy mustache."

"Big Ed, you mean."

"Yeah. Fuckin' Big Ed." Uh-oh. She was looking at him kind of funny. He made his voice nice and gentle, like he was some favorite uncle. "The music business is tough, Norah, got to warn you."

"But even so," Norah said, "he always answers my calls, every single time."

Maybe he doesn't love you anymore. A clever little joke, since Pirate was pretty sure of its truth, but best kept to himself. "He said he'd call. He wants the Rick, after all. Don't he just love that old guitar?"

"It means a lot to him."

"He'll be playing it soon," Pirate said. "Like with the angels up in heaven."

"Huh?" said Norah.

"Just saying he plays like an angel," Pirate said. "One of those expressions—just means he plays real good."

"Yeah, I know. You, uh, play nicely, too."

"Shucks," said Pirate.

Lightning cracked across the sky, a big thick crevice, like a glimpse of a place where everything was white-hot. Pirate saw a lake in the distance, all black, and two big houses, lights in the windows. They rolled up to a closed gate.

"This is it," Norah said.

"They got a gate?"

"Maybe there's someone in the gatehouse," Norah said. "Try honking."

Honking didn't seem like a good idea. Pirate just sat there, thinking, the wipers going way too fast. Norah interrupted, not his chain of thought, because there were no links yet, but still: it put him on edge.

"What are we doing here, again?" she said.

Pirate turned to her. "A little stoned?"

"Not much."

"But some," Pirate said. "Maybe I better do the thinking for both of us. I got you your dad's address book, remember?"

"Of course. Thanks."

"Then we're square, right?"

She answered correctly. "Right."

"And that address book—we can't just do nothing."

She looked confused. "I guess not."

The rain banged on the roof, drumrolls piled on drumrolls. Lee Ann had tried so hard to tell him the name of her killer: first actually naming him, and then—how horrified she must have been at his *Goddamn right, we'll get the bastard*—even then, with just a few more breaths to go, she'd tried again, telling him to bring the address book. Why? So he could see that name, Kirk Bastien, on Johnny Blanton's calendar; see that name and take vengeance. Why else? He would never have another partner like Lee Ann. Vengeance was his: Who had a better right?

Pirate pulled the car over a little, angling the headlights on the gatehouse. Dark inside, unoccupied, but he saw a small sign: when guard off duty buzz for admission. Pirate swung the car around, bringing the buzzer in reach from Norah's side.

"Buzz," he said.

"Me?"

"You know him, right?"

"Who?"

He wanted to smack her. And what's more, Pirate realized at that moment how in some way Norah's beauty had gotten in the way of Lee Ann and him being what they could have been. But that was for later. He took a deep breath. "Kirk Bastien, who we've been talking about."

"Not really," Norah said. "I know his brother better, but I haven't seen him either in a few years. There are no kids up here and—"

"How about we just buzz and see what happens?"

Norah laughed, her mood changing quickly. "Sounds like a plan." She slid down her window. Rain pelted in. "What do I say?"

"Who you are." And if that didn't work? Pirate had no idea.

"That's easy," said Norah. She buzzed.

A woman came on the speaker, almost right away. "Yes?" she said.

"Hi, this is Norah Jarreau."

There was a little pause. "Oh, hi. Not sure, but I don't think your father's here right now."

"Huh?" said Norah.

"Were you expecting him, or—" the woman began. "Anyway, I'll buzz you in. I'm Mindy, Duke's, um, fiancée."

"Nice to meet you," Norah said.

Both women laughed. The buzzer buzzed. The gate swung open. Pirate, who'd had trouble following the back-and-forth, drove through.

The driveway curved toward the lake. There were lots of buildings, but two real big ones. One had a tower at the top, the other did not. It was raining so hard Pirate couldn't make out more than that.

"Where?" he said.

"Not exactly sure," said Norah.

"But you've been here." Uh-oh. Too loud?

Norah's eyes were wide, like she was scared or something. "I told you—it's been a long time. But he's the younger brother."

"So?"

"So wouldn't the older one get the tower?" Norah said.

"Yeah." Norah was smart enough, when she was straight.

"Weed has some negative effects," Pirate said. That came without a thought, proving that he would have been a pretty good uncle after all—maybe still could be.

"Thanks for the advice."

He didn't like her tone, but a question arose in his mind, more important. "Uncles," he said.

"What about them?"

"Need a brother or sister for that, correct?"

"I guess so."

Pirate did have a sister, much older, unheard from in years. She lived in New Mexico, or possibly Alaska. He'd never liked her.

Pirate drove into the parking area near the house with no tower. All at once it stopped raining, just like that.

"Wow," Norah.

Had to be a good sign. They got out of the car. Pirate went around to the trunk, opened up.

"What are you looking for?" Norah said.

"Flashlight."

"I don't think there is one."

"No problem," Pirate said, closing the trunk; but not before, real quick, he grabbed the tire iron and stuck it down his pant leg.

They walked up a seashell path to the front door. Sounds of rushing water came from everywhere. Pirate got distracted by them, was barely aware of Norah, a step or two behind him, dialing her cell phone.

"Hello?" she said.

Hello? She'd reached someone? How was that possible?

"I'm calling for Joe Don Yeller," she said. "Who's this?" She listened for a few seconds and spoke again. "You're a nurse at Mercy Hospital? I don't—"

The next moment, Norah was lying facedown on the seashell path, the cell phone a few feet away. Pirate stamped on the cell phone, but not on Norah. On the other hand, what to do with her? This wasn't fair.

Norah rolled over, sat up. She groaned in pain, but didn't look worse for wear to Pirate; she did look scared, though, maybe even terrified.

"Why'd you do that?" she said, her voice rising. Pirate had no experience handling hysteria, knew he'd be useless.

He knelt down, took her by the hair, not too hard. "Have to be partners now," he said. "Don't fuck up."

But she did fuck up, big-time, screaming the loudest scream he'd ever heard. He jerked her upright and raised his free hand high. At that moment, the door of the house with no tower opened. A man stood in the doorway, lit mostly from the back, but Pirate recognized him, this blond rich guy, from that brief meeting at Vito's—the fanciest restaurant he'd ever been in. Maybe he'd lost some weight, but Pirate knew his enemy: Kirk Bastien, mayor of Belle Ville.

"What's going on out there?" he said, shielding his eyes. "Norah? Is that you?" He stepped outside.

No time for more questions, nothing left but action. Pirate

let go of Norah, charged forward, reaching for the tire iron. "This is for Lee Ann," he cried out at the top of his lungs. Bastien took a step back, raising his hands. Behind him, a tall tanned woman appeared. By that time, Pirate was in range. He swung the gleaming wet tire iron with all his might—the great rain of his strength!—and just as he did, the tall woman shouted, "Duke!"

Duke, not Kirk? Did that mean this was the brother, and therefore the wrong guy? Why was he finding this out now, too late? Meaning too late to stop the tire iron, although Pirate was able to slow it down and alter the path a little, bringing it lower, keeping the hard steel from connecting with his forehead. Instead, it caught him somewhere in the middle of the face. Christ, what a mess. Norah had fucked up the whole tower analysis, her logic all wrong. Pirate almost threw up.

And Norah? She was standing there with this look on her face, like he was a monster. He grabbed her, dragged her out to the car. That was when the Rick came in handy. Pirate ripped out the D and A strings, used them to bind Norah's hands and feet. She struggled a bit, tried screaming again, this time screaming something about Joe Don. He tore a strip off his soaking shirt and put a stop to that, then threw her over his shoulder. This was all taking too much time. He had to face the fact that Norah was nothing but a burden to him now.

gates at the Bastien compound on Lake Versailles ng open. The rain had stopped a few minutes before, but as Timmy drove through, there was a boom of thunder, deep and rolling, followed by a sizzling sound from the sky, and rain came pounding down. Nell saw two cars in front of Duke's house: a cruiser with the chief's star on the side, and the Miata. Timmy parked beside them. Nell jumped out, was soaked to the skin in an instant.

"Maybe you should stay in—" Timmy began.

The front door was wide open. Nell ran in. Duke lay on the floor, face bloody, jaw at a strange angle. The new girl-friend—the name wouldn't come—knelt beside him, rocking back and forth, a bloody towel in her hands.

"The ambulance is coming," she said. "The ambulance is coming."

"What happened?" said Timmy. "Where's the chief?"

"And Norah?" Nell said. "Was she with Alvin DuPree?"

"The ambulance is coming."

Nell raised her voice. "Answer me," she said. "Was she with DuPree? A man with a patch?"

"Oh, God," said the girlfriend. She looked terrified.

Duke stirred, looked right at Nell. His lips moved and he spoke one toothless word, his voice so weak she almost missed it. "Sorry," he said.

"Shh," said the girlfriend, "shh. The ambulance is coming."

Nell ran outside, headed for Kirk's house at the end of the driveway. Timmy caught up. He'd lost his hat. His hair was plastered down flat; he looked like a little kid. "Maybe it would be better if you—"

She cut him off. "Have you got your gun?"

"Of course."

They ran. A lightning bolt streaked across the sky, from one horizon to the other. Then came thunder, so loud it deafened her. Nell's hearing didn't recover till they'd reached the house. She heard running water everywhere.

They stepped up to Kirk's wraparound porch. Timmy knocked on the door. It opened. Clay stood in the doorway, a gun in his hand. Kirk was beside him, wearing shorts and flip-flops. He had a thick bloodstained bandage wound around one of his thighs and his hands were cuffed in front of him with zip-strips. Clay lowered the gun.

"Officer," he said, speaking to Timmy but watching Nell, his voice not his own, more like a machine talking, "Mr. Bastien is under arrest for the murder of Lee Ann Bonner. I read him his rights."

"Yes, sir."

"I've called in backup."

"Yes, sir."

"Mr. Bastien has a bullet in his leg that we need to match with Ms. Bonner's revolver," Clay said.

"Yes, sir."

"Where's Norah?" Nell said.

"Norah?"

"For God's sake—DuPree might have her."

Clay stopped meeting her gaze. He looked sick.

"And is that the only murder you're arresting him for?" Nell looked right at Kirk. "What about Johnny? And Nappy Ferris?" Kirk's face showed nothing.

"Timmy," Clay said. "Draw your weapon and guard him. I need a moment with my wife." By the time he got to that last word, the mechanical edge in his voice was gone. Sirens sounded, cutting through the noise of the storm. Clay took Nell's hand, drew her down the hall.

"Before you say a word," she said, "I know everything." Even how actually destroying the tape must have been unbearable for him, a step too far, leading to the Dumpster, Bobby Rice's locker, the long wait for Bernardine and exposure. "With the exception of why," Nell added, withdrawing her hand.

Clay closed his eyes, actually shuddered, the vein in his neck throbbing.

"Did Duke pay you off?" she said. "Was that it?"

He shook his head.

"He just simply asked you? You framed DuPree out of friendship?"

Clay nodded. He opened his eyes, looked deep into hers, a look totally honest, as far as she could tell. "You mean everything to me," he said. "Does it ruin our life together? No possible recovery?"

Kirk had tried to bury her, out on the reef. Did Clay have any suspicion of that, even the slightest? He was the one who'd brought in the broken anchor. Nell took a step back.

"I don't know," she said. He winced, as though struck by some inner pain. "And this isn't the time. Norah's out there somewhere."

Clay's face turned businesslike; Nell could feel the effort that took. "I'll find her," he said. "I promise."

"Just do it," Nell said.

He nodded, showing no emotion at all, like an obedient soldier. They went back to the door. Timmy faced Kirk, gun pointed at his chest.

"That's not necessary," Clay said. "Lock him in the back of your patrol car. Then we search the grounds." Timmy lowered the gun. Nell could see patrol cars driving up, high-intensity lights already moving near the gatehouse. "He won't get far on foot," Clay said. "And if he does have Norah, keeping her safe is his only play."

That made sense, but Nell felt no better.

They walked out on the porch, Timmy beside Kirk, Clay and Nell behind. Lightning flashed again but less intense, and the thunder that followed seemed farther away. A pre-monition came to Nell: that somehow everything was going to be all right. The next moment she heard a strange rush of air, like a breeze that had gained force blowing through the wraparound porch, and Alvin DuPree came bursting out of the shadows.

"Clay!" Nell said.

But not fast enough. DuPree had a metal bar of some kind in his hand. He brought it down with crushing force on the back of Kirk's head. Kirk was still slumping to the floor when Timmy's gun went off. DuPree grabbed his chest, toppled over—the metal bar pinwheeling away—rolled down the stairs and came to rest on his back, blood spreading on his shirt, lots and lots.

Clay leaped down to the ground, gun in one hand, held it at DuPree's head. "Cuffs, Timmy."

Timmy ran down the steps, pulling a zip-strip from his pocket.

"Hands out front," Clay said.

DuPree put his hands out front, or one of them; with the other, his right, he seemed to be adjusting his eye patch. What was he . . . ? Nell remembered: *My power lives in this secret place.*

"Clay!"

DuPree's right hand was moving, very fast, darting toward Clay's neck and that prominent, throbbing vein. Nell dove. She saw a tiny flash of steel. Then came a slicing pain down her left side, from just under her armpit all the way to her waist. She knocked Clay over, landed on wet grass, her wound on fire.

Timmy gazed down at her. "Oh my God," he said. He glanced around wildly, then pointed his gun at DuPree's head and pulled the trigger.

Clay knelt beside her. "Are you okay?"

"I think so."

His eyes were very dark. "That was wrong," he said. "You shouldn't have saved me."

Police and rescue came, by the dozen. They found Norah down at the boathouse, bound and gagged and with a possible concussion, but alive. They took Nell and Norah to the hospital. The best plastic surgeon in town came and stitched Nell up. The best radiologist took pictures of Norah's head. Two hours later, they were back home on Sandhill Way.

They sat at the kitchen table: Nell, Norah, Clay. He made a full confession, admitting everything Nell already knew.

"And what happened on the reef?" she said.

"I didn't realize," he said. "There was no reason for him to do it."

Nell believed him: the reason—sharing her plan to use hypnosis with Kirk—she'd concealed.

"Why didn't they just build the gates properly in the first place?" Norah said.

A smile, faint and quick, crossed Clay's face: the smile of a proud dad with a bright kid. "Duke never knew anything about Johnny Blanton. Kirk kept it to himself. He decided there was no way they could afford to do it right. They'd be ruined."

Silence fell. Nell still loved him with her heart, but not with her head. "I think you'd better leave," she said.

Joe Don lay in a coma. Norah visited every day. Nell started going with her. Each time, she would get the strange sensation that she could feel the love between the two of them, like something in the air. She liked being around that feeling.

Norah told Nell that Joe Don had written a song for her, "Norah's Song." He'd laid down a simple track at a studio in Baton Rouge, just voice and rhythm guitar. Nell liked it. They took the CD to the hospital the next day.

"Listen to this, Joe Don," Norah said.

He lay on the bed as always, motionless, intubated, eyes closed, head wrapped in bandages. Norah turned on the machine.

> *Saw your face*
> *Down the hall*
> *Nothin' else*
> *Matters at all.*

Joe Don made a soft sound, like a purr. One eye opened. It fastened on Norah. He smiled.

Clay resigned from the force. No charges were brought. Duke, his face repaired as well as it could be, gave him the deed to Little Parrot Cay; everything he owned was threatened by lawsuits anyway. Clay moved down there and turned the place into a small resort for divers and fishermen.

A few tracks from Joe Don's album leaked onto the Internet, caused a little buzz. Only a month or so after getting out of the hospital, he landed a gig at the Station Inn in Nashville. Norah went back to Vanderbilt in the fall. The three of them—Nell, Norah, Joe Don—had a nice Thanksgiving in Belle Ville. Nell made the corn bread from Clay's grandmother's recipe.

That might have been a mistake, because around that time she started missing him terribly. Maybe nothing would have come of it, if he hadn't called. But he did call.

"I loved that essay," he said.

"What essay?"

"Norah's essay on Garibaldi. I hadn't even heard of him, believe it or not."

"She sent it to you?"

"I read it out loud to the guests."

Nell could picture it. Picturing it gave her pleasure.

"Saw a big turtle this morning," Clay said. "Loggerhead. Must've weighed a hundred and fifty pounds."

She could picture that, too.

"You'd have liked it," Clay said.

Nell ended up booking a flight. Even though there'd been no divorce, she'd stopped wearing her wedding ring. On the day of the trip, she didn't put it on, or even bring it. She boarded the plane with no expectations.

Acknowledgments

Many thanks to my editor, David Highfill, my agent, Molly Friedrich, and my wife, Diana.